SOUL CAGE

Also by **TETSUYA HONDA** and available from **TITAN BOOKS**

THE SILENT DEAD

SOUL CAGE

TETSUYA HONDA

TRANSLATED BY **GILES MURRAY**

TITAN BOOKS

Soul Cage
Print edition ISBN: 9781785651717
Electronic edition ISBN: 9781785651724

Published by Titan Books
A division of Titan Publishing Group Ltd
144 Southwark Street, London SE1 0UP

First Titan edition: July 2017
2 4 6 8 10 9 7 5 3 1

First published in Japan by Kobunsha Co., Ltd.

This is a work of fiction. Names, places and incidents are either products
of the author's imagination or used fictitiously. Any resemblance to actual
persons, living or dead (except for satirical purposes), is entirely coincidental.

A CIP catalogue record for this title is available from the British Library.

Printed and bound in Great Britain by CPI Group (UK) Ltd.

PROLOGUE

I read somewhere that prisoners on death row got a cigarette and a bean-jam bun just before their execution.

Tadaharu Mishima was lounging by himself, eating a bean-jam bun. Someone must have doled them out to the work crew at the three o'clock break, and Mishima had either saved his or pocketed a second one. It was white and powdery on the outside with smooth, creamy paste on the inside.

I couldn't bear to look at him, so I turned and stared out the window. Work had ended for the day, and the sun was streaming straight into the building. We were up on the ninth floor, level with the late-afternoon sun.

The building was like a great black shadow: a huge gravestone in the vast graveyard of Tokyo. But I could hear the song of the cicadas. . . . Or is my memory playing tricks on me?

I turned away from the window and looked back at the room. Because of the sudden contrast, everything seemed to have fused together in one dark mass—the bare concrete walls, the burlap sacks crammed with rubble, the profile of Mishima as he perched on top of them.

All I could see was the silhouette of a face eating the silhouette of a bun—wordlessly and slowly.

I lit a cigarette to get my courage up. I felt a tiny burst of heat at the end of my nose. I inhaled, then expelled the smoke.

"Is there . . . like . . . *nothing* you can do?" I asked.

The jaw stopped moving. An instant later, it resumed its chewing motion, as if Mishima had had an idea, then changed his mind. His face was calm and emotionless. His eyes were unfocused. His gaze drifted around the empty room, then out into the corridor and off somewhere far, far away.

"No. It's hopeless."

He didn't speak the words so much as sigh them.

"But there's got to be something you can do. How about personal bankruptcy? I'm happy to go and speak to Mr. Tobe for you."

Mishima took another leisurely bite of his bun.

"Personal bankruptcy? I tried that already . . . ages ago. It didn't work. I needed money and just ended up borrowing more. . . . Look, the kind of people I was dealing with, I knew what I was getting into . . . I mean, whatever, man. It's not a big deal."

Mishima looked straight at me. His face was covered in dirt and grime. The sweat on his forehead had almost dried.

"Have you got any idea how it feels? My boy's hungry, and the best I can manage is, 'Sorry, kid, there's nothing in the house to eat today.' The boy's so hungry he picks the straw out of the tatami mats and tries to eat that shit—until

I smack him, that is. I smack his hands, punch his head, kick him in the legs and back." Mishima paused and looked down at his feet. After a moment, he shook his head and looked back up at me. "One thing I never do, though, is hit him in the face. Never. Hit a kid in the face and you get visible bruising. Then someone raises a stink about child abuse and, next thing you know, they've taken your kid away from you. I keep telling myself, 'If you've got to hit your kid, then hit him in the face. It'll be better for him that way.' But I can't. I always end up stroking his damn face when I mean to smash it...."

Mishima lowered his eyes and stared at the round, white, half-eaten bun in his hand.

"Children's cheeks are so soft and smooth. They have this sweet smell. When I hug my boy and rub my face against his, it's got to hurt. There's my stubble, plus my face is always filthy.... And you know what the kid says to me? 'Daddy, why are you crying?' What can I do? I just tell him, 'I'm sorry. I'm sorry for being such a shit dad.'"

My cigarette had burned all the way down to the filter. I tossed the butt out the window, pulled the pack out, and gestured for Mishima to help himself. When he said no, I took one.

He looked up at me and hesitated a moment before asking, "When did you find out about me?"

"Pretty much from when you got here."

"You knew, huh?"

I nodded. The cloud of smoke floating in front of me

quivered and began to break up.

"Yeah. I couldn't really help it. I mean, it's unusual to be working as a scaffold builder at your age. I just heard rumors. Vague stuff."

"Oh yeah?" sighed Mishima. "If you know so much, how come you think I've got any choice?"

I tried to reply, but the words wouldn't come.

A great jumble of memories welled up inside of me, like a physical weight inside my chest. But I couldn't talk to Mishima about my own past. I had no right.

Have you thought about the effect this will have on your little boy? I wanted to ask him. Damn stupid question. Of course he'd thought about his kid. He must've tied himself in mental knots before making the decision. God knows, I knew the thought process he'd been through—probably better than anyone.

"I'm just trying to help, man."

In the end, that was the best I could come up with.

Mishima snorted derisively.

I felt bitterly ashamed. What I'd said sounded so cheap and facile. But what else *could* I say, for fuck's sake?

"All right, then, you'd better go," I murmured.

Mishima got to his feet, cramming what was left of the bun into his mouth. Patting the dust off the seat of his pants, he picked up a battered hard hat from the floor.

"Listen, man, I'm really sorry for getting you into this mess in the first place," I said. "Anyway, you'd better go."

The floor joists creaked as Mishima trudged out of the

room. When he got to the corridor, the sound changed; I could hear sand scrunching on cement as he forced himself reluctantly forward.

I just stood there, watching my cigarette burn.

There was an empty soda can at my feet. I dropped my cigarette butt into it and listened as the butt went out with a sad fizzle.

Hearing the clanking of metal, I stuck my head out the window. Mishima was standing on the scaffolding three windows down. He had placed his hard hat onto his head without bothering to do up the chin strap. He looked up at a length of scaffolding above his head, stretched out his arm, and applied his wrench to a joint clamp.

He stayed in that position for a while, quite motionless. He wasn't actually tightening anything, just staring up at his hand.

A gust of warm wind swept across the evening sky.

Eventually, Mishima's right foot began to edge silently forward. One centimeter. Two centimeters. Now, just a millimeter or two.

I knew that if I kept watching, chances were I'd yell out before he'd done what he had to do. Which was the last thing I should do—for his sake, more than anyone's.

The moment the heel of his right foot finally slid into the air, I felt a shiver of horror go through me, and I clasped my hands to my mouth.

His back slowly tilted forward. His hard hat came off his head and tumbled straight down. As his body angled forward, he finally lost his footing completely and plunged from the ninth floor.

It was only a matter of seconds. It felt long and short at the same time.

Gravity had some fun with him on the way down: he hit the scaffolding once, bounced, did a midair somersault, and kept on falling.

Just before he hit the ground, there was a loud splat, then a heavy thump, like when you drop a bag of cement.

His body lay sprawling on the dusty ground.

"Oh my God!"

The site foreman, the security guard, and a handful of construction workers ran over to him.

"He fell," I yelled down. "There. He fell from there."

I was three rooms away from where it had happened. No one had any reason to suspect me of anything. It had all gone exactly as planned.

Despite the accident, work resumed on schedule the very next day. The inspection or investigation or whatever they call it was all over and done with in less than twenty-four hours.

Two or three days later, I was gazing out the same window, thinking that the sunset was the same as on that day, when I noticed a tiny figure at the gate of the construction site.

•

I don't remember anything about my mother. Dad told me she got sick and died. I never believed it. My guess is that she ran away. Given the kind of person Dad was, running away would be the sensible thing to do.

My dad was a complete loser, addicted to gambling though he never won a red cent. Most days we didn't have so much as a grain of rice in the house. On the rare occasions when Dad came up with dinner, the best he could manage was a can of chicken. He made a big song and dance about it, but I knew he'd won it from a pachinko parlor. Some of those places aren't allowed to give out cash prizes, so they hand out stuff instead.

My dad mostly worked in construction. He probably did odd jobs—taking the trash out, carrying stuff up to people, or, at a stretch, site security. Whatever it was, I doubt he had any special know-how or was a qualified construction worker.

I was only a kid then, but it was clear to me that my dad was physically weak and morally spineless. He was a loser who could never make up his mind about anything. The man had no backbone, no balls.

He wasn't too bad when I was in nursery school. Things only really went to shit when I moved on to grade school. The guy couldn't even afford to buy me a decent pencil case. A couple of pencils, an eraser, and a notebook—that was enough to wipe out my dad's whole budget.

He wasn't a store clerk's idea of the dream customer either. He had on a filthy running shirt and ripped-up work pants. He was unshaven and gave off this sour smell of grime and sweat—plus a touch of cheap booze whenever he opened his mouth.

The store clerk looked disgusted, and even though I was just a kid, I felt desperately embarrassed.

"This one is three hundred yen," the clerk said. "It's the cheapest pencil case we stock."

In the end, my dad just gave up on the idea. I used an elastic band to keep my pencils together.

In second and third grade, life became halfway decent. I don't know why. Perhaps Dad lucked into money—or someone lent him some. Either way, he always had my lunch money waiting for me, and I had new clothes instead of ragged old ones. There was enough rice in the house, plus some meat and fish to go with it too!

That didn't last. By the time I was in fourth grade, we were short of food again. Dad was usually able to give me money for my school lunch, but all there was at home were scraps of bread for breakfast and dried squid for dinner.

Not surprisingly, I got bullied at school.

The other kids called me "poor," "smelly," and "dirty." I was like, *Thanks, guys, I don't need you to tell me that.*

Still, I did my best to fight back.

"Come on, then. Calling me names doesn't hurt *me*. But if I punch *you*, you'll feel it all right."

Being called names actually hurt me a lot. I was just trying to be a smartass, the way kids do.

I wasn't big, but I was quick on my feet and had guts,

so getting into a fight was no big deal. Still, I was careful not to overdo it. That wasn't about being nice to the other kids; I was being nice to *me*: I simply didn't have the energy.

After school, I'd go back to the shoddy two-story timber-frame apartment block where we lived and try and get Dad to make me something to eat. When he was out, I'd try and fix something for myself. Of course, whether my dad was there or not, it didn't mean there was anything to eat.

"Sorry, buddy . . . I had a good look around, but there's nothing in the house. . . . Sorry, buddy."

I'd nod sympathetically, while thinking, *Yeah, right. The way you smell, there must have been plenty of booze in the house.*

As I drifted off into the comforting world of daydreams, I'd start picking at the tatami mats.

Suddenly, Mom was back with us, rustling up a hamburger and a steaming bowl of rice for me. Delicious! "You should come and live with me," Mom would say in my dreams. I had no idea what she looked like in reality, so I'd give her the face of actresses I'd seen on TV. I didn't need her to look sweet and pretty. I wanted someone who looked tough enough to deal with whatever life threw her way.

Then, a hand reached out and smacked me, bringing my daydream to an abrupt end.

"What the fuck you doing, kid?"

I opened my eyes. Without realizing it, I'd ripped a lump out of the tatami mat and was about to put it in my mouth.

"Oh," I stammered. "Sorry, Dad."

"You're so hungry, you'll eat tatami?"

"No, Dad."

"Are you really that hungry?"

Actually, yes, I really am that hungry.

"No, I'm fine," I answered after a moment. "I had seconds at lunch at school."

"Don't lie."

Oh, come on. Do you really have to hit me?

"I'm fine. Honest, I am."

"Shut up, kid."

And off we went again. My broke, crappy old dad taking out his frustrations with the world on poor little me. He was a loser who went crazy whenever he had to face the fact that he was a loser. I knew what was coming and steeled myself.

My best strategy was to pull my knees up to my chest, curl up in a ball, protect my face, make myself as small as possible. My drunken dad was such a total failure he couldn't even do a decent job of beating up his grade-school–age son.

Like a rain squall, his rage would quickly pass, and my dad would pick me up and hug me.

"I'm sorry, Kosuke. I'm sorry for being such a lousy father."

You loser! The only thing you can teach me is to be as unlike you as possible. You're weak and gutless. You can't even follow through: if you're gonna hit me, don't start hugging me halfway through the beating.

"Why are you crying, Daddy?"

You were the one who was hitting me! I'm the one who should be crying here, Dad!

"Kosuke."

Must you hug me? You stink. I don't want your stink rubbing off on me.

I'd have preferred being rolled up in a gym mat and jumped on by the other kids in school to being hugged by him.

Anyway, this dad of mine died the summer after I finished fifth grade. He fell at work from the ninth floor of an apartment block.

Our phone had been disconnected ages ago, so I got the news in person from a detective who showed up at the door. When I heard him out dry-eyed, he patted me on the head and complimented me on being a tough little guy.

Being tough had nothing to do with it. I felt stunned and stupefied. That's how pitifully weak I was.

Sure, you were a crap dad, but you tried to work so we could buy food. Sure, you lost it every three days and beat me up, but we always made up by bedtime. How am I meant to make it without you? A schoolkid like me can't play the slots. I can't work construction. How about delivering papers? Is a fifth grader allowed to do that?

I assumed they'd stick me in an orphanage. An orphanage would probably be better than this shitty apartment without a stick of food in it. Sure it would. How did I get into one? Who was going to take me? Should I ask someone at school to set it up? Would the detective take care of it?

Right at that moment, I didn't need to worry about that. They took me to a sort of hospital in Otsuka. It wasn't a normal hospital. I didn't see any nurses, and the place was crawling with police.

"You're the only family your father's got, kid," said someone. "I'm sorry, but we need you to identify him for us."

I said okay. What else could I do? They led me into this bare white room and took me over to a bed covered with a white sheet.

All of a sudden, I was afraid.

The detective who'd come to the house said that Dad had fallen from the ninth floor. The ninth floor! That was three times taller than my school!

"His face is a bit . . . well . . . so I'm going to have you look at his tummy and his chest. Is that all right?"

I was wondering what exactly was meant by his face being "a bit, well . . . ," when the sheet was pulled back.

I retched, gasping for air.

My dad's body had this greenish tinge. That's how I remember it. There were several sets of black stitches on the body. *How am I supposed to identify this?* was my first thought. Then I took a good look and recognized the chest hair as my dad's, and the round, sticking-out belly button, which was undamaged.

"Yes, that's him," I whispered. "That's my daddy."

That was all I could manage before a second wave of nausea hit me.

A message came for me at the school two days later.

It was from Kinoshita Construction, the company Dad worked for. They wanted me to come and pick up his things.

"Will you be all right? Can you get there all by yourself?"

My teacher, Mr. Masuoka, was a very nice man. He photocopied a map for me and lent me money for the train fare. I thanked him and headed for Kinoshita Construction. I'm not proud of it, but even as a kid, I was kind of hoping that there might be some money in it for me.

The directions they'd given me were for the construction site where Dad had died. I was pacing anxiously in front of the big metal security shutter at the entrance when the security guard came out of his little prefab cabin.

"Are you Tadaharu Mishima's kid?"

When I said I was, the guard took me to another, bigger prefab hut, where the air-conditioning was going full blast. There must have been four or five adults inside, all wearing identical pale green boiler suits—all except one, that is. He was dressed differently. He had on a white shirt, unbuttoned to show his chest, and black pants. He had a five-o'clock shadow and small brown sunglasses. I still remember how he had a cigarette dangling from his lips and the way his short-cropped hair stood straight up on his head.

"Thanks for coming, kid. I'm impressed. Really impressed."

The man made an effort to be friendly.

"This is your dad's duffel bag. Is that right?"

I nodded. The man asked me to check the contents. I recognized everything in it. There was even a little money in my dad's wallet—six hundred yen.

"Okay, kid, you take the duffel home with you. And take this too. It's incense money from the company. Money to say we're sorry for your loss. You'll need cash for one thing and another. Spend it wisely."

They had also included what they owed Dad for overtime and other benefits.

"Thank you very much, sir. Good-bye."

I took the money with a bow and left the hut.

After just a couple of steps, I opened the envelope to peer inside. There was a hundred thousand yen in there. *Wow!* I was over the moon—and nervous about having that much cash on me.

I made my way back to the front gate, then turned around for a last look at the construction site.

The building was eleven stories high and covered in scaffolding. My dad had fallen from the ninth floor. The detective told me that he'd been building the scaffolding when he fell.

The metal scaffolding glowed faintly in the light of the setting sun. In my childish imagination, it looked like a gigantic cage for a humongous monster.

Did the monster eat my dad? Or had Dad jumped down to escape from the monster?

Get me out of here! Get me out! Help me! Kosuke, help!

I pictured my father, his blubbering face all scrunched up with fear. Suddenly I felt sorry for him. The hundred thousand yen I had on me was the price of his life.

I didn't cry. For some reason, however, I felt acutely thirsty.

The metal boards they put on the ground for the trucks to drive over were wet. They'd been spraying water to keep the dust down. There had to be a spigot nearby.

As I looked around, I heard a voice.

"Hey, are you Mishima's boy?"

I spun around. Before I could reply, the man continued.

"Of course you are. You've got your dad's eyes."

Must you say that? I thought to myself.

The man squatted down in front of me and looked into my face. He was handsome, with a striking-looking nose. I guessed that he worked there, but he wasn't all grimy like my dad.

A whiff of sweat wafted out from the collar of his polo shirt. Oddly enough, it didn't disgust me.

"Your dad and I were pals. We were working together right at the end."

It was the first time I'd imagined my dad having friends.

"I guess you came alone, huh? Well, I'm alone too. How about you and me have dinner together? You can order all your favorite things. My treat."

All my favorite things. . . .

My stomach started rumbling. It actually hurt. It was like my intestines were tying themselves in knots.

"Come on, let's go. I'm not planning to kidnap you, you know. If you're frightened, you go first. Go into whatever restaurant you want and order whatever you like. How about it? Sound like a plan?"

I wasn't afraid of him abducting me or anything. If anyone was dumb enough to kidnap me, there was nobody to pay even a penny in ransom. I'd completely forgotten about the hundred thousand yen I had on me.

"We've got us a deal, then. What's your name?"

Kosuke, I told him.

"Kosuke, huh? Nice name. Mine's Takaoka. Kenichi Takaoka. Pleased to meet you."

And that was how I met the old man.

PART
ONE

1

CHIYODA WARD, TOKYO
TOKYO METROPOLITAN POLICE HEADQUARTERS

Reiko Himekawa was having coffee with Kazuo Kikuta in the canteen on the seventeenth floor of the Tokyo Metropolitan Police headquarters. Kikuta was a sergeant in Himekawa's squad and just a little bit older than she was.

"What's wrong, Lieutenant? Why the long face?"

"Oh, no reason."

It was three o'clock in the afternoon of Thursday, December 4. The canteen overlooked the Imperial Palace grounds. It was so bright and sunny that it was easy to forget how cold it was outside.

"Are you still having dreams about Otsuka?"

Reiko looked up. Kikuta was resting his chin in his hands and gazing into her eyes. It was an atypical pose for him.

Shinji Otsuka had been a cop in Himekawa's squad. On August 25 this year, he'd been killed while investigating a series of murders. He was only twenty-seven. Two years younger than she.

Kikuta had hit the nail on the head.

"Yeah." She paused. "He's been showing up in my dreams a lot recently. It's always the last time I saw him in Ikebukuro. It's rush hour. He's got no idea what's coming as he gets off the train and makes his way through the crowd. And then—this is the part where the dream departs from reality—Otsuka always turns back and waves at me with this goofy grin on his face. . . ."

Reiko's voice quavered. *Take a sip of coffee and get a grip on yourself.* Her hand refused to obey, and the words started pouring out uncontrollably.

"I say, 'Don't go, Otsuka, don't go.' For some reason, though, he can't hear me, and off he goes, still with that goofy grin on his face."

The waitress came over, and Reiko discreetly turned away to hide her face.

"Everyone talks about me having a sixth sense. It's bullshit. God, I wish I did! Then I could have warned him."

"So you're still putting yourself through the wringer, Lieutenant."

Kikuta was holding out a handkerchief. Reiko shook her head and began looking through her handbag. She couldn't find a handkerchief or even a Kleenex. Should she use the napkin on the table?

"Think I will take that after all."

Kikuta was about to stuff the handkerchief back into his

pocket. He stopped mid-motion and, with a grin, handed it to her.

"It's not healthy to obsess about it."

Kikuta's chunky fingers closed around the handle of his mug. His lips were thick and slightly chapped, and his chin was a mass of dark stubble. There was something endearing in his simple, vigorous masculinity.

"What do you mean?"

"I mean those dreams. It's not your fault, Lieutenant. If you start going down that route, then it's Director Hashizume and Captain Imaizumi who are ultimately responsible. They're the ones who assigned Otsuka to Ikebukuro."

"That's not what I'm talking about."

"But it's the same thing. Remember what you're always telling us? How the criminal is the only one who is guilty, and that no one else should blame themselves? You mustn't blame yourself, Lieutenant. And that's exactly what you're doing. For one thing, Otsuka wouldn't have wanted you to. He loved being a cop, and he took his job—and that investigation—seriously. That's the reason he's always smiling. I mean, *Otsuka is smiling at you in your dreams*, right?"

"Hey, take it down a notch. You're yelling."

"Sorry," mumbled Kikuta. The small black eyes that were such a bad fit with the great meaty slab of his face darted anxiously around the room.

Reiko suddenly saw a funny side to what Kikuta had been saying. She pressed the handkerchief to her mouth. "You're about the last person I'd expect to say that sort of thing."

Kikuta's eyes widened.

"What do you mean?"

"I mean that sort of new age, spiritual stuff: '*Otsuka is smiling at you in your dreams. . . .*'"

Kikuta put his mug down on the table with a shamefaced grin.

"Perhaps it's because 'that sort of thing' is popular right now."

"Do you believe that stuff, Kikuta? Spiritualism? Communicating with the 'other side'?"

"Nah, not really. How about you, Lieutenant? Women are usually more into that sort of thing than men."

"Oh, *women* are, are they? I'm not a big one for generalizations myself."

Did she believe in it or not? That was a question worth pondering.

She certainly thought about the people she loved who had passed on. Did that mean she believed in the spirit world? Hardly. She had no sense that there were invisible beings out there, smoothing her way. When she went to the family grave, she thanked her ancestors as you were supposed to do, but as far as she was concerned, she herself was responsible for what she had achieved.

As for the idea of a personal guardian spirit—that, she rejected out of hand.

"Hmmm," she grunted. "I'd have to say that I'm not much of a believer . . . I think."

"That's what I thought."

Reiko felt slightly annoyed.

"Are you trying to tell me I'm not a normal woman?"

"That's not what I meant."

"What did you mean, then?"

"I just thought skepticism was more *you*, Lieutenant. That's all."

"And 'more me' means what, exactly?"

Kikuta looked flustered.

"What's with the third degree? The Reiko Himekawa I know tends to be skeptical and look at things in a more detached and rational way. The Reiko Himekawa I know wouldn't fret over all the hypotheticals with Otsuka—what if this, what if that—it's a bottomless rabbit hole. No, the Reiko Himekawa I know would just come out and say, 'The only person at fault here is the murderer—and that's that.'"

Reiko could feel herself getting angry.

That's what you think of me, is it?

Still, if people tended to see her as brisk, decisive, and businesslike, that was because it was the image she chose to project. As a woman in her twenties, there was no way she could move up the ladder at the Tokyo Metropolitan Police without some careful image-management.

Reiko had been appointed a squad leader in the Homicide Division soon after making lieutenant at twenty-seven. It was a nearly unprecedented achievement, but still, a woman could not be a woman in a work environment like the police. She had to be more of a man than the men if she wanted to avoid being treated as a joke.

Still . . .

To Kikuta, if to no one else, Reiko made an effort to show her feminine side. She thought they were close enough for that. She thought that he liked her.

It hasn't worked out too well. He doesn't understand me one bit.

She'd known all along that Kikuta was never going to win any prizes for sensitivity. His emotional obtuseness got on her nerves, but she was willing to overlook it as a lovable defect. The truth was, she had her own vulnerabilities, and she wanted his support. She thought he could at least sense her needs without her having to be explicit.

What a bummer!

She wasn't going to transform herself and suddenly become all clingy and dependent, girly-girl style, just for his sake. She was too proud for that, and her rank as lieutenant obliged her to be a little more formal and stiff. Sometimes, though, she felt like she had a metal board strapped to her back.

"Perhaps we should make a move," said Reiko, consulting her Longines watch. Kikuta reached for the check and sprang briskly to his feet.

"I'll deal with this, Lieutenant. You go ahead."

You're the soul of tact when it comes to unimportant things, Reiko thought to herself.

"It's okay."

"Seriously. You should go first." Kikuta's large head suddenly loomed in toward her. "You need to redo your makeup. Anyone can tell you've been crying."

28

Reiko shuddered. The skin around her eyes flushed.

Was Kikuta being sensitive or obtuse? She wasn't quite sure.

Worse than that, what was she coming to if she needed a man like him to tell her that her makeup needed fixing!

When Reiko got back to the big open-plan office on the sixth floor, everyone else on the squad was at their desks.

Sergeant Tamotsu Ishikura, the veteran of her team at forty-seven years old, had his nose buried in the newspaper as usual.

Officer Kohei Yuda was poring sleepily over a textbook for his promotional exam. With Otsuka gone, his position in the group had risen a notch.

Otsuka's replacement was Officer Noriyuki Hayama. He was deep in an old case file.

Hayama was highly competent. Despite joining the force out of high school, he'd been appointed to the Homicide Division when he was only twenty-five. He was tall and handsome, but he didn't let that go to his head. When he was working a case, he went about things quietly and methodically. He'd only been with Reiko's squad for three months, and, as far as she could tell, he was a model detective.

If Himekawa was going to be picky, then perhaps Hayama was a little gloomier than she would have liked. When the squad went out for a communal booze-up, he barely smiled or spoke. Even when Yuda got so wasted that he started sticking chopsticks into his nose, mouth, and ears in his best Hellraiser imitation, Hayama's only response was a solemn nod. He certainly knew how to wreck the mood.

There was also something about him that hinted at insubordination. It was nothing Reiko could put her finger on, just a certain irritating superciliousness. She'd gotten so annoyed that she'd asked him flat out if working with a female lieutenant was a problem for him. "Problem? No," he'd replied, flatly. Worried that pressing him too hard would make her look immature, Reiko opted to let sleeping dogs lie. Perhaps he'd thaw out in time.

Sergeant Kikuta was the fourth and last member of Reiko's team. Unit 10 of the TMPD Homicide Division consisted of the Himekawa squad and the Kusaka squad— and they were a whole other set of oddballs.

"Lieutenant?"

Ishikura pushed his newspaper to one side and cocked an eyebrow at Reiko. He wanted to tell her something in confidence.

Reiko walked around the clump of pushed-together desks until she was standing next to Ishikura. Kikuta, who was sitting on the far side, discreetly strained to listen in.

"What's up, Tamotsu?"

Much older than the rest of them, Ishikura gave off quite a different vibe from the others in the squad. Reiko didn't dislike it; if anything, just the opposite. Of late, she found middle-aged male stolidity increasingly appealing.

"Toyama is definitely up to something," murmured Ishikura. "A moment ago he left the room with Kusaka. Perhaps there's been a development in that business this morning."

Toyama was a sergeant on Kusaka's squad. "That business this morning" was a rumor about Director Hashizume bringing back an object from Kamata Precinct in Ota Ward.

"Have you got the lowdown on whatever it was?"

"It was in an ice chest. Hashizume took it to the crime lab and gave the head of Forensics a hard time about needing the results fast. That's all I know."

At present, the members of Homicide Unit 10 were the only people on standby at TMPD headquarters. There were three levels of readiness: A, B, and C. Level A meant standing by at headquarters; B was standing by at home; and C meant on call but free to go about your business.

There wasn't much difference between being on level C and being on vacation. With the recent squeeze on department finances, however, C had been temporarily shelved, and for the last three days, both squads in Unit 10 had been at the desks on level A, while Unit 3 was on level B.

This meant that if there was a murder anywhere in Tokyo today, Reiko's team would have to work with Kusaka's squad on the case. This would be a problem. The Kusaka squad and the Himekawa squad were at daggers drawn; or to be precise, Lieutenant Himekawa loathed Lieutenant Kusaka.

Reiko wasn't short of reasons. She detested everything about Kusaka, from his looks and the sound of his voice to the way he handled his cases. Through sheer dumb luck, they'd not had to collaborate on any cases over the last few months. Sadly, it looked like that happy state of separation was about to come to an end. Reiko was just going to have to suck it up.

"Any idea what's going on in Kamata?"

"That must be what Toyama is trying to find out. My guess is they've put a gag order on it."

All sorts of horse-trading went on behind the scenes before a task force was formally established, whether between different divisions of the TMPD, between the TMPD and the local precincts, or between the police and the media. The fact that the detectives hadn't heard anything formally yet probably meant one of two things: either the incident was too insignificant to deserve its own task force, or it was a delicate and complex case and things were moving slowly. It was the latter scenario that Reiko thought more likely—and it was the one she was hoping for.

If you wanted to make a name for yourself in this department, it was far better to solve one big case than to fool around with a bunch of smaller ones. Big cases drew media attention, and the bigger the noise the media made about you, the more of a reputation you got inside the force. The best possible thing was to singlehandedly solve a case that made major headlines, like the Mizumoto Park murders earlier this year.

It's a shame that someone else walked off with all the credit for that one.

Reiko gazed out across the office at the vast rows of desks. There was a cluster of men around the coffee machine near the door on the far side. It was Sergeant Mizoguchi, and Officers Shinjo and Itoi—all of them members of Kusaka's squad.

"Hey, Tamotsu, have you seen the captain?"

Reiko was talking about Captain Imaizumi, the head of Unit 10.

"He went out about ten minutes ago."

"Did someone come in to fetch him?"

"Not that I saw."

As Reiko and Ishikura were talking, Kusaka and Toyama reappeared in the doorway. They seemed to be relaying information to the other three members of their squad, deliberately keeping their voices low.

Were they planning to keep whatever they had found out to themselves so they could be a step ahead when the task force was set up?

Come on, Reiko! Why must you always think the worst of other people?

Reiko walked over to the group. She could hear Kikuta's footsteps right behind her.

"Hey, Lieutenant Kusaka, any interesting scuttlebutt come your way today?"

Kusaka stared blankly back at her with his small black reptilian eyes. As usual, his thin lips were clamped together in a straight line.

"Scuttlebutt? What's that?"

That voice—deep, heavy, joyless.

"I know you've been gathering info. What did you find out?"

"You've got the wrong end of the stick. I just went to the bathroom."

"Oh, and you're so pally with your squad mates that you always take them with you for a communal piss?"

"Watch it, Himekawa. Dirty talk like that's not going to help you find yourself a husband."

Reiko caught the hint of a smirk on his face.

"Thanks for the marital counseling, but I'd prefer if you stayed off that topic in the workplace."

"Sorry. I misspoke."

Officer Itoi, who was standing in front of Kusaka, sniggered. Reiko ignored him.

"So what's going on? In the crime lab, I mean?"

"Like I said, I just went to the bathroom—"

"A man of your caliber, Lieutenant Kusaka—I'm sure you can retrieve useful information even when it's just floating around in the toilet bowl."

Kusaka flinched and snorted with disgust. Reiko simply kept staring at him.

"Listen, Himekawa, if you're so keen to get some information, how about finding it out for yourself? Being on standby level A isn't supposed to mean getting all lovey-dovey with your subordinates and taking them out for coffee and a nice view."

The bastard! He must have seen me and Kikuta!

"Which just proves I was right. You weren't in the bathroom."

"Did I say it was me who saw you? I've had enough of this chitchat. It's a waste of time."

Tapping Toyama on the shoulder, Kusaka headed over to his desk.

"Hey, just a minute. Are you trying to give me the slip?" Kusaka glared at Reiko.

"You shouldn't try and copy Stubby, Himekawa. You're way too young to be able to browbeat information out of me. Try again in ten years' time."

Kusaka spun on his heel and marched off, his subordinates in tow.

Me? Trying to copy Stubby?

Stubby was the nickname of Lieutenant Kensaku Katsumata, a squad leader in Unit 5. He was ex–Public Security Bureau and a classic old-school cop in the worst possible sense. His method of investigation was a combination of foul language, violence, and bribes—and he excelled at all three.

Stubby's the last person on Earth I want to be compared to!

Reiko heard footsteps in the corridor and turned to see Director Hashizume and Captain Imaizumi in the doorway.

"Listen up, everyone," announced Imaizumi. "We're going to be setting up a task force for a murder over in Kamata. Everyone needs to get over to that precinct right now."

Director Hashizume looked like the cat who ate the canary and was clearly desperate for a chance to sound off.

"What's going on, Director?" Reiko asked.

Hashizume cleared his throat rather theatrically, then announced: "It's because I kicked their asses and told them get a move on. They insisted that they needed a minimum of nine hours. I knew that if they got it together, they could do it in seven."

"Do what, sir?"

"DNA analysis. On some bloodstains and a hand. Sure enough, the DNA was a match."

Now it was all starting to make sense. The "something" that Director Hashizume had brought back in the cooler was a human hand.

"You'll get a proper briefing over in Kamata. I need you all to get a move on," said Captain Imaizumi. "It's already 3:20. If it gets dark, we'll have lost a whole day."

2

Kamata Police Station was about five minutes' walk from Kamata train station.

When they arrived, Reiko and her squad took the elevator to the sixth floor, walked past the cafeteria, and to a large conference room. Reiko slipped off her coat and had a look around.

It all looks well prepared.

The desks had all been arranged in long rows facing the front of the room. Around twenty investigators—from Kamata and neighboring precincts, Reiko guessed—were already there.

"Hi there, Lieutenant Reiko."

I just can't believe it! Of all people: Hiromitsu Ioka!

"What the *hell* are you doing here?" growled Kikuta.

Reiko had to slide between the two men and physically restrain Kikuta from grabbing Ioka by his jacket lapels.

"Just cool it, Kikuta. Ioka, what are you doing here in Kamata? Last I heard, you were over in Kameari."

Ioka gave a bucktoothed smile, flushed up to his jug

ears, and stared at Reiko with his round bug eyes.

"I got transferred again. I've been based here since October."

"You've got to be kidding. It's just too weird. Three times in one year, you've transferred to precincts my team gets sent to. That's not natural."

Ioka squirmed in his chair and rubbed his hands. Reiko shuddered at the all-too-familiar sight.

"You know why, Lieutenant Reiko? It's because our destinies are intertwined. That's an incontestable fact, isn't it?"

"I damn well hope not. Anyway, like I told you before, don't call me by my first name."

"You're so cute when you're bashful."

"Ioka!" bellowed Kikuta, his face purple with rage. "How come you're always in the right place whenever a murder's committed? Are you committing these crimes yourself just to have an excuse to see the lieutenant?"

Oh please. Get real, thought Reiko to herself. Ioka himself seemed quite unflustered.

"My old pal Kaz Kikuta."

Kaz?

"You creep, you can't talk to me like that—"

Reiko guessed that Kikuta had been about to say that a lowly officer like Ioka had no business being so familiar with a sergeant like him when Ioka lifted a hand and cut Kikuta off. Ioka reached into the inside pocket of his jacket, pulled out his badge wallet, then flapped it ostentatiously open and shoved it into Kikuta's face.

"I'm happy to report that I just made sergeant. In other words, Brother Kaz, you and I are now the same rank."

Kikuta scowled ferociously, spluttered, and sank into silence.

That explained Ioka's move to this precinct. Any detective who passed the promotional exam was rewarded with an automatic transfer.

"Maybe you finally made sergeant, but you've still got two years' less on the force than me," Kikuta barked at Ioka.

"You lot, shut the fuck up," bellowed Captain Imaizumi, drowning out the tail end of Kikuta's outburst.

The group exchanged looks and shrugged.

Reiko's head slumped forward. She knew nothing about the case yet, but she already had a bad feeling about it.

A few minutes later, the truck arrived from the TMPD HQ, and all their equipment—everything from phones, computers, and radios to basic office supplies—was brought up to the sixth floor.

There were now over forty investigators in the room, waiting to be briefed. In addition to the two squads from Homicide Unit 10, there was the Mobile Unit and the detectives from Kamata and the neighboring precincts. The top brass sat facing them at table along the front of the room.

"Good afternoon, everybody. I'm Director Hashizume from the Homicide Division. Captain Imaizumi here is going to brief us on the case, so I want everyone to listen carefully. Captain?"

"Thank you, Director," Imaizumi began. "This morning, what appears to be the left hand of an adult male was found in the back of a white minivan. The vehicle was a Subaru Sambar, license number Shinagawa 480-Hi-2956. It was illegally parked on the street in the West Rokugo neighborhood of Ota Ward."

Why only a hand? Reiko wondered idly, as she picked up her notebook and dutifully jotted down the details.

"Based on fingerprint evidence and the testimony of the individual who led us to the hand, we have been able to confirm that it belongs to a Mr. Kenichi Takaoka, forty-three years old, living at Hope Mansions, Middle Rokugo, here in this precinct. Takaoka is unmarried and lives alone. The hand was in a tightly sealed plastic bag. The plastic bag was from a convenience store. From the large quantity of blood in the minivan, we can assume that the blood loss was fatal. The forensic team is currently examining the van and running tests on it. We will let you know the results when we can.

"Now I want to tell you how the case came to our attention." Imaizumi turned to the next page of the file in his hand. "Just after six a.m., Sergeant Toshimitsu Iwata from Kamata Precinct received a verbal report about the discovery of a large pool of blood in a rented garage in Middle Rokugo. The person who reported the blood was Kosuke Mishima, a twenty-year-old male. The garage in question is rented by Kenichi Takaoka. Takaoka has his own business, Takaoka Construction, which does subcontract work on big construction projects. Kosuke Mishima is employed by Takaoka Construction.

"Mishima arrived at work early this morning. As soon as he opened the garage door, he noticed that the minivan they use for work was missing and that the concrete floor of the garage was wet. He also noticed a peculiar odor. Not recognizing it as the smell of blood, he walked straight into the crime scene. As soon as he realized he was standing in a pool of blood, he called Takaoka's cell phone, but no one picked up. He then went to Takaoka's apartment; no one was in. He made a beeline for Zoshiki Police Station. Sergeant Iwata, after hearing what he had to say, called the Kamata Precinct. He also put out an alert on the missing vehicle."

Damn! Realizing that she'd forgotten to write down the address of Takaoka's apartment, Reiko snuck a look at Ioka's notes and cribbed it from there.

"An officer from the West Rokugo station had noted the presence of an illegally parked vehicle on the Tama River embankment at 2:00 a.m. that morning. Since no one had actually called in to complain about the van, the officers waited until 5:00 a.m. to draw warning chalk lines in the asphalt around the tires. At 6:17 a.m., Lieutenant Hideo Tanaka, who was monitoring the radio in the West Rokugo police station, heard the bulletin about the license number and called Kamata Police Station to inform them of the location of the van. At 6:52 a.m., Lieutenant Tanaka went with Kosuke Mishima, who had a spare key for the minivan, to examine it. That is when the lieutenant discovered the shopping bag containing Kenichi Takaoka's hand at the far end of the bed of the truck. I should add that the electric saw believed to have been used to sever the hand was later found in the garage."

Reiko skimmed through her notes and composed a simplified timeline for herself. Early that morning, twenty-year-old Kosuke Mishima informed a local police officer that his firm's minivan wasn't in its garage and that the garage itself was awash with blood. The van had been illegally parked at the Tama River embankment at 2:00 a.m. or earlier. When the police opened up the van in the morning, they found a plastic bag containing Kenichi Takaoka's severed hand.

"We've taken samples from the blood in the garage and in the vehicle, as well as from the severed left hand. All the blood samples were type A, and the DNA was also a match in every case. From the sheer quantity of blood that was spilled, we have to accept that Kenichi Takaoka is dead. What we're dealing with in this case is the disposal of the body of someone who probably met an unnatural death, likely as not murder. That's why we've set up a task force HQ to investigate the case."

At the end of the day, it was a murder investigation with no corpse. From studying similar cases in the past, Reiko knew they tended to be tricky.

"Now we'll explain how we're going to tackle the investigation."

At this point, Director Hashizume took back the

microphone. "Thank you, Captain. For today, we need you to split into two groups: one group will do a house-to-house canvass near the river where the van was found; the other will make inquiries in the vicinity of the garage and the victim's home. Lieutenant Himekawa of Homicide will head up the team at the riverside, and Lieutenant Kusaka, also of Homicide, will lead the garage team."

The standard practice on task forces was to pair up one TMPD detective with one detective from the local precinct.

"I'll deal with the riverside canvass first. I want Lieutenant Himekawa of Homicide and Sergeant Ioka from the Kamata Station to handle Sector One. Sector One is the area immediately around where the vehicle was found."

"What!" she burst out.

Why do I get landed with Ioka, of all people?

Ioka, who was sitting one row in front of her, cleared his throat meaningfully.

"Did you hear me, Himekawa?" said Hashizume. "I need verbal confirmation."

"Ah, yes, sir," she stuttered. "Of course, sir. Excuse me, sir."

"Hiromitsu Ioka, sir. Understood, sir. I'm your man, sir."

Under the table Ioka had both fists clenched tight in a gesture of determination.

"It's love bringing us together again," he whispered with a little cackle.

"Oh, shut it."

Reiko suppressed the urge to smack Ioka and listened to the rest of the assignments being doled out instead.

"Sergeant Kikuta of Homicide and Sergeant Ato of Kamata Station will handle Sector Two, which is block two, numbers thirty to thirty-three."

There was a long pause before Kikuta replied.

"Yes, sir."

"Yes, sir."

This wasn't good. Kikuta was behaving oddly. His voice was like the whining of a beaten dog.

Hashizume wasn't the sort of man to pick up on details like that; he plowed right on.

"Sector Three is Sergeant Ishikura from Homicide and Officer Yoshino from Kamata Precinct. You'll handle block two, numbers thirty-four to thirty-seven."

"Yes, sir."

"Yes, sir."

When Hashizume had finished assigning the sectors for the riverbank canvass, Reiko left the other investigators in their huddle and hurried over to Imaizumi at the front of the room. He was busily sorting through some files.

"Captain?"

Imaizumi turned and looked at her over his shoulder with an arch smile.

"Yes? Got something to say to me?"

She went and stood next to him and pretended to help him with the files.

"You bet I do. Do I *really* have to team up with that clown Ioka again?"

Imaizumi's shoulders were quivering with suppressed

laughter. She should have known. The whole thing was just a joke to him!

"You're just going to have to suck it up. Director Hashizume's the one who makes the decisions here."

"And how does he do that? How does he assign teams?"

"He draws up a seniority-based list of everyone from the TMPD and the local precinct, then he flips it to pair off the most senior investigators with the most junior ones. It's quite an art, you know. For the investigators from the other local precincts and the Mobile Unit, he went by alphabetical order."

Goddamn! She'd always known Hashizume was a hopeless ditherer, but that really took the cake.

"I see," she said, with a resigned gulp. "I'll just have to run with it for today, but can you pair me up with someone better tomorrow?"

"Huh? What do you mean, 'better'? Ioka's a hardworking detective who's solved plenty of smaller cases. They tell me he's seen as a topflight cop around here. . . . At least, that's what their chief of detectives told me."

Reiko had her doubts about any department that seriously regarded Ioka as a "topflight cop."

"Anyway, enough of that. Let me deal with these files here."

Reiko, who wasn't in the mood to finish this conversation, started leafing through a file she'd taken from Imaizumi's pile.

It was a report on the scene where the severed hand had been discovered. As far as Reiko could see from the sketch diagram, the Tama River embankment was a normal road, accessible to ordinary traffic. You needed to climb down a mound to get to the riverbank, and from there it was a further twenty or thirty meters to the water's edge.

"Only the left hand was found in the vehicle, Captain. With the river being so close, doesn't it make sense that the rest of the body was dumped in the water?"

"Maybe. The forensics team is going over everything within a fifty-meter radius of the van, right up to the river's edge where it's quite overgrown. I've told them to look out for shoe prints and bloodstains that might have been left when the body was moved. Look, this is the interior of the minivan where the hand was found."

Imaizumi flipped open another file. There were photographs of the vehicle from every conceivable angle.

The minivan contained a single row of seats, at the front. Everything behind them was used for storage. A separate platform had been fitted above the bed of the van to create two long, deep shelves. On the upper shelf there was a looped length of electric cable; what looked like a tool case; a number of small, unmarked cardboard boxes of unknown contents; and a portable light inside a protective wire cage.

According to the report, the bag containing the hand had been found at the back of the bottom level. Reiko peered at the picture, but with the upper shelf blocking out the light, it was hard to see anything on the lower shelf, let alone right at the back of it.

"You think the perp simply forgot one of the hands

when he was disposing of the body?" she asked.

Imaizumi nodded. "Or maybe some random passerby came along, and he hightailed it before he had time to dispose of the whole body. That would also account for his leaving the vehicle behind."

Sensing someone behind her, Reiko spun abruptly around. She had expected to see Ioka. She was wrong. It was Kusaka, and he was standing right on her heel.

"Making assumptions like that at such an early stage will only hinder the investigation going forward."

Imaizumi gave an exaggerated shrug of his shoulders.

"Loosen up, Kusaka. I'm expressing a personal opinion, that's all."

"Except that if you issue directives based on those personal opinions, the whole investigation will be skewed."

"What are you talking about?"

Kusaka's eyes were stern. He was almost frowning.

"I'm talking about the instructions you gave the forensics team to focus on looking for shoe prints and bloodstains at the crime scene. Limiting the scope of their search like that will infect them with an unconscious bias."

And there it was! The Great Kusaka Doctrine in all its glory—the idea that assumptions or preconceptions of any kind only serve to impede an investigation. Believe only what you have physically seen or heard. Reiko wondered what to call it. Anti-preconceptionism, perhaps?

More than that, how the hell did Kusaka manage to eavesdrop without us noticing?

Imaizumi scratched his neck and grinned sheepishly.

"Maybe you're right, Kusaka. I was premature in restricting the search like that. I'll issue a new set of orders to eliminate any risk of bias."

"Please do. Now, if you'll excuse me."

Kusaka spun on his heel and marched out of the room. All the other investigators assigned to the garage area canvass followed. As far as Reiko could tell, about half the investigators assigned to the riverside area had already gone too.

She sighed.

"That guy's impossible to work with. He's a goddamn nightmare. I mean, the crap he spouts—like some goody-two-shoes greenhorn freshly graduated from the special investigation course."

Imaizumi grinned at her.

"You shouldn't take that attitude. You are who you are, and Kusaka is who he is. The two of you balance each other out nicely. The force would be pretty screwed up if it were made up of only people like you and me! It'd be like some silly quiz show on TV: everyone in a race to press the buzzer and spew wild guesses about the identity of the perpetrator."

Reiko knew that when Imaizumi was a detective his style was similar to hers—he went with his gut. He might have spoken with a little more tact, but she couldn't stop herself from smiling.

"That's not a very nice thing to say."

"Yeah, yeah, whatever. Come on, get moving. Your partner's waiting."

Ioka was standing by the door, eagerly rubbing his hands.

"So he is." She paused. "Anyway, Captain, I'm depending on you to get me a new partner for tomorrow." *Please.*

"Uh-huh. I'll think about it."

Reiko pulled on her coat, switching her bag from hand to hand as she did so.

It would be seriously cold canvassing the area at this time of year.

The perpetrator in this case was already starting to piss her off.

3

From the road, Reiko looked down at the river as it curved and flowed off to the left. She was standing on the precise spot where the illegally parked van had been found.

Long withered grass covered the riverbank. An area fifty meters wide and thirty meters long around the van had been sealed off, all the way down to the water. Not even the detectives were allowed inside. Around twenty forensics technicians were hard at work with their high-powered flashlights and magnifying glasses. The light was fading fast, and the working day was almost over.

Damn, though, it's cold. Seriously cold.

She had tried to psych herself up for the cold, but it was worse than she'd expected.

I'll buy myself a down jacket.

She'd be hitting the big three-oh next year. For her birthday this year, she'd bought herself a Burberry Blue Label trench coat to commemorate the final year of her twenties. She adored the color—it was dark beige, almost brown—and the design was fabulous. Its only failing was the length: it was too short to keep out the cold, and she was freezing from her butt down.

"Lieutenant, your legs are trembling. Shall I rub them for you?"

"Pi–piss off," she said, her teeth chattering with cold. "And shut up."

The morning weather forecast said today would be "on the warm side."

Bellyaching wasn't going to make things any better. It was almost five o'clock already, and it wasn't going to get any warmer as night fell. The only way to stay warm was to move around.

Reiko's cell rang. She looked at the display to see who was calling. "Tokyo Medical Examiner's Office," it read. It had to be Kunioku. Dr. Sadanosuke Kunioku was the source of everything Reiko knew about forensic pathology. Despite being on the verge of retirement, the old coroner was her drinking buddy—though he insisted on telling everyone he was her boyfriend.

"Hello?"

"Hi there, sweetheart. You're on standby at police headquarters downtown, right? Fancy coming out with me tonight or tomorrow? I've got my eye on this dobin mushi place in Ueno. Shall I make a reservation?"

"Sorry. I won't be able to make it for a while. I just got assigned to a new task force."

She ended the call and snapped her phone shut.

"What's up, Lieutenant?"

"None of your business."

I need to concentrate and start focusing on the canvass.

The neighborhood canvass was the first stage of any investigation and often the most crucial. The area around the crime scene was divided into distinct blocks and everyone there was interviewed.

Reiko had been assigned ten teams of two for her canvass. Seven teams, including the pairs with Kikuta and Ishikura, were going to handle the residential area along the road, while three teams—Reiko's, Yuda's, and Hayama's— would interview anyone they found on the riverbank.

There was a running track about two hundred meters off to the left. A group of kids was busy practicing sprinting. Probably from the local high school, guessed Reiko.

"Nori, those kids over there. Go and talk to them."

"Yes, ma'am."

Hayama marched off down the road with his partner, a sergeant from Kamata Precinct.

"Kohei, I want you to talk to anyone coming in this direction—people walking their dogs, jogging, out for a stroll, whatever. Have they seen anyone suspicious hanging around? Do they notice anything that's different today from yesterday? Nothing's too small."

"Yeah, yeah, I know the drill."

With a frown of annoyance, Yuda headed off to the right with his partner.

"How 'bout we do that spot over there?"

Ioka was pointing to a piece of ground just outside

the tape. He had a point. There were several people either following the tape up the embankment or turning around when they found they could go no further. Reiko shook her head.

"No. Our first order of business is over there."

There was a tent rigged out of white tarpaulin down by the river. As far as Reiko could tell, it was the only makeshift shelter nearby.

"Why do you think there's only one homeless guy living around here?"

Ioka pointed past the running track off to the left. "There's a cycling track and a baseball ground over that way. That means decent toilets and running water. Naturally enough, most of the homeless prefer to live around there."

"All the more reason to ask this guy what he's doing on his own here, then."

"Maybe he's just antisocial."

As they walked along the embankment, they encountered an old man detouring around the sealed-off zone. He was small and looked to be in his seventies; nonetheless, he was walking at a good clip.

"Excuse me. Sir?"

The man, who had a cap pulled down low on his forehead, raised himself to his full height and tilted his head to look up at Reiko, who was roughly five foot six. She leaned down a little so that her eyes were level with his.

"What's the problem?"

His eyes were milky and clouded behind wrinkled eyelids.

"Sorry to accost you out of the blue like this, sir. Do you often come walking here?"

Reiko's voice was a little louder and a little shriller than she would have liked. She was doing her best to sound relaxed. With men of this age, the best approach was to treat them like you would your own granddad.

Me, his granddaughter? Perhaps I'm pushing my luck. . . .

The old timer cracked a smile and nodded slowly. Operation Granddad was progressing well so far.

"Every single day of the week."

"Always at this time?"

"Normally a bit earlier. I like to get home before it gets dark, you see."

"Do you ever come out here at night?"

"At night? No, never. Might be dangerous." He paused a moment. "Why? Has something happened?"

Reiko shook her head, then went into a half-crouch and pointed with an exaggerated gesture to make sure the old man could follow her finger.

"Can you see that tent over there, sir?"

"Huh? Oh yes, that one."

"Has it been here long?"

"Been there for ages," declared the old man with a brisk nod. "One year, maybe two. . . . In the summertime, I see the fellow there fishing in the river, happy as can be."

"Is that right?" answered Reiko, amused at his chattiness. "You've seen the man who lives there. Can you tell me what he looks like?"

"What he looks like? ... Let me see."

There was a long pause.

"Having trouble remembering, sir?"

"No, sorry, I can't remember his face. What I will say is that I think it's outrageous. Sometimes in summer I forget what I'm doing and walk that way—and, oh my God, the smell! It's enough to make the nose drop off your face. It's a disgrace."

"I see. Have you noticed anything else odd, a bit out of the ordinary, when you've come walking around here? A suspicious-looking person, perhaps?"

The old man shook his head rather vacantly. Perhaps he was getting cold standing there; he had started clenching and unclenching his black-gloved hands.

I know how you feel, gramps. It's freezing.

Reiko pulled her badge wallet out from inside her jacket, flipped it open, and showed her ID.

"I'm with the Tokyo Metropolitan Police Department. We had an incident here earlier today. That's why we're asking the residents if they noticed anything out of the ordinary. If you don't mind, could I get your name and address? We may need to ask some follow-up questions."

"No problem at all," the old man answered cheerily. He gave his name as Shinsuke Tayama, his address as West Rokugo block 1, number 38, and provided his phone number.

Reiko waited until Ioka had finished jotting down the man's details, then held out her hand.

"Yes, Lieutenant?"

"Give me one of your name cards."

"Sure, here you go."

Reiko's own cards didn't have the phone number of Kamata Police Station, so giving them out wouldn't be of much use.

"Here you are, Mr. Tayama. Give us a call at this number if anything comes to mind. We're a 24/7 operation, so you can call any time."

They thanked the old man for his assistance, and after watching him go on his way for a moment or two, Reiko and Ioka resumed walking themselves.

Ioka peered around Reiko to inspect the riverbank.

"So, Lieutenant, are we going to pay a visit to the tent?"

They got to the corner of the sealed-off section and started walking down the slope through the withered grass toward the flat section of riverbank.

"You bet. That guy might have had a ringside seat when the perp was dumping the body."

"But the old geezer just now said he stinks to high heaven."

"There's nothing to worry about. There'll be no smell in cold weather like this."

Suddenly she squealed as she lost her footing.

"Careful!"

She felt a hand grab her right elbow and another encircle her waist. Ioka was a small man and rather highly strung; Reiko was startled at the lean strength in his arms.

"Thanks."

"My pleasure, I assure you," he sniggered.

He kept holding her as they made their way down the rest of the embankment.

"Hands off now."

"How can you say that? I'd die if anything happened to you, Lieutenant Reiko."

"Be my guest."

Even when they reached the flat part of the riverbank, Ioka wouldn't let go.

"I told you, hands off."

"There you go again. You're adorable when you get bashful."

"I'll bash you, if you don't watch out."

She jerked her arm a couple of times until Ioka had to let go.

"Dammit, what are you thinking?"

"Thinking? I'm thinking of you, Lieutenant Reiko, you and nothing but you."

"Put a sock in it. Try focusing on the crime for a change."

"How can I?"

Still, Ioka did pick up the pace. In the last few minutes, night had fallen, and it was now pitch dark. The white tent, which had been so easy to see from the top of the embankment, was now hidden among the tall weeds that grew in profusion by the water's edge.

"Ioka, have you got a flashlight?"

"Leave it to me," he replied as he whipped a flashlight out of his bulging shoulder bag. It was surprisingly big.

"Nice. I'm impressed."

"You can always rely on me."

"Switch it on, then."

"Here goes," giggled Ioka.

A small patch around them was suddenly illuminated.

Looking around, Reiko spotted a gap in the high weeds over to her right. She headed for it, and the light came bobbing after her. Ioka was doing a poor job of directing the light at the ground under her feet.

"Give the thing to me," Reiko said, grabbing the flashlight out of Ioka's hands.

"The ingratitude!"

Through the weeds, about three meters ahead, she could see the black surface of the river; the tent was a little way over to the left, on slightly higher ground. The homeless guy must have chosen the place because it would stay dry even when the water level rose. There was no light on inside the tent.

"Come on."

"Are you serious?"

Reiko carefully made her way toward it.

The tent looked square. The entrance, which was on the side facing the river, was a black aperture. The occupant must have just done his laundry; three pairs of grimy socks were hanging just outside.

"Smells pretty bad to me."

Reiko blew the air out of her lungs. Ioka was right. The place stank of rotting garbage.

What if the rest of the chopped-up body has been dumped right here?

Reiko peered into the flap, hoping against hope. Inside, it was too dark to see anything without the flashlight.

"Hello?"

Her voice sounded a little funny because she was trying not to breathe through her nose.

There was no reply.

"Anyone home?"

Still no response. Reiko directed the beam of the flashlight into the tent. The interior was bigger and tidier than she had expected.

While the floor was just bare earth, there was a square table with a portable gas stove and a spice rack on it at the back right. A little way closer to her was an old-fashioned TV set. Reiko also noticed a gasoline-powered generator (which wasn't switched on), a bookcase full of magazines, and a chest of drawers.

But where does the guy sleep?

At that moment, a little mound in the middle of the back wall of the tent burst into life. There was a rustling sound, and a head with a woolly hat on emerged.

"What's going on here?"

It hadn't occurred to Reiko that the pile of cardboard over there could be a bed. Now she could see that the man was wrapped up in a comforter or a blanket under it all. Reiko's immediate impression was she wasn't dealing with someone storing a dead body on the premises.

"Sorry to barge in like this. No one answered, so—"

"You from the municipality? What you doing here so late."

His voice was a horrible rasp.

"We're not from the municipality. We're the police."

Now Reiko could see the man properly—if *properly* was the word. He was scowling so fiercely, his face was so grime-blackened, that it was impossible to know what he really looked like.

"Cut it out, will you? I know you're just winding me up."

"No, sir, we are the police."

"What you doing turning up unannounced in the middle of the night? You're not gonna tear this place down, are you? Where am I supposed to go on a freezing night like this?"

"That's not why we're here, sir."

Thinking she might be used to the smell, Reiko tried breathing through her nose. Big mistake. The old man was right: getting too close in summer would definitely cause your nose to fall off.

"Listen, we're not here to ask you why you're here or to move you along. . . . Were you aware that the police have been working just outside your tent since early this morning?"

The man coughed and brought a hand up to shield his eyes.

"Hey, turn that thing off, will ya? It's blinding me."

"I'm sorry."

She wasn't pointing the beam directly at him, but to

someone who'd just woken up, it probably felt painfully bright.

Reiko switched off the flashlight and everything went black. She would have felt nervous had she been alone.

"Did you not notice them?"

"Huh? Notice what?"

"Like I said, that the police have been poking around in the grass just over there."

More rustling. As far as she could tell, he wasn't getting up; perhaps he had lain back down again.

"No, I'd no idea. Lately, I've not been feeling too good. I've been in bed . . . , the whole day."

"In bed all day?"

"Yeah, except for when I went for a piss. About where you're standing now."

Eager though she was to jump aside, Reiko didn't want to give the homeless guy the satisfaction.

"Very interesting. There was a small white van parked on the embankment up there from late last night until early this morning. Would you know anything about that?"

"What's that about the embankment?"

"I asked if you were aware that a small white van was parked there from late last night till early this morning."

The man exploded into a spasm of coughing. It sounded nasty. Reiko hoped it wasn't TB. She waited for the noise to subside.

"Nah, didn't see nothing. Last night, today, just taken a piss over there. Never looked at the embankment."

It was plausible enough. You couldn't see the

embankment from down here. To do that, you'd have to get out of the tall weed patch or go down to the river's edge.

"Did you hear anything? Any noises?"

A pause.

"When?"

"Last night or early this morning."

"Naah," the man grunted and sank into silence. "What kind of noises, anyway?"

"Could be anything. Branches breaking, someone prowling around, the sound of car brakes."

Reiko nearly added "the sound of someone dumping something in the river," but thought better of it.

"I get you. It's always pretty noisy around here. There's the dogs, the birds, the crows who come to steal the trash. . . ."

As Reiko's eyes got used to the darkness, she was gradually able to make things out. The man wasn't completely lying down; he had his head propped up on his arm and was looking at her.

"So did you hear anything?"

The man was overcome with another violent coughing fit.

"Are you all right, sir?"

There was no reply. The coughing went on and on, accompanied by a slithery rustling of newspapers and cardboard.

What am I supposed to do in a situation like this?

As a human being and a government employee, Reiko felt that she should go over, rub his back, ask him how he felt, maybe even arrange for him to go to a hospital.

But as a policeman, that wasn't her job, and she loathed dirty people. She actually preferred a decomposed dead body to a dirty living one. All corpses smelled bad; that was just the way they were. She put up with them because it was part of her job. Now, here she was, confronted with someone who was alive and smelled bad, and she wanted nothing to do with him. It didn't seem quite right.

The guy was sick, so, yes, she felt sorry for him. At the same time, she wanted to ask him how he could seriously expect to stay healthy when he lived like this. Some people ended up homeless despite doing everything they could to fight against it. But if the guy's only problem was a lack of grit, then he needed to pull his socks up and make an effort to return to normal life. Living this way was dangerous: he was putting both his health and his safety at risk.

The man eventually stopped coughing.

"Why you still here?" he grunted. "I can't tell you anything . . . that you want to know. . . . Shit, I don't even know what fucking time it is. . . . Why'd you imagine I'd know anything in the first place anyway? Go on, get out of here. Leave me alone."

That was the first proper answer Reiko had got out of him and it had made her ears prick up.

Why'd you imagine I'd know anything in the first place anyway?

She didn't know why that particular phrase bugged her. Was it something in the tone of his voice? Was it because of the long pause before he said it? Was it the words themselves?

Sounded a little bit legalistic and roundabout to me . . .

Reiko asked the man if he had a cell phone, even though she suspected the question was a waste of time.

"No, I don't," came the answer in a tone that as good as said, "Duh! You stupid bitch."

Reiko asked for his name. Takeshi Iizuka, he said, and even spelled it for her. She asked him to call 110 and ask for Kamata Police Station if he happened to remember anything.

No answer.

All she could hear was his stertorous breathing. Or was the man snoring?

4

It was just after 7:30 p.m. when Reiko and the other investigators in her group got back to Kamata Police Station. Somebody had taped a sign reading "Tama River Dumped Body Task Force" to the door of the room.

The instant she entered the room, Captain Imaizumi, who was sitting at the table up at the front, waved her over with an extravagant gesture. Reiko walked across the room, deposited her coat and bag on a seat in the middle of the front row, and turned to face him.

"What is it, sir?"

"Who've you left stationed at the crime scene?"

"I left four investigators on the scene: Nori's team and Sergeant Shimoda's team—Shimoda is from the Major Crimes Division here at Kamata. There's a temple on the embankment, and they let us use a room on the third floor overlooking the crime scene. The men are under orders to patrol the area on a rolling basis. Once the meeting here's over, I'll send another couple of teams across to relieve them. I'll speak for Nori and Sergeant Shimoda at the meeting."

"Good work. Go and sit down."

"Thank you, sir."

Ioka handed her a seaweed-covered rice ball when she got back to her place. It was pickled plum flavor. Reiko had picked it up in the convenience store on the way back to the station. Ioka must have taken it out of the package and wrapped the seaweed around the rice himself.

"What the hell! I told you I'd do it myself."

"Don't say that. It's a labor of love."

God, this man just wears me out! My nerves are shot.

"Thanks but no thanks. With seaweed, I prefer to roll my own."

"I'm not good enough for you?"

There was a sudden sharp crack. Ioka yelped and grabbed his head with his hands. Kikuta, who was in the row behind, must have smacked him in the head.

"What!" Ioka spluttered. "What are you doing, Brother Kaz?"

"Sorry, *bro*. My hand must have slipped."

"Sure it did."

"You calling me a liar? All right, bucktooth, want to take this outside?"

"Will you two just knock it off," snapped Reiko, glaring at them. Kikuta pouted and looked away.

Oh, please. You're not a child.

In the meantime, the remaining investigators had returned. Kusaka and his squad were back, and they sat in a row to the left of Reiko and her team.

As Captain Imaizumi picked up the microphone, Reiko hurriedly crammed the last of the rice ball into her mouth.

"Okay, let's get this meeting under way. Everyone, stand at attention! Bow toward the front."

Including the forensics teams, there must have been over fifty investigators in the room. At the front of the room was Senior Superintendent Nakamura, the commander of Kamata Police Station; Superintendent Miyagawa, Commissioner of the Homicide Division; and Captain Kawada, Chief of Detectives of the local precinct, alongside Director Hashizume and Captain Imaizumi, the chief of Unit 10.

The official head of the task force was the director of the TMPD's Criminal Investigation Unit, but he was too lofty a being to put in a personal appearance. Even Director Hashizume wouldn't be there all the time. That meant that in practical terms it was Captain Imaizumi who was leading this particular task force.

"I'd like to kick things off by giving you an update on the hand that was found," began Imaizumi. "We believe it was severed around four centimeters below the wrist joint from the palmar side, using an electric saw that cut through both the radius and the ulna."

Reiko flipped through the bundle of documents she'd been given until she came to the photographs of the hand. She found one that showed the hand as it was when found at the scene and before cleaning.

The hand was slathered in its own blood and had turned a lurid pinky-red that looked nothing like normal human skin. It reminded Reiko of pickled red ginger garnish.

"We examined an electric saw found in the garage. After comparing the shape of the blade with the marks on the cut bones, we concluded that the saw was used to sever the wrist. Traces around the on-off switch and the grip on the upper part of the saw show that someone used it while wearing cotton work gloves. We couldn't lift any prints off of it."

Reiko flicked through a few more pages until she came to a photograph of the saw. It was old and heavily used. There was a piece of green electrical tape wrapped around the power cord about halfway down.

"Any questions?"

No one said anything.

Reiko glanced off to one side and saw Kusaka wearing a pair of silver-rimmed spectacles, craning forward, busily taking notes.

"Okay, we'll move on, then. Let's hear from TMPD Forensics on the garage."

"Yes, sir," said Lieutenant Ijizu from the CID Forensics Department, making his way to the whiteboard at the front of the room. He'd already drawn a floor plan of the garage on it.

"I'm going to tell you what our inspection of the garage's interior and environs turned up," he began. "As you can see from this diagram, the garage is rectangular, with a width of 3.7 meters and a depth of 6.2 meters. It's located at the far left of a row of three rental garages of identical size, which stand at a distance of 1.6 meters back from the road. Seen from the road, this garage has a window on the left-hand wall. Since there's shelving running around all three of the garage's internal walls, there's stuff blocking the window from the inside. From the street you can just about tell if the light's on or not, but you certainly can't see inside.

"There's a lot of construction hardware—nails, metal fittings, lengths of timber and other building materials, leftover pieces of plywood—either sitting on the shelves proper, or leaning up against them. I'll spare you the gory details, but suffice it to say that pieces of flesh and blood spatter were found in all directions, and the victim had lost enough blood to more or less cover the entire cement floor. From this, we conclude that the body was dismembered and cut into a minimum of six or seven pieces at the scene.

"The next thing is fingerprints," continued Ijizu. "We found six sets of prints in addition to those of Kenichi Takaoka, the victim, and Kosuke Mishima, his employee. We ran them through our database, but none of them came up as having any priors. Two of the six were found on boxes of building supplies on the shelves, so it's quite possible that those particular prints originated outside the crime scene. Now I'd like to draw your attention to this metal pole-hook used to open and close the garage's roller-shutter door."

Ijizu held up a clear plastic bag with the pole inside.

"We found a complete set of prints—both the right and the left hand—on this pole-hook. They don't belong either to Takaoka, the victim, or to Mishima, the employee who was first on the scene. It's legitimate to speculate that the

TETSUYA HONDA

suspect left them in a moment of carelessness when he used the pole-hook to pull the door shut with ungloved hands."

Kusaka immediately raised his hand.

"Lieutenant Ijizu, I'd prefer if you refrained from speculation of any kind."

Ijizu gave Kusaka an icy stare, nodded curtly, and went on.

"I'll proceed, if I may. The next thing is shoe prints. Because the floor was almost entirely covered with blood, we only managed to locate three shoe prints: these were Mishima's sneakers, then a second set of sneakers, and finally some leather shoes. Since Mishima told us that Takaoka always wore sneakers for work, I think it's reasonable to assume that the leather shoes—"

Ijizu wanted to say that the leather shoes most likely belonged to the suspect; after his earlier run-in with Kusaka, however, he opted for tactical vagueness.

"—belong to a third person of identity unknown. Traces of the same bloody shoe prints were also found on the stretch of concrete between the garage and the road. The fact that they are pointing toward the street suggests that the owner of the shoes trod in the blood *inside* the garage and then went outside. We also found the same shoe prints on the pedals of the abandoned van.

"In the garage, we found a roll of translucent plastic sheeting of the kind contractors use to keep things clean when they're working."

"How much of it was left?" boomed Kusaka from the back of the room. Reiko's head swiveled around. This

72

time he hadn't bothered to raise his hand.

Ijizu grimaced and jerked his shoulders angrily.

"Two meters precisely. We also detected gloved fingerprints on this sheeting. We think it's possible that this sheeting was used to wrap up the dismembered body parts prior to transportation."

There was an edge to Ijizu's voice. He was clearly exasperated. He continued with his report, going into very precise detail. There was nothing in it that struck Reiko as truly game-changing.

"If there are no questions about the garage, then we'll move onto the next item," said Imaizumi. "The results of the forensic testing of the vehicle."

"Thank you, sir."

Sergeant Minuo of TMPD Forensics got to his feet. His findings didn't add anything to what Ijizu had said.

They had managed to pull some prints off the driver's seat. They had also found impressions from cotton work gloves that had absorbed a large quantity of blood, but the prints were far dirtier than those on the electric saw in the garage because the gloves had slid around on the upholstery. There were some more partial glove prints on the driver's door, on the sliding door on the passenger side of the van, and on the handle of the back hatch, but these only provided evidence of the suspect's movements around the vehicle and were unlikely to be of much use until they had him in custody.

When they found the van, continued Sergeant Minuo,

all the doors were locked and the key was not inside.

So whoever had chopped up Takaoka's corpse had wrapped the pieces in plastic sheeting or stuffed them into plastic bags, loaded them into the minivan, and then driven it to the Tama River embankment. There he locked the vehicle and abandoned it. But what had he done next?

I don't want to be Kusaka-like about it, but it's probably best to not to speculate for now.

"Thank you, Sergeant Minuo," Imaizumi said. "Can we move on to the forensics report on the riverbank?"

Sergeant Moroi, also from TMPD Forensics, got to his feet. Most of his report was devoted to the blood traces they'd found in the stretch of grass by the river.

There had been a light rain the night of the crime, and Forensics had expected all the blood traces to be washed away. Amazingly, however, they'd located a series of bloodstains in a more or less straight line from where the van was parked down to the river's edge.

The bloodstains were all distributed within a lateral span of roughly four meters. This suggested that the suspect had made multiple trips from the van to the river, following a roughly similar path every time. Eventually the rain must have washed all the blood off the soles of his shoes, because they couldn't determine in which direction he'd gone after disposing of the corpse.

They'd retrieved a number of items from the scene: a small white button, some scraps of nylon, an unidentified fragment of red plastic, pieces of eggshell, a thick wooden cooking skewer, a dog collar, a broken cell phone, one ten-yen and two one-yen coins. . . .

"We didn't find any fingerprints or blood traces on any of the above items. That brings my reports on the riverside to an end."

"Any questions?" barked Imaizumi. "Right, then: next up is the canvass in the neighborhood of the garage. Who handled Sector One?"

"That's me, sir," replied Kusaka, getting to his feet. The guy sitting next to him—was that Sergeant Satomura from Kamata Precinct? Reiko wasn't quite sure.

"We interviewed all the residents of Middle Rokugo block two, house numbers one to five. The first person we spoke to was Hideyuki Tanaka, age thirty-two. He works in the post office and rents the garage beside Takaoka's. He lives in Middle Rokugo, block two, number three, in a detached house which he shares with his parents. The parents were also present when we conducted the interview. They are Masayuki Tanaka, a sixty-eight-year-old retiree, and his wife, Shizuko, a seventy-one-year-old homemaker. Hideyuki is an only child. Hideyuki has a car—a Mazda Demio. It is iris blue mica, which I can best describe as pale blue with a hint of purple."

God help us! Kusaka's canvass reports always followed this pattern. He regurgitated every trivial factoid in the most excruciating detail.

Reiko had taken him to task about it more than once. *Leave out the irrelevant stuff and just give us the key points,* she'd said. Kusaka had completely ignored her. Early on in the process, he argued, no one was qualified to judge what might or might not be relevant. For example, he might claim that if you didn't know, say, that the little sister of the person renting the garage next door to Takaoka's had moved up to Aichi Prefecture after her marriage four years ago, then you couldn't safely eliminate her from the scope of the investigation.

During one meeting, Reiko had gotten so exasperated that she'd blurted out something sarcastic about the need to take meteor strikes into account.

Kusaka had counterpunched by explaining that, whenever he was assigned to an investigation, he would only set out for the crime scene after checking the local weather on an hour-by-hour basis. "Any fool could tell if there'd been a meteor strike," he said, "but let me assure my female colleague that in the current case I have not encountered any evidence of freak events near the crime scene: no lightning strikes, no tornadoes—and no meteors either."

Reiko had been so furious she'd thought she was going to spontaneously combust.

Kusaka's approach reminded Reiko of a man grabbing everything he could get his hands on, sifting it through a sieve, and then plucking out any big lumps that stayed behind. She preferred to stick her hand right into the sieve and pull out what felt important.

What annoyed Reiko most was how Kusaka managed to contemplate every possible angle without his investigations getting bogged down. He was both thorough *and* fast. His reputation was so good that his nickname in the prosecutor's office was Mr. Guilty Verdict. Strange as it was, Reiko had to accept that the man was widely trusted and respected.

I've got my own personal reasons for disliking him.

Kusaka was still droning on. Reiko summarized everything he'd said so far in her head.

Several local residents heard the sound of angry male voices coming from the garage at around 9:30 p.m. The whine of an electric saw got on the nerves of a student studying for the university entrance exam in the house opposite; when he checked his watch, it was 10:40 p.m. Another resident, who was strolling along the street in front of the garage around the same time, reported seeing a van parked on the street outside.

That's the gist of what you had to say. And how long did it take you?

If any of the households Kusaka had visited owned a dog, he'd be sure to inform you of its color and breed. If anyone was sick, he'd give you the name and address of the hospital they were in.

You bombard us with so many factoids it's impossible to write it all down.

Glancing to one side, Reiko noticed that instead of taking notes, Ioka had turned Kusaka's report into a manga. It was surprisingly well done.

I've got my doubts about you too, my friend. Is it so smart to treat life as one big joke?

Eventually, Kusaka concluded his report. Needless to

say, no one had the energy to ask any questions.

"Okay then," sighed Imaizumi. "Next up is Sergeant Toyama, who handled Sector Two."

"Yes, sir."

None of the reports from the precinct detectives added anything new to what Kusaka had said about the garage area. Once they were done, it was, at last, Reiko's turn.

"Thanks," said Imaizumi. "We'll move on to the riverbank canvass now. Himekawa, I believe that's your department?"

"Yes, sir."

Reiko believed that the best way to deliver her reports was by distilling the important points and aiming for maximum brevity. It wasn't about getting back at Kusaka. She simply had her own style, one that worked for her.

"My report will also incorporate information from Officer Hayama and Sergeant Shimoda. They've both stayed behind with their partners to keep an eye on the crime scene. When we got to the riverside this afternoon, there were plenty of people there—people walking their dogs and jogging, a group of high school kids from the school athletics club. They all come to the river regularly in the late afternoon; none of them had any knowledge about a van left on the embankment last night. There was also a tent belonging to a homeless man. The occupant—his name is Takeshi Iizuka—has been feeling unwell for the last couple of days. As he's been in bed the whole time, including, of course, the last twenty-four hours, he claims not to have noticed the forensic investigation taking place in the immediate vicinity of his tent, let alone the van parked up on the road. He also said he heard nothing suspicious.

"Sergeant Shimoda spoke to an Akio Ishikawa, a twenty-year-old male residing at West Rokugo, block three, number eight. Ishikawa spotted the parked minivan as he was driving home sometime after midnight. He got home just after 12:30 a.m., and since it takes five minutes maximum to drive from where the van was parked to his house, we can place the van on the river embankment at 12:25 a.m. Mr. Ishikawa does not recall seeing anyone inside the vehicle or noticing anyone suspicious nearby. Remember, of course, that it was raining at the time.

"Various other residents spotted the van when they looked out of the windows of their homes. They either couldn't recall the precise time or provided times later than that of Mr. Ishikawa, so in the interests of simplicity I will omit their testimony. That brings my report to an end."

"Any questions?" asked Imaizumi.

Kusaka prodded his glasses higher up his nose with his index finger, but said nothing.

The first case meeting ended with the investigators who hadn't had a chance to speak briefly introducing themselves to the group; then Director Hashizume droned on for a while about how important it was to keep the details of the investigation secret.

Most of the investigators stayed behind after the

meeting. They dragged their chairs into a circle and began devouring the beer and takeout food someone had ordered in.

That wasn't Reiko's idea of fun. She preferred to head out to a local pub with Kikuta and the rest of her squad. Today, however, that wasn't an option. She had to take part in the executive meeting to assign the sectors for the next day's canvass and decide who was going to handle what aspect of the inquiry into the victim's family, friends, and associates, which was also starting the next day.

Normally, the executive meetings were held away from the main room of the task force. Maybe the police station was busy and there wasn't another room available—or maybe the Kamata people were plain disorganized. Either way, they ended up having to hold their meeting in a corner of the big room where everyone else was eating and drinking. Six people took part: Director Hashizume, Captain Imaizumi, Captain Kawada (the chief of detectives in Kamata Precinct), Lieutenant Tanimoto (Kamata CID's head of major crimes), Kusaka, and Reiko.

Captain Imaizumi again took the lead. Director Hashizume acted like an observer, refusing to get directly involved. Reiko guessed that he was trying to come across as a broad-minded boss willing to delegate to his subordinates; as far as she was concerned, though, it was just a pose, and the man was failing to live up to his responsibilities. On this one point, she suspected that she and Kusaka saw eye to eye.

Imaizumi wrote out a list of the names of all the investigators on the case.

"We're going to have to throw a lot of manpower at the inquiry into the victim's family, friends, and associates," grumbled Imaizumi. "There's a ton of people to talk to."

Kusaka nodded. "That's right, sir. In terms of Takaoka's work associates alone, we'll need to talk not just to the construction company where he worked before setting up in business for himself, but also to all the different outfits he currently does business with—contractors, architects, scaffolders, plumbers, electricians, gas fitters, hardware merchants, demolition contractors, scrap merchants—plus all his clients on top of that. As a sole proprietor, Takaoka dealt directly with a lot of different people."

Kusaka was reading the list from the initial statement of Kosuke Mishima, Takaoka's sole employee. It was Captain Kawada, the Kamata chief of detectives, who'd interviewed him.

"Obviously, tomorrow we'll need someone to interview Kosuke Mishima in greater depth," said Reiko, keen to snare the job for herself.

An unexpected obstacle presented itself: Kusaka.

"Hold your horses, Himekawa. There's something I need to ask you."

Reiko had a bad feeling about this, but with only six people, the meeting was too intimate to just blow Kusaka off.

"Uh-huh?"

"How is it that the name Hiroshi Maekawa did not feature in your report just now?"

"Pardon me?"

Who the heck is Hiroshi Maekawa?

"You've no idea what I'm talking about."

This doesn't look good. Have I messed up?

"I don't. Who is he?"

"Hiroshi Maekawa is a seventy-four-year-old man who lives in the sector I covered for the door-to-door in the garage area. At 5:30 this evening, Maekawa went power walking along the riverside—where you were supposedly making your inquiries—before returning home at 6:30 p.m."

So damn what?

"Maekawa informed us that no one from the police approached him while he was on the riverbank. In other words, you completely overlooked a man who went from the area where the body was dismembered to the area where the body was disposed of and back again. That sounds like a very sloppily run canvass to me."

"You can't be serious?"

Reiko was angry. What was Kusaka trying to imply? That they should have waylaid every single person who came anywhere near the riverbank?

"No excuses, please. Here we have a man who traveled between the two crime scenes less than twenty-four hours after the incident took place. You'll agree, I think, that he could quite feasibly have gone to check up on the progress of the police investigation or to verify that he'd not left any evidence behind."

"What was your impression of Maekawa? Did he strike you as suspicious?"

"I don't deal in impressions, Himekawa. What I can assure you is that there's no need for concern. Maekawa has an alibi. He works part-time as a security guard and was on the job all last night. I was able to confirm that with his employer over the phone. If anything suspicious comes up later, I will, of course, look into his alibi more deeply. You made a basic blunder, Himekawa, and there's nothing your famous sixth sense can do to compensate for it."

Yeah, yeah, I know. Applying imagination to a case is an instant black mark in your book. God knows, I've heard that often enough before.

"What do you want me to say? What about the road along the embankment that we've reopened to traffic? Am I supposed to stop every single car and question the occupants?"

"Is it doable?"

"*What!*"

"Listen, Himekawa, I'm not asking you to do anything extraordinary here. You like your outer space analogies, don't you? Okay then, think of it like this: I'm not saying that the man in the moon's a suspect. What we have here is a human being who traveled between the two crime scenes. You missed that. That's inexcusable for the leader of a numbered squad."

A numbered squad in Homicide was the elite of the elite in the Tokyo Metropolitan Police. Being a squad leader came with serious responsibility.

Oh shit!

Reiko sighed heavily and bowed her head in apology.

"I messed up. I'll be more careful in the future."

The fact that Kusaka didn't get loud or angry, even when he was tearing a strip off you, was some consolation. None of the investigators scarfing down their dinner in the same room would ever guess that Reiko had just been subjected to some pretty rough justice.

Kusaka looked from Reiko to Imaizumi.

"Captain, *I'd* like to interview Kosuke Mishima tomorrow."

You've got to be kidding!

Kusaka's timing was perfect. There was nothing Reiko could do.

Damn it! That's what this whole Maekawa episode was about.

As far as Reiko could tell from skimming through Mishima's statement, he and Takaoka, the victim, spent most of their waking hours in one another's company.

Interviewing Mishima was obviously the quickest way to get up to speed on Takaoka. As the person closest to him, Mishima was most likely to know about the victim's personal enmities, woman troubles, money problems, whatever.

Reiko was furious at the way Kusaka had swooped in on Mishima, but now wasn't the time to try and wrestle him back. She didn't have a leg to stand on.

Although Captain Imaizumi kept an eye out for Reiko, he didn't practice favoritism. "A fuckup by any other name is still a fuckup," was one of his favorite sayings, as was, "You can't do what you can't do." That was the sort of boss he was.

"There is something you can do, Himekawa."

Kusaka had pulled his glasses down to the tip of his nose and was peering at Reiko over the upper rim.

"What's that?"

"Mishima has a girlfriend. He claims to have been at her workplace at the time that the crime is thought to have occurred."

Kusaka was reading from Mishima's written statement.

I've got a copy of the statement too. And, believe it or not, I can read as well!

Michiko Nakagawa. Nineteen years old. Studying hairdressing while working part-time at a diner.

"Why don't we let Himekawa handle the girlfriend, captain?" Kusaka said to Imaizumi. "They're both young women. Might be a good fit."

"Sounds good to me," replied Imaizumi, after a second's hesitation.

Kusaka looked around.

"Are you all right with that, Captain Kawada?"

As a captain, Kawada was one rank above Kusaka. In a task force, however, the rules were different: Homicide always had the whip hand, and regular seniority counted for little.

"That's fine by me."

"Good, that's decided, then."

Reiko had been like a rabbit caught in the headlights.

She had lost her chance to interview Mishima, a key actor in the drama, and been fobbed off with Michiko Nakagawa, a minor player in the supporting cast.

That's why I hate working with this guy.

The executive meeting dragged on until midnight.

5

It was day two of the task force.

The moment the morning meeting ended, Lieutenant Kusaka hurried over to the CID offices on the third floor. Kosuke Mishima was coming in for voluntary questioning.

Sergeant Takehiko Satomura, who'd been designated as Kusaka's partner at the morning meeting, poured him a cup of tea. An easygoing man of forty-two, Satomura was a couple of years Kusaka's junior.

"He should be here any minute. Here, have some of this."

Captain Kawada, who was sitting on the other side of the table, reached out and took another cup from Satomura without removing the cigarette from between his fingers.

"That Lieutenant Himekawa, she's quite something," said Kawada, breaking off for a slurp of tea.

"And 'something' means?"

"She's tall, a looker, and tough as nails. Mentally, I mean."

Kusaka grinned sourly. "When it comes to strong-

87

mindedness, Himekawa's in a league of her own. She's a damned good cop, though."

"I got the impression that you two don't get on so well," said Kawada, tentatively.

"How so?"

"How so? It's her eyes, I guess. There's something a bit, I don't know, harsh in the way she looks at you."

Kawada chuckled under his breath. *Oh, so a cup of a tea and some nice juicy gossip about feuding homicide detectives is your idea of a nice break, is it?* thought Kusaka.

"You're wrong. Himekawa and I have differences of opinion—that's only to be expected in the course of an investigation—but it has nothing to do with whether we 'get on' or not. Life in a numbered homicide unit is no cakewalk. We haven't time to be all buddy-buddy when we're on the on the job."

"Sorry, I spoke out of turn," murmured Kawada, shrugging as he put his teacup on the table.

One thing Kusaka could not do was state categorically that Reiko Himekawa did not detest him. In fact, she hated him, and he had no idea why.

As far as he could recall, he hadn't said anything to her that would qualify as gender harassment, nor had he tried to sabotage her career. He simply couldn't conceive what had triggered her dislike for him. It dated back to her first day with Unit 10, and they had never warmed to each other since.

Kusaka refused to believe that their very public clashes,

whenever he criticized or wrong-footed her in meetings, had anything to do with it. In the end, she just didn't like his type. That was no skin off his nose, provided she did her job right. Besides, even if they got on like a house on fire, he wouldn't have been a jot less critical or left her on a job that he judged she wasn't up to handling properly.

Still, that didn't mean he liked it when outsiders started griping about her. He was willing to fight in her corner—provided she didn't go too far.

She's a loose cannon. She's got no idea about the impact of her behavior on other people.

Kusaka, however, was quite sincere when he described her as a damned good cop. That and their characters' being polar opposites were two different things.

"I think that's our boy," said Kawada, looking over toward the door. Kusaka swung around and saw a young man standing in the doorway. He looked slightly different from the driver's license photo Kusaka had seen in the file.

Kosuke Mishima wasn't tall. Kusaka put his height at roughly five feet, six inches. His hair was cut short and dyed a fashionable light brown. He had typically Japanese features: small, alert eyes, and features compressed into the middle of a broad face. He was stockily built, and the first impression Kusaka got was one of toughness.

"Thanks for making the time to come and see us," said Kusaka.

An anxious expression flashed across Mishima's face. Perhaps he wasn't keen on having to talk to someone other than Kawada, who'd taken his statement the previous day.

"My name's Lieutenant Kusaka. I'll be interviewing you today. Could you come this way, please?"

Kusaka went out into the passageway and indicated Interview Room III on the far side. It wasn't the most reassuring place for an ordinary civilian, but the Kamata CID office was just too noisy for a serious interview.

The young man looked from Kusaka to Kawada, cocking his head inquiringly. Kawada nodded brusquely but stayed in the CID offices. Satomura pushed open the door of the interview room. Mishima went in first, followed by Kusaka, with Satomura bringing up the rear.

The room was a typical interview room: small and rather claustrophobic.

"Could you sit over there?" said Kusaka, pointing to the chair on the far side of the table. He took a seat on the side closer to the door.

Satomura deposited his laptop on the table and went out again to prepare some more tea.

"Sorry to get you to come in early like this. I hope we haven't disrupted your work schedule," said Kusaka, making small talk in an effort to get Mishima to loosen up.

"Not really."

"Are you working near here today?"

"No, over in Kawasaki. I was asked to provide an estimate for redoing someone's kitchen by . . . by the old man."

The old man . . .

Mishima's voice trailed off, and his face contorted.

"Frankly, after what happened to . . . uh . . . Mr. Takaoka, I've got no idea if the kitchen job's on or not."

"Won't you be taking over the business?"

"Me? I'm not ready."

Satomura came back in and dished out the teacups. Mishima stared at the steam rising from his cup to avoid eye contact.

"I see," replied Kusaka. "Did you and Takaoka handle most of the jobs that came in yourselves?"

"We did, yeah. We call ourselves a construction company, but we're a tiny little outfit, really. We've got a roster of regular clients, and we get work by calling around and asking them if they need our help with anything. Sometimes they hook us up with new clients. That's how we got this Kawasaki kitchen job. Occasionally, big contractors get in touch and ask us to work as part of the team on large-scale jobs. Normally, though, we do stuff that the two of us can handle. I didn't do a whole lot by myself."

"You were with Takaoka most of the time, then?"

"Most of the time, yeah."

"But sometimes you worked separately?"

"With jobs that came directly to us, Mr. Takaoka handled the money side of things, collecting payment, you know. He also handled the preliminary site inspection and drawing up cost estimates. When he had something like that to do, he'd go off and leave me working on whatever job we were doing."

Collecting payment?

"The jobs you handle—what sort of sums are we talking about?"

Mishima gave a little shrug.

"I don't know a whole lot about the money side of things. Don't think we handle anything above ten million yen. I'm guessing, three, four, maybe five million is about as high as we go."

"Collecting payment—was it ever problematic?"

Mishima swallowed and shifted in his seat.

"Problematic? Sorry?"

"I mean, was there ever any trouble with clients refusing to pay up?"

"I can't say it *never* happened."

A second later, Mishima's head jerked up. He looked at Kusaka with a startled expression on his face.

"What? You think that might have something to do with the old ma—I mean, Mr. Takaoka—being murdered?"

"At this stage, we really don't know," replied Kusaka gently. "Mr. Mishima, if I may? The first time we heard the name Kenichi Takaoka was yesterday. We knew nothing about him then, and things are not all that different today. What kind of person was he? How did he spend his time? What kind of people did he socialize with? Did he have any problems? These are the sorts of things we need to know. From what you told Captain Kawada yesterday, we're pretty confident that you are the person who knows the most about Kenichi Takaoka. Can you think of any reason why this might have happened? Did you notice any signs?

Can you think of an event that might've acted as a trigger? Of course, it doesn't have to be as obvious as that. It could be something that struck you as odd, maybe about Takaoka himself, maybe about someone he hung around with. Tell us everything you know. Nothing is too small."

Mishima cocked his head to one side.

"To be honest, I don't think not being paid was much of a problem for us. It'd be serious if someone tried to wriggle out of paying for a five-million-yen job, but nothing like that ever happened. It was more like someone saying, 'Give us a discount of two hundred thousand,' or, 'Come on, why not round it down to the nearest hundred thousand?'"

Mishima was silent for a few seconds. He was having trouble getting the words out.

"Yeah, mainly it was stuff like people demanding a discount if they thought our work wasn't up to snuff, or if we'd damaged something, you know, like scratched the floor. Screwups like that, nine times out of ten, I was responsible. Sometimes the client would beat the price down by three hundred or five hundred thousand yen. Discount or no discount, though, Takaoka always paid me my full day's wages. Business wasn't always easy, but Takaoka was a stubborn bugger. I'd be like, 'It's me that messed up, so take it out of my wages.' He never did. He was always like, 'It's fine. It's not your problem. Don't worry about it.'"

While Kusaka wasn't prepared to write off the whole money-trouble angle right then and there, from what Mishima had just said it looked unlikely.

"I'm afraid that we now need to revisit ground that you went over yesterday with Captain Kawada."

Kusaka flipped the file on the table open. Mishima's eyes widened, his jaw tightened, and his face went pale.

"Is it the pho . . . the photographs?" he stammered.

Kawada had warned Kusaka that Mishima had vomited when shown the picture of the severed hand yesterday.

"I'm afraid that identifying the victim is always unpleasant," explained Kusaka gently. "Since Takaoka has no direct family, you're the only person we can ask. Do you understand? One thing that I can do is to cover the injured part."

Kusaka pulled a photograph of the hand from the file. He covered the severed wrist with his hand and pushed the picture across the table toward Mishima.

"You identified this hand as Takaoka's based on a distinguishing mark on it?"

"Tha-that's right. It's this scar here at the base of the thumb."

Sure enough, there was a scar at the join of the thumb and the index finger.

"How did Takaoka get it?"

Mishima exhaled loudly. He turned away from the photograph as if averting his eyes from something unholy.

"It was about two years ago, when we were doing some renovation work in a house. Takaoka was slicing through a wooden pillar with a circular saw. Turned out there were some old nails stuck in it. The blade hit a nail, the saw jumped, and the blade cut into the old man's—sorry, I mean Takaoka's—hand. That's how he got the scar."

"Were you there?"

"Yeah. The old man bled like a stuck pig. It was kind of funny. I mean, he cut himself, but *I* ended up puking all over the place at the sight of blood. He'd sliced through a nerve and couldn't use the hand for a while. The index finger's still pretty useless now. Thank God it was the left hand."

The story certainly sounded convincing.

"Any other distinguishing marks on the hand?"

Mishima shot a quick glance at the photograph. Inspecting it carefully was the last thing he wanted to do.

"The fingernails? Contractors like us are always lifting hard and heavy objects. The skin on your hands toughens up, and your fingernails thicken and harden."

Mishima placed his hands on the table. Kusaka saw that the boy's nails were about three times thicker than his own. The nails of the hand in the photograph were the same.

"But that would be true for any contractor?"

"Uh, I guess so, yeah."

"So I should take only the scar as definitive proof that this is Mr. Takaoka's hand?"

"Isn't that enough?"

Mishima pouted impatiently. There was still something of the teenager in him.

"That's fine. I just needed to confirm the basis for your identification of the hand."

Kusaka returned the photograph to the file. In an effort

to lower the level of tension, he started talking about the weather. Today was looking a little cloudy, he said.

Mishima was hoping that the rain would hold off until at least late afternoon. A roofer friend of his was planning to strip the tiles from an old house nearby and replace them with new ones. Rain would force him to postpone the job.

Kusaka sipped his tea, grunting from time to time. "Incidentally," he broke in. "Could you tell us how you first met Takaoka?"

Mishima sat upright in his chair. A faraway look came into his eyes.

"My dad died when I was in fifth grade. He fell off the scaffolding of an apartment building that was under construction. Takaoka was working on the same site for a different subcontractor....When I went there to collect my dad's things, Takaoka introduced himself....I guess he felt sorry for me. He knew that I had no family left."

Could Mishima remember the name of the company his father worked for? Kinoshita Construction, said the young man, volunteering that Takaoka had been working for Nakabayashi Construction, a medium-size general contractor, at the time. Kusaka guessed that Kinoshita Construction was probably there as a subcontractor to the larger Nakabayashi.

Mishima sighed and sipped his tea.

"After that, I was put in this orphanage in Shinagawa. Takaoka used to come and visit me there all the time. He'd swing by on weekends and take me out to amusement parks or for meals or whatever."

Kusaka asked the name of the orphanage. Mishima informed him that it was the Shinagawa Mercy College.

"A few months before I was due to graduate, Takaoka asked me if wanted to work with him. He explained that working on different jobs all around Tokyo he'd built up a good network of potential clients and was planning to set himself up as Takaoka Construction, a proper business. I was over the moon."

Mishima went quiet for a moment.

"Both my parents were dead. Academically, I was nothing to write home about. I've got no special talents. Yet here was this guy treating me like his own flesh and blood. I jumped at the chance. I said yes, right then and there. From that moment, I really saw Takaoka as being—I don't know—a father or a big brother, someone very special, anyway. I was so thrilled."

Kusaka then asked Mishima detailed questions about Takaoka's business. Mishima provided the names of several clients he hadn't mentioned to Kawada yesterday, but he warned that, without access to Takaoka's notebook, the names and addresses he was giving them might not be one hundred percent correct.

"You've been working with Mr. Takaoka for five years?"

Mishima did a quick mental calculation.

"Guess so."

"Did Takaoka have a girlfriend?"

Mishima cocked his head.

"Uhm, no. Never. Kind of strange, isn't it?"

"That reminds me—do you happen to have a recent picture of Takaoka?"

So far, the task force HQ had only managed to get their hands on one photograph of Kenichi Takaoka: an ID photo from the database of the motor vehicles department.

"I'm not sure. I need to have a look at home."

"Please bring in any photos you find. We'll copy them and give them back to you as fast as we can."

"Yes, sir."

As far as Kusaka could tell from his driver's license picture, Takaoka was quite handsome, definitely someone that women would find attractive. So maybe he swung the other way?

"Should I take it that Takaoka was not . . . uh . . . very *interested* in women?"

"Hey, he wasn't, you know, like that."

Mishima placed the back of his right hand flat against his left cheek in the Japanese gesture for "gay."

"When he had money to burn, he would go out to hostess clubs. And we went to . . . uh . . . like those soapy massage parlors a few times together. No, the old man liked pussy as much as the next guy. There's no doubt on that score."

"My apologies," Kusaka said. "I didn't mean to imply anything."

He had, but no matter.

"Was there some joint he went to regularly? A 'main squeeze' he liked to spend his money on?"

"No ... not unless he was going someplace I didn't know."

"You did your own thing in the evenings, then?"

"Generally, yeah. I mean, occasionally we'd have dinner together. We always went to the same three places: a little local restaurant, a grilled chicken joint, or a pub."

Kusaka jotted down the names of the places: Mantei Bistro, Okada BBQ, and Bar Fujikawa.

"Mainly, we did our own thing. I mean, we're not fags or anything."

Mishima was clearly riled. Kusaka, reckoning that a further apology would only make a mountain from a molehill, just ignored the remark.

"That reminds me, do you have a girlfriend?"

Mishima looked a little uneasy. Was he just being shy, or was it something else? Kusaka couldn't tell.

"I don't know if she's really my, like, girlfriend."

"What about a certain Michiko Nakagawa, age nineteen, studying hairdressing. Have you two known each other long?"

Mishima's thick eyebrows twitched.

"What's that got to do with anything?"

"Let me explain. We know that you were with Ms. Nakagawa at that time the incident occurred. I just need a few more details about your relationship, so I can explain the background to the satisfaction of my colleagues."

Mishima snorted and puckered his lips. The kid was just going to have to get with the program. In any investigation, the police had to confirm the alibis of everyone involved.

It was a cast-iron rule. They also needed to be alert to the possibility of close relationships leading to false testimony. The risk was greater when the relationship was a sexual one.

"We met a bit over a month ago."

"Where?"

Mishima hemmed and hawed and looked off to one side. Was it really so hard to recall something so recent?

"At the place she works. The Royal Diner, the Route 15 one, a little way past Kawasaki City Hall."

Kusaka knew that already.

"That's quite far from where you live, isn't it?"

"I drop in on my way back from work."

"And you got to know one another that way?"

"I've always liked the Royal Diner. I go whenever I have a job in Kawasaki."

"Correct me if I'm wrong, but if you're driving back from Kawasaki, the diner's on the wrong side of the highway for you. Isn't that a little inconvenient?"

Mishima scowled.

"What's your problem, man? You don't believe me?"

"It's not that I don't believe you. It's just that I had a look at a map and wanted to ask you. Me, I'd probably drive on until I found another diner on the same side of the road."

"Well, me, I don't. Like I said, I like the Royal Diner."

"You had the girl in your sights. I can understand."

Mishima groaned and leaned back in his chair.

"Did you speak to her first or did she speak to you?"

"What's that got to do with anything? Give me a goddamn break, will you?"

"I need you to answer my question."

"Why?"

Why indeed? Kusaka was only putting pressure on Mishima because he didn't feel he was getting full cooperation from him.

"As I said earlier, I need you to explain the nature of your relationship *now* to preempt any questions that might come up *later*."

"It was me," said Mishima grudgingly. "I made the first move. I'd seen her a few times and thought she was cute. I think she recognized me and we got chatting. . . . You know how it is."

"Was Takaoka ever with you?"

"Maybe one time."

"How come? You said that the two of you normally drive back from work together?"

"I don't fucking remember."

With a sudden movement, Mishima half rose from his chair and strained across the table, his nostrils flaring.

"Fuck you, man. Maybe it was twice. Maybe three times. What the fuck does it matter? You can't seriously think it's got anything to do with what happened to the old man."

"We don't yet know if there's a connection or not. That's the reason I'm asking. I'm not trying to be deliberately provocative," said Kusaka, in his most soothing tones. Mishima sank back into his chair.

Best to take another timeout for small talk. Cars would be as good as topic as any.

"I hear you've got a Subaru Impressa. Did you take out a loan for it?"

"Nah, I paid all cash."

"Expensive?"

"It was a steal. I got it secondhand."

PART TWO

1

I was sent to Shinagawa Mercy College, an orphanage in Shinagawa Ward. The folks at City Hall must have set it all up. The buildings were on the old side, but the place itself was all right.

I had plenty to eat, and they gave me new clothes too. And no one bullied me anymore. I thanked my lucky stars every single day of the week.

"You're settling in well," the principal told me. "That's great."

In fact, there was some pretty nasty stuff going on. You see, there was this older boy who was really mean to the girls. He also forced the weaker boys to hand over their candy and whatever pocket money they'd saved up. The high school kids lived in a separate dorm some way off campus. As a result, the ninth graders like him were free to throw their weight around if they wanted to. No way was I going to put up with that, though.

"Think you're tough, new boy?"

"What's your problem, Hiroki? Everyone hates you, so

you take it out on grade-school girls. It's pathetic."

"You cocksucker."

I started it. I wanted Hiroki to attack me. And I was ready for him. I had this piece of broken metal railing I'd found near the school. Even now, I've got to say it was a darn good weapon—hard and easy to handle. I'd used a saw to cut mine to the perfect length: thirty centimeters.

I pulled the metal bar out the back of my trousers and got things going by whipping Hiroki across the shins. I knew right away who was going to win. I stomped all over Hiroki. By the end, he was bawling like a baby, saying how sorry he was. I called my classmates over and got them to pull his trousers down, then made him kowtow in the dirt and say sorry to them all directly. For the last act, I made him do a thousand squats—with his little dick out all the time, of course—and whacked him on the shins whenever he showed any sign of slowing down. Hiroki had made everyone's lives hell, so none of the pupils told on me to the teachers.

Did I take Hiroki's place as the big bully of junior high? Nope. I guess I'd earned some sort of authority, or whatever you want to call it, but I never bullied the younger kids. Ever. I swear it.

I reckon the old man was the reason I never lost my shit and ran wild.

Because of him, I got to do stuff all the other kids wanted to, but never could. The old man did things like take me to Disneyland or get me a nice juicy steak for lunch. I felt a bit guilty around the other kids. I was luckier than them, so

I did my best to be nice to them all. If it wasn't for the old man coming around the way he did, maybe I'd have ended up a second Hiroki. At least, that's my take on it now.

It was my third year in junior high. The old man had taken me out to lunch. We ate all sorts of things, steak, noodles, whatever. That day, I remember, we were having okonomiyaki pancakes. The old man was eating a pork pancake with a beer to wash it down and I was having beef with oolong tea. The place has shut down now, but, God, the okonomiyaki there was good.

"Studying hard for your high school entrance exams, Kosuke?"

"Me?" I answered. "Nah, study's not really my thing."

"How're you going to get into high school, then?"

"High school?" I shrugged. "Dunno."

Truth is, I was sick of school. What use were factorization and quadratic functions for a guy like me? No, I just wanted to be the total opposite of my dad; I wanted to get out there and start earning money for myself ASAP. I was just a kid, but I was pretty fired up.

"If you don't go to high school, what are you going to do?"

"Thought I'd get some sort of job, I s'pose."

"It's a tough world out there, kid. You need to think a little harder."

I knew that. Unless you had some special talent or a skill or were a really driven kind of person, it could be hard for a high school grad to find a job. That was why I liked the idea of doing the same thing as the old man: all a construction worker needed was a few tools and some know-how, and you could make a living anywhere, without the need for college. As long as you put in the work, you could learn everything you needed on the job, and it only took a few years.

Thinking back on it, maybe the old man invited me to lunch and asked me about my future plans to set me thinking in that direction. If he did, I'm fine with that. He may have influenced me, but he never forced me to do anything.

"If the idea of working as a general contractor isn't too much of a turnoff, you should come and work with me, Kosuke. Recently, I've been thinking about striking out on my own. I'm going to call myself the Takaoka Construction Company—yeah, I know it sounds a bit high-falutin'!— and start handling jobs directly myself."

Waves of heat were drifting up from the iron griddle on the table in between us. I felt something similar inside me: a wave of hope welling up in my chest.

"Will you give me a job?"

In my excitement, I grabbed hold of the table so hard that I knocked over my glass and spilt my tea all over the griddle.

"Yikes!"

"You idiot! Oh, shit."

A great cloud of steam billowed up toward the ceiling. All the other customers started yelling and shrieking; then the fire alarm went off. At the end, me and the old man, we were literally groveling in front of the manager, saying we were sorry. "He's a no-good kid. I just don't know what to do with him," said the old man, cuffing me on the head a few times. I had to suck it up.

The instant we were out on the sidewalk, though, the two of us burst out laughing.

Good times. I'll never forget that day.

I was impatient to get started. I was due to graduate junior high in April, but I began my apprenticeship over the winter vacation.

The trouble was, the whole building trade more or less shuts down over New Year. All I did was help polish off one small job that was all but finished anyway and then go to the warehouse of a big contractor the old man worked for to help them with their big year-end cleanup.

The old man's friends were surprised to see me. "Hey, Ken," they'd say to the old man. "How come you never told us you had a grown-up kid?"

In construction, plenty of guys bring their sons into the business. The old man told his pals that I was the son of a relative. Hearing him say that made me feel kind of proud. The other guys accepted me on the spot.

I remember one funny thing that happened during my very first job. We were putting the finishing touches on this newly built house when I came across this book in the trash. It was a step-by-step manual for putting up a door or something like that. Anyway, I asked the old man if it was really okay to bin it. I mean, I didn't want to throw out anything important. The old man didn't reply. When I looked at him to see if he'd heard me, he was staring straight past me. There was something savage in his eyes, like a wolf stalking its prey.

The light was fading, but I saw this man standing in the street, just outside the front door. I recognized him. It was the guy who gave me the money when I went to pick up Dad's things after he died.

I remember what he was wearing. He had on this fancy black overcoat and a bright red shirt underneath. I could just see the collar. He wore sunglasses even though it was evening. As a kid, I hadn't realized how tall he was.

A few seconds later, he caught sight of the old man and grinned in our direction. "See you later," he said to whoever it was he was talking to outside, and then he went off. And that was that.

Snapping back to himself, the old man turned to me.

"Oh, yeah," he mumbled. "I was looking for that."

He plucked the book from my hands and wandered up to the second floor.

Looking back on it now, I think those two must have known each other for a long time.

When I graduated, I moved out of the orphanage in Shinagawa to live with the old man in his apartment in Middle Rokugo in Ota Ward. He had a couple of rooms. The place was kind of run down, but it had a bath and a toilet, so it was comfortable enough. For me, it was home.

Working in construction is no walk in the park. You need to be strong, but you've also got to do the job right. Like when you're carrying something, you've got to be careful not to bump into anything and damage it. Plasterboard panels are like that: they're heavy and bulky, but if you don't put them down gently, they'll snap in half.

I had my share of accidents. The old man was always giving me a hard time, like, "Kosuke, be careful. Those materials cost money." I was constantly having to say I was sorry.

On top of that, there's always loads of dust and grime floating around construction sites. Stick a towel up your nose after a day's work, and the thing comes out black. You're getting shit in your eyes all the time too. There's all that loud machinery, like electric saws. One of the guys I worked with wore earplugs all day. He was unusual, though; really into music and high-end audio gear, so . . .

At the beginning, I couldn't do anything right.

"You've got to hit nails straight to get them to go in straight. They'll bend if you hit them off-center. You're holding the hammer wrong."

"A good workman is as only good as his tools. Use a carpenter's square that's squiffy and it'll screw everything up."

"You're not ready to use the circular saw. Fetch an ordinary saw and cut this manually."

"The metal hook at the end of a tape measure makes it hard to read. If you want accurate measurements, you're better off starting from ten than the zero mark."

I had a lot to learn—a bit of basic architecture; a ton of terminology; how to handle my tools; the names of different kinds of wood and other building materials; how to cut them up and assemble them; how to bang in nails right; the right order to do jobs in; how to give a job a nice finish; how to work well with other contractors. It wasn't so hard, if your head was screwed on right. I mean, everything was there right in front of you. It was the first time in my life I realized that learning could be fun.

"You're writing all this down! You're more serious about this job than I thought."

I was kind of embarrassed when the old man came across my notebook. I'd christened it my "Builder's Bible," and I updated it every day while the old man was in the bath. It was my prized possession.

"Hey, boss, how do you spell that wood we used today?"

"Cedar? That's *S-E-E-D-A-H*, I think."

The old man was even worse at reading and writing than me. He couldn't even spell half our clients' names. Like Kinoshita Construction, where he had a bad habit of getting the *K* and the *C* the wrong way around.

I started out at five thousand yen a day. The old man paid me every couple of weeks.

"You don't need to pay any rent while you're here with me. Use the money to buy yourself tools. If you have your own gear, you'll treat it with the proper respect."

After a year, the old man hiked my daily wage to eight thousand yen. I was able to move out of his apartment into a place of my own. The old man helped me find one: it was a small studio with an even smaller bathroom. It cost me sixty-five thousand a month. I felt kind of bad: it was a whole lot newer and nicer than the old man's pad.

"Here," he said, handing me a couple of envelopes on the day I moved out. "Use this for the deposit. Today's a special day, after all."

One of the envelopes was one of those fancy ones used for gift giving. The other had the logo of a big foreign insurance company on it.

"Thanks. What's this one for?"

"That? It's an insurance policy. If something happens to me, you're the beneficiary. It's not a whole lot of money, but provided you do the paperwork, you'll get something."

I felt hot and cold shivers going up my spine.

"I don't know what to say, boss. . . ."

I loved the fact that he treated me as family. At the same time, the idea of something happening to him frightened and upset me.

"I don't deserve this."

The old man reached out, grabbed hold of the hand in which I was clutching the two envelopes, and looked deep into my eyes.

"There are two policies in the envelope; one's for you, and the other's for someone else. It's a bit complicated. Basically, I haven't told the other person about the policy; that means they might not hear the news about my death. I want you to make sure that doesn't happen. If anything happens to me, open up the second policy and get in touch with the beneficiary so they can claim the insurance money. Okay? You promise to do what I'm asking?"

I felt a bit overwhelmed. It was all so new: having someone who trusted me; having to deal with big, unfamiliar ideas like death, the uncertainty of the future, insurance payouts, mystery beneficiaries.

Whatever my feelings, I had no business turning the old man down. He was the only family I had.

"Sure, boss," I said, as I sniffed back the tears. "But I don't want to think—"

He gave me a mighty smack on the back.

"Don't be such a crybaby, Kosuke. Everybody has life insurance. When you get married, you'll see. It's the most natural thing in the world."

I often thought it funny that the old man didn't have a woman in his life, so when he came out with that spiel about things being "a bit complicated" with the "other person," I just thought to myself, "Aha, so there is a woman in the picture after all."

I remember a conversation we had just before I turned eighteen. We were having a meal of deep-fried pork cutlets in a soba restaurant at the time.

"Listen, Kosuke. You should get yourself a driver's license."

I'd been thinking the same thing.

"I want to go," I explained. "The thing is, I'll be too

worn out to take lessons in the evening after work, and the lessons are probably booked solid on weekends."

"Have you heard about those intensive courses where you go off and stay somewhere and do nothing but practice all day? It's way cheaper than learning here in Tokyo, and you stand a better chance of passing the test too. You know Satoru? His daughter went to Iwate Prefecture to get her license. School was nice, apparently."

Satoru was a plasterer we sometimes worked with.

"It would make my life a lot easier if you could drive," continued the old man.

"I could go and pick stuff up at the hardware store for us by myself."

"Exactly," he replied. "And *I* could have a drink or two on the way back from work."

"Oh, so *that's* what this is really about."

The old man was obsessed with the scheme. He offered to lend me the money so I could enroll right away and sent off for all the brochures and application forms himself.

Next thing I knew, he'd set the whole thing up, and I was going to a driving school in Fukushima Prefecture.

It worked out well. Somehow, I didn't have most of the problems student drivers do, and I ended up getting my license in sixteen days, the minimum time possible. I enjoyed the change: it was my first time out of Tokyo.

When I got back, life only became that much harder.

"Hey, Kosuke, nip down to the hardware store and pick up a new drill bit for me, will you? Here's the size."

"Get down to Maruyoshi, the builders' merchant. They called to say the skirting boards and crown moldings we ordered have come in."

"These nails you bought are hopeless. We're going to use them for this gutter, so we need a darker color—brown or chocolate brown. These silver ones will stick out like a sore thumb. They need to be exchanged. Oh, and pick up a couple of rafter beams while you're at it."

"Do you need two-by-fours or two-by-sixes?"

"You retarded? Can you see any two-by-sixes in this house? They're for the ceiling joists in the living room there. Of course I want two-by-fours."

"Sorry, boss. Be right back."

"Unbelievable."

Suddenly, there was this horrible whiny, screechy noise; next thing you know, the old man had dropped the saw and was writhing on the floor.

"Boss?"

"You okay, Ken?"

Matsumoto, the electrician, rushed over. That was when I noticed the old man's left hand.

"Oh shit, look at that."

"Ken, are you okay?"

The old man was very far from all right. There was a jagged, gaping wound on his hand between the thumb and the index finger.

"Call an ambulance, Kosuke," hissed Matsumoto.

"I'm fine, Matsumoto."

"Not with a cut like that, you're not. Bring me a towel, Kosuke. A clean one."

The blood was pumping out, streaming out . . .

"Kosuke, what are you doing, standing there looking all goggle-eyed? Didn't you hear me?"

An icy spasm worked its way up from my stomach to my chest, neck, and head. My stomach turned over, and I was loudly and violently sick.

"What the fuck, Kosuke!"

I couldn't help myself. Since the day I'd been taken to see my father's corpse, I couldn't bear to see blood or cuts or anything like that. Throwing up was just a reflex action.

"Looks like the kid needs an ambulance more than me, huh?"

In the end, Matsumoto walked the old man to a nearby surgery. They left me lying on the bare wood floor surrounded by puke and with a wet towel on my head, staring up at the beams and joists of the unfinished ceiling.

2

Reiko was responsible for looking into Kenichi Takaoka's past. At the executive meeting the night before, however, it had been decided that she should interview Michiko Nakagawa, Kosuke Mishima's girlfriend, so that was the first thing on her agenda today.

The girl lived in a one-room apartment in Wataridamukai-cho in Kawasaki Ward. Reiko called to set up an appointment, then she and Ioka hopped on the train, going four stops from Kamata to Hatchonawate, and then one stop on the Nambu Line to Kawasaki-Shimmachi, the nearest station. (Obviously, Reiko's request for a different partner had been turned down.)

"Lieutenant Reiko?" said Ioka in a wheedling voice, as they walked along beside a fence surrounding a primary school. He was wearing a pair of cheap leather gloves and rubbing his hands together.

"I warned you before not to use my first name."

"There doesn't seem to be a whole lot of love lost between you and Lieutenant Kusaka . . ."

A cold gust of air blew into Reiko's collar. She shivered and jerked her head.

"Why'd you say that?"

"The executive meeting last night."

"What the hell, Ioka! Were you listening in?"

"These great big ears of mine pick up everything."

Stuffing his bag under his elbow, Ioka grabbed his ears and flapped them at her. It was quite a performance.

"Especially information to do with you, Lieutenant Reiko."

"You're like the wolf in Little Red Riding Hood."

She thought that might get a laugh.

"Oh, ha ha," he said acidly.

Reiko couldn't figure out how Ioka's moods worked. His unpredictable behavior wore her out.

"So why are you at each other's throats?"

He just doesn't know when enough's enough!

"We're not. It's just . . . normal. It's like not getting on with the neighbors. Just one of those things."

"But you're not neighbors. You're in the same homicide unit."

"No. Kusaka's in a different squad in the same unit. That means he's my enemy. I need to keep my guard up or I'll be toast."

Ioka smiled.

"What's the creepy grin for?"

"The way Kusaka treated you, I can't believe he's much of a hit with the ladies."

What, not like you, Casanova?

The remark was on the tip of her tongue, but she stifled it. She wasn't going to let Ioka trick her into talking about matters of the heart. No way.

With his smarminess and his suggestive jokes, though, Ioka probably cut quite a figure in the sordid world of suburban hostess clubs, she thought.

Why am I wasting time thinking about crap like this?

They had reached their destination: Sun Heights, Wataridamukai-cho. It was a three-story block. They examined the rack of mailboxes in the lobby: there were twelve apartments all told.

"Wow, this place is quite swish."

Ioka was right. The building—brand new and still immaculate—was done out in varicolored tiles designed to evoke autumn leaves.

Reiko's watch said 10:28. Perfect timing.

"Ready?"

They walked down the first-floor external corridor to room 102, second from the end, and pressed the bell.

"Yes?" came a shy voice.

The voice was low and husky, especially for a girl of nineteen. Perhaps she'd drunk too much last night or had a touch of flu. Or was she just annoyed about them coming around?

"This is Reiko Himekawa of the Tokyo Metropolitan Police Department here. We spoke on the phone earlier."

"Oh, uh, of course . . . I'll open the door."

They heard the clinking as she unlatched the door

chain. The door opened a crack. A gust of warm air with a distinctly feminine scent came out.

"Good morning. Miss Nakagawa?"

Reiko held up her ID. She always made a point of doing this, especially when dealing with women who lived alone. It helped put them at ease.

"As I said on the phone, we want to ask you a few questions about your friend Kosuke Mishima. May we come in?"

"Be my guest."

Michiko pushed the door wide open. She stiffened briefly when she noticed Ioka in the background but gestured for them both to come inside.

Reiko guessed that Kosuke Mishima had probably contacted her. How close were they? Was their relationship sexual yet? The closer they were, the more careful Reiko would need to be.

Michiko led Reiko and Ioka to a small table, then turned to the kitchen unit.

"Make yourselves at home."

"Thanks."

It was a single room of modest size. With just a bed, a TV, and a chest of drawers, it already felt cramped. There were piles of hairdressing and beauty magazines arranged around the walls. Reiko had expected something more stylish and tasteful from an aspiring hairdresser.

Where were all the normal cutesy, playful knickknacks most girls her age had? There were no Mickey Mouse or

Miffy Rabbit stuffed animals, nor posters of singers like Kazuya Kamenashi or movie stars like Brad Pitt. The room reminded Reiko of a prison cell. Or was she being uncharitable? Either the girl was unusually serious, or else she was just plain hard up.

The girl boiled some water in the kettle and served them tea. Lipton.

"Here you go."

"Thank you."

"Thanks. That looks delicious."

Michiko's eyes darted to Reiko's folded coat, which was sitting on a chair.

"Oh, I'm sorry. Let me hang that up for you."

"Really, that's fine," countered Reiko tersely. There were things in the pockets, so she didn't want anyone else handling it.

The girl bowed discreetly and lapsed into silence.

Seems like a sensible girl.

Michiko was slight and around middle height. The chest beneath her knit sweater was flat, and her denim-clad legs were almost repellent in their thinness. Her features were regular, with a hint of squiffiness. She had buckteeth and over-prominent gums that were on show whenever she opened her mouth to speak. Not as bad as Ioka's, though.

What was that theory of Otsuka's?

Reiko suddenly remembered how Otsuka, her deceased squad mate, had lectured her about his preference for girls with a minor physical flaw like buckteeth or a snub nose, and the complex to go with it. "They're actually the cutest ones," he'd insisted.

Now she finally understood what Otsuka had been getting at. There *was* something rather charming about the way Michiko hesitated before speaking and the care she took to keep her mouth shut tight when she wasn't saying anything. She was insecure—in a delightful way.

Ioka swallowed down the last of his tea.

"That hit the spot," he said with a contented sigh.

Picking up her cup, Reiko took a sip.

"I'm sorry to have phoned you so early this morning. I hope we're not disrupting your day?"

Michiko picked up her cup.

"I do have school today," she said blankly. "But I arranged to take the day off."

"Oh, I'm sorry. If we'd known . . ."

Michiko shook her head.

"I didn't feel so good when I woke up this morning and was planning to take the day off anyway."

"Either way, we're inconveniencing you. Are you feeling better?"

"I'm okay, thanks."

"We'll get this interview out of the way as fast as possible, I promise. Let's get started. First, can you tell us about your relationship with Kosuke Mishima?"

"He's . . . a friend," she replied with no hint of shyness.

"What kind of friend?"

Michiko cocked her head.

"He was a customer at the diner where I work. He used to come in quite a lot; he's about the same age as me, so we ended up friends."

"I see. What can you tell me about the day before yesterday?"

The girl's jaw tightened briefly. Subtle enough, but that was definitely an emotional reaction.

What's that about?

"The day before yesterday? I was on the late shift from ten. Mishima came in not long after I started."

She called him Mishima. Wouldn't most girls refer to their boyfriend by their first name or have a nickname for them?

"How long did Mishima stay?"

"Until just before midnight, I think. . . . Yes, that's about right."

"Was he alone?"

"Yes. He was reading, I think."

Not wanting to come across as an inquisitor, Reiko nodded casually and let a little time elapse before her next question.

"By the way," she asked with a smile. "Do you remember what he ordered?"

"Seafood gratin followed by coffee, I think."

"Can we confirm that at the diner?"

"Confirm what?"

"That Mishima was alone."

Michiko said that, yes, she thought that the day before yesterday shouldn't be a problem. At the restaurant, they recorded the number of people in a group, as well as gender and age.

Whether the manager would share the data with them was another matter.

Michiko looked first at Reiko and then at Ioka.

"Has . . . something happened?"

Had Kosuke already filled her in? Or hadn't he told her anything yet? Either way, he didn't have much information to share.

"Yes, something has. I'm afraid that Kenichi Takaoka, Mishima's boss, is dead."

She barely flinched. Was that significant?

"Mr. Takaoka was like a second father to him."

"Yes."

"You used the word *dead*. Do you really mean that he was killed?"

Reiko let a moment pass, then nodded gravely.

"We can't yet say so with complete certainty, but, yes, we believe that to be the case. The investigation has only just started, so there's a great deal we still don't know."

Reiko broke off to take a sip of tea.

What's this girl really thinking?

She radiated grayness, drabness.

There was also a hint of twitchiness, of nerves about her. Was she hiding something, or was she just high-strung by nature? With her frank answers and ready eye contact, her personality seemed robust enough. Of course, that could just be a professional gloss she'd acquired working as a waitress.

I'll probe a little deeper.

"You live alone?" Reiko asked, letting her eyes run around the room. A shadow flitted across Michiko's face.

"Starting two months ago, yes."

"What about your parents?"

"My mother died when I was a baby. And my father—" The words caught in her throat. "He died early October this year."

Reiko clasped her hands and bowed her head. Ioka, seated beside her, did the same.

"We're sorry for your loss."

"Thank you."

"Was he sick?"

Michiko shook her head blankly.

"It happened at work. An accident."

"How awful," said Reiko, and left it at that. It was a deliberate ploy: create a silence and wait for the other person to fill it. She wasn't proud of herself, but she wanted Michiko to talk.

"He was working on a construction site, when he slipped and fell from the scaffolding on the tenth floor of the building. The body was in a bad way; he hit the scaffolding on the way down. The face was uninjured, though. I identified him."

He died at a construction site?

Was there any link between her father and Takaoka and Mishima? The other two men worked in construction too.

Reiko nodded sympathetically.

"What was your father doing at the time of the accident? Affixing sidings to the external wall, something like that?"

"No, he was what people in the trade call a 'kite'—someone who erects the exterior scaffolding. They were getting all the ladders and gear in place for the next phase of construction work."

"Had he always been a scaffolder?"

Michiko gave a shrug. She seemed to be getting bored with this line of questioning. Reiko, however, wasn't planning to step back quite yet.

Once again, she just kept quiet and waited.

It was Michiko whose patience gave out first.

"He used to be a salesman for an apartment developer. He switched to the construction side a few weeks before he died."

Although Reiko was keen to ask why he had made the switch, she stopped herself. There was no harm in being discreet. For now, all she needed Michiko to do was to confirm the alibi of the man who'd discovered the crime scene.

"There's just one question I need to ask you, more for reference than anything else," blurted out Ioka. "Could you tell us the name of the firm your father was working for when he died?"

His voice was the same idiotic singsong as always. Michiko's face registered no emotion. She appeared to be staring into the empty space between the two of them, as if there were a third person sitting there.

"Kinoshita Construction," she replied. "I think it's

based in Setagaya. I'm not too sure though."

"Kinoshita Construction? Thanks."

That brought the interview to a close. Reiko jotted down the task force's phone number on one of her name cards and handed it to Michiko.

They were already out in the passageway when Michiko called them back.

"What is it?"

"I just wanted to ask, is Mish all right?"

The question could mean several things. Did they regard Mishima as a suspect? How was he holding up after losing his surrogate father? Did Michiko need to worry about him being in possible danger?

From the interview, Reiko had got the impression that Michiko and Mishima weren't all that close. The girl calling them back to inquire about "Mish" showed that in fact she cared about him deeply.

Reiko gave her an encouraging smile.

"He's all right," she replied. "If you're worried about him, give him a call. I'm sure he'll be pleased."

Reiko smiled again and Michiko, looking relieved, smiled back.

She's a sweet kid, really, thought Reiko to herself.

Reiko and Ioka took the train back to Kamata, where they headed for the municipal government office. Reiko handed over a formal written request and in return was presented with Kenichi Takaoka's resident's card. The information on it included a record of all the places that Takaoka had lived. He'd moved to the Kamata area twelve years ago; prior to that, he'd lived in South Hanahata in Adachi Ward, in east Tokyo. They would have to go and visit his previous residence in the next day or two.

"Lieutenant Reiko, I'm famished. How about you?"

"Half past one already? Shall we get some lunch here?" Reiko gestured at a branch of Matsuya, the beef-and-rice fast-food chain.

Ioka looked unenthusiastic.

"Fine, I'll go by myself, then."

She crossed the street and went in; Ioka followed reluctantly.

"I was hoping we could go somewhere a little more romantic."

"Exactly what I *don't* want. Here we get served fast and can get out fast."

With lunch out of the way, they headed back to Kawasaki.

When they got to the Royal Diner, two-thirds of the tables were empty.

"Welcome to the Royal Diner. Is it just the two of you today?"

Content to be treated as an ordinary customer for now, Reiko nodded. The waitress, who looked about the same age as Michiko, led them to a table.

After they sat down, the waitress launched into her spiel about the day's specials and how to use the electric bell to order.

"Excuse me, miss," interrupted Reiko. "We need to see the manager or whoever the person in charge here is."

When the waitress looked a little skeptical, Reiko whipped out her badge. The girl's face tensed. With a jerky bow, she dashed into the back of the restaurant.

In under a minute, the manager—he said his name was Saito—came over to their table.

They both got to their feet.

"My apologies. I know you must be very busy. I'm Lieutenant Himekawa of the Tokyo Metropolitan Police, and this is Sergeant Ioka, my colleague."

"Afternoon."

They all bowed, and Saito sat down with them at their table.

"How exactly can I . . . ?"

"It's not you we're here for, Mr. Saito. I believe you have a Miss Michiko Nakagawa working as a waitress here?"

"That's correct."

No visible reaction.

"Do you happen to know a Kosuke Mishima? A friend of Miss Nakagawa's?"

Saito repeated the name dubiously.

It only needed Reiko to provide a few further details before Saito nodded brightly.

"Michiko's boyfriend? Oh, yes, I know him." His face became clouded suddenly. "Why? Has something happened?"

Interesting. The restaurant staff apparently saw Mishima as Michiko's boyfriend. . . .

"To him, no. We were hoping you could consult your billing data and tell us, first, if he was here the night before last, and, second, if so, around what time."

Saito looked dismayed.

"I'm terribly sorry," he said, with a small tip of the head. "Unless you have a warrant, I'm not at liberty to share that data with you. We have strict rules about privacy."

Reiko had expected as much.

"I understand. What about you, Mr. Saito? Were you out on the restaurant floor around 11:00 p.m. the night before last?"

"Yes, I was on the graveyard shift. I took the occasional break, but basically I was here all night."

"Do you remember seeing the young man here that night?"

Saito nodded.

"Uh-huh, he was definitely here. I got the impression that he and Michiko had come here together."

"What do you mean?"

"Well, the boyfriend got here first. It was unusual for him to come when she wasn't here, and just a minute or two later, she showed up and started sorting out the drinks behind the counter. They came in so soon one after the other, my guess is that they arrived here together. The interval was just long enough for her to change into her uniform."

"Do you remember how long Mishima stayed?"

"He normally sticks around about an hour and a half, maybe two. It was probably the same that night. If it'd been shorter than usual, I'd have picked up on it."

"Were you out here when he left?"

"I was. Any normal customer, I'd probably not have noticed, but as he's Michiko's young man, I guess I keep a special eye on him."

What exactly did that mean?

"Does the restaurant have any rules about staff fraternizing with customers?"

Reiko hooked her left and right index fingers together. Saito chuckled and shook his head.

"No, we don't. Obviously, I'd have to have a word with any waitress who spent all her time yapping with a particular customer, but Michiko isn't like that. She's a young girl. It's good for her to meet people."

The manager frowned suddenly.

"Something on your mind?"

"Not really," Saito murmured, looking a little agitated. "I don't know. Perhaps I'm just imagining things, but Michiko did seem a little . . . odd that night."

"Odd?"

"It was nothing major. When I asked her to do something, she was slower to respond than normal. And the jobs she normally handles very efficiently—things like collecting the dirty plates from tables—one of the other girls was always getting to it first and doing her job for her. When she realized what was happening, she apologized."

Saito paused a moment. "Yes, and she seemed a bit jumpy, a bit edgy. This customer knocked his glass off the

133

table and it smashed. It happens all the time, and we're all used to it. That night, she seemed not just startled but almost *frightened* at the noise. Yeah, now that I think about it, she wasn't her usual self."

Sensitive to loud noises. Easily startled. On edge.

Reiko had an idea what might have been behind the girl's behavior, if Saito's impression was right, of course. She had been in a similar psychological state herself once.

Something nasty happened to Michiko Nakagawa that night. Chances are it was physical violence.

3

Kusaka and Satomura had finished their interview of Kosuke Mishima, and the two men were now having lunch in the cafeteria at Kamata Police Station. Kusaka was having chop suey with a side order of udon noodles in broth. Just watching how much cayenne pepper mix Kusaka put on his food was making Satomura's eyes water.

"That Mishima's typical of kids today. Flies off the handle for no reason."

"Typical? . . . Perhaps."

Kusaka pictured the face of Yoshihide, his fourteen-year-old son. Would Yoshihide be surly and uncontrollable in a few years' time?

"What do you think, Lieutenant?"

"About what?"

"Do you think Mishima could have been involved in the crime?"

Kusaka tilted his head to one side and began poking his chopsticks at his noodles. He didn't want to discuss the investigation where there was a risk of being overheard.

Everyone in the police station was supposed to be on the same side, but as far Kusaka was concerned, anyone who didn't belong to the task force might as well be from Mars. He wasn't big on sharing his opinions with other people even at the best of times.

"Shall we discuss that later?"

Satomura got the message. For the rest of the meal, he just made general chitchat.

Kusaka suggested they take a little break after lunch. The two men went back to the CID office, and Satomura stayed there while Kusaka picked up the papers and headed back up to the big room where the task force was based. He hadn't had time to skim the five main newspapers that morning, and he wanted to see what was in the news.

By now, the mobilization of Homicide Unit 10 would definitely have reached the reporters assigned to the Tokyo Metropolitan Police Department. The real question was what they knew beyond that. Did they know that a task force had been set up here in Kamata? Had any of them got wind of a large-scale forensic investigation being conducted on the bank of the Tama River?

Kusaka couldn't find anything in any of the morning editions. No one yet had enough to work the material up into a story.

The top brass were determined to avoid any leaks. Imaizumi hammered that point home at the end of every meeting. The reason that the higher-ups—and that included Kusaka—were so fanatical about secrecy was that it was possible that the perpetrator hadn't yet realized he'd forgotten the left hand inside the van.

Luckily for them, the only person outside the police who knew about the hand was Kosuke Mishima. So if anyone they hauled in for questioning mentioned anything about a hand in a vehicle, it would be proof positive that they were connected to the crime. This advantage, however, would only last as long as they could keep the story out of the news.

Sharing anything with the media was often a double-edged sword: it was useful in eliciting information from the public but likely to invalidate whatever aces they had up their sleeves. It only needed one hack to get suspicious and call around all the different Tokyo precincts to find out where Unit 10 Homicide was working and learn about the task force. Kusaka wanted to delay that for as long as possible.

The top priority was to make sure Director Hashizume kept his mouth shut. The man had been promoted from Community Policing and had no background in investigation. To make things worse, he was excitable, unpredictable, and loved shooting his mouth off. Hashizume could quite easily spill the beans if he thought it would make him look good, the rest of the team be damned.

Thank God that Captain Imaizumi was heading up Unit 10. Sure, the man was a little too prone to follow his gut, but his judgment was basically sound and practical. He was a good guy to have as a boss. Provided Imaizumi kept

Hashizume on a tight rein, Kusaka was confident that he could get out there and do his job without undue worry. Still, those hacks were so persistent, and it only needed one of them to get their teeth into someone on the task force, and then . . .

Kusaka assigned a number of sergeants from Homicide to chase up Takaoka's work associates, while he and Satomura focused on Takaoka's relationship with Mishima.

First thing in the afternoon, they set off for Shinagawa Mercy College, the orphanage where Mishima had spent some four and half years of his life.

They met the principal, a Ms. Noriko Shimizu. She'd been vice-principal when Mishima was at the school. She looked distraught when they explained the reason for their visit.

"Poor Kosuke. He must be quite devastated."

Apparently, Takaoka had made quite an impression.

"I remember him," she told them. "He was a handsome man, very well-built."

She met with Kusaka and Satomura in a small staff room rather than an office.

"We heard that Mishima came here after losing his father, who was his only living relative, in an accident at work."

Ms. Shimizu gave a pained frown.

"That's right," she sighed. "At one time the police thought it might have been a suicide."

That was news to Kusaka.

"Did they tell you that?"

"They did. Apparently, Mishima's father had quite significant debts. There was some question about whether or not his life insurance would pay out. The dispute didn't drag on, so I suppose there must have been a verdict of accidental death in the end."

Suicide dressed up as an accidental fall? Insurance fraud . . .

Kusaka had no idea if Mishima's father's death had any connection to the case they were working on, but it was certainly something worth exploring.

"You don't happen to know roughly what scale of debts he had, do you?"

"No, the police never told me. They did ask me to let them know if Kosuke had any visitors here."

Clearly the local police had been highly suspicious at the time.

"And did he?"

Ms. Shimizu shook her head and smiled.

"No—well, only Mr. Takaoka. He was such a lovely man. He took Kosuke out on weekends, for lunch or for little trips. He was very sweet to him."

"Is that sort of thing common here?"

"Well, maybe not common, but it does happen. It's not unusual for a relationship that starts like that to end up with both sides agreeing on a formal, legal adoption. Even if things don't get officialized like that, people want to be helpful. . . . Did you ever read *Daddy-Long-Legs*? You know, the story of the orphan who has her college education paid for her by a mysterious benefactor? That sometimes happens here too."

"Was there ever any talk of Takaoka adopting Kosuke?" inquired Kusaka.

Ms. Shimizu shook her head.

"Never. I do my best not to be pushy, but I did once ask Takaoka why he wasn't interested in it. Because he was single, was his answer. Did he get married later?"

"No, he was still single at the time of his death."

"Oh, I see."

Kusaka straightened his shoulders and cleared his throat as the prelude to his next, important question.

"This is something I'm very keen to know. You don't happen to remember which precinct the policeman who asked you to keep an eye on Kosuke's visitors came from, do you?"

Since he had no idea that there had been anything suspicious about Mishima's father's death, he hadn't bothered to touch on the topic at all during his interview of Mishima that morning.

"Let me see . . . Kosuke used to live in . . . I think it was Mitaka. Of course, I've no way of knowing if his father had his accident near there or not."

"Of course not."

Kusaka would just have to wait and see about that one.

"You've been most helpful."

The interview enabled Kusaka to verify what he already knew about Mishima and Takaoka's relationship, and about

Takaoka's character. The speculation about Mishima's father's death had come completely out of left field. Since he'd gone in with low expectations, the result was more than satisfactory.

They said their good-byes and left the school.

As they went out of the gate, two little boys with satchels on their backs skipped past them. Was school out already? Kusaka checked his watch. It was just after half past two.

Their next stop was Gotanda, where they visited the offices of Nakabayashi Construction, the general contractor where Takaoka had worked before going into business for himself.

The company's seven-story head office building was right on the main road. At the reception desk, Kusaka asked for the head of the company's general affairs division. He and Satomura were led up to a meeting room on the second floor.

A couple minutes later, the division director, a Mr. Kurihara, came in. He was short and plump.

"You're from the Metropolitan Police? Please, have a seat."

"Thank you."

Kusaka wasn't the sort of person who knew or cared about designer labels, and he couldn't identify Kurihara's suit. All he knew was that it looked expensive; the same was true of the gold watch—was it a Rolex?—on the man's wrist.

Kurihara threw himself into an armchair, leaned back, and crossed his stumpy little legs.

"Why are you here?"

His tone was hardly friendly, but then few people welcome a visit from the police. Kusaka knew better than to attach much importance to his manner.

"Do you remember a man by the name of Tadaharu Mishima who worked for Kinoshita Construction? He died nine years ago in an accident at one of your building sites."

Kurihara shrugged and stuck out his lower lip.

"I only joined the firm four years ago. I'm afraid it's before my time."

"Can we meet with someone who's been here longer?"

"Off the top of my head, I have no idea who might remember that particular incident. Give me some time and I'll make inquiries. If it's someone who's out on site today, they won't be back till six-thirty or seven at the earliest."

Kurihara clearly wanted nothing to do with them. A tactical withdrawal seemed in order.

"That's very helpful. When you find someone, give me a call at this number."

Kusaka wrote his cell phone number on his name card and passed it across. Kurihara examined it briefly before putting it into his card case. He handed one of his own cards to Kusaka.

"I'm looking forward to your call," said Kusaka, giving a little bow. Kurihara stayed in his seat and didn't see them to the elevator.

•

They parked themselves in a coffee shop from which they could keep an eye on the lobby of the Nakabayashi office. Nothing appeared to be out of the ordinary, just men with briefcases bustling in and out.

"There's something not quite right about that Kurihara guy," murmured Satomura.

Kusaka gave a barking laugh. There was certainly something a bit dodgy about Kurihara.

"Will you keep an eye on things here, Sergeant? I'm going to go and check a few things on the computer. If anything happens, call my cell."

"Sure."

Kusaka picked up the check, paid, and left. Through the glass, he could see Satomura lighting a cigarette as he watched the building on the far side of the street.

Kusaka turned and walked off. The wind was cold, and he crammed his hands into his pockets.

When Kusaka reached the plaza outside the station, he stopped and looked around. He spotted signs for three Internet cafés. He wanted the quietest place with the smallest number of kids in it. One of the three advertised "private rooms," a "no-smoking zone," and a "chilled-out atmosphere." That sounded like what he wanted.

He ducked into the doorway beneath the sign and marched up the stairs to the second floor.

The sign-up procedure was a matter of seconds. Opting

for the ninety-minute package, Kusaka settled down in the numbered booth assigned to him. Once upon a time, he used to lug his laptop around with him all day, but now, with Internet cafés everywhere, that was no longer necessary. He could carry his own office with him on a single memory stick smaller than a tube of lip balm. The downside was all the membership cards that he ended up with, but that was nothing compared to the weight of a computer.

Kusaka put his glasses on, launched the browser, and went to the home page of a business database. When the search page opened, he typed "Nakabayashi Construction" and pressed enter. The key data of the company appeared on the screen, including a list of the board of directors. Kusaka opened another window and Googled all the names. He then repeated the process for the company founder, the main investors, the group companies, consolidated subsidiaries, and affiliated companies. Kinoshita Industries was one of the affiliates.

Kusaka then widened his search to affiliates and consolidated subsidiaries of Nakabayashi's affiliates; any other companies that the founder had established; companies Nakabayashi had acquired; and companies Nakabayashi had restructured and revived by sending in its own staff.

After nearly an hour, a shadowy pattern was beginning to form. A little later, he encountered a name that made sense of it all: Toshikatsu Tajima.

Now I get it.

On his memory stick, Kusaka opened a data file he had built up of individuals associated with "antisocial forces," as the yakuza were euphemistically referred to. Yes, he was right. Toshikatsu Tajima was the younger brother of Masayoshi Tajima. Masayoshi was the first-generation boss of the Tajima-gumi, an organized crime group that was part of the Yamato-kai Syndicate.

Kusaka worked out the linkages based on the names he'd pulled up over the last hour. Toshikatsu Tajima's daughter Miyuki was married to a Michio Ogawa, who had set up Zell, a construction company, with his own capital. When Zell became insolvent and ceased trading, Ogawa had given his backing to Tatsuo Nakabayashi, a licensed first-class architect who was a Zell executive director. Nakabayashi had then become president of a new company, Nakabayashi Building Enterprises, which took over all of Zell's business, and was also the parent company of Nakabayashi Construction. Kusaka noticed that although Michio Ogawa was no longer on the board of Nakabayashi Construction, three Nakabayashi directors also served on the board of a company called New Tokyo Industries, where Ogawa was president. One way or another, the link to organized crime was still in place.

What did it all mean? Kusaka thought Nakabayashi Construction was probably a front; although it might look like any other company from the outside, the Tajima-gumi could be using the firm for their own ends and helping themselves to the lion's share of its profits.

I need to get to the bottom of this right now.

Kusaka took out his cell phone and called Captain

Imaizumi. He wasn't going to make it back to the precinct in time for tonight's task force meeting.

It was eight o'clock before Kusaka and Satomura were finally able to talk to a Mr. Ikawa, the man in charge of Nakabayashi's construction projects in Tokyo's southern segment.

"You've some questions about an accident that happened nine years ago?"

"That's correct. It involved a Tadaharu Mishima working for Kinoshita Construction. Do you recall the incident?"

On the surface, Ikawa was an ordinary Japanese businessman, but like the man they had spoken to that morning, he radiated hostility. *Another chip off the same old corrupt block*, thought Kusaka.

"Uh-huh, I remember."

"How about the fact that Mishima had some very heavy debts?"

Ikawa jerked briskly to one side.

"No, that I didn't know. Mishima worked for Kinoshita Construction, not for us. Why should I know anything about him?"

"I had a look at your corporate brochure. Nakabayashi has its own division that erects scaffolding and preps building sites—exactly what Kinoshita Construction does, in other words. How's that aspect of the business organized?"

Ikawa scratched his neck.

"Yeah, we have our own in-house division that handles

that line of work," he growled. "Sometimes, though, when they've got a lot on their plate, they need to call in an outside contractor. The weather has a big impact in the construction business. We can draw up nice, well-organized schedules, but if the weather doesn't cooperate, schedules get screwed up and we can end up with two big jobs to do at the same time. That's when we call in Kinoshita. They provide general laborers to make up for temporary manpower shortfalls or to handle specific jobs like erecting or dismantling scaffolding. Does that answer your question?"

"It sounds like a very practical arrangement." Kusaka paused a moment. "And what can you tell me about Kenichi Takaoka?"

Ikawa repeated the name to himself once under his breath, then his face lit up with recognition. "Oh, you mean Ken Takaoka? Tall, handsome fellow with a Roman nose? Sure, I remember him."

Takaoka's looks seemed to make a strong impression on everyone.

"Don't tell me something's happened to good old Ken?"

Kusaka sidestepped the question with a meaningless grunt. "When did Takaoka leave Nakabayashi?"

"Uhm . . . five, perhaps five and a half years ago."

"Do you know why he quit?"

"Uh-huh," replied Ikawa, in an easygoing tone. In his mind, Takaoka and the Mishima incident were obviously two quite separate things. "Here at Nakabayashi, we specialize in building quite sizable apartment and office buildings. Ken was keen to work on smaller-scale, neighborhood projects—single-family homes, basically. There was nothing we could do for him there. I mean, that's not the business we're in."

"So there was no bad blood between him and Nakabayashi when he quit?"

Ikawa threw himself back in his chair, batting away the idea with an extravagant wave of his hand.

"Absolutely not. We don't kick up a fuss every time one of our workers leaves us. In the building trade, everyone job-hops. That's just the way it is. Ken was with us for five, maybe six years—that's a pretty good stint. Anyway, when you're putting up big buildings, you don't really need skilled carpenters. As long as they can knock shit into shape, anyone one will do. Some of the guys are easier to deal with than others, but at the end of the day, it's just a job. If someone says they're moving on, we're like, good-bye and good luck. The laborers seldom come to this office; people like me, we only see them when we go on site. So we don't give them farewell parties or anything."

"I get the picture."

Tadaharu Mishima, who was drowning in debt, had died in a fall at one of Nakabayashi's construction sites. It seemed likely that his life insurance payout had gone to pay off his debts.

Perhaps the majority of Nakabayashi's employees were good, honest people. Nonetheless, Kusaka had strong grounds for believing it was a front company for the Tajima-gumi.

Kenichi Takaoka, who had worked at Nakabayashi, had become a surrogate father to Tadaharu Mishima's son after his death.

And then Kenichi Takaoka himself . . .

"So how's old Ken doing these days?" asked Ikawa. "I bumped into him a while back at a site in Kawasaki. Is he doing okay?"

"No." Kusaka looked into Ikawa's eyes and shook his head. "Kenichi Takaoka is dead."

"What—!"

Ikawa was speechless with shock. Experience told Kusaka that the man's reaction was genuine. Still, that was just his impression, not an unassailable matter of fact.

4

At the morning task force meeting, Kusaka provided a short, bare-bones account of his interview with Kosuke Mishima and of his visit to Nakabayashi Construction.

It was so unlike his usual performance, Reiko suspected him of underplaying his hand.

What was Kusaka doing all last night?

Reiko was no fan of Kusaka's normal rapid-fire, ultra-detailed delivery, but his suddenly turning all cagey like this made her uncomfortable. Had he found a valuable lead that he didn't want to share? Was he so far ahead that she was going to end up shut out of the case? The idea was torment.

I've got to admit, I'd do the same thing myself. Perhaps that's the only reason I'm so suspicious of him. . . .

Reiko wasn't usually so self-critical, but the thought helped her calm down.

"Time to mosey along, Lieutenant?" said Ioka.

"Let's go."

She slipped her arms into the sleeves of a down jacket she had bought the day before. Kikuta, who'd been sitting one row behind them during the meeting, turned his back on Reiko without a word and headed for the door.

What's your problem? What's the cold-shoulder treatment about?

Was Kikuta too stupid to realize that she was as unhappy about being paired up with Ioka as he was? She couldn't stop the guy from flirting with her, and it wasn't her fault that he'd been promoted to the same rank as Kikuta. When Kikuta had lost his temper and lunged for Ioka, she had to intervene; but for Kikuta then to indulge in a mega-sulk because she'd "taken Ioka's side" was downright childish.

The man's an idiot.

Ioka was ready. He stood there, twisting and squirming, as he waited for Reiko to make the first move.

What a bunch of clowns!

Reiko grabbed her Coach bag and headed for the door.

The sooner we solve this case, the sooner this task force will be dissolved and we can all calm down.

Their assignment for today was to see what they could discover about Kenichi Takaoka's past life from a visit to South Hanahata in Adachi Ward.

A shock awaited them at their destination.

"It *says* it should be right here."

"What a screwup!"

On the site of the "previous address" listed on Kenichi Takaoka's resident's card stood a towering fourteen-story apartment block.

It was clearly newer than the rest of the buildings around it. Would anyone in the neighborhood remember Kenichi Takaoka? After all, he had moved out twelve years ago.

They quickly found the caretaker's office. The caretaker was a scrawny old fellow of around sixty. His face reminded Reiko of those yellow pickled radishes you see hanging from the eaves of farmhouses in the countryside.

"I'm afraid can't help you. I only moved to this area three years ago, so anything earlier than that . . ."

"Do you know anyone who's lived around here a long time?"

"Let's see . . . I know. If you turn left out here and go down the street, you'll come to a barber. They've been here a long time, I think."

Reiko and Ioka went straight there. The barber's shop occupied the first floor of a four-story apartment block and looked clean, new, and rather trendy. When they went in, Reiko's fears were confirmed: the owner was a man in his thirties.

"Twelve years ago? I was working as an apprentice over in Shinjuku then. I wasn't here."

"Who was running the place then?"

"My dad. But he passed away six years ago."

"I see. And your mother?"

"She died two years after him."

"Do you know anything about the house of a Mr. Takaoka, which was on the site of the new apartment building just up the road?"

"I'm sorry, I don't. Anything to do with real estate, you'd be better off talking to the Takenotsuka people."

Takenotsuka turned out to be a small realty agency a few doors down the street.

"I'm sorry, madam, the boss is out right now," the middle-aged woman, who was the only person in the office, told them. "There's another agency you could try in block 2, directly opposite the primary school. Maruzen, it's called. They might be able to help you."

Maruzen was only a five-minute walk away. The place was deserted.

"This is a ghost town."

"Don't say that."

They spent the better part of an hour walking around the neighborhood with nothing to show for their trouble. As a last resort, they visited the local police station and asked the duty officer to show them the record of their home visits. If home-visit records were kept properly updated, they could provide valuable information—things like how many people were in a family along with their dates of birth. Sadly, that was not the case here.

"Well, Officer, it looks like you guys don't take your home-visiting duties over-seriously."

The officer, who looked around forty, was wary of them. He mumbled an apology, but he sounded blasé, and his chin was thrust out defiantly.

"Can you at least tell us who the local realty agents are?"

"That won't be a problem."

The officer's tone changed. Suddenly he was brisk and perky.

"Here we have Yoshizawa Real Estate," he said, gesturing at the large, detailed map of the neighborhood on his desk.

"We've been there already."

"How about this one? Maruzen?"

"Nobody home."

"Okay. This one here is Suzuki Real Estate Sales."

Ioka duly jotted down the address.

"Any more?"

"There's Sanko Home Sales here. That's the lot, I think."

"Got it. Thanks."

Sanko Home Sales was the closer of the two, so they went there first. It turned out to be the local office of a large real estate chain. All the employees who'd been working there twelve years ago had been rotated out to other offices.

They finally got lucky at the last place they went to.

"The big apartment block? You mean Green Town Hanahata? Sure, I know all about that place."

The boss of Suzuki Real Estate Sales was Taichi Suzuki, a portly man of fifty or so. He was more than happy to share what he knew with them.

"It was quite controversial. They had to displace quite a few people in order to build it. There was quite a cluster of small shops and flats there, back in the day."

Reiko looked around the office.

"Have you got a map from twelve years ago?"

"Sure."

"Can you show us this address?"

She showed him the address they'd gotten from Takaoka's residence card. Suzuki went to the steel bookcase, took down a large file, and opened it very deliberately.

"That particular address," he said, peering at the house-by-house map, "was the Takaoka Store."

"A family business?"

"Yes, it sold cigarettes, candy, and a few toys as well. Toward the end, it wasn't doing too well."

Reiko pictured the little candy store close to her family home in Minami-Urawa. Just by the front door, there was a sliding window for selling cigarettes to passersby, and inside, bags of colored gumballs hung from the ceiling. The lighting was a single fluorescent tube, and there was a bizarre hodgepodge of stuff for sale: superhero utility belts for kids, and snacks like sugar-coated wheat-bran sticks and vinegared squid. Reiko liked the large sugar-dusted boiled sweets best, with sour vinegar seaweed a close second. Tamaki, her younger sister, detested seaweed; she always went for the roasted soy flour sweets.

"Tell us about the Takaoka Store. Whatever you can remember."

Suzuki nodded, then promptly leaped up from his chair with a great display of urgency. All he did was prepare three cups of tea.

"Thank you," Reiko said, accepting a cup.

Looks like he's settling in for a good long talk.

As he sipped his steaming tea with a faraway look in his eyes, Suzuki reminisced about the store.

"A married couple ran the place. I remember my dad telling me that the store was already there when he set up this business, so that's a good fifty years ago. I used to buy stuff there myself when I was a lad. That's how old the place was!"

Suzuki then went off topic and held forth on the subject of novelty candy. The business didn't seem to evolve much: Suzuki had bought the same brands of candy in his childhood as Reiko in hers.

"I've seen a few stores that specialize in retro candy recently," chimed in Ioka. "There's one in the Sunshine Sixty shopping mall in Ikebukuro."

They'd never get back on topic if Ioka encouraged Suzuki.

"Japanese Plum Jellies were my favorite," said Suzuki. "Delicious."

"I like the way they turn your tongue bright red."

"What? You have those jellies over in Kansai too?" Reiko asked.

"What do you mean? I'm a Tokyoite, born and bred."

Wow, that really is a revelation.

After a while, the interview got back on track.

"Anyway, the plan to put up this big apartment building got the go-ahead, and the residents started receiving eviction notices. My son was about to switch from primary to junior high, so that would be . . . let's see . . . around fifteen years ago."

"You said there was some controversy or trouble with the development?"

"The whole 1980s stock-market and real-estate bubble was already over by then, but there was plenty of nasty harassment."

"Tell me more."

"They'd do things like smash up people's water mains or gouge out the eyes of their pets. There was a noodle shop a couple of doors down from the Takaoka Store; they got the worst of it. A case of food poisoning put the place out of business. There were all sorts of rumors: people said that the customers who got sick were plants and that the butcher who supplied meat to the place was in league with the developer—things like that."

In Tokyo fifteen years ago, land-sharking of that kind had been rampant, though not always easy to detect. But with land prices in decline since then, there was much less of it these days.

"Do you happen to know who the developer was?"

"A firm called Nakabayashi Construction. They're based in the Shinagawa area."

Nakabayashi Construction . . . ?

The name sounded familiar to Reiko.

Yes, it was at the meeting this morning. Didn't Kusaka say something about Takaoka having worked at Nakabayashi Construction before striking out on his own?

"What about the Takaokas? Did Nakabayashi use the

same sort of strongarm tactics on them too?"

"I'm not sure," replied Suzuki, pursing his lips. "The husband was long dead by then. The wife tried to make a go of running the store on her own, but it didn't work out, and the place soon closed down. Come to think of it, the wife was probably dead as well when the problems with the new apartment building started. . . . Yes, yes, that's right. The noodle shop was still running at the time of her funeral. Yes, she died before the trouble started."

"But the Takaokas had a son," Reiko said.

"How did you know that?"

"Kenichi."

"I'd forgotten his name."

Suzuki murmured "Kenichi Takaoka" to himself a few times in an effort to jog his memory. It didn't seem to have much effect.

"The son didn't take over the store?"

"No one does that anymore. There's a convenience store on every street corner, fewer children around, and vending machines for people who wants cigarettes. I think the son went to college and then got a white-collar job."

Kenichi Takaoka was a college graduate who'd worked in an office job before he became a carpenter.

"What sort of company did he join?"

Surely it wasn't Nakabayashi Construction?

Suzuki scratched his head. "A gas company? No, no, no. The gas company was the boy from the noodle restaurant. I'm sorry, I really don't know."

"No problem. Is there anyone else around here who might?"

Suzuki reached inside his jacket and pulled out an electronic calculator no bigger than a name card.

"Do you know how old the Takaoka boy is now?"

"Forty-three."

"Forty ... three ... ," Suzuki repeated. His fat fingers tapped the tiny keyboard with surprising deftness.

"He's quite a bit younger than me, but I can think of a few people born the same year who still live around here. I'll get in touch with the newsagent's daughter and the son of the people who run the florist for you. The best thing would be to find someone who was in his year at school, or just above or below him. They'd have played together. They'd know him."

"Great. We really appreciate your help."

Reiko took out one of her name cards, scribbled the number of her cell on it, and gave it to Suzuki, asking him to call if he found anything out. Suzuki took her card politely with both hands and scrutinized it.

"You look a bit like that famous actress, Lieutenant Himekawa. I've been trying to remember her blasted name ever since you came in, but it's just not coming to me."

"I'm sure you'll remember before our next meeting," said Reiko, as they said their good-byes. She was hoping that Suzuki was thinking of someone good-looking, at least.

She and Ioka took the bus back to Takenotsuka Station. Since it was still too early for a proper lunch, they went into a doughnut joint. Reiko had a shrimp gratin pie with a chocolate French doughnut and an Americano coffee. Ioka plumped for a double chocolate French cruller.

"That's girly food, Ioka. They're horribly sweet. *What?* You're having five of the things!"

"What's the problem? I've got a sweet tooth."

Reiko wasn't keen on sitting at a table for two with Ioka. She didn't like the enforced intimacy. Unfortunately, she had no choice; it was the middle of the day, and the place was packed. Reiko opted for a table beside the window, where no one could eavesdrop on them.

"I love *all* doughnuts. Why don't we share?"

"No, thanks," said Reiko coldly.

She was surprised to discover that the victim's parents had run a candy store—even more that Takaoka had been to college and had an office job for several years.

"Do you really think Takaoka was a graduate who'd had a white-collar job?" she mused. "Being a qualified carpenter is a skilled trade. It's not something you can pick up in just a year or two. Quitting a desk job to become a tradesman—it's an unusual choice to make."

She sipped her coffee. Ioka, meanwhile, was lavishing all his attention on his doughnuts.

"Even odder is his decision to work for the very company that evicted him from his own house. *And* gouged out the eyes of the neighborhood cats and dogs. *And* put the noodle restaurant next door out of business by staging an outbreak of food poisoning. Would Takaoka knowingly work for them after all that?"

Ioka was munching away intently.

Reiko picked up her shrimp gratin pie.

"I wonder if the yakuza were involved?"

Ioka looked up from his plate, hastily swallowed what was in his mouth, and leaned toward her.

"Didn't you know, boss?" he said, in a low voice. "Nakabayashi Construction's a front company for the Tajima-gumi."

"*Really?*"

It was just as well that Reiko's mouth was full, otherwise the whole restaurant would have heard her surprised exclamation.

"Really."

"Why didn't you say anything when the name came up at the meeting this morning?"

"I thought everyone knew."

You are a complete and utter dolt.

"You should have said something."

"Lieutenant Kusaka would just have given me a hard time. 'What, you think I didn't know that?' No thanks. I don't need the grief."

"You need to be diplomatic. Just preface your remarks with a phrase like, 'As I'm sure you are aware.'"

"Brilliant! Lieutenant Reiko, I don't know how you think of these things."

God, he wears me out.

Hopelessness was like a crushing weight on her shoulders.

"Are you sure about Nakabayashi being a front for the Tajima-gumi?"

"Sure I'm sure. I went out for a drink with a pal of mine from the Shinagawa Precinct. He's in the Organized Crime Investigation Division. We were on the subject of organized crime, so I thought I'd ask him about Nakabayashi. He says it's a conglomerate with its fingers in all sorts of pies—there's Nakabayashi Real Estate, a Nakabayashi Residential Sales, and they're in the hotel business too. My guess'd be that Nakabayashi Real Estate were the ones doing the dirty tricks to get people out of their houses over in South Hanahata, not Nakabayashi Construction."

"Is there anything else? Have you told me everything I need to know?"

"There is one more thing," said Ioka, with a grin. "Today, Lieutenant Reiko, you look ravishing."

The buffoon! She wanted to grind her pie into that stupid mug of his!

5

Kusaka was already there when Reiko and Ioka got back to the big room in Kamata. He was busy typing up his report. Ishikura and Yuda from her own squad were there too.

"How was South Hanahata?" asked Ishikura, as he poured a couple of cups of tea. He wasn't the designated tea maker for the squad; they'd just happened to come back after he'd brewed a fresh pot for himself.

Reiko thanked Ishikura. She was quite happy to make tea herself when it was needed. Gender stereotypes about Japanese working women being nothing more than glorified tea ladies didn't bother her, and bossing around an older man just because she could wasn't her idea of fun.

"We learned a decent amount about Takaoka's background. Not so sure of its relevance to the case, though. How about you?"

Ishikura had been making inquiries related to Takaoka's work life.

"We didn't turn up anything. Takaoka was a complete boy scout. Paid his suppliers on time and never cut corners.

Everyone says that Mishima's a lovely young man and that he and Takaoka were, if anything, closer than a real father and son. No one has any idea why he could have been murdered."

Kikuta came back. He and his partner, one of the local precinct detectives, had also been speaking to Takaoka's work associates.

"Hey, how's it going?" said Reiko.

"All right. You?"

Kikuta didn't make eye contact.

I've had it up to here with you!

"Kikuta, come with me. *Now.*"

She grabbed him by the sleeve and began to drag him between the rows of desks. He just grunted and kept his eyes fixed on the ground. When Ioka got to his feet to follow them, Reiko gestured him back into his seat.

"Stay here and write up our report. Properly."

She tossed him the file and strode to the door. Kikuta followed in silence.

Reiko marched up the stairs. Kikuta trudged dutifully after her.

When they got to the seventh floor, the site of the infirmary and the dojo, there was no one around. She walked to the door of the darkened dojo, made the requisite bow of respect to the empty room and went on in.

Standing on the duckboards beside the shoe lockers, she turned to face Kikuta. The angle of the light meant that she couldn't see his face properly, while he could probably see hers.

"What's your problem?"

The shadow didn't respond.

"Why are you carrying on like this? Are you upset about something?"

Once again, there was no reply.

"What is it you expect *me* to do? The way Ioka's behaving—I mean, this is the third time you've worked with him, right? You should know, that's just the way the guy is. You're just going to have to put up with it. I hope you don't think that I actually *enjoy* his shenanigans?"

The only sound was heavy nasal breathing. What was Kikuta up to now? Impersonating a water buffalo?

The air smelled of stale sweat. Over to one side, Reiko noticed a door. Probably led to a storeroom, she thought.

Reiko peered over her shoulder into the darkened dojo. A white lump loomed vaguely up out of the dark floor: a heap of folded futons beneath the window overlooking the main road. The TMPD detectives assigned to the task force used them for sleeping. Reiko herself had been staying in a nearby hotel for the last couple of days.

The streetlight outside must have turned red. The noise of traffic suddenly went quiet.

"Would a kiss cheer you up?"

Hadn't Kikuta heard? He was so close, he must have.

"Would a kiss from me cheer you up, I said?"

Kikuta said nothing. He just stood rigidly to attention.

Oh, for goodness's sake!

Reiko placed her hands on his broad shoulders, pulled

herself up on her tiptoes, and kissed him square on the mouth.

The texture of his lips was like the skin of a steamed sweet potato.

Kikuta gave a loud gulp.

"Perhaps I shouldn't have."

Reiko took her hands away, patted Kikuta on the shoulder and took a step sideways. She'd have been quite happy for him to smother her in a bear hug. He seemed to have no intention of doing so.

"We need to be getting back now, Sergeant Kikuta."

"Yes."

She went back out into the brightly lit corridor. Kikuta followed. The sound of their footfalls echoed in the passageway.

"Kikuta."

"Yes."

"You're an idiot."

"Yes, ma'am."

Reiko walked faster. So did Kikuta.

She skipped down the stairs. Kikuta fell in step behind her.

Not long afterward, the evening meeting began.

The first order of business was to hear the report of Lieutenant Kusaka.

"This morning I had the opportunity to speak briefly to Kosuke Mishima. As you know, it was Mishima who was first on the crime scene. This was his second interview with us."

This time, his report was classic Kusaka: excruciating

detail on everything from Takaoka Construction's business practices to the most recent developments of the case, all delivered at machine-gun speed.

He left nothing out: the Kawasaki kitchen renovation job; the difficulty of estimating costs making Mishima skeptical about his ability to run the business alone; the fact that Takaoka occasionally had trouble getting paid but that the sums involved were not large enough to derail the business; how Mishima was always paid on time; and how Mishima had identified the hand because of a scar and had in fact been present when Takaoka cut himself.

Kusaka then began to explain how Mishima and Takaoka had first met.

"Tadaharu Mishima, Kosuke's father, was working as a scaffolder for Kinoshita Construction nine years ago when he lost his footing and fell from the ninth floor."

Reiko and Ioka exchanged a look.

At the meeting that morning, Kusaka had mentioned that Takaoka used to work for Nakabayashi Construction. This, however, was the first time anyone had said anything about Kosuke Mishima's father being employed by them too.

Other people must have realized that Kusaka had come up with something new and interesting. A buzz of excited chatter broke out.

Kusaka paused for a moment. Reiko raised her hand.

Imaizumi, who was sitting at the front of the room, pointed to her. "Okay, Himekawa. Fire away."

"Thank you, Captain," she replied, without getting to

her feet. "You couldn't make it back for last night's meeting, Lieutenant Kusaka, so I don't think you're aware that the father of Michiko Nakagawa, Kosuke Mishima's girlfriend, also died in an accident at a Kinoshita Construction site. It was a fall in his case too."

Kusaka turned and looked at her. The white glare of the fluorescent lights was reflected in his glasses.

There was a drawn-out silence.

Kusaka was at a loss for words.

A twenty-year-old boy and a nineteen-year-old girl. A builder and a waitress who was studying hairdressing. A boyfriend and girlfriend in a normal relationship—except for the fact that both their fathers had died in identical accidents, albeit years apart, when employed by the same company. . . .

"I'm at fault here." Kusaka's power of speech seemed to have returned. "I haven't had time to review all yesterday's reports yet. When did Michiko Nakagawa's father die?"

"It was a couple of months ago. He'd only just joined Kinoshita."

"Did the girl tell you how she got to know Kosuke Mishima?"

Reiko flipped back a few pages in her notebook.

"Let's see. Oh yes. He was a frequent visitor to the diner where she works. Being more or less the same age, they got chatting and ended up becoming friends."

"That tallies with what Mishima told me."

Kusaka turned to face the front.

"There's one thing I'm doubtful about: Mishima told

me that he went to the diner because it was 'convenient' when he was on his way home from jobs in Kawasaki. The trouble with his story is that the Royal Diner is actually located on the wrong side of the highway for traffic going in that direction. When I pointed this fact out to Mishima, he was very insistent about that particular restaurant chain being a favorite of his; his manner changed and he became quite aggressive."

Imaizumi lolled back in his chair and crossed his arms on his chest.

"What's your interpretation?"

Kusaka looked down at the floor and slowly exhaled.

"I think he's lying. I don't believe that the two of them met by chance. I'm willing to accept that the children of two men who both worked for the same company could go out together. But the idea that the children of two men who both worked for the same company *and died in similar accidents*, even if several years apart, should start a relationship based on a random meeting at a roadside diner strains the limits of credibility."

"Meaning?"

Imaizumi was deliberately forcing Kusaka to deal in impressions and guesswork, knowing that there was nothing the man hated more.

"Meaning, sir, that it's not impossible that the meeting was the result of intention on somebody's part."

"Whose part?"

"That, I don't know."

"Who do you think?"

Kusaka's jaw clenched.

"If push came to shove, I'd probably go with Mishima having initiated the meeting. Of course, it could have been a third party, though I've no idea who."

"Good. Keep going."

Kusaka cleared his throat and pushed his spectacles high up on the bridge of his nose.

"Mishima told us that Takaoka invited him to come and work for him not long before he graduated from junior high school. Takaoka was still an employee of Nakabayashi Construction at that time—"

"Excuse me!"

Ioka had thrust his hand into the air and was waving it about.

Oh, the idiot.

Didn't he know that it was rude to interrupt a speaker in full flow? That was doubly true with Kusaka. Sure enough, when Kusaka turned around to face them, his eyes glowed with cold fury.

"What do you want? Can't you wait a min—"

Ioka plowed on, jumping to his feet.

This won't end well, thought Reiko.

"Yes . . . uhm . . . I mean no. Anyway, as I'm sure you're aware, Lieutenant Kusaka, Nakabayashi Construction is a front company for the Tajima-gumi."

Ioka's syntax was a mess. On top of that, he had interrupted Kusaka, a superior officer, not once but twice.

Silence fell on the room. A heavy, cold silence. Being buried alive probably felt rather like this, Reiko thought to herself. Ioka's hand was still sticking hopelessly up in the air.

"And so? That was precisely the point I was about to address. I'm very well aware about the relationship Nakabayashi has with the Tajima-gumi."

Ioka gurgled something incoherent.

"So if you want to say anything, kindly wait until I've reached the end of my report."

Ioka sagged visibly. He reminded Reiko of katsuobushi, those flakes of dried tuna that people sprinkle on their food. Dancing around merrily from the effects of the heat one moment; flaccid and inert the next, as they soak up the sauce.

"I'm sorry, sir."

Poor Ioka looked ready to burst into tears. Reiko couldn't very well laugh at his misfortune; she, after all, was the one who'd encouraged him to speak out.

"Thank you. Now, to get back to what I was saying. . . ."

Kusaka then proceeded to explain how Nakabayashi Construction and the other firms that belonged to the Nakabayashi Group had been established with capital provided by Masayoshi Tajima, the first-generation boss of the Tajima-gumi, a branch of the Yamato-kai Syndicate, and by Michio Ogawa, who was married to his brother's daughter.

"I've not yet managed to confirm that Kinoshita Construction was set up based on an injection of capital from the same Ogawa. What I do know is that Nakabayashi Construction does a significant amount of business with

Kinoshita Construction and outsources plenty of site-prepping and scaffolding-related projects to them. I have yet to review the two companies' accounts, but I have spoken testimony from a Seiichi Murai, a thirty-nine-year-old employee of Chiba Building Materials, a company that does business with Nakabayashi, to the effect that Kinoshita Construction gets three or four large-scale projects from Nakabayashi every year.

"Let's turn our attention to Tadaharu Mishima, Kosuke Mishima's father. When Tadaharu fell to his death nine years ago, his life was insured for twelve million yen. Kinoshita Construction both paid for the policy and was the designated beneficiary. I found this information in the records of the Takaido Precinct CID—that's the precinct that certified Mishima's death as an accident. Their records also show that Tadaharu declared personal bankruptcy thirteen years ago, four years prior to his death. It seems to have been of little use to him. His financial situation remained precarious, and he eventually went through illegal channels to borrow money. At the time of his death, he had debts of almost ten million yen.

"A finance company by the name of Joy Credit rolled up and took over all of Mishima's debts. Joy Credit has definite links to the Tajima-gumi. I haven't yet been able to establish any link between Joy Credit and Kinoshita Construction. However, according to the current principal of Shinagawa Mercy College, the police informed the school that Tadaharu's life insurance covered his debts in full. Unfortunately, I have not yet managed to track down the detective who was in charge of Mishima's case."

Goddammit! How could he possibly have found out so much in such a short time?

It was some consolation to Reiko that she'd managed to surprise him with her nugget about the fathers of both Kosuke Mishima and Michiko Nakagawa dying in accidents at Kinoshita Construction building sites. In Tadaharu Mishima's case, it was even looking as though Kinoshita might be guilty of insurance fraud.

Hashizume, the director of Homicide, suddenly put his palms flat on the table and leaned aggressively forward.

"What exactly are you investigating here, Kusaka?"

Kusaka plucked his glasses off his nose.

"I'm probing the alibi of Kosuke Mishima, the person who discovered the crime scene in this particular case. I'm examining Mishima's relationship with Michiko Nakagawa, the person who provided him with an alibi; and I'm also looking into the circumstances surrounding the death of Tadaharu Mishima, the event which led to the first encounter between Takaoka, the victim, and Kosuke Mishima."

"Do you think any of it has a direct bearing on Takaoka's murder?"

"That, I do not know."

"If you don't know, then why go into such painstaking detail?"

"It's precisely because I don't know that I'm investigating all of this. Nothing I'm doing is a waste of time."

Hashizume had leveled the same accusation at Kusaka many times before. Today was just another rerun.

"There simply isn't the time for you to chase down every tidbit of information that you blunder across."

"I don't believe that my progress is particularly slow compared to any of the other investigators on this case."

"All I'm trying to say is that a man of your abilities would make even faster progress if you narrowed your focus slightly."

"That's exactly what I'm trying to do, in my own way. I made a conscious decision, for instance, *not* to delve into the background of the principal of Shinagawa Mercy College."

"Why not treat Tadaharu Mishima the same way, then? Even if you suspect that insurance fraud had something to do with his death, it's nine years since it happened. The statute of limitations has run out."

"I'm not trying to build a case here. I'm just trying to see if there is a causal relationship between that incident and the murder case we're working on."

"Based on what? The father of the person who discovered the crime scene dying in an accident nine years ago? Are you serious?"

"Absolutely. And I don't plan to abandon this particular line of inquiry until I can find positive proof that no connection exists."

Kusaka and Hashizume were oblivious to everyone else in the room. Looking around at the forty or so investigators there, Reiko detected signs of impatience in a good many of them.

She turned to the front of the room and caught Imaizumi's eye. He nodded knowingly and cleared his throat loudly, forcing Kusaka to stop talking.

"So, have you anything else to report to us, Lieutenant?"

"Yes, sir. I need to give you an account of my interview with Mitsuru Kurihara, Nakabayashi Construction's head of general affairs, and Hidehiko Ikawa, the man in charge of construction sites in the south segment of Tokyo."

"Go right ahead."

Kusaka resumed his normal, rapid-fire delivery.

"Neither of the two men could tell me anything about Tadaharu Mishima; Ikawa, however, clearly remembered Takaoka. Takaoka quit Nakabayashi around five and a half years ago, after having worked there for five or six years. There was no disagreement or unpleasantness of any kind behind his decision to leave. That brings my report for today to an end."

"Any questions? No? All right, Sergeant Mizoguchi, you're up next."

"Yes, sir."

Mizoguchi got to his feet.

"Since yesterday, I've been going over the articles we found in our search of Kenichi Takaoka's apartment. I've not come across anything massively significant. Takaoka's bankbook shows that he ran his business primarily on a cash basis: whenever there was an incoming payment to his work account, he seems to have withdrawn the same amount the following day. He treated his bank account like a mailbox. The current balance stands at twenty-three thousand yen. He seems to have used cash rather than direct debit to pay for his utilities. All in all, getting a handle on his finances isn't going to be easy."

That was the end of Mizoguchi's report. Short and sweet. Sergeant Toyama was next.

"I've got something . . . pretty big to report."

He sounds pretty sure of himself, with his dramatic pauses!

"Today, we visited the outlets of all the insurance companies in Takaoka's neighborhood. There were twelve in total. It turned out that the Omori South branch of Act Insurance had issued a policy for him."

A wave of excitement rippled through the room. Everyone sat up straighter in their chairs. All eyes were focused on Toyama.

"In fact, it wasn't one policy they issued, but two. Takaoka took them both out at the same time, four and a half years ago. The first policy pays out ten million yen, and the beneficiary is Kosuke Mishima. However, the payout on the second policy is for fifty million."

A tense silence.

Fifty million yen! That's serious money.

"The beneficiary of the second policy is a Ms. Kimie Naito, a forty-nine-year-old woman who lives alone and runs a restaurant in Kitasenju, Adachi Ward."

South Hanahata, the site of Takaoka's original family home, was also in Adachi Ward, and Kitasenju wasn't that far from Kenichi Takaoka's current address in Ota Ward.

They all fell into Tokyo's northern segment.

Imaizumi frowned and raised a finger.

"What connection does the woman have with Takaoka?"

"I don't know yet," Toyama replied. "All I can say for sure is that they're not related."

"Did you check out the restaurant she runs? Have a look at where she lives?"

"Yes, sir. The restaurant consists of a counter that sits six and three low tables on a raised dais. It can probably accommodate twenty people, tops. Kimie employs no staff and takes care of everything herself. She lives above the restaurant. The place is very popular. She serves a prix fixe lunch, and it was packed at lunchtime."

Imaizumi grinned.

"You ate there?"

"Yes, sir. Today's lunch was grilled yellowtail fish, chicken-vegetable stew, and miso soup and pickles on the side. The flavors were a little on the strong side for my taste, but it was good. The clientele's mixed—the regulars seem to be local office workers plus a smattering of laborers. We haven't had the chance to visit in the evening, but there were plenty of bottles of shochu with nametags on the shelf behind the bar, so it's probably doing well. According to a local realty agent I interviewed, Kimie owns the place outright."

"You've not yet spoken to her?"

Toyama shook his head.

"No. Today we just passed ourselves off as a couple of first-time customers. That's concludes my report for today."

"Good work, Toyama. Starting tomorrow, I want surveillance on Kimie Naito. Right, who's next? Officer Shinjo."

Neither Shinjo, nor the person who spoke after him, had anything of significance to report. Eventually, Reiko's turn to speak came.

"Today we made some initial inquiries in the neighborhood where Kenichi Takaoka used to live. Unfortunately, there's no longer ..."

Reiko went on to explain that an apartment building had been erected on the site of the Takaoka family home and that they hadn't managed to locate anyone who knew Takaoka from when he lived there. A local realty agent who'd lived in the neighborhood for decades had promised to help her with that, she said. Takaoka's parents had owned a small candy store. Takaoka had found himself an office job after graduating from college instead of taking over the family business. The plan to build the apartment block postdated the death of both parents. There'd apparently been friction when the local residents were thrown out of their homes.

"The developer of the new apartment building was Nakabayashi Construction," Reiko continued. "But the theory is that another Nakabayashi company, Nakabayashi Real Estate, handled the evictions."

The response of the top brass and the other investigators was rather muted this time. The involvement of the Nakabayashi Group certainly got everybody's attention, but Kusaka, by getting in first, had stolen Reiko's thunder.

Imaizumi gave Reiko a quizzical look.

"Seems strange for Takaoka to get a job with Nakabayashi after something like that happened in his own neighborhood."

"I'm with you there, sir. According to Lieutenant Kusaka's report, Takaoka quit Nakabayashi five and a half years ago, after having worked there for five or six years. That would suggest that Takaoka joined Nakabayashi Construction almost immediately after they'd kicked him out of his own home. I mean to look into that tomorrow."

"Is that everything, Himekawa?"

"Yes, sir."

"Any questions?" Imaizumi said to the room.

There were none.

PART
THREE

1

It was a summer evening.

I remember the shadow of the huge steel shutter; the damp, freshly hosed earth; the thick metal slats they put down for the heavy trucks to drive on.

I remember Kosuke, loitering there.

"You've got your father's eyes," I told him.

That wasn't what I was really thinking.

No. I saw my son in him. Kosuke was eleven. My son—at least in my memory—is always five years old. The two boys had a lot in common even so.

Podgy, innocent faces; big, wide-open, upturned eyes; suntanned skin; spindly shoulders; muscular legs from running around all day long; sneakers worn without socks.

Getting a grip on my emotions, I squatted down in front of the lad. I did my best to sound cheerful.

"I was a friend of your dad's," I said.

The reality wasn't quite so simple. What was I really? An observer? An accomplice? A hypocrite, only looking out for Number One?

Where did I get off posing as Mr. Nice Guy? What could I do for a poor little bastard like this boy? Give him a slap-up meal? Wow, big deal! Like filling up his little belly would make any real difference. Like it would make me feel better about the crimes I'd committed—and the punishment I knew I deserved.

In fact, the time I spent with little Kosuke was sheer bliss.

His little hand in mine as we thread our way through a crowd. The excited looks we exchange as I hold up the restaurant menu and ask him what he wants to have. The fun of us both eating the same thing. The boredom of waiting in line for amusement park rides. The souvenir snaps we take with costumed cartoon characters. The sight of his face when he dozes off on the train home. His weight when I carry him on my back. The words he mutters sleepily in my ear. "Daddy! Daddy!"

My heart is racing. I am happy again.

What more can I do for the boy?

It became an obsession with me.

What more can I do for him? It's about more than money, about something the old me could never do, something that the new me seems to have lost. . . .

Gradually the gray, gray city began to get its color back. It no longer felt like a giant graveyard.

Time started to mean something again. A week became more than seven units of seven days. My Sundays were no longer a yawning blank; they were a treat, a new start, precious time off.

The heat of the summer, the cold of the winter—I enjoyed it all. But I'd be lying if I said I didn't feel guilty for getting my zest for life back. Man cannot live on bitterness alone. I needed to move things forward. I needed to put my unforgivable crime behind me.

I felt—or rather, I remembered how to feel—the joy of having someone who depends on you; the deep contentment that comes from being needed.

I was determined not to screw things up this time. Above all, I wanted to protect the little boy. I wanted to give him everything he needed to make a go of life. I didn't have much in the way of money, but I was ready to give him everything else I could.

I'm a wicked man, I know, but all I ask is that you let me share in your innocent joy of life, even just a little.

I'd just handed in my notice to Nakabayashi Construction, where I'd been working for the last six years. I was at a building site in Nakano, laying the floor in a new apartment complex. It was my last job for them.

"Mr. Ta-ka-o-ka?"

Someone was calling my name in a mocking singsong voice. When I turned, I saw a man—no, *that man*—standing in the doorway.

It was Makio Tobe, from the administration department of Kinoshita Construction. He was wearing his trademark long black coat that was out of place on a building site. He started walking toward me. His black enameled shoes made a hard, ringing sound on the wood of the floor.

Ignoring him, I went back to work.

I pointed the nail gun at the floor and squeezed the trigger. A nail shot out, then another. It sounded like a pistol fitted with a silencer, as in the movies.

"I heard you're leaving Nakabayashi?"

The air compressor feeding air to the nail gun wheezed and groaned.

"You know that you can never run away from me, don't you, Mr. Takaoka? Ever."

His voice was soft and wheedling. With a note of insanity.
Oh shit!

"Are you listening to me, Ken-i-chi Ta-ka-o-ka?"

I kept working the nail gun. One. Two. Three. Four. Five.

"You weren't going to bother to say good-bye to me— me, the man who set you up with this job! That's not very friendly, is it?"

Switching on the safety, I put the nail gun down on the floor.

The compressor went on groaning.

I got to my feet and stood to attention in front of him.

"Thank you for everything you did for me. After leaving Nakabayashi Construction, I'm planning to set up my own business—"

"You taking the fucking piss?"

Tobe launched a kick at an empty soda can on the floor that we'd been using as an ashtray. It smacked into the cream plasterboard wall, leaving a dent and a grimy stain.

"You shut up and listen to me. You've no fucking right to do what you want with your life unless you get my fucking permission first. You should know that. After all, you are *Kenichi Takaoka.*"

"Yes . . . I know."

From beneath the window I could hear the spoken warning alarm from a truck backing up. "Danger. Truck reversing," it repeated, over and over again.

"I'm not trying to run away. I just wanted to start working on different kinds of jobs—smaller ones."

"What about your digs? Planning to move?"

"No, I'm staying in the same old place."

The craziness that swirled around Tobe with the unpredictability of a tornado suddenly blew itself out.

"Oh yeah?"

"That's right. It's just like you say, Tobe: *I am Kenichi Takaoka.* Changing jobs or moving house will never change that. I know that."

Tobe didn't seem to be interested anymore.

"Okay. You spooked me, Takaoka. That's why I lost my shit."

He grinned at me as he rubbed the stain he'd made on the wall.

"Sorry 'bout this. You're going to stick wallpaper up here, right? It won't be a problem?"

"It's fine. I'll use putty to smooth it out."

Tobe went back to rubbing the wall with his grubby palm.

"Let's go out for a drink together this evening, my friend.

Your own private farewell party. Do you know Patio, the hostess club near the station? Meet me there when you finish."

Tobe wasn't interested when I said that I wasn't dressed properly for a fancy-pants joint like that. I knew he'd fly off the handle again if I protested and yell at me about thinking I was too good to share a jar with him, so I thanked him and agreed to go.

By the time I got to the club, Tobe was pretty wasted.

"Hey, Takaoka, my man," he crowed. "Over here. Come on. Sit yourself down."

He indicated a seat between two girls on his left. There was a third girl sitting across the table from him.

"This here's my man Takaoka. He's my best buddy. Quite a hunk, eh?"

"Ooh, he's gorgeous."

The whole experience was humiliating—just as I'd expected. Those nightclub girls have a sixth sense: they can sniff out who's got money and who doesn't. In order not to wreck the atmosphere, they made a show of being "nice" to me, but there was a subtle difference in how they treated me and how they treated Tobe. I was an inferior being. With Tobe and me, it was blindingly obvious which of us had more dough.

"Hey, hey, Mr. Tobe," twittered the girls. "What's your blood type?"

"Me? I'm Type F. Know why? 'Cos I'll fuck anything that moves."

In hostess clubs, men with money can get away with just about anything.

"Stop it!" squeaked one of the girls. "My boobs are ready to pop out with laughing. No, seriously, what type are you?"

"A serious, responsible fellow like me? I'm type A."

"You're kidding! I'd never have pegged you for an A."

"Yes, I had you down for a B," chimed in another girl. "Strong, passionate, and independent—you've got to be B."

"Yes, Mr. Tobe, you should go and get your blood tested again, but *properly* this time."

All three girls exploded with laughter. I managed to force a smile.

"How about you, Mr. Takaoka? What type are you?"

"Me? . . . Actually, I'm A too."

There was another outburst of laughter.

"You're pulling my leg! You two—the same blood type. No way."

"Mr. Tobe's wrong. *Definitely.*"

The hostess sitting between Tobe and me got to her feet. "Excuse me. I'll be right back."

I slid across the banquette to Tobe.

"Sorry to bring this up here," I whispered into his ear. "That business with Tadaharu Mishima from four years ago—is it all taken care of? All finished?"

Tobe popped a cigarette between his lips. The girl sitting opposite reached over and lit it with a blue plastic lighter.

"You betcha," he grunted. "Heard you were there when it happened. Did the cops haul you in for questioning?"

"Nah. I just gave them a statement there."

"You see what I mean? No problemo."

"That's not quite what I mean."

How could I ask him the question I wanted to ask without bringing Kosuke into it?

"What I mean is, are all Mishima's debts settled for once and for all?"

Tobe blew out a big cloud of smoke and nodded breezily.

"Yes, indeedy. Hey, that's what the whole thing was all about, right?"

"So it's a clean slate now?"

"Yessir. I'd forgotten about the whole darn business till you brought it up."

I felt a huge sense of relief. Going to that sordid dive hadn't been a complete waste of time after all.

After staying a little under an hour, I decided to make a move. Tobe seemed to have got whatever had been bugging him out of his system. He clapped me on the shoulder and wished me good luck.

"If you have any more problems, just give me a call. You know that I'm here to help, Mr. Ta-ka-o-ka."

I bowed, turned on my heel, and left the club.

I prayed I'd never have to see him again.

I thought we were done with each other, but Tobe kept popping up when I least expected.

I wasn't surprised that he kept tabs on me, but I was

surprised that he came out to check up on me in person. Either he was worried about me—or else he just had way too much free time.

Tobe kept showing up, even after Kosuke started working for me. The last thing I wanted was for him to find out about the boy.

Sure, he'd told me that the whole business with Tadaharu Mishima was over and done with. The thing is, a guy like Tobe is always looking for ways to stir up trouble. Now that Kosuke was earning decent money with me, what was to stop Tobe telling him that his father's debt was still outstanding and insisting that he pay it back—with some outrageous interest charges stuck on top for good measure? Those guys wouldn't think twice about doing something like that.

I worried that by having Kosuke near me, I was exposing him to danger. Still, at least he was where I could keep an eye on him and help him out, if things went south. Tobe frightened me, but the idea of parting with Kosuke frightened me much more. I took my life one day at a time. "Stay strong and there's nothing Tobe can do to Kosuke," I kept telling myself.

Kosuke hadn't been any great shakes at schoolwork, but he wasn't by any means dumb. He picked up the job fast, and he was a whole lot tougher and stronger than I'd thought.

He worked hard, ate well, and slept like a log. By the time he was sixteen, after a year on the job, he was so burly you could hardly recognize him. He was on the road to becoming a first-rate carpenter-tradesman.

I started the boy at five thousand yen per day and bumped him up to eight starting his second year. I can't remember all the stages, but I know that I raised his wages to eighteen thousand a day as an eighteenth birthday present. That was very generous, and I didn't have much leeway for any further wage increases after that. If the boy wanted to earn more after that, it wouldn't come from his regular wages—he'd need to start bringing in jobs himself. That was what I was training him up to do.

There was Kosuke and me. And all the guys we worked with on a regular basis.

We had our problems. Sometimes we'd get to the end of a job, only to have the contractor cut our fee on the grounds that Kosuke had misread the plans and not done what the client wanted. In a way, though, that was a good experience. For both of us.

Whatever happened, I always paid Kosuke exactly what I'd promised him. When he protested, I forced him to take it anyway. Was I being soft on the boy? No. Kosuke knew what my paying him meant. It meant that I expected him to do the job right the next time—something that's a whole lot more challenging than swallowing a one-off pay cut. Sure enough, Kosuke never made the same mistake twice. That was what made me proudest of all.

One day in mid-October this year, we were working on a house when Matsumoto, the electrician, came over and hissed in my ear.

"Hey, Ken. It looks like Kinoshita Construction are up to their old tricks."

"Up to their old tricks?"

I nervously scanned the room. Kosuke was out front having his three o'clock tea break. Matsumoto and I were alone together.

"Where?"

Matsumoto wrinkled his nose in distaste.

"At one of Nakabayashi's places, a block of condos they're building in Musashikosugi. A newbie scaffolder fell from the tenth floor and was killed. The guy wasn't properly trained. What the hell are those guys thinking?"

My heart was pounding so hard my chest hurt.

I didn't need to ask. I knew that Tobe was behind it.

"Akimoto at the building suppliers told me. He thought there was something not quite right about it. Apparently this guy turns up on site, and you can see from the get-go that no way is he a pro. He's there a couple of weeks, mainly carrying pipes and fittings and shit around the place, driving the dump truck, whatever, then—splat, sayonara baby."

I remembered the way Tadaharu Mishima had died. It had been ugly, brutal.

"It turns out—I got this from Shimatani, the architect—that, surprise, surprise, the poor bastard who did the high dive had debts. Classic mistake: he'd acted as guarantor on a friend's personal loan. Guy's name was Nakagawa; Shimatani knew him from this real estate developer where he'd worked in sales. So Shimatani's like, 'Never expected to run into you here,' and Nakagawa makes a quick exit. Whoosh! Gone! Shimatani thought that was odd, so he does a little asking around. One of the managers at the developer said he had to give Nakagawa the boot. He'd found him with his hand in the corporate cookie jar."

The skin on the back of my neck broke out in prickly goose bumps and my armpits were drenched with sweat.

"I don't know exactly what happened next, but I'm guessing that Nakagawa ended up in hock to loan sharks. It's exactly the same thing that happened to Kosuke's dad, right? Up shit creek without a paddle. So they fix him up with a job at Kinoshita and tell him to throw himself off the scaffolding when no one's watching, then they dress it up as an accident and pocket the insurance money themselves. Officially it goes to Kinoshita, but Nakabayashi's in on it too, I reckon."

"What's this 'same thing' that happened to my dad?"

Kosuke was standing in the passage just outside the room, holding a plastic bag from the convenience store.

"Oh, nothing, Kosuke."

Kosuke wasn't going to be fobbed off like that. He ignored me and started peppering Matsumoto with questions.

"What did you mean about him throwing himself off the scaffolding when no one's watching?"

Kosuke grabbed Matsumoto by the shoulders and shook him. The electrician was distraught. "Mean?" he croaked. "Nothing."

"Getting fixed up with a Kinoshita job when there was

no way out—what was that about? Huh? Tell me."

"Stop it, Kosuke," I said, trying to pull him away.

Slapping my hands off, he wheeled on me in a fury.

"Did you know about this, boss?"

"No," I eventually stammered.

"Now that I think about it, you were working for Nakabayashi when my dad died, weren't you? Was it really an accident, or did my dad get the job at Kinoshita just so he could kill himself too? Did you fucking know, boss? Did you know what he was going to do?"

I couldn't say anything. Even when Kosuke grabbed hold of me and started shaking me, I couldn't utter a word.

"You fucking answer me! Did you know that my dad had been told to kill himself to clear his stupid debts? You knew, but you didn't try to stop him?"

"Kosuke, that's enough," Matsumoto pleaded.

"You said you were my dad's friend. I don't think so, man. You just stood to one side and let him die. Or, what, were you in on it? Were you? Huh?"

"Kosuke," shouted Matsumoto. "That's enough."

The electrician grabbed Kosuke in a full nelson and pulled him off me.

"Kosuke, you mustn't speak like that to Takaoka. Never speak like that to this man. Never, you hear."

Kosuke was on his hands and knees on the plywood subfloor. He looked dazed, bewildered.

"Think about everything Takaoka's done for you, about how he's trained you. It's not his fault. And it wasn't just him—

it was the whole lot of us, we all knew what was going on."

I grabbed the electrician by the elbow.

"Matsumoto, stop it."

"No, Ken, let me have my say. You've got no idea, kid. Ken here, who's not even family to you, he made the rounds, visited everyone in the trade. 'Please look out for the boy,' he says. 'Any problems with him, you tell me first. He's my responsibility, one hundred percent. I'm going to train him up right, so let's not worry about teething problems.' This man here's done a ton of things for you—a ton of things—that few real fathers would do for their own flesh and blood. I won't stand by and hear you insult Ken. You should be ashamed of yourself."

Kosuke slowly pulled himself to his feet and stumbled out of the house.

Neither Matsumoto nor I made any move to go after him.

I went and picked up the shopping bag Kosuke had dropped in the passage. It contained three drinks, a packet of soy-sauce-flavored rice crackers, and a little bag of chocolates. There was a can of Pokka coffee for me, Ito-en green tea for Matsumoto, and a Coke for Kosuke. When we asked Kosuke for "the usual," that was what he'd get us.

Matsumoto sighed.

"Maybe I was too aggressive with the boy."

I was hardly in a position to criticize.

I handed Matsumoto his tea, and the two of us sat down and had a smoke.

The cigarette had a vile, bitter taste.

2

They were sitting in a diner not far from Mishima's apartment.

"Sorry to bother you on your day off," said Kusaka.

Mishima gave a jerk of his chin but kept his eyes fixed on the tabletop.

"Not a problem," he murmured.

It was an ordinary working-class diner of the kind you could find anywhere in Tokyo. It served bacon and eggs on toast for breakfast and spaghetti or rice omelet for lunch. Most of the customers came alone and ate with their noses buried in newspapers or manga.

All three men—Sergeant Satomura was there too—were having bacon and eggs.

"We talked about Michiko Nakagawa in our last interview. I'd like to ask you a few more questions about her."

Kusaka watched Mishima carefully. He couldn't detect any visible reaction.

"Michiko's father, Noboru Nakagawa, died two months ago. He was killed in a fall at one of Kinoshita Construction's building sites. . . . Did you know that?"

Mishima reached for the pack of cigarettes that was sitting on the corner of the table. He lit one with a disposable lighter. His hand was steady.

"No, I had no idea."

That was an important statement.

Mishima's father and Michiko Nakagawa's father had both been killed in accidents on construction sites that belonged to Kinoshita. Mishima had categorically stated that he knew nothing about the circumstances of Nakagawa's death.

He has to know.

Everyone on the task force was convinced of the fact. Whether Mishima was guilty of Takaoka's murder was another matter, but Kusaka now knew that the boy was happy to perjure himself.

There's definitely more to this than meets the eye. I need to be careful.

"Okay. Now, on another matter. Kenichi Takaoka had a life insurance policy that named you as the beneficiary. Can you tell us anything about that?"

Kusaka noticed a flicker in Mishima's eyes this time. It looked like he'd been prepared for questions about Michiko's father, but the topic of life insurance had caught him off guard.

"I remember the old man saying something about it."

"Did he give you any documentation?"

Their search of Takaoka's apartment hadn't turned up anything insurance related.

"Uhm. I don't recall him doing so."

Takaoka had taken out both life insurance policies four and a half years ago. According to Kusaka's calculations, that was roughly a year after Mishima had begun working with him.

"All right. Now, have you ever heard of a woman called Kimie Naito?"

Again his eyes darted to one side. This time the movement was even more pronounced. Despite Mishima's denials, Kusaka's conviction that he knew about Noboru Nakagawa's death was getting stronger all the time.

"I'm sorry, Naito who?"

"Ms. *Kimie* Naito."

Mishima cocked his head. He took a drag on his cigarette, then swiveled in his seat so that he could blow the smoke away from Kusaka and toward the nearby tables.

"Does she live in Shimoshakuji?"

"You think you know her?"

Mishima took another pull on his cigarette, then stubbed it out in the ashtray.

"Not sure. We once did a job at the house of a Mr. Naito. Perhaps his wife's name is Kimie. I really don't know."

"They lived in Shimoshakuji?"

"Yeah. It was a big place, so we nicknamed it 'Chateau Naito' as a joke. . . . Or were they called Saito, not Naito? I'm starting to get confused."

"How long ago was this job?"

"Two . . . maybe three years back. We can check it in Takaoka's notebook easily enough."

The person of interest for Kusaka was a Kimie Naito who lived in Kitasenju in Adachi Ward. Whoever this person in Shimoshakuji, Nerima Ward, was, it definitely wasn't her.

Kusaka scrutinized Mishima's face.

In response to his first question about Noboru Nakagawa, the young man had coolly denied any knowledge of him. With the life insurance, he had admitted to being aware of the policy but claimed not to know where the documentation was. In response to the question about Kimie Naito, he'd thought hard and dug up a job he'd done for someone with the same name.

If Mishima was playacting, the guy was quite a performer; otherwise, he'd genuinely not heard of Kimie Naito. Kusaka had the sense that it was the latter. Of course, that was just a supposition.

"Fine. Feel free to call me anytime at all, if you remember anything."

Mishima promised he would and added that he'd have a look at his journal to see if he'd mentioned anything about the Naito job in it. That was a bit of a surprise. Kusaka hadn't pegged Mishima for a journal-keeping kind of guy.

In the afternoon of the next day, Monday, Kusaka and Satomura went to visit Kinoshita Construction in Todoroki, Setagaya Ward.

The office was in a modest four-story building surrounded by a low wall. Its reddish-brown exterior looked run down, and from the lived-in feel of the windows and balconies of the upper floors, Kusaka guessed they were used as apartments.

The Kinoshita office occupied the front part of the first floor.

Kusaka pushed open a glass door decorated with the company name and came to a counter. There were three people in the room: two women in uniform and a man in a suit. There was a large whiteboard on the right-hand wall. It seemed to be for assigning and scheduling work.

"Excuse me?"

"How can I help you?"

The woman who was seated nearest to the counter got to her feet. She was on the young side and wore glasses.

"We're from the Tokyo Metropolitan Police Department. Apologies for dropping in unannounced like this. Is the president here by any chance?"

The girl bowed, gave a watery smile and, after asking them to please wait a minute, headed for a door on the left side of the room. She knocked and popped her head inside.

A few seconds later, a fattish man who appeared to be in his midfifties stuck his head around the door.

"Can I help you?"

He was frowning but not in a hostile way.

"Very sorry to barge in on you like this," began Kusaka politely, displaying his badge. "We're from the Tokyo

Metropolitan Police. We need to ask you a few questions. Is this a good time?"

"Sure, sure. My name's Kinoshita. I'm the president of the firm. What do you need to know?"

"We'd like to ask you some questions about Noboru Nakagawa, who died in a fall a couple of months ago, and Tadaharu Mishima, who died the same way nine years ago."

Kinoshita began to look a little uneasy.

"Uh, I see. Well, why don't you come right on in?" He gestured for them to come into his office. "Ms. Yashiro?" he asked, turning to the woman who'd announced their arrival. "Would you make us some tea?"

Kinoshita's office was big, with one of those old, solidly built partner's desks and a suite of armchairs in it. The lounge part of the office was decorated with an oil painting of Mount Fuji, while behind the desk hung a framed calligraphy scroll with four hand-painted ideograms. "Carry through your original idea," it said. The only bad feature was the windows. The next building over was so near that they admitted almost no natural light.

After the ritual exchange of name cards, Kinoshita indicated for them to sit down, and Ms. Yashiro brought in the tea. She caught Kusaka's eye when he thanked her. For a moment she looked as if she was about to say something, but she just bowed and slipped out of the room.

Frowning and sipping his tea, Kinoshita spoke without being prompted.

"Those incidents you mentioned . . . I should say that

the police conducted a full investigation both times and deemed them to be accidents."

"We're aware of that, sir. We're actually here today to ask you some questions about events *after* the accidents took place."

"After?"

Kusaka nodded, his eyes fixed on Kinoshita.

"Kinoshita Construction received a payout of twelve million yen for a life insurance policy it had on Tadaharu Mishima."

"Oh, that's quite——"

Kinoshita was obviously about to launch into an explanation that insuring workers was no more than standard practice. Kusaka held up his palm to silence him.

"Yes, I know. The construction business being what it is, on-site accidents are a fact of life, and insurance payouts help compensate and support the bereaved families."

Kinoshita was looking at the edge of the coffee table in an effort to avoid eye contact.

"Something I'm wondering about," Kusaka went on breezily. "When he died, Tadaharu Mishima had debts of nearly ten million yen. Did you know?"

Kinoshita swallowed nervously.

"Yes, the police told me."

"And what about Noboru Nakagawa? Did you hear anything about him having money troubles?"

An anxious sigh.

"I don't know. Doesn't ring a bell."

"No? Even though the accident only occurred a couple of months back. Can you think of anyone here who might know?"

Kinoshita raised his head in surprise, taking care to avoid eye contact.

"Is there somebody we could talk to here who's better informed than you?"

Kinoshita's eyes were darting frantically this way and that. The man was a soft touch compared to the bastards over at Nakabayashi.

"You're the company president. Do you personally handle welfare and benefits for your staff?"

"No."

He replied more from reflex than intention.

"So who does?"

Kinoshita made incoherent spluttering sounds.

"Seventeen people work at this company," said Kusaka. "Twelve of them are construction workers who work on site. Ms. Yashiro, the lady who served us this tea—does she handle health and welfare benefits?

"No, she—"

"All right, what about the second woman? Or the man in the suit at the back of the room?"

Kusaka lapsed into silence. Kinoshita contemplated the expanse of the empty coffee table. He seemed to be thinking.

Kusaka noticed a shogi board about fifteen centimeters high on the floor in the corner of the room behind the big desk. He imagined that Kinoshita was reviewing his options like a shogi player mulling his next move.

"It's my wife who handles insurance," was his next gambit.

"Is she here?"

"No, she's out."

"When do you expect her back?"

"She won't be in again today."

"Where's she gone? Is she out of town?"

"I don't—"

"Mr. Kinoshita?"

Kinoshita was looking increasingly distraught. He thrust a hand into his inside jacket pocket, rifled around, then clucked his tongue fretfully when he couldn't find what he was looking for.

"Excuse me," he stammered.

He got to his feet and went to his desk to fetch a pack of cigarettes. There was only one left. After sticking it between his lips, Kinoshita crumpled the cream-colored packet in his fist. He lit the cigarette with a desktop lighter and breathed out a thick cloud of smoke.

"Where were we? Uhm, oh yes, insurance.... Insurance is handled by the general affairs department, by Mr. Tobe."

"Is that the gentleman next door?"

"No, Tobe's not in today."

"Taking the day off?"

Kinoshita brusquely shook his head.

"He only handles insurance for us, nothing else, so he has his own ... uhm ... unique style of working."

"When do you expect him in the office?"

"Gosh. Well, probably not today."

"How about tomorrow?"

"I really can't say."

Kinoshita insisted that he was unable to get in touch with Tobe and had no idea when he would come in, either. Although Kusaka found it hard to believe, he decided not to press him any further and asked for Tobe's details instead.

His full name was Makio Tobe, he was forty-one, and he lived in Yutenji, Meguro Ward.

Kusaka and Satomura left the offices of Kinoshita Construction with a promise to return.

"Why didn't you put the squeeze on him, Lieutenant?" Satomura asked in a low, tense voice, looking intently at Kusaka.

"I don't think Tobe's been in the office for more than a week," Kusaka replied.

"What? How come?"

"I took a good look at the magnetic scheduling board on the way out," continued Kusaka. "There were three nameplates in the 'Currently in the Office' section: Yashiro, Kawakami, and Niki. The Niki nameplate was red like the Yashiro one, so I'm guessing red is the color for female employees and Niki is the name of the second woman we saw. Kawakami's got to be the fellow in the suit. I couldn't see a nameplate for President Kinoshita. Most of the other employees' nameplates were in boxes representing different building sites. There was one nameplate right at the edge of the board, outside the grid entirely. The name on it was Ito. I'm guessing that the edges of the board are for people on leave or away on vacation. Did you notice Tobe's nameplate?"

Satomura shook his head.

"It was sitting on the twenty-eighth. It's a one-month scheduling board, and today's the seventh of December, so that has to mean the twenty-eighth of last month. All the other nameplates were in the 'Currently in the Office,' 'Out on Site,' or 'Pending' boxes. Tobe's was the only name in the schedule grid. That has to mean something."

"Excuse me," came a voice from behind them.

They turned around. It was Ms. Yashiro, the woman from Kinoshita Construction. She was wearing a moss-green coat over her uniform and panting; her breath formed little clouds of white vapor.

"What is it?"

"I . . . uh . . . I wanted to talk to you about Makio Tobe." Her glasses began to mist over.

Without being aware of it himself, Kusaka was staring at her so hard that he looked positively angry.

Ms. Yashiro had about an hour to spare, so the three of them went to a dowdy local café.

"So, what can you tell us about Tobe?"

The girl gulped down a whole glass of water and ran

her eyes around the café's interior.

"I overheard some of what you were saying to the boss. Has Tobe done something bad connected with insurance? Are you going to arrest him?"

"Why do you think we'd want to do that?"

Their coffee arrived. The girl stared at the black liquid in her cup.

"Why? Because the guy's a total bastard, that's why."

"A bastard?"

"He's a yakuza. A gangster."

"That's a serious accusation. As far as we can see, Kinoshita Construction is a normal, regular company. Why should it want to put a yakuza on the payroll?"

The woman exhaled slowly. It looked like an attempt at keeping her emotions under control.

"Are you familiar with a firm by the name of Nakabayashi Construction?"

Kusaka shot a glance at Satomura.

"Yes, we know it."

"Nakabayashi's a front for the yakuza."

"We've heard the rumors too. What's the connection to Tobe?"

"I don't know his official status at the firm, all I know is that he was seconded to Kinoshita from Nakabayashi. He told me so himself."

Kusaka's mind began sparking, making connections.

"That would explain why he never comes to the office more than one or two days a week. And why he never does a stroke of work when he's here."

"He wasn't in today?"

"No. He's not been in for a while."

"How long since he was last there?"

The girl counted the days by tapping her fingertips on her knee.

"He showed up last Wednesday. Briefly. I think that's the last time he was in."

Kusaka's guess of November 28 had overshot the mark. Last Wednesday was December the third—the day Takaoka was murdered. If Tobe had been a no-show since then . . .

Maybe it's just a coincidence, but it's definitely intriguing.

"What did you mean when you said that Tobe never does a stroke of work?"

The girl grimaced.

"Me and the other woman at the office, we have this room we use as a changing room. Tobe's always barging in on us there. It's not just the things he says—he tries to feel us up, you know, grope us. That's just a regular day at the office for him. When he made a move on me, the president heard the noise and physically intervened, pulled him off me. So I was okay, but my coworker—you saw her just now—well, he did the same thing to her. She says she's fine and he didn't do her any serious harm, but my guess is that something bad happened and she's not okay at all. He's just so—"

The woman drank a mouthful of coffee in an effort to calm herself.

"He always stinks of booze. He never comes to the office in the evening when the guys who work on the construction sites are back in. He's happy to throw his weight around with girls like us, but the construction workers, even the older guys, could wipe the floor with him. That's the sort of sneaky bastard he is."

"So why do you think the president keeps a troublemaker like him on the company books?"

The girl dropped her gaze to the floor, looking more uncomfortable than ever.

"I'm not sure about this, but there was this one time when the president was out and we heard two people shouting at each other up on the third floor. Then, Tobe comes strolling down the stairs, with this big grin plastered across his face. The man's got no business going to the boss's flat up there, none at all. Mrs. Kinoshita is younger than her husband and quite pretty. Maybe something happened between them that Tobe is using for leverage. . . . I'm guessing that Mr. Kinoshita can't get rid of the bastard, even if he wants to."

Although Kusaka was careful to take everything the woman said with a grain of salt, he was getting a sense of the kind of man that Tobe was.

"Why don't you quit?"

Ms. Yashiro jerked upright.

"No way. Except for that pig Tobe, everyone at Kinoshita is good people. The guys who work on-site, Kawakami the accountant, Mr. Kinoshita, his wife—they're all really nice.

It wouldn't be fair for me to run off and leave them."

She leaned across the table toward Kusaka.

"Can't you arrest that pig Tobe?"

"We have no cause," explained Kusaka, with a shake of his head. "But if you're willing to file a complaint about what he did to you, then we'll do everything in our power to help. I get the impression that's not something you want to do, though."

The woman's shoulders sagged and her head lolled forward.

"It's no good then. . . . That's what I thought."

Kusaka took the opportunity to mentally review everything they had learned so far.

Tobe had been seconded to Kinoshita Construction from Nakabayashi Construction, where he was in charge of insurance. It looked highly likely that he was involved in insurance frauds linked to both Tadaharu Mishima and Noboru Nakagawa. It still was too early to know if there was a link between those frauds and Kenichi Takaoka's murder, but Kusaka thought it was more likely than not. And there was the fact that Tobe hadn't been seen at Kinoshita Construction since the murder on the third.

"Filing a complaint for sexual assault is quite a complex business, Ms. Yashiro. There's also a very real possibility that you could lose when the case comes to trial. On the other hand, if Tobe is involved in the case we're investigating, we may very well arrest him for that."

Her black eyes opened wide with excitement.

"So, Ms. Yashiro?"

"Yes?" she said, a solemn expression on her face.

"I'd like to ask you to do a couple of little things for us. First off, we'd like you to provide us with Tobe's cell phone number. Then—if it's okay with you, of course—we'd like you to keep calling him until he picks up, then say whatever you need to say to get him to come into the office. Call us immediately when you make contact and call us if he just happens to shows up at the office anyway. Do your best to keep him on the premises. We'll come around right away. Can you do that?"

Ms. Yashiro nodded and rapidly punched a number into her cell phone.

"Hey, Niki, is that you? Yeah, I'm fine. I'm talking to the police. Could you text me Tobe's cell number? Yeah, the police want it. Great. Thanks. Later."

A minute later a jingle erupted from her cell phone. It was the opening bars of a song Kusaka knew—something by the Beatles, though he couldn't remember the song's name.

3

Reiko had spent the last few days interviewing people from South Hanahata who'd known Kenichi Takaoka when he lived there. Taichi Suzuki, the proprietor of Suzuki Real Estate Sales, had tracked them down for her.

They'd all been at primary and junior high school with Takaoka. And they all said the same thing: they'd not been in touch with him at the time he was evicted him from his house.

"He didn't really stand out from the crowd at school."

"He just sort of blended into the background."

"He was the class wimp. Everybody bullied him."

"I don't remember much about him."

Takaoka really was Mr. Forgettable!

The photographs Reiko showed them didn't do much to jog their memories.

She also pursued other lines of inquiry, but it was difficult trying to uncover details from more than a decade ago. Some local residents remembered a candy-and-toy store run by a couple called Takaoka; none of them remembered them having a son.

Things weren't looking promising.

Her phone rang. It was Suzuki the real estate agent again.

"You remember the noodle restaurant I told you about, the one a couple of doors down from the Takaoka Store?" said the estate agent. "Well, I managed to track down the owner's son. I've got his contact details for you."

Reiko called him immediately. They arranged to meet in a coffee shop next to the Kinokuniya bookstore in Shinjuku.

She pressed the redial button on her phone as soon as she and Ioka got there. A man sitting at a table by the window overlooking the big boulevard outside reached for his phone while scanning the restaurant. She caught his eye, bowed, and went over to his table. He was a good-looking, stylishly dressed man in his early thirties.

"Good afternoon. Are you Yuji Sawai?"

"That's me. So you must be . . . uhm . . . Lieutenant Himekawa."

After exchanging name cards, Reiko and Ioka sat down opposite Sawai. According to his card, Sawai worked in human resources for a well-known appliance company.

Sawai was having a coffee, so Reiko and Ioka ordered one each themselves.

"Suzuki says that you're interested in Ken Takaoka from the Takaoka Store?"

"That's right. Were you two friends?"

The waitress returned with Reiko's coffee. She waited until she'd left before she went on.

"Before we start, though, I just need to ask for your age for our records."

Thirty-eight, said Sawai with a grin. He certainly didn't look it. Reiko had pegged him as two, possibly three years her senior. He looked like a model or an actor.

"That makes you five years younger than Takaoka?"

"Yes. He looked after me when I was little. We used to walk to primary school in the same group. Just for my first year."

"What was he like?"

"Rather shy and timid, I suppose. He was very sweet to me—like a big brother. He was crazy about Japanese language and literature, and really good at it. You know how you have to write book reports over the summer vacation? Well, Ken Takaoka did most of mine for me. The guy was such a bookworm that he'd read almost all the assigned books anyway. And he could adjust his writing style and vocabulary. Like, when I was in first year, he wrote all my reports in the style of a first-year student. It was brilliant. All I had to do was copy what he'd written into my exercise book. Yeah, he was good to me."

That dovetailed with how Takaoka had given Kosuke Mishima a job and behaved like a surrogate father to him, but the bit about him being good at Japanese was a surprise.

"What about your school handicraft and engineering projects? Did he help you with those?"

Sawai shook his head.

"That was one subject Ken was complete crap at. He

was more of an arts than a sciences kind of guy. I was always better at handicrafts than him. I'd have been happy to give him a hand, but getting help from a kid five years his junior—he'd have died of embarrassment!"

Takaoka was "crap" at handicrafts and engineering!

Her confusion must have showed in her face. Sawai glanced anxiously at Reiko, then at Ioka.

"Is Ken in some kind of trouble?" he asked tentatively.

"Uhm . . . we'll get to that later."

Since Reiko hadn't told Suzuki that Kenichi Takaoka was dead, Sawai had no way of knowing either.

"When was be the last time that you saw Takaoka?"

Sawai's face clouded over.

"It was one or two weeks before he was forced out of his home."

"Go on."

"Twelve years ago," he said, through gritted teeth. "I was still in the sales department back then, crisscrossing the city by car every day."

"What about your parents' restaurant?"

"They'd already had to close the place. They got set up. A fake food-poisoning episode."

"We heard about that," said Reiko.

"You knew?" Sawai exclaimed in surprise.

"Suzuki told me."

"That old chatterbox," Sawai murmured, with an affectionate smile.

"I'd only just started working when the restaurant shut

down. I wasn't yet earning enough to fully support my parents. They'd lost their livelihood and were in a state of shock. My two sisters saved the day; they got jobs instead of going to college. Not that I could've paid their tuition anyway."

He lowered his eyes and sighed.

"After what happened to us, I couldn't forget about what everyone in the old neighborhood was going through. I had this sales call to make nearby, so I thought, Why not drop in for a look? It was a graveyard—no lights, no people, nothing. There was one house down a back street where the lights were on. It was the Takaokas' place. The father and the mother were dead, but Ken was still living there. That got me thinking about old times, so I parked the car and went over to the house."

Reiko imagined a cluster of unlit, decrepit old houses standing on the site of the new apartment building. "Graveyard" was perhaps an exaggeration, but she knew similar neighborhoods—sad, bleak places that felt as though time had passed them by.

"I didn't want to shout in case Ken thought I was a heavy sent in by the land sharks. I knocked and rang the bell and said, 'Hey, it's me, Noodles Sawai.' Nobody came. They hadn't got around to demolishing the house next door. There was this alley running between it and the Takaokas' where we used to play as kids.... It was more like a gap than a proper walkway. I had to turn sideways and edge down it. I wanted to go to the back of the house because I knew I could see into the living room from there...."

Sawai's face contorted horribly.

"...What I saw was Ken squatting in the passage in between the living room and the bathroom. He was holding this great big carving knife in his hands, just staring at it.

"I knew exactly what was going on," went on Sawai. "He was psyching himself up to kill himself. So I banged on the window and shouted his name. I was just about to smash the glass, when Ken turned and looked at me. It took him a while to recognize me. I just kept saying, 'It's okay. It's me, Yuji.' Eventually the tension left his body, and his face sort of melted into this slack-jawed, idiot grin—I know that's not a nice way to put it—and he came over to the window."

Sawai sighed. A deeper, longer sigh this time.

"I went around to the front door and he opened up for me. He was still holding the knife. The thing was completely brown with rust. It was a piece of garbage. I just lost it and started yelling at him: 'What the hell are you doing with that thing?'"

Sawai was getting so emotional that he was having trouble getting his words out. Even Ioka looked upset.

"And then, grown man that he was, he burst into tears. 'I want to sharpen this damn knife, but I can't find a whetstone anywhere,' he said. 'I've been looking and looking and looking and I just can't find one.' I noticed he had these bumps and bruises on his forehead.... Lieutenant, have you ever heard of a firm called Nakabayashi Real Estate?"

Reiko nodded.

"When I asked about his bruises, Ken told me he'd gotten

into a fight when he was drunk. That was an obvious lie. Ken was the last person to get involved in a pub brawl. He was timid and quiet, not a fighter. He just wasn't equipped to handle the harassment Nakabayashi subjected him to. They'd do anything to get the residents out."

Takaoka afraid of physical violence? Takaoka no good at handicrafts and engineering? A nonentity whom the other kids pushed around, according to all his old classmates. How could you reconcile that with Takaoka, the powerfully built carpenter who'd taken Kosuke Mishima under his wing?

"I can't get in trouble for something I did ten years ago, can I?" said Sawai, suddenly all sheepish and awkward.

What's this about?

"I'm afraid that I took Ken out for a drink. I was probably over the limit when I drove him home."

Sawai hung his head apologetically.

Reiko looked at him with mock sternness.

"As long as you're more careful now."

"I never drink and drive."

"The police are a whole lot stricter about that sort of thing these days."

"You certainly are," said Sawai, scratching his head in embarrassment.

"So while we were having that drink, Ken told me what was going on." Sawai's face darkened. "How the real estate people made his life hell by calling his phone day and night, and how changing his number was no good because they always managed to get hold of the new one. They'd even stuffed a dead cat into his mailbox. It was awful."

Reiko felt a sense of mounting indignation. However, her annoyance—*anger* would be too strong a word—was directed more toward the victim than the wrongdoers.

"Takaoka should have gone to the police. Confiding in you wasn't going to do him much good."

Sawai glared disgustedly at Reiko, then his gaze moved to her name card on the edge of the table in front of him.

"Lieutenant, I see from your card that you're from the Tokyo Metropolitan Police."

Was it something to do with all the police dramas on TV? These days, even ordinary civilians seemed to be well aware of the difference between the TMPD and the local police.

"That's correct."

"Up on your lofty perch there, it's probably hard for you to imagine what a bunch of useless deadbeats most local cops are. Someone sticks a dead cat in Takaoka's mailbox. What happens? Some plod from the nearest police station trundles by, gets him to fill out a couple of stupid forms— and that's the end of the matter. Finished. Bye-bye. They didn't investigate. They didn't even modify their foot patrols at night to keep a closer eye on the Takaoka house. We couldn't prove it, but all of us at the time thought that Nakabayashi had paid the cops off."

Sawai had the wrong idea about Reiko's background. She certainly hadn't started her career in the TMPD headquarters in central Tokyo. After graduating from the Police Academy, she'd served time in three local precincts—Shinagawa, Himonya, and Yotsuya—before being transferred to headquarters. She knew about life at the precinct level, and God knew, she'd seen with her own eyes how bone-idle and corrupt the local cops could be. She'd seen them reduce plenty of ordinary people to tears.

"I wasn't aware that Takaoka's case was handled negligently," she said quietly, tilting her head in a bow. "I'm very sorry. I know that my apology is too late to make any difference, but as a police officer, believe me, I'm ashamed."

She sympathized with Sawai. Even so, her apology was mainly a ruse so she could push on with her questions.

In the seat next to her, Ioka also bowed his head.

Sawai leaned in toward her.

"I wasn't angling for an apology. You're from a completely different branch of the police force. I'm the one who's out of line."

"The way you've described things, wouldn't it have made more sense for Takaoka to get out of his house as fast as he could? In a way, he was lucky. I know *luck*'s not quite the right word, but with both his parents dead, he was free to move out, especially if he was in physical danger."

"I thought so too," Sawai agreed. "But that night, he explained the situation. His parents had run up debts and mortgaged the house to repay them. Ken was steadily paying it off, but it seems the outfit that issued the mortgage was crooked, and there was something not quite right about the lien that they held against the house. My guess is that there was bad blood between the mortgage firm and the Nakabayashi people, and that the mortgage company was preventing Ken from fully settling his debts as a way of keeping him in the house. I suspect they were using him to block the construction of the Nakabayashi apartment building."

"I see what you're saying."

Reiko found herself thinking of those well-worn phrases about "debt spirals" and "the inescapable cycle of poverty."

"Ken changed jobs quite a lot. I think he was in the sales department of an English-language textbook company at the time. Declaring personal bankruptcy would have been one way for him to clear his debts, but if his employer heard about it, they'd probably have fired him. . . . You know what employers are like. Paranoid. They think that people with debts are going to steal company funds. You're damned if you do, damned if you don't."

The evening sun was streaming into the restaurant at a low angle. The teaspoon in Sawai's saucer gleamed like a fragment of a fallen star.

"I wasn't able to give Ken any practical advice. I just told him that I was there for him and that he could call me anytime he wanted."

"You said this meeting took place one or two weeks before Takaoka moved out?"

"That's just me guessing. A couple of weeks later I went back to the neighborhood, and the Takaoka house, the house beside it, and our place had all been knocked down. All that was left was an empty lot. I just assumed the problem with the mortgage had been sorted out. I called Ken's cell, but it was offline. I thought he'd moved somewhere else to make a new start."

Reiko could see that Sawai was just itching to ask her what Takaoka was doing now, so she decided to put him out of his misery.

"Takaoka moved to Ota Ward and began a new career as a construction worker and a carpenter."

"Ken? A laborer? Him?" Incredulity was pulling Sawai's handsome face all out of shape. "That's simply not possible."

"From what I heard about him, I felt the same way. Apparently, though, he did really well. He even took on an apprentice."

"But that's crazy. Ken was a stick insect of a man. Way too frail and spindly for manual labor."

Frail? Spindly? Kosuke Mishima had dropped off a recent photo of Takaoka at the police station for them. He looked anything but spindly—muscle-bound was more like it. Sawai had known Takaoka a long time ago, so the man could have changed . . . somewhat. But still . . . does anyone change that much in twelve years?

"Just hang on a second." She turned to Ioka. "Give me the photograph."

Ioka flipped open his personal organizer and slid Takaoka's photograph out of the flap on the inside back cover. "Here you go," he said with a chuckle. Reiko grabbed it, turned it the right way up, and presented it to Sawai.

"This is Kenichi Takaoka, right?"

Sawai frowned in astonishment.

"Who the hell is that?" he said gruffly.

They all looked at one another.

"It's Kenichi Takaoka," said Reiko.

Sawai looked her directly in the eye and shook his head.

"No way. There's no way that is Ken Takaoka."

"How come?"

"Look at this guy. He's tough, he's never been afraid of anything in his life. He's got eyes like a wolf. Old Ken was more like an underfed sheep. He had droopy eyes and a saggy face. He was like an old man minus the wrinkles."

He grinned.

"Sorry, Lieutenant, but this looks like a case of mistaken identity to me."

I refuse to believe it. It was there in black and white on the man's resident's card. He'd lived at that address in South Hanahata before moving to Middle Rokugo. That was beyond doubt.

"What happened to this fellow?" Sawai asked.

Half dazed, Reiko managed to tell him that "there had been an incident" and that the man was dead.

Sawai displayed no surprise. "Poor fellow," he murmured, shaking his head.

After parting from Sawai, Reiko and Ioka strolled down Shinjuku Boulevard. It was already dark.

Kenichi Takaoka isn't Kenichi Takaoka.

The words ran around and around inside Reiko's mind.

"I've got no idea what's going on with this case

anymore," burst out Ioka. "It's crazy."

He pushed a little see-through bag toward her.

"What's that?"

"Dried squid."

"What are you doing carrying that stuff around with you?"

"It's good to chew on when you're feeling peckish—and when your brain is tangled up in knots. It helps you think. Fancy some?"

"Don't mind if I do."

They wandered on down the street, occasionally popping strips of dried squid into their mouths.

Kenichi Takaoka is not Kenichi Takaoka. Where had they gone wrong? Where had their investigation taken a wrong turn?

Okay, let's think this thing through.

Takaoka's childhood friend Yuji Sawai was adamant that the man in their photograph was not the Kenichi Takaoka he knew from South Hanahata. And she believed him. The boy with the weak personality whom the other kids had all picked on, who was good at Japanese but hopeless with his hands—he could not be the same person as Takaoka, the builder who lived in Middle Rokugo.

"You like my squid?" asked Ioka.

Reiko mumbled something incoherent.

Is it crazy to think that the Nakabayashi Group murdered the Kenichi Takaoka whose parents ran the local candy store? That they killed him and got someone else to take his place? And that he took over the name Kenichi Takaoka and went to live in Middle Rokugo? An identity swap would certainly help explain how "Kenichi Takaoka" worked as a builder for Nakabayashi.

No, that doesn't hold water. Sawai said that there was another firm holding the mortgage for the Takaoka house and that that firm and Nakabayashi were at daggers drawn. Nakabayashi would only be shooting itself in the foot by killing Takaoka and making already prickly negotiations over the land rights even worse. No, for Nakabayashi, murdering the candy store kid would definitely have been a bad move.

"Wow, Lieutenant, you're really chugging that squid down."

How about suicide? Is that a realistic possibility?

From what Sawai had told them, it sounded as though Takaoka had been driven to a state of paranoia. He might well have succumbed to a suicidal impulse and taken his own life.

Let's try on this chain of events for size.

Takaoka tops himself. Some Nakabayashi goon swings by to put the screws on him, only to find him dead in the house. Said goon knows that this is the worst possible outcome for his employer. With Takaoka dead, his land will fall into the hands of a rival developer, and Nakabayashi's scheme to build a shiny new block of apartments will collapse. They need Takaoka alive.

That's it. That's the key!

So they brought in someone to take the dead man's place and got him to sell the land to them. It wasn't the time to haggle over money. They'd probably paid whatever price the mortgage company

228

had asked for, dissolved the mortgage lien, changed the owner-ship of the land to their name, and then demolished the house. Demolishing the house was also a handy way to get rid of the physical evidence of the suicide and the identity swap.

"Lieutenant, you're not supposed to polish off a whole packet in one go. You've finished the lot."

"Go buy me some more."

"You'll get sick."

But hang on a second! Why had they gone so all-in on the identity swap? If they needed a substitute, then why not find some serious, white-collar Nakabayashi employee who'd look the part and use him for just as long as was necessary? Why opt for a burly laborer and keep the deception running for years afterward?

It was too weird. Reiko knew she was missing a vital piece of the puzzle.

She needed more squid to get her brain working faster.

4

Officer Noriyuki Hayama had been keeping watch on Kimie Naito for three days now.

Forty-nine years old and single, Kimie ran Naitos, a little restaurant-cum-bar in Kitasenju, which did a nice line in set lunches. Asking around, Hayama learned that she'd opened the place more than ten years earlier.

He and his partner, Sergeant Nomura, had each gone to Naitos on separate days for lunch. The day Nomura went, there was fried mackerel on the menu, and it was a vegetable stir-fry when Hayama went. There was only one dish a day on offer, and even that was half prepared in advance.

They needed to be careful about making too many repeat visits. They would get noticed. For now, with no link established between Kimie Naito and Kenichi Takaoka, they needed to stay under the radar. Hayama and Nomura were keeping a discreet eye on the restaurant from a parking lot diagonally across the street.

At a 10:02 a.m., a high-sided truck drew up in front of the restaurant.

"It's the same truck that came yesterday and the day before," commented Nomura.

Today, though, it was a different driver. Hayama wondered if Nomura had picked up on that. It probably didn't mean much, so Hayama contented himself with making a mental note of the fact.

"That lieutenant of yours," began Nomura. "She's quite a woman."

Nomura had taken a major shine to Reiko Himekawa. He lost no opportunity to steer the conversation around to her, and when he did, his language lost some of its usual formality.

"Is it true she doesn't have a boyfriend?'

"Search me. I've only been in Homicide three months."

"What's your sixth sense say?"

"I really don't know. I'm pretty obtuse about that sort of thing. Sorry."

They'd now spent almost three full days watching from a car in the parking lot. Late last night, a relief team had been sent over, and they'd gone back to the police station for a bath and a short nap before participating in the morning meeting. They took turns making inquiries around the neighborhood, but that took up a maximum of two hours a day. Hayama thought of stakeouts as a crucial component of detective work; Nomura thought otherwise.

"Talk about drawing the short straw. Here we are doing surveillance on some middle-aged broad, while Ioka, that monkey with his buckteeth, gets to pair up with Lieutenant Himekawa. *Ioka, of all people.*"

Sergeant Kikuta had told Hayama that the Himekawa squad and Sergeant Ioka were linked together by some sort of unfortunate karmic bond. Nomura probably wouldn't understand. Worse yet, any explanation he provided might give Nomura an excuse to go on about Himekawa even more. In the end, Hayama opted to say nothing.

Hayama too had his own views on the lieutenant, but they were quite different from those of most of the other male detectives.

His attitude stemmed from an experience back when he was a fourteen-year-old junior high school student. His parents had planned his whole life out for him: making sure that he aced his exams at the end of primary school and won a place in a big private school that "fed" students from its own junior high school into its own high school and then to a major university. Unfortunately, something happened that drove his life off the rails.

It was the autumn of his second year at junior high, and he was on his way home from basketball practice. He was walking along one of those Tokyo streets with just a painted line indicating the sidewalk, rather than raised paving or a metal guardrail. He recognized the girl who was walking down the street ahead of him. She had been his home tutor for the junior high entrance exams. At the time, she'd been in her final year at one of the local universities. Now, however, she was a fully fledged adult.

A shadow suddenly burst out of a side street and appeared to engulf her.

It was a man wearing sweats and a hoodie.

The whole thing only took a second. There was no scream, just the sound of a body crumpling and crashing onto the black asphalt.

The hooded figure ran off to the left. A man in a suit came running from further down the street.

"What happened? Miss, are you okay?" Then he started yelling. "Oh my God! Somebody call an ambulance! Now!"

That brought all the local residents out into the street. Hayama just stood there, rooted to the spot. A patrol car arrived along with the ambulance; the police asked if anyone in the crowd had seen anything. Hayama's legs were like jelly. They refused to carry him over to them.

The girl—her name was Reiko Arita—died from stab wounds. As there was no boyfriend or other male in her life for suspicion to fall on, the police classified the case as a random assault.

Hayama never stopped reproaching himself. Why hadn't he come forward to tell the police what he saw? He'd had a pretty good look at the attacker—knew his build, what he was wearing. Information that could have helped the investigation.

The memory of the shadowy figure continued to terrify him, though. When he was lying alone in bed, he shuddered at the thought of that shadowy figure hunting him down and killing him to keep his mouth shut.

The fear went on. And on. And on.

Hayama decided to skip university and become a cop. He joined the police force four years later, right out of high school. He wanted to prove to himself that he wasn't a coward. He also dreamed of making detective and personally reopening the unsolved Reiko Arita case. (Now that he'd actually made detective, he knew what a pipe dream that was. But he hadn't quite given up; the commitment was still there, and he still had four years until the statute of limitations ran out.)

He was doing his best to remake himself as someone who would not fear the shadowy killer anymore. He had the confidence that came from being part of the police force; the physical strength he'd developed through his martial arts and other training; his investigative know-how; his knowledge of criminology and the law. Hayama devoted every waking moment of the day to making himself a better cop. He was a new creature: genus, policeman; species, detective.

He was still a little short of his goal. But his hard work was definitely paying off: he'd been appointed to the Homicide Division at an extraordinarily young age. And Homicide was where he had encountered Reiko Himekawa, his squad leader.

She was taller. She looked different. In fact, the only thing that Reiko Himekawa and Reiko Arita had in common was their first name. For Hayama, though, that banal fact was rich in meaning.

And then there was the voice . . .

When Himekawa addressed him as "Nori" and asked him if he'd completed his case report, it always brought back memories of his tutor asking him if he'd done his homework assignments.

Each time Himekawa spoke to him, the sense of the obligation he was under to the murdered Reiko tightened its grip. "I must never forget her," he thought. The stress must have been written on his face.

Misinterpreting his expression, Himekawa never stopped asking him if he had a "problem" with her. He knew he came across as having an attitude, but the reasons behind it were just too heavy. In the end, he always deflected her questions with a curt "no." In his heart, though, he wanted to open up to Himekawa and tell her the truth, sometime.

Things started getting interesting around two thirty in the afternoon.

Kimie Naito came out of the restaurant, locked the door behind her, and headed down the street. Instead of her normal work getup of scarf and apron, she had on a black duffel coat over a brown skirt. It wasn't high fashion, but, in her own way, she was dressed for going out. She had a large paper Uniqlo bag squeezed under her arm.

"Let's go," said Hayama.

"About time. Let's goddamn go."

The two detectives set off after Kimie on foot. Hayama was planning to hail a taxi if she took the bus. Luckily for them, she opted to walk the fifteen minutes it took to reach Kitasenju Station. She took the train two stops to

Kameari, dismounted, walked for five minutes, and went into a large building.

It was Kameari Central Hospital. A large sign in the lobby listed all the different departments: internal medicine, surgery, dermatology, pediatrics, cardiology, and so on.

"You think she's sick?" asked Nomura.

"You guess is as good as mine," Hayama replied.

Without stopping at the outpatients' reception counter, Kimie made straight for the elevator.

"She's probably visiting someone," Nomura muttered.

Hayama badly wanted to tell Nomura to shut up. As what Himekawa referred to as "a homicide detective in an elite numbered unit," he should just come out and say it, despite his partner being older and of higher rank. But he couldn't bring himself to do it. In situations like this, he'd just clam up and let things be. It made life easier.

Kimie got out on the fourth floor and registered at the nurse's station. They sneaked a look at what she'd written in the register.

Name: Kimie Naito
Patient visited: Yuto Naito
Relationship: Aunt

Kimie vanished into room 505. As far as the two men could tell from their vantage point in the passageway, it was a six-bed ward. Hayama noticed the name Yuto Naito in the list of patients on the door. He rolled his eyes at

Nomura, and the two of them strolled casually on by.

"Kimie herself isn't married," whispered Nomura. "If she has a nephew, it has to belong to her brother or sister."

"I'll see what I can learn."

Hayama left Nomura to keep an eye on the door of the ward and headed back to the nurse's station.

There was a woman sitting behind the counter. From the number of bands on her cap, Hayama guessed that she was the head nurse. She had a narrow face, looked the nervous type, was probably in her midthirties.

"Excuse me, miss?"

To keep things discreet, Hayama held his badge up right against his chest when he showed it to her. The woman nodded rather tensely and asked what he wanted.

"You have a patient called Yuto Naito in room 505? How old is he?"

The woman leaned over the counter and looked down the corridor toward the ward. For a while, she didn't reply. She was probably wondering how much she was allowed to tell a cop who hadn't flashed a warrant.

"He's eighteen."

"What's wrong with him?"

She hesitated a moment.

"He was in a car accident."

She sighed. Hayama guessed that the boy must be in a bad way. The nurse looked him straight in the eye. She'd made up her mind to be frank.

"Yuto was transferred to this hospital around four years

ago. He's been in the state he's in now for thirteen years. He's conscious but unable to talk: he's quadriplegic and mute."

Hayama did some quick math in his head. The accident happened thirteen years ago. Yuto would have been five at the time and Kimie Naito thirty-six; Kenichi Takaoka would have been thirty, Kosuke Mishima seven, Tadaharu Mishima thirty-six, Michiko Nakagawa six, and Noboru Nakagawa thirty-two.

"Do you know any of the details of the accident?"

"I don't. As I said, Yuto was in a different hospital back then."

"Do you know which?"

"I'm afraid I don't. For information like that, you're better off contacting our administration department."

That was fair enough. Hayama didn't want to push his luck. It was time to step back.

"I understand. Thanks very much."

He went back to a small rest area just off the passage and updated Nomura on what he'd found out.

"I'm heading for the nearest library to see what I can find out about the car crash," he said. "You stick with Kimie."

Nomura's mouth turned down at the corners.

"Yes, sir," he muttered.

The nearest library was about a kilometer from the hospital. The old newspapers were available in miniaturized bound format. Hayama pulled out all the volumes from thirteen years ago, piled them on a reading table, and began trawling through them all. As long as he limited his search to accidents featured on the local city news page, his task was not that forbidding.

Yuto Naito, five years old. Yuto Naito, five years old . . .

As he was skimming through one of the volumes, his phone rang. It was Nomura, telling him that Kimie was on the move. He ordered Nomura to call him if she stopped off somewhere or else when she get home, then hung up and returned to flipping the old newspapers.

Yuto Naito, five years old. Yuto Naito, five years old . . .

He found what he was looking for in well under an hour: it was an article from the morning edition of Monday, May 28.

> At around about 5:45 p.m. on May 27, Kazutoshi Naito (31), a construction worker from Umeda, Adachi Ward, Tokyo, was driving along the Kawaguchi section of the expressway in Saitama Prefecture when he lost control of his car. It skidded onto the median where it flipped over. There were two passengers in the car: Asako Naito (26), who died as a result of the severe head injuries she sustained, and the Naitos' only son, Yuto (5), who is in critical condition. Kazutoshi himself suffered serious injuries to his chest. Eyewitnesses report seeing a dump truck with a Saitama number sideswipe the Naitos' car, causing the loss of control.

The Kawaguchi police are looking for the driver of
the truck.

Hayama took careful note of the age of the people
involved. Kazutoshi Naito was thirty-one and Asako
twenty-six.

The man probably blamed himself, not the truck that
sideswiped him, for his wife's death and his son's quadriplegia.
Where was he now? What was he doing? What sort of state
was he in?

Hayama went out into the lobby of the library, flipped open
his phone, and called one of his preprogrammed numbers.

"Himekawa here."

"This is Hayama."

"Hi, Nori. What's up?"

"Kimie Naito went on a walkabout this afternoon. She
visited her nephew, Yuto, in Kameari General Hospital.
He's eighteen and quadriplegic. He was in a car crash
thirteen years ago. I'm at the library now. I went through
the old newspapers. According to them, Yuto's parents were
a Kazutoshi and an Asako Naito, but Asako, the wife, was
killed in the crash. Kazutoshi himself was badly hurt. I'm
guessing that Kazutoshi is Kimie's younger brother."

"How old was Kazutoshi at the time of the accident?"

Typical Himekawa, thought Hayama. He'd dumped a
ton of information on her, but she'd absorbed and processed
it all at high speed.

"Thirty-one. Which would make him forty-four now."

"Did the papers say anything about his job?"

"Just a second." Hayama checked his notes. "Yes, he worked in construction."

"Really."

Himekawa went quiet. Hayama knew what that meant: she was thinking. He pictured her gazing off into the middle distance with that strange look that managed to combine serenity and tension. Like a leopard sizing up its prey.

"Nori," she said abruptly. "Call Captain Imaizumi and tell him to look into that relationship. You've still got time to nip into the city office and do some checking."

Hayama looked at his watch. It was 4:28 p.m.

"What exactly do you want me to check up on?"

He heard a snort at the other end of the line.

"If Kazutoshi Naito's alive or not, of course."

"What do you mean?"

"My hunch is that we'll find that Kazutoshi Naito's dead."

A chill of excitement shot up Hayama's spine.

"Got you."

Hayama ended the call. He was about to get in touch with Imaizumi at the task force HQ, when he had an incoming call. It was Nomura.

"Yes, hi."

"It's me, Nomura. I followed Kimie back to the restaurant. When we got there, I spotted a suspicious person lurking behind one of the nearby electricity poles. Any guesses who?"

"No," said Hayama.

"Kosuke Mishima," Nomura announced. "How does he even know where Kimie Naito lives?"

"Any direct contact?"

"No, Kimie didn't even notice him."

"Did Mishima make you?"

"I don't think so. The guy's never seen me before. We walked right past each other and there was no reaction on his part."

"What was he doing?"

"He just sort of looked at the restaurant a while and then wandered off, climbed into a little truck parked some ways down the street, and drove off."

"You're certain it was Mishima."

"Yep. He was wearing an orange down jacket with a stain on the right shoulder. I took down the license number of the truck, so we can look that up too."

Hayama wasn't sure what was happening. He just knew that the case was gaining momentum. He felt it in his bones.

"I'll come and pick you up. You need to attend the evening meeting at the station tonight. I'll call ahead and get them to send a relief to take over the stakeout."

"Very good," replied Nomura. The note of relief in his voice was audible.

5

The atmosphere at that night's task force meeting was electric.

Reiko dropped the first bombshell.

"To sum up, then, we think it a very real possibility that the victim in this case—the man whom we believed to be Kenichi Takaoka—is not Kenichi Takaoka after all. The Kenichi Takaoka who resided in South Hanahata—Takaoka's address prior to Middle Rokugo, according to his resident's card—was a weak, bookish boy who was bullied at school, worked at a series of different office jobs after university, and was selling English-language textbooks when he was finally evicted from the family home. When I showed Yuji Sawai, the son of the family who ran a local restaurant, our photograph of Kenichi Takaoka, he insisted we had the wrong man."

Reiko was delighted at the impact her report was having. The top brass were clearly having trouble getting their heads around the implications.

"So, if the dead Kenichi Takaoka isn't the real Kenichi

Takaoka, then who on earth is he? We have some interesting information to share with you on that very point. Officer Hayama, would you do the honors?"

Hayama got to his feet.

"I found out today that Kimie Naito has, or had, a younger brother, Kazutoshi Naito. Kazutoshi died at the age of thirty-two, a year after a car crash that killed his wife and made his son a quadriplegic. From a visit to the Nishiarai Police Station in Adachi Ward, I learned that Kazutoshi Naito committed suicide on April twenty-ninth, twelve years ago. He hung himself on the first floor of a building that was under construction. The developer was ... Nakabayashi Construction."

The room exploded with surprised chatter. Reiko was pleased at the effect they were causing.

"The Nishiarai police found nothing suspicious and handled Kazutoshi's death as a straightforward suicide. I plan to go back tomorrow and take an in-depth look at the case file and any other available documentation." Hayama paused for a moment. "I also need to report that Sergeant Nomura witnessed a man he believes was Kosuke Mishima hanging around in the vicinity of Kimie Naito's restaurant. Either someone here told Mishima where Kimie lives, or he already knew her address."

Kusaka put up his hand. Imaizumi nodded permission to speak.

"I did mention Kimie Naito's name in the course of my interview with Mishima, but I said nothing about her living in Kitasenju. Captain Kawada took his first statement back on the first day, but we didn't yet know about the connection to Kimie Naito when they spoke. Now we need to find out if anyone else here has had direct contact with Kosuke Mishima."

"Well?" growled Imaizumi.

No one said anything.

"Good," Kusaka continued. "Mishima claimed not to have heard the name. There was nothing suspicious in his manner when he denied knowing her. He could have been pretending, but I'm more inclined to think that he found out about her some time after our interview."

Imaizumi cocked his head.

"Any ideas, Kusaka?"

"Yes, sir. As I reported at a previous meeting, Mishima wasn't entirely sure if he had got any insurance-related documents from Takaoka or not. He hasn't contacted me about it, but assuming he's found them, he could well have found Kimie Naito's address, since she's the beneficiary of one of the policies."

Reiko was on tenterhooks. Was Kusaka about to steal her thunder? Not this time, apparently, as he brought his remarks to an end there.

"Thank you, Kusaka. Hayama, have you said everything you need?"

"Yes, sir."

Reiko raised her hand.

"Yes, Himekawa?"

Reiko got to her feet for the second time that evening.

"The Kazutoshi Naito whom Hayama mentioned just now lost his wife and, to all intents and purposes, his son, in a car crash thirteen years ago, then took his own life a year later. The first thing we need to check up on is whether Kazutoshi's death triggered any life insurance payouts. The second thing is the chronology of events: Kazutoshi Naito's suicide and Kenichi Takaoka moving to his present Middle Rokugo address happened very close together. We also have grounds to think that our Kenichi Takaoka was not, in fact, the real Kenichi Takaoka. Putting all that together, I believe that the victim, whom we are referring to as Kenichi Takaoka . . ."

The room was hanging on her every word. Reiko took a moment to savor all the attention.

". . . could well be Kazutoshi Naito."

"I object."

Kusaka had his hand in the air.

"What are you basing your theory on?" he asked.

What an idiotic question! I just told you.

"Why do I think Kenichi Takaoka is not the real Kenichi Takaoka? Okay, consider the fact that the fake Takaoka arranged for Kimie Naito—someone with whom he had zero contact—to receive a fifty-million-yen payout on his death. People normally choose a family member as their beneficiary, very occasionally people opt for someone to whom they have a very special obligation. We don't know how the fake Takaoka justified his choice of beneficiary to the life-insurance company, but if Takaoka is in fact Kazutoshi Naito, then everything falls neatly into place. Now, do you remember what Yuji Sawai told me about the South Hanahata Kenichi Takaoka? That he'd been harassed so badly he looked ready to commit suicide at any time. Who reduced Takaoka to that state? The Nakabayashi Group."

Nobody was sticking up their hand to make silly objections now. Reiko felt that her big reveal was proceeding nicely.

"Let me throw out a possible scenario. The real Kenichi Takaoka takes his own life—maybe he hangs himself, we don't know—in the family house in South Hanahata. Somebody working for Nakabayashi Real Estate comes across the body, transports it to one of Nakabayashi Construction's building sites and does whatever 'stage dressing' is needed. Kenichi Takaoka's death would have been a major spanner in the works for Nakabayashi's ongoing attempts to buy the land. They were desperate to keep his death under wraps. They decided that the best way to do that was to keep Takaoka 'alive' by putting someone else in his place. That 'someone else' was Kazutoshi Naito.

"Yuto, Kazutoshi's son, was a quadriplegic after the crash. The medical-care costs for him during that first year were probably astronomical. That's something we need to look into, as with Kazutoshi's financial situation. For now, let's assume that Kazutoshi was in dire financial straits. He might well have toyed with the idea of committing suicide to provide a decent chunk of money to his sister, Kimie, and his boy."

She examined the faces of the brass at the table at the front. It was fine. She could keep going.

"The Nakabayashi Group cleverly exploited that situation. Substituting Kenichi Takaoka's body, they made it appear that Kazutoshi Naito had committed suicide on their building site. His death triggers the payout of Kazutoshi's life insurance to his sister, Kimie. As next of kin, Kimie was probably the one who had to identify the body. Obviously she knew that the corpse was not that of her brother, but she chose not to say anything. That suggests to me that Kazutoshi had briefed her about his scheme in advance.

"There was something else that had to be dealt with—transferring Takaoka's family register to Kazutoshi to provide him with a viable new identity. My guess is that Nakabayashi took care of this in return for Kazutoshi helping them get their hands on Takaoka's house for their development project. Kazutoshi then 'became' Kenichi Takaoka and started his new life in Middle Rokugo. As Kenichi Takaoka, he witnessed the 'accidental' death of Tadaharu Mishima, whose son, Kosuke, he later got to know. . . . Note that there is an age difference of just two years between Kosuke Mishima and Yuto Naito. For the fake Takaoka to want to help little Kosuke, bewildered at the loss of his father, strikes me as the most natural thing in the world . . ."

Uh-oh. Why's Director Hashizume leaning forward like that? This doesn't look good.

"Kazutoshi Naito, or Kenichi Takaoka as he now was,

then took out a new life insurance policy, and once again designated Ki—"

"Himekawa, hold it. Just stop."

Damn. End of the line?

"Yes, sir?"

"With you, it's always the same. There you go, building more of your castles in Spain."

"Excuse me, sir?"

"The circumstantial evidence we currently have cannot support your theory."

"Oh, I think it does, sir. Our Takaoka is not the real Takaoka; Kimie Naito had a brother around the same age as the real Takaoka; both the real Takaoka and our fake Takaoka were under tremendous financial pressures. And then you have Nakabayashi, like a great spider whose web entangles them all."

"Easy on the metaphors, Himekawa."

"Sorry, sir. But if we pull together all the leads we currently have, you see—"

"We need to give it more time. This is all premature."

"It's simple. All we need to do is to find people who knew Kazutoshi Naito and show them a photograph of Kenichi Takaoka. That's the quickest way to prove that Takaoka is really Naito."

Hashizume slammed his fist onto the desk.

"So damn what? What's that got to do with our case? I don't care if our victim is Takaoka or Naito—I want to know who killed him."

You're such a sweet man. NOT.

"So stop faffing around and find me the murderer pronto. All this fake Takaoka this and real Takaoka that—it does my head in."

Duh! That's why I was explaining it.

"Sir, the victim's background is an important part of—"

"That's enough. Stop it, Himekawa. Just shut up. Come back and deliver another report after you've followed up all your leads and can build a convincing case. If you want to tool around expounding crackpot theories, please go and do so elsewhere. Right, who's next?"

Captain Imaizumi took over the mike.

"Kikuta, it's your turn."

"Yes, sir."

Out of the corner of her eye, Reiko saw Kikuta casting anxious glances in her direction. She nodded discreetly to let him know that she was fine with him going ahead.

No one else at the meeting had anything earth-shattering to report.

The main investigation was at a standstill: the search team scouring the river hadn't found any more body parts, and the investigation into Kenichi Takaoka's family, friends, and associates hadn't turned up anyone with a possible motive for murder. The only point of possible interest was gossip to the effect that the homeless people based by the baseball ground beside the river were living it up, with boozy barbecues on a daily basis.

Hashizume, however, wasn't interested in that either.

"So damn what?" he said contemptuously. "Homeless people sometimes win the lottery too, you know. Besides, the meat they're barbecuing—they probably filched it from a trash can somewhere."

Now the only person left to speak was Kusaka. He was normally the first person to deliver his report, but he'd been a little late back to the police station this evening, so his name had been pushed down the list. He was scheduled to speak after Reiko, but a call had come into his cell, so he had been out of the room then too.

Reiko scrutinized Kusaka's face. He exuded self-confidence. Not a good sign.

"In my report yesterday I mentioned Makio Tobe, the person who handles insurance for Kinoshita Construction. I've been making additional inquiries about him and found one or two points of interest."

Kusaka flipped open the file on the table in front of him.

"Makio Tobe is forty-one years old. His mother, Yuko Tobe, died six years ago, at the age of sixty-two. Yuko was the mistress of Masayoshi Tajima, the first boss of the Tajima-gumi."

The room began buzzing. "I can't believe the far-out shit people are coming out with today," Reiko heard one precinct officer say.

"However, some people believe that Makio Tobe is not Yuko's son. They believe that his biological mother is actually Miyuki Ogawa. Who is she? Let me explain. Masayoshi Tajima has a younger brother called Toshikatsu. Toshikatsu

Tajima chairs a real estate management company and is not directly involved in organized crime. Toshikatsu had only one child—Miyuki, a daughter. Miyuki is married to Michio Ogawa, the founder of Nakabayashi Construction. According to rumor, she had a child when she was forty—Makio Tobe—and Masayoshi was the father. In other words, Miyuki had a child with her own uncle, related to her by blood. I got this information from several ex-Tajima-gumi people—I can't reveal their names—so there's a good chance it's more than just malicious gossip."

"That's all very interesting," grumbled Hashizume. "But again, so what?"

Imaizumi indicated to Kusaka to keep going.

"Thank you, sir. Tobe attended a public high school, where he made a name for himself as a troublemaker, though more in the lady-killing than the fighting department. He was adept at squeezing money out of his girlfriends and always had loads of cash and a posse of hangers-on as a result. After leaving school, he worked in some capacity for the Nakabayashi Group—perhaps his birth mother, Miyuki Ogawa, helped set this up—though he did little in the way of serious work there. For the last ten or so years, he's hung his shingle at Kinoshita Construction. That's about everything I've learned about him so far."

Kusaka shuffled the papers in the file in front of him.

"Oh, one more thing I should mention. . . . Tobe seems to deploy the same talents he showed at school in his work life. That's how he managed to get the insurance companies to issue numerous policies for Kinoshita Construction employees where the company is simultaneously the signatory and the beneficiary. As you know, life insurance in Japan is sold primarily by an army of door-to-door saleswomen. Tobe specialized in seducing them. Once they were his lovers, it was easy for him to get them to modify or falsify policy documents and to bypass their companies' screening processes. My source here—again, I won't be naming names—is an insurance saleswoman, no longer employed there, who herself had a sexual relationship with Tobe."

Kusaka raised his eyes from his file and looked at the executives at the front of the room.

"Tobe has not come into the offices of Kinoshita Construction since Takaoka's death on the third of December. I believe that locating him should be a matter of absolute urgency. That brings my report to an end for today."

The report was both concise and dense. Hardly Kusaka's usual style.

Who is Makio Tobe, serial womanizer, insurance fraudster . . . ?

Hashizume had once again launched himself halfway across the table.

"What the hell's got into you all today? First it was Himekawa, and now it's you, digging up all this peripheral information! I want my investigators to do their digging in the center of the problem, not around the edges."

"I believe, sir, that you will find that my approach and Lieutenant Himekawa's differ materially in a number of points."

What the fuck?

Reiko was annoyed, but she held her tongue.

"It's the goddamn same to me, Kusaka," Hashizume snapped. "Let me ask you a question. Do you have any clear grounds for thinking that this Tobe guy bumped off Takaoka?"

"No, sir. But it's to get to the truth of the matter that I'm trying to track him down."

"All right, what motive would Tobe have for whacking Takaoka?"

Kusaka exhaled loudly through his nose. Reiko understood the frustration he felt. She sympathized despite herself.

"Of course," he began. "I cannot speak to the reliability of Himekawa's report—"

"Now just a minute, Kusaka," she interrupted, smacking a hand on the table.

He turned and stared at her with cold, reptilian eyes.

"If I've annoyed you, I'll apologize later," he snarled. "For now, just shut up and listen, okay?"

You bastard! You complete and utter bastard.

Kusaka turned back to the front of the rom.

"For the sake of argument, let's accept Himekawa's hypothesis that our victim, Kenichi Takaoka, was in fact Kazutoshi Naito. It's highly possible that Tobe was involved in arranging the identity swap. In that case, Kenichi Takaoka aka Kazutoshi Naito would have witnessed Tobe putting his fraud schemes into action. In addition to his own case, he might have witnessed the cases of Tadaharu Mishima and Noboru Nakagawa and possibly others we don't know about. Maybe he thought he knew enough to turn the tables and start blackmailing Tobe."

A spark ignited somewhere deep in Reiko's brain. Something was moving in there, but what it meant, she didn't yet know.

"Tobe wasn't going to take that lying down, so he murdered the fake Takaoka." Kusaka went on. "There's one other possible scenario we should consider, though the methodology is different from the Mishima and Nakagawa cases. What if the victim arranged his own murder?"

There was a ferocious scowl on Imaizumi's face. "What?" he exclaimed. "Are you seriously proposing that the fake Takaoka hired Tobe to kill him in order to trigger the insurance payout to his sister Kimie?"

"I'm only saying that it's one not totally impossible scenario—"

"I've said it over and over again already tonight," interrupted Director Hashizume. "Let's get back to reality."

Hashizume looked down the front table at the other brass, with an exasperated look on his face. None of the other brass backed him up. Reiko felt a little sorry for him.

After the task force meeting came the executive meeting. Reiko consulted her watch when it was finally over: it was just before ten.

The other members of her squad were already at the local bar. If she went and joined them now, she'd be several drinks behind, stuck at the table with a bunch of drunks. Instead, she decided to try out the sauna at a sports center near the station. As she was getting her things ready, she took a look in her makeup bag: she was out of cleansing lotion. Shouldn't be a problem. There was a convenience store on the way.

Reiko pushed a change of clothes and her makeup bag along with her cell phone and wallet into her shoulder bag and walked out of the station. A little way ahead of her was a familiar-looking figure wrapped in a coat.

"Captain!"

Imaizumi stopped, and Reiko scampered up to him.

"Are you going for dinner?"

"No, going to buy a razor."

Imaizumi's stubble was thick and legendary for its toughness. Apparently, electric razors couldn't handle it; the only thing that worked were cartridge razors with three or four blades, which Imaizumi would use once and then have to throw out.

"At the convenience store?"

"Yeah. You?"

"I'm going for a sauna, but I need to drop into the convenience store on the way. I'll go with you."

Imaizumi was walking very slowly. He must be exhausted, thought Reiko. Still, it meant more time to talk.

"You know, Captain?" she began.

"What?"

"No, it's nothing in particular. I mean, it's not like it's something that started today. . . ."

"Spit it out. I know it's about Kusaka."

Reiko couldn't suppress a grin.

"The two of us, we're apples and oranges, complete opposites. I just can't get my head around Kusaka's hatred of theorizing of any kind. I never have and I never will."

Imaizumi smiled drily. "Did you know that Kusaka once worked with Katsumata in Homicide Unit Four?"

"I had no idea."

Imaizumi nodded knowingly. "Back then, Kusaka was still a sergeant, and Katsumata had just made lieutenant. The two of them hated each other's guts. They had raging arguments in meetings."

"What were you doing back then, Captain?"

"I was a lieutenant, but in Unit Nine. What I'm about to tell you is mostly secondhand."

"Right."

They'd arrived outside the convenience store.

"Just wait here a second, Captain."

The conversation with Imaizumi was more of a priority than buying cosmetics.

She nipped in and emerged with a couple of canned beverages. She handed a coffee to the captain and kept the corn soup for herself.

"Or would you prefer the soup, Captain?"

"I'm fine with coffee."

They pulled off the tabs, clinked cans, and took a swig. The hot liquid turned their breath into thick white clouds of steam in the night air.

"Anyway, the long and the short of it is, Kusaka was set up—by Katsumata."

Reiko frowned quizzically at Imaizumi. He took another swig of coffee, then continued.

"They were both on a task force that was handling a robbery-murder in Kyodo, in Setagaya Ward. Kusaka figured he knew who'd done it, and the higher-ups on the case all encouraged him to bring his suspect in. The only person who didn't actively support the move was Katsumata, Kusaka's immediate boss. But he just kept quiet. He stood back and let Kusaka arrest the wrong man."

"Why?"

"To take him down a peg, I guess. Katsumata knew that Kusaka was a good detective, and for him, that was a good enough reason to engineer a pratfall. This sergeant who worked the case with them told me that Katsumata even faked evidence designed to lead Kusaka to the wrong guy. Kusaka's suspect had been in custody several days, when suddenly Katsumata brings in a completely different guy—the real perp—and proceeds to demolish Kusaka's case. Kusaka was hung out to dry by his superiors: he got all the blame, and his reputation took a big hit. At the time, he was doing his promotional exams for lieutenant first grade, and they failed him—he didn't even make lieutenant second grade.

"Since then, Kusaka won't allow himself—or anyone else—to speculate about cases. He conducts his investigations flawlessly and always builds a rock-solid case. Talk about unintended consequences! Katsumata lived to regret his dirty trick. He's been grumbling for years about having created a Frankenstein's monster."

Imaizumi tipped the last of his coffee down his throat and threw the empty can into the trash.

"You don't need to hold back. Feel free to demolish Kusaka's theories, if you don't buy them. In a way, that's what Kusaka wants."

"You're joking," burst out Reiko in surprise.

"Kusaka has a great deal of respect for you. I know he does, believe me. Even if he doesn't show it. The guy's got a bigger heart than you think."

Imaizumi patted Reiko on the shoulder and walked through the automatic doors of the convenience store.

"I'll see you tomorrow, then. 'Night."

The door whooshed slowly shut behind him.

Oh, dammit! I forgot the cleansing lotion!

Following him inside now, however, didn't seem like right thing to do.

PART
FOUR

1

didn't expect to get much out of Matsumoto, the electrician, so I started to probe some of the other old guys we worked with.

The plasterer, the lumber merchant, the plumber, and the guy at the building supply store—they all knew about Nakagawa's accident, but none of them knew anything about his family. They hadn't been friends with him, after all. I eventually met an architect who'd helped out at Nakagawa's funeral. By a stroke of luck, he had the details of the man's only child, a daughter.

She was called Michiko and lived in an apartment in Wataridamukai-cho in Kawasaki Ward. The architect gave me her cell phone number.

That evening after work, I went straight around to her place. She was out. The next day I went a little earlier, probably around eight o'clock, but had no better luck. It was only on my third visit that I managed to see her.

I got to the front of her building at half past seven. No sooner had I arrived than the door to her apartment opened and a delicate little girl, whose arms and legs looked to be about half the thickness of mine, came out and locked the door behind her. She had on a plain gray half coat and jeans. Where was she going that late in the evening? She certainly wasn't dressed up for a night out.

She walked in the direction of the local train station. I followed her from a distance. After about ten minutes, I was surprised see her walk in the back entrance of the Royal Diner on Route 15. I'd driven past the place more times than I could count, though I'd never actually stopped there.

I went inside like an ordinary customer. The girl appeared at exactly eight o'clock. I called her over and ordered the beef curry set dinner with a Coke to drink.

"Thank you, sir. Let me repeat your order to you."

She was pretty enough, though she looked a little worn out. A male server brought me my curry and salad, but she brought me my Coke.

My only goal that day was to give her the once-over. I went home without trying to talk to her.

After that I continued going to the Royal Diner, a couple of times with the old man, mostly by myself. On nights when I went and found that the girl wasn't working there, I'd have a quick snack, then walk over to her place, leaving my car in the diner parking lot. I'd go to the back of her building because I could see if the lights in her place were on from there. Sometimes they were, and sometimes they weren't.

I wondered if I was doing the right thing. She had now gotten to know my face at the restaurant, though our relationship was only that of a waitress and a customer. Maybe it would have been better if I'd dropped in on her at her place without letting her get to know my face first. I was worried that accosting her after I'd already been to the diner so often would make me look like a stalker.

One night I was watching her place from the street out front when something happened that changed everything.

The door of her apartment was thrown open and someone came out. All the lights had been off when I'd checked earlier, so I'd thought no one was home. But it wasn't the girl who came out; it was a man. He was tall with closely cropped hair and wearing a long dark coat. Shutting the door behind him, he stumbled toward me. When he passed under one of the streetlights, I got a good look at his face.

It was him.

It was the man who'd given me the money after my father died. The man that the boss had looked at so strangely when he appeared at that house we were working on. The man who worked for Kinoshita Construction. . . .

He glanced casually at me and walked on by. He hadn't recognized me. What was going on? I stayed in the street feeling rather helpless.

A little later, the door of number 102 opened for a second time. This time it was the girl. She had on the same gray half coat I'd seen before, but this time her legs were bare and her feet were thrust into a pair of sandals. With one hand she was pulling her coat collar shut, while she held something in the other.

Was it a cup? No, it was a jar.

She plunged a hand into the jar, picked up a handful of white powder, and sprinkled it outside her door. She did it again. Beneath her open collar, I caught a glimpse of almost painfully white skin.

I guessed that it was salt. Some kind of purification ritual, perhaps? Her hand began moving faster and faster; eventually she just turned the jar upside down and spilled whatever salt was left on the ground. Then she squatted on her haunches and started bashing the jar on the cement.

A brittle, hollow sound.

She was still on the ground, clasping her head in her hands, when I walked slowly over to her.

"Excuse me, miss?"

First she was bewildered; then, after a moment, she recognized me. She scowled in astonishment.

"You?"

She scrambled to her feet, pulling the sides of her coat shut over her chest, stepped back and turned sideways to me.

"What's going on? What are you doing here?"

I picked up the plastic jar. She wrenched it out of my hands, her face on the verge of tears.

"Listen, I . . . uh . . . owe you an apology. The truth is, I've been coming to the diner because I knew some things about you. Like that man who came out of here just now— he's from Kinoshita Construction, isn't he?"

Her scowl grew fiercer.

"What business is that of yours?"

"There's something I've got to tell you. It's about your father."

The girl's chin jerked upward and her long hair billowed around her head. She spun around, shoving me backward as she did so, pulled the door open, and jumped back inside. As she pulled the door shut behind her, I tried to wedge my foot inside, but she was too quick.

"Miss Nakagawa, you've got to hear me out."

I was banging on the door now. It made a distinctive dull thud I recognized—steel plate over a paper core. The door must have been quite new: there was almost no give in the rubber seal of the aluminum doorframe, and none of the normal rattling.

"Miss Nakagawa, please. Open up. I've got to talk to you."

I knew she was standing just on the other side of the door. I could feel her there.

"Please, Miss Nakagawa. It's not the sort of thing we can talk about here on the doorstep."

The door flew open and smacked me on the forehead. Fireworks exploded somewhere behind my eyes. Green ones.

"Damn, that really hurt."

"Keep the noise down. The neighbors'll complain."

Peering down through the one eye I could still open, I saw a bar of white light lying across my feet. When I looked up, I found the girl glaring at me through the partially opened door.

She shivered.

"Okay, I get the message. I'll get changed and then I'll let you in. Wait there."

She slammed the door shut. I heard the key turning in the lock and the chain being slid into place.

I picked up the plastic jar.

It was cracked, and a piece of the lip had snapped off.

Ten minutes later, she opened the door and let me in.

I didn't want her to get the wrong idea about me, so when she gestured for me to take a seat at the table, I sat on the floor, my back against the wall, in the formal seiza position, my heels tucked under my bottom. The room itself was so small, where and how I sat probably didn't make much difference.

The girl was wearing jeans and a knit jersey; for some reason, she looked physically bigger here than she did at the restaurant. Maybe she felt more *real* to me here in her own room. I don't know.

I told her my name and that I'd worked for a while with her dad on a building job. It was a lie, but I was worried that things might get too emotional, too fast, if told her what we really had in common.

I began by telling her that there were some pretty ugly rumors swirling around Kinoshita Construction and that her father's accident wasn't the first of its kind. I asked her if her father had any debts. She didn't say anything to that, so I put forward my theories about what the company was up to. Most of it was based on what happened to my dad and me. From her reaction, it looked like I was on target.

I was careful not to move too fast. It wasn't easy, but I just kept talking, slow and steady, until she began to believe me.

"He started out by saying that Kinoshita Construction would take care of me," she explained. "Because Dad was working for them when he died."

Apparently, Makio Tobe had found her new apartment for her and handled the move. She'd been wary at first, but in the end it was thanks to him that she'd been able to put her life back together, she said.

"The company had insured my father's life for fifteen million yen. Tobe said that the money could cover all my school fees, and my living expenses for quite a while too."

School, in her case, meant beauty school; she was studying hairdressing.

"The minute I moved in here, his whole attitude changed. He said that all the money from the insurance money had gone to pay back what my dad owed and that he couldn't give me a red cent. He told me that I owed him—for the deposit and the key money for this place, plus my moving expenses and the fees for two terms of school. Well over a million yen, all told."

"That's a fortune."

She smiled sadly.

"Learning to be a hairdresser's an expensive business, you know. We have to buy all our own equipment—combs, brushes, scissors, whatever—and the school I go to is private, so tuition there costs way more than at a public school. The fees are more than a million a year. The rent here's over ninety thousand, but I haven't got the money to move out now. Dad only had thirty thousand yen in the bank when he died."

She tilted her head and stared up at the blank white ceiling. She was trying to blink back the tears. It didn't work. They streamed from her eyes and slid down her cheeks to her throat. I stared at her long, white neck; at the straight black hair that tumbled onto her shoulders.

"Tobe told me that Kinoshita Construction wouldn't be able to take care of me after all and that he needed me to sign all these documents acknowledging responsibility for my father's debts. Then he dumped all these bits of paper on the table and yelled at me to sign. I was terrified. I knew that signing anything would only make things worse for me, so I said no. And that's when—"

Her body was racked by a sob.

"That's when he told me to strip. 'Take all your clothes off for me right here, right now, and I'll cancel all your debts and take care of you till you graduate.'"

I didn't want to catch her eye, so I looked off into the corner.

"I've dreamed of becoming a hairdresser since I was a girl. Dad always encouraged me. I didn't want to lose that dream, so ... fuck it, what's it matter anyway? It's not like it cost me anything to do it. I've got no boyfriend ... nobody who cares."

She was clasping the edge of the table. She lowered her head onto her little bunched fists and wailed.

I didn't know what to do. I just sat there quietly as my

legs went numb beneath me.

Maybe I should have gone around the table, put my arm around her shoulders, told her that everything was okay. I was pretty sure she'd shove me aside and tell me to get my hands off. She'd be right. Nothing was really okay.

Not helping her wasn't an option, though. My mind was made up. I knew that Kinoshita Construction had set up her father's death to pay off his debts. I knew that Tobe had then exploited the situation to take advantage of her. I racked my brains: how could I help her escape from the awful situation she was in?

"You've got to stop."

Her sobbing let up a moment, then redoubled in force. It was almost a retching sound.

"You mustn't let him come here anymore."

I felt like I was getting through. She'd stopped sobbing now and was breathing heavily.

"I can probably help you with the money side of things. There's this old guy, Mr. Takaoka. He's got my back. He's kind of like a father to me. I'll talk to him. And I've got savings of my own too. You said a million yen, right? I'm sure we can raise that much."

She lifted her head, slowly and unsteadily, and looked right at me. Her breathing had normalized. There was an icy smile on her face.

"You goddamn hypocrite!"

What was she talking about?

"Don't pretend you don't know what kind of girl I am,"

she sneered. "That I'll fuck anyone—for money."

She cackled wildly.

"That's not what I meant—"

"Did I misunderstand you? You don't think I'm worth the money? That I'm overselling myself?"

"I never said that."

"But that's what you mean. You fork out the money and I dump Tobe and become your sex friend instead. Hey, I'm cool with it. At least you could pass as my boyfriend. If you're going to pay me, then come on, let's have a party right now."

The girl crossed her arms in front of her and grabbed hold of the hem of her jumper.

"What the hell are you doing?"

With a single deft movement, she peeled the jumper over her head and threw it to one side.

Under the cold white fluorescent light, her skin looked as white and fragile as a sheet of paper. There was something pitiful about the tiny breasts beneath the pink bra.

Her hands moved to the belt in the waistband of her jeans.

"How about a quick fuck? If you like the goods, we can formalize our little arrangement. If you don't, then it's no obligation, no commitment."

"Don't talk like that."

"Don't worry. This is my life. You don't need to play Mr. Nice Guy with me. I know I'm not supermodel material."

"Stop it, please."

I got to my feet, pulled the duvet off the bed behind her,

SOUL CAGE

and draped it around her skinny body. As I did so, I noticed several fresh stains on the sheet on the bed.

Looking away, I wrapped the girl in my arms.

"I like you, but not in that way. Anyway, you've got to stop saying those things."

She was like a kitten in my arms: a soft, warm bundle of fragile bones.

"I was lucky. I had Takaoka. When my dad died, the old man was there to help me out. You—you've got no one. Tobe's a scumbag. He's not what you need."

A hand emerged from a gap in the duvet. The nails, I noticed, were cut short. The fingers crawled questioningly over the cloth until they reached my arm.

"You're so warm," she said.

At that moment her alarm clock went off. I'll never forget the sound.

The girl never knew when Tobe would come round. Her phone would ring suddenly in the evening and it was him, announcing that he was heading her way and she should be at home for him. He didn't care if she was supposed to be working or had a school assignment to do. Once, she'd got back late and kept him waiting outside; he'd bitch-slapped her to teach her a lesson.

After the night we spoke, I went round to her place every day as soon as work was over.

"You must be really into her," the old man said after I

275

told him I'd got a girlfriend. I didn't say anything about her connection with Kinoshita Construction. The last thing I wanted to do was to worry the old man.

"Is it the girl at the diner?"

"Yeah."

"She's a nice girl?"

"I guess she is."

"Good to hear there are some of them around."

I wanted to introduce them to one another. Not yet, though. Not yet.

"I know I'm jumping the gun here, but are you guys thinking of getting married?"

Although we weren't even boyfriend and girlfriend yet, I'd already made up my mind.

"I'd like that, yeah, at some point. . . . Haven't said anything to her though. I mean, she's a student. We'll have to wait a few years."

"What about her parents?"

"They're both dead."

When he asked me her name, I pretended I was too embarrassed to tell him. In fact, I was just worried that he might figure out the link between Michiko Nakagawa and Noboru Nakagawa, the dead construction worker.

"Okay, son, I understand. You can introduce us properly when you feel that the time is right."

"Will do, boss. Okay, got to run."

As soon as work was over, I'd go back to my place, have a quick shower, jump back in the car and head for her apartment. She was usually in when I got there.

"I'm coming. Oh, you poor thing. It's freezing out there."

"I'm fine. Don't worry about it."

Going over to her place became a part of my routine. If she hadn't rustled something up for dinner, we'd eat out nearby. After dinner, I'd drive her to the diner. Sometimes I'd call it a night and go home; often I'd go to and collect her at the end of her shift and drive her back home.

Sometimes we'd walk instead of taking the car. Now and then she'd link arms with me. I never pushed for anything more. I didn't want anything to start between us until the Tobe business had been properly sorted out.

That day came sooner than I had expected.

December 3. It was a depressing day. It had been drizzling for hours.

"Hi, this is Michiko here."

I'd just got in from work when she called. A desperate note in her voice told me everything I needed to know.

"He called?"

"Yes. He's coming here at seven. Kosuke, I'm afraid."

I looked at my watch. It was six thirty.

"I'm on my way over. Don't let him in, whatever you do."

"I know. Please be quick."

"I'll be right there. Promise."

I ended the call, dashed out to the parking lot, and jumped into my car.

Keep cool. You've got plenty of time.

To calm myself, I repeated the phrase like a mantra throughout the drive.

I normally left the car in a parking lot around the corner, but that night I parked right in front of her building. It was the right thing to do. Tobe was already there, banging on Michiko's door.

I grabbed something from the glove box and ran toward him.

"Open the fucking door, woman," he was yelling. "You'll be sorry."

Since pummeling the door with his fists wasn't having much effect, Tobe switched to kicking it. That was when I charged him.

He grunted, staggered to one side and crashed to the ground.

"What the fuck! Who the fuck are you, punk?"

I placed myself between him and the door.

"Don't come round here again. Out of here. Scram."

Tobe blinked and peered up at me through the drizzle. He dragged himself slowly back onto his feet. He wobbled once but managed to keep his balance.

I took a step toward him.

"Did you hear what I said? Don't come around here no more. Using the profits from an insurance swindle to get your hooks into a dead man's daughter—you make me sick."

Tobe inspected me with curiosity.

"You're very well-informed, you fucking know-it-all."

"Yes, I do know it all. You know why? Because you gave

me some money too: a hundred thousand yen. I needed it. I was grateful. I had no idea about all the double-dealing dishonest shit that lay behind it. You dirty, greedy little rat. What was your cut? One million? Two?"

His eyes suddenly widened.

"Hah! I know you. You're the kid who works with Ken Takaoka."

"Real quick on the uptake, aren't we. Booze addled your brains?"

"You said one hundred thousand yen, right? Are you . . . are you . . . *that little kid*?"

"Bravo, full marks. Maybe you've got a couple of brain cells left after all."

Tobe's shoulders began to shake. He was laughing.

"Oh, you've got to be kidding. You're telling me that you've got the hots for that piece of skirt in there?"

I didn't reply. Talking with him about her would only soil our relationship.

"Damn it, boy. The girl's a whore. A million yen was all it took for her to spread her legs and, hey, presto, pussy on tap for yours truly. What's to like in a cheap slut like that?"

"Shut up."

"Oh, I've got it: it's that bristling bush on that scrawny body of hers. Turns you on, huh?"

I felt like something caught in my throat. I couldn't breathe. Or speak.

"Every time I come around to ride the bitch she starts out blubbing—and then ends up moaning like a fucking porn star. '*Ooh! Aah! Ooh! Aah!*' Her tits aren't up to much, but her nipples—they stand up like soldiers and just fucking *beg* for it."

The bastard! The total bastard!

"Let's try it doggy style, I say, and she rolls right over and wags her little butt in my face. You had her that way yet? Up the shitter? She fucking loves it, man."

Suddenly I could breathe again. I heard myself roaring. The sound came from somewhere deep inside of me and burst out of my throat.

I pulled the iron bar out from under my waistband, lunged forward in a half squat and swung it as hard as I could at Tobe's shins.

He went down again with a crash. I kicked him. Stomped all over him. Called him every name I could think of.

"Stop it, please stop!"

Tobe was sprawling on the ground. His clothes were soaked through. He was trying to grovel with his forehead pressed on the ground to let me that know I'd well and truly defeated him. Except I wouldn't let him.

It was Michiko who made me snap out if it.

"That's enough. Stop or you'll kill him. Then you'll be in serious trouble."

Tobe was squatting on the ground like a school kid cowering under the desk in earthquake drill. He was shivering and laughing all at the same time.

2

Since the evening meeting of December 9, Reiko had been trying to make sense of everything.

There was the fake Kenichi Takaoka who was actually Kazutoshi Naito. There was Makio Tobe, the insurance fraudster and serial womanizer. Somewhere in the background, there was the Tajima–gumi, part of the Yamato-kai Syndicate, and their front company, the Nakabayashi Group.

There were the two young people who had been deprived of their fathers by Kinoshita Construction: Kosuke Mishima and Michiko Nakagawa. And then there was Kimie Naito and her nephew, Yuto Naito, who was in fact Kazutoshi's birth son.

Makio Tobe was the one common thread that linked them. She wasn't sure how much he and his murky history had to do with the Takaoka murder case, but the fact that no one had seen him since December 3, the day of Takaoka's death, had to mean something.

On December 11, Sergeant Ishikura was dispatched to unearth information on the late Kazutoshi Naito. By speaking to several people who'd known Naito, Ishikura was able to establish that Kenichi Takaoka of Middle Rokugo was almost a dead ringer for Naito. Ishikura also identified the firm where Naito was employed when he committed his suicide: it was a subcontractor for Nakabayashi Construction.

Ishikura also paid a visit to Kawaguchi police station, which handled the Naito family car crash thirteen years ago, and was able to sweet-talk them into showing him the accident report. Comparing the fingerprints in the accident report with those of the severed left hand in the minivan proved that Kenichi Takaoka of Middle Rokugo and Kazutoshi Naito of Umeda were one and the same person.

There was just one problem.

According to the family register, Kazutoshi Naito was dead. The male victim whose death they were investigating had lived his life as Kenichi Takaoka. That was who everyone had believed him to be. For reasons of convenience as much as anything, the task force decided to continue to refer to him by that name. Mainly because she had been first to spot the identity switch, Reiko would have preferred to use the Naito name, but in the end, did it really matter much? The victim was Kenichi Takaoka. No need to make an issue of it.

Reiko identified fatherhood as a common theme that ran through the lives of both Kazutoshi Naito and his subsequent alter ego Kenichi Takaoka.

The man had abandoned his original identity so that

his sister Kimie could get a payout for his supposed death. The sum involved, they discovered, was twenty-six million yen. It was needed to fund hospital care for Yuto, the man's quadriplegic son. The fact that Kimie was now taking care of the boy supported this interpretation of events.

Takaoka subsequently became a sort of surrogate father to Kosuke Mishima. His motivation wasn't hard to understand. Having shed his old identity, he had to stay away from his own son; instead, he gave Kosuke everything that he couldn't give to his own flesh and blood. Everything that Kenichi Takaoka did was driven by the same powerful sense of fatherhood. Reiko was certain of it.

But what was the connection between that and Makio Tobe? What sort of situation had Tobe got into that he had to kill Takaoka?

So far they had no evidence that Tobe stood to gain from the murder of Kenichi Takaoka. If anything, it was the opposite: Takaoka's death had shone a light on his identity swap, which looked like the first step in a trail leading all the way to the door of the Tajima-gumi. Why would Tobe want to set off a chain reaction that would bring the TMPD down on their heads? Then again, given the kind of man Makio Tobe was, he probably didn't get unduly torn up about the unintended consequences of his actions.

The man had vanished, leaving behind one of the victim's severed hands and the vehicle he'd used to transport the body. Seeing Takaoka's murder as spur-of-the-moment, rather than a calculated killing, made more sense.

Everything in the man's history pointed that way. The product of incest or not, Tobe was still the child of the first-generation boss of the Tajima-gumi. That hadn't been enough to guarantee his spot in the Nakabayashi Group, the gang's front company, and he'd been kicked downstairs to Kinoshita Construction, a corporate minnow by comparison. The man was a notorious weakling who probably didn't have what it took to be as a proper gangster.

He'd ended up carving out a niche for himself at Kinoshita as a low-grade swindler who exploited his talent as a womanizer to run insurance scams. He worked at Kinoshita for years. How did Tobe and the fake Takaoka first cross paths? At what point did Kosuke Mishima get involved? What about Michiko Nakagawa?

If fatherhood was the driving force behind Takaoka's actions, perhaps trying to protect Kosuke was what got him in trouble with Tobe?

Tobe and Kosuke Mishima first come in contact with one another nine years ago. Tobe had either murdered Mishima's father and made it look like an accident, or forced the man to take his own life. Whichever it was, Tobe was responsible for the death of his father.

Maybe that was what this was about.... Maybe Kosuke was planning to let the world in on the dirty secret of what Tobe was up to. No, that was impossible. When Kosuke's father died nine years ago, Kosuke was only eleven. He could hardly have figured out the mechanics of insurance payouts at that age. Let's say that he'd recently started asking questions?

But why nine years later? Why now?

Try another tack. What if Michiko Nakagawa acted as the trigger? Michiko's father died just a couple of months ago. The girl was already nineteen. That was old enough for her to be suspicious. But how could she have contacted Kosuke Mishima—or even known that his father had been killed in a similar accident to hers? It was much more likely that Kosuke initiated contact. . . .

What brought the two of them together? There must have been something. . . .

Whatever it was, they met and became increasingly suspicious about the "accidents" both their fathers were involved in.

Then what? How did one get from there to Takaoka's murder?

Perhaps the two youngsters had approached Takaoka for advice. What would Takaoka have said to them? Takaoka probably knew all about what Tobe was up to. How would he have acted?

Takaoka took being a father very seriously. Did he take it seriously enough to consider exposing Tobe's crimes? But exposing Tobe would also expose Takaoka's own false identity and nullify the new life insurance policy he'd taken out as Kenichi Takaoka, preventing his sister from getting any benefits in the event of his death. The police would also go after him for stealing the family register of the real Kenichi Takaoka, which was a serious crime. . . . Or would the statute of limitations have already expired on that one?

Takaoka's only remaining connection to his quadriplegic son, Yuto, was via the insurance policy of which Kimie was the designated beneficiary. As a father, reckoned Reiko, he wouldn't want to jeopardize that by exposing Tobe's crimes.

Okay, where did that hypothesis lead? To Takaoka choosing to protect Tobe by persuading the two youngsters to back off?

It was doable enough. All Takaoka needed to do was feign ignorance of what Tobe was up to. Had something happened to prevent him from allaying the youngsters' suspicions with a simple bluff?

What?

Reiko had no idea.

The top brass restructured the investigation around three priority areas and made some major changes in the assignment of personnel.

Firstly, they decided to place Kimie Naito, Kosuke Mishima, and Michiko Nakagawa under twenty-four-hour surveillance, with at least one pair of investigators watching them all the time. That meant two sets of two investigators, each pair covering one twelve-hour shift, for each of the three subjects. Reiko and Ioka were one of the teams assigned to Michiko Nakagawa.

Twenty-six detectives, including Kusaka and Kikuta, were assigned to the second priority, which was to locate Tobe. They interviewed his girlfriends, visited insurance companies, made the rounds of all the pubs and clubs he frequented, and talked to his friends. They made inquiries in Middle Rokugo, where the body had been dismembered. They also put under surveillance the residence of Miyuki Ogawa, Tobe's biological mother; the headquarters of the Tajima-gumi; and the offices of the Nakabayashi Group.

Last priority was the search of the river and the riverbank. With so much time having elapsed, it looked like the least promising aspect of the whole investigation.

Investigations, however, have a habit of defying expectations, and, sure enough, on December 15, one of the search teams discovered what looked like the torso of Kenichi Takaoka. They found it in the river around four kilometers downriver from where the van had been parked.

The first Reiko heard of it was when Imaizumi called and ordered her over to the forensic pathology department of Tomei University Hospital. The autopsy was already under way when she arrived. Around ten people were in the dissecting room watching, including the Special Assistant to the Director of the Ministry of Justice, the autopsy recorder, the public prosecutor, and a representative from the Mobile Forensics unit. Director Hashizume, Lieutenant Kusaka, and his partner Sergeant Satomura were sitting on a bench in the hallway outside.

"Sorry I'm late. What's the story here?"

Kusaka, who was a bit of a gadget head, took his precious digital camera out of his briefcase, clicked a few buttons on it, and passed it to Reiko.

She scrolled through the pictures of the torso.

The torso was a ghastly, livid white—probably because all the blood had drained from it—and the head and limbs were gone. The head had been cut off just below the jawline, leaving the neck in place, while the arms had been severed at the shoulder and the legs at the hip joint. In shape, it was like an elongated pentagon.

"It's in surprisingly good condition," Kusaka volunteered.

He was right. It was far better preserved than Reiko had expected.

Hang on! There's something odd about this body.

Assuming it had been dumped in the river on the night of the third, it had spent twelve days in the water. That was ample time for the fish to start eating the thing.

There's no sign of any scavenger activity on the body. How come?

Reiko felt a vague sense of unease. Still, she could hardly resolve any doubts she had based on a few tiny images on the back screen of a camera.

She handed the camera back to Kusaka.

"Remarkable lack of damage."

"It's possible that for much of the time it was in the water it was protected somehow. For example, it could have been wrapped in plastic sheeting."

Reiko grabbed the camera out of Kusaka's hands as he was about to switch it off.

"Just a minute," she said. "Did you notice this part of the neck here? This big gouge mark?"

A semicircle of skin on the left of the pharynx was missing.

"I see it, yes. Wonder what caused it. Looks like the work of fish to me."

Reiko grunted noncommittally.

The autopsy ended after ninety minutes. The Metropolitan Police crime lab sent over the DNA data they had extracted from the various crime scenes so that a DNA comparison could be made.

The chief pathologist withdrew to his office after the autopsy to draw up his report. Meanwhile, Fujishiro, Special Assistant to the Director of the Ministry of Justice, came out into the corridor to talk them through the findings.

"We found no wounds on the torso that could have been the cause of death," he explained. "The analysis of the stomach contents is still ongoing, but judging by the condition of the organs, we can also rule out poison as the cause of death."

"Did the torso's blood type match with the other blood samples?" interrupted Hashizume, scratching his temples.

Fujishiro and Hashizume both had equivalent ranks, but in this particular instance Fujishiro had the greater authority.

"The basic blood type is the same," replied Fujishiro. "We can't confirm that they're from the same person until we've finished the DNA test on the torso."

"Is there a rush on dismembered bodies here today? You can't turn around the test any faster?"

"Let us focus on doing our job right, Hashizume. Your job is to just sit tight and wait for the results. If the DNA doesn't match, that'll mean we've got a second dead body on our hands. In that case, I'll recommend that the chief of Homicide set up a second task force in Kamata."

"Like hell you will! That precinct can't handle another goddamn task force. The place will implode! God knows, the quality of the food the canteen serves is vile enough already. The thought of living off rice balls from the convenience store until we've cleared this case is getting me down."

Reiko was very much on Fujishiro's side, though she couldn't come out and say so.

Why would a high-ranking civil servant care about your stupid stomach?

Oblivious to his own lack of tact, Hashizume made a great show of examining his watch.

"When will we get them?"

"What?"

"What? The DNA test results, of course."

It was ten past four.

"The crime scene DNA data was delivered around one hour ago," Fujishiro replied. "My guess is they'll need till midnight to get a result."

Hashizume scratched the crown of his head.

"That's no damn good. No damn good at all. I need it by nine. Can you get it to me by nine?"

"In six hours? Out of the question."

"Last time they did it in seven."

"That was the central crime lab at TMPD headquarters."

"Big deal. Get them to do it an hour faster. They can do it, if they try."

"What kind of idiot are you? What's 'trying' got to do with anything? You want the technicians to sing songs to the PCR equipment and the automatic analyzer so the machines will complete the job faster? You've no idea what you're talking about, so I advise you to keep your stupid mouth shut."

Ioka, who was standing behind Reiko, burst out laughing.

Hashizume wasn't going to give up.

"You need to think about the investigators working the case. We haven't got a cause of death, and the DNA analysis is going to take hours. If we get your report in the middle of the night, it'll be too late for our evening meeting."

"Then do your meeting later."

"I can't do that. After the general meeting for all the investigators, we have the executive meeting. The executive meeting often runs all night."

Well, that's a lie. Besides, you're usually asleep during it.

"Let me lay out the bottom line: we can't do what we can't do."

"Yes you can. I know you can."

Reiko was beginning to be impressed by Hashizume's sheer bullheadedness, when someone tapped her on the shoulder.

"I'm going back to Kamata," Kusaka said. "Call me if anything comes up."

He walked briskly down the corridor.

Watching this Punch-and-Judy show all evening's not my idea of fun either, you know.

But Reiko felt strangely reluctant to leave.

What was bugging her?

It was something about the photographs of the torso. She felt as though a gray mist had rolled in and enveloped her mind in murk.

Fujishiro obviously won the pissing contest with Hashizume. It was two in the morning before the DNA test results arrived from Tomei University Hospital.

"About time," grumbled Hashizume, yawning. "That stuck-up bastard."

The rest of the executive team ignored him and skimmed through the report.

The DNA test proved that the torso belonged to the same person as the blood from the garage, the blood in the minivan, and the severed left hand.

The report on the torso was along the lines of what Fujishiro had told them in the hospital.

No wound that could have caused death was found. There were no significant abnormalities in the internal organs. It was suggested that the cause of death was "something other than suffocation or blood loss." Absence of congestion or anemia in the internal organs excluded poisoning, strangulation, or choking; beating, which would result in massive bleeding from the head, was also ruled out.

What other means of killing are we left with, then?

In the section about distinctive physical marks, the report mentioned "scars consistent with cholecystectomy for acute calculous cholecystitis"—scars left by an operation to remove gallstones, in layman's terms.

As far as Reiko could see, the report didn't attempt to explain the reasons behind the semicircular patch of gouged-out skin on the left of the pharynx that she had noticed in the photographs. The pathologist had noted its location and measured it. The diameter of the semicircle, which was seven centimeters long, was flush with the top of the severed neck; the gouge was 1.2 centimeters in depth.

"Anyone have any thoughts about this missing patch of skin here?" she said.

None of the five other people there—Director Hashizume; Captain Imaizumi; Lieutenant Kusaka; Captain Kawada, the head of detectives at Kamata; and Lieutenant Tanimoto, from the Kamata Major Crimes Unit—bothered to reply. They were probably just too tired.

"Captain, look. You see how the skin's been gouged out at the throat? What do you think it means?"

Imaizumi's only response was a grunt. The copy of the report in front of him was open to the page about stomach contents, and he made no effort to turn to the relevant photograph.

"What's your take, Lieutenant Kusaka?"

"Got to be fish, I'd say."

"Wouldn't there be some mention of tooth marks with fish?"

"The skin's so macerated that the tooth marks dissolved."

"If that's what had happened, the report would say so."

"No. Like I said, skin maceration would eliminate any telltale signs."

This is a waste of time. Everyone's worn out. Their brains aren't firing on all cylinders.

Reiko couldn't come up with an explanation either. She was as hopeless as the rest of them.

After a night's sleep, Reiko had an idea.

The next morning, as soon as the meeting ended, she made a copy of the text of the autopsy report, scanned and printed all the photographs on a high-quality photo printer, and put it all into an envelope.

"Hey Ioka, the post office is in that direction, right?"

"Shall I take you?" said Ioka, with a smirk.

"Thanks, but no thanks."

Reiko went to the post office in Kamata and sent the package by express mail. Then she phoned Dr. Kunioku, her friend in the Tokyo Medical Examiner's office.

"Hello, Doctor? It's me."

"Hiya. What's up?"

Kunioku's voice was not quite as perky—or was *smarmy* a better word?—as normal.

"You sound a little down, Doctor."

"I can't believe the way you're behaving, saying, 'Hello, it's me,' as though nothing's happened."

"Okay, why are you sulking?"

Was it because of the way she'd turned down his

invitation to dinner the other day?

"Sulking? Nursing a broken heart is more like it."

"Don't let's go overboard. Listen, Doctor, I've got a favor to ask you."

"How can you treat me like this! No small talk; no 'I'm sorry.' Just straight down to brass tacks."

Reiko decided that ignoring him was probably her best tactic.

"Just listen, please. We've comes across an interesting body in the case I'm on right now. The pathologist at Tomei University Hospital was unable to specify a cause of death. I need to get a second opinion from the leader in the field, and that's why I've just posted all the documentation to you. Promise me you'll have a look, Doc?"

There was a long silence at the other end.

What now?

"Doc, you still there?"

"So you won't be delivering the file by your own fair hand?"

"Oh, I didn't think of that. I'm afraid it's already in the post."

"What should I do once I've looked it over?'

"Let me know what you think. Phone or e-mail are fine."

"Not for me, they're not. I'll only look at what you sent if you come in person to discuss it with me."

Reiko had been expecting something like this.

"Provided you've got some observations worth listening to, I'm happy to go."

"I'm not falling for that trick. Promise me you'll come regardless of my findings—otherwise I'll use your precious documents as toilet paper."

"Don't come whining to me when you get hemorrhoids."

"Oh, you didn't know? My nickname is 'the man with the iron colon.'"

"Potty mouth. Such a crude sense of humor."

The old fellow was back to his normal cheeky self.

"The file will reach you tomorrow. Have a look as soon as you can."

"How's it coming? DHL? Bike courier?"

"No, by express post."

"I'm strongly opposed to these recent moves to privatize the post office."

"I haven't time for that now. Treat me to your best lecture on the subject next time we meet. Take a good look at the file. *Please.*"

"There's this fabulous dobin mushi restaurant I know in Ueno. I thought—"

Reiko hung up.

Good. That's the body out of the way.

3

Most of the investigators had left the station house, but Kusaka stayed behind. He wanted to watch the press conference. It was going to be held at 10:00 a.m. in the conference room where the task force was based.

There were around thirty journalists there. Most were newspaper reporters, but there was also a smattering of TV correspondents.

The Kamata station commander and his deputy were sitting at the head of the room along with Wada, the chief of TMPD Homicide, and Director Hashizume. The precinct commander did the talking.

"At 11:00 a.m. yesterday morning, we were notified that something that appeared to be a human torso had washed ashore in the South Rokugo section of the Tama River. Officers went to the scene and confirmed that it was indeed the torso of an adult male. We are now working in conjunction with the Tokyo Metropolitan Police Department, and our task force is doing its best to establish the identity of the victim."

The top brass must have felt there was sufficient doubt surrounding the real identity of Kenichi Takaoka to keep his name back for now.

"The torso is that of a male in his forties. We have not yet recovered the head, arms, or legs. That is all we have to share with you for the time being."

One of the journalists raised his hand. The deputy station commander pointed to him. He identified himself as Ozeki of the *Daily News*.

"My sources are telling me that you've been conducting quite a large investigation since the beginning of the month focusing on an abandoned vehicle. Is there a link between the two incidents?"

"That is currently under investigation," came the bland reply.

The next question was from Furuta of the *Tokyo Sun*.

"I've been hearing rumors of extensive house-to-house canvassing in the Middle Rokugo district since the start of the month. Would you care to comment?"

"An investigation is ongoing there."

"Do you believe the two cases are linked?"

"I cannot comment at the present time."

Hashimoto of the *Nippon Times* asked the next question.

"My sources tell me that the vehicle you found on December fourth on the embankment of the Tama River contained a severed hand. Have you DNA-tested the hand and the torso?"

The room went very quiet. The rest of the reporters

looked shocked. Kusaka was every bit as taken aback. If that much information had leaked, it meant that either someone in TMPD headquarters or someone on the task force was shooting their mouth off.

He wondered how the station commander was going to wriggle out of that question. He would have to improvise. The chief of Homicide leaned over and whispered something into the commander's ear.

"We have indeed conducted DNA tests," said the commander. "But we are still awaiting the results."

Though better than a flat-out denial, it was hardly the ideal response. Kusaka would have preferred that the whole severed hand angle had been kept quiet.

"When will you get them?"

Wada whispered into the commander's ear again. The journalists at the front of the room stared at him intently.

"We expect to get the results sometime tomorrow. We will make a public announcement the day after."

Hashimoto of the *Nippon Times* was nothing if not persistent. It was obvious that he'd done a lot of digging around.

"With a dismembered corpse, you must be treating this case as a homicide. Can you give us a cause of death?"

"We were unable to locate any lethal wounds or visible signs on the torso that were identifiable as the cause of death."

"In that case, is it fair to assume that the victim died from injuries to the head?"

"That we don't yet know."

Knowing that the station commander's response was

unlikely to keep the *Nippon Times* journalist quiet, Chief Wada picked up the microphone and leaned forward sternly.

"This is an ongoing investigation. All we can tell you is this: previously we found a hand and yesterday we found a torso. Thank you, ladies and gentlemen. That will be all for today."

"The hand—is it a left or a right hand?" yelled someone.

"This press conference is officially over," barked chief Wada, with an air of finality. Director Hashizume gestured at the station commander and the four men filed out of the room, bringing the event to a rather anticlimactic end.

Now everyone and their dog knew that a torso had been found in the Tama River and a severed hand found in a vehicle. *Fine,* thought Kusaka, *the real investigation starts now.*

Kusaka had spent the last few days trying to find the trail of Makio Tobe. Kinoshita Construction was the natural place to start.

According to Ms. Yashiro, Tobe had last been seen in the Kinoshita offices at around 3:00 p.m. on December 3.

Ms. Yashiro was having a cup of tea with her two coworkers and Mr. Kinoshita, the president of the company, when Tobe burst in. Although he smelled of drink, he didn't appear to be downright drunk.

Tobe walked up behind Ms. Yashiro, commented on how stiff she was, and began to give her a shoulder massage. It didn't take long for him to slide his hands down and start fondling her breasts. When Kinoshita, the CEO, and Kawakami, the accountant, told Tobe to knock it off, Tobe clapped Kawakami hard on the back. "I'm just playing around, man," he said. "Just joking."

He then leaned down and nuzzled Ms. Niki, the other woman in the office. When Kinoshita roared at him, Tobe smirked and headed for the toilet. He emerged a few minutes later, and stalked out of the office without a word—and without having done a stroke of work.

Another witness placed Tobe in a slot machine parlor not far from Todoroki Station between 3:30 and 5:30. One of the women working on the floor remembered him because of the way he'd tried to grab her ass every time she went by. "Oh God, he's not *still* here!" she'd thought to herself at 5:20. Ten minutes later, she noticed that he had gone. The woman was able to provide a positive visual ID based on a copy of Tobe's driver's license and a photograph that Kinoshita Construction had provided. Kusaka made doubly sure by having the manager show him the CCTV footage from the day. It confirmed that Tobe had entered the parlor at 3:27 and left at 5:22.

With the time of Takaoka's murder placed at around 9:30 in the evening, that left four hours unaccounted for. Where had Tobe gone when he got fed up with playing the slots?

Kusaka dropped in to all the local bars and sleazy massage parlors. No joy there. Tobe's trail went cold at the slot machine parlor.

Several teams of investigators were making inquiries in Yutenji, Meguro Ward, where Tobe lived. While none of the local residents had seen Tobe since the day of the crime, it turned out that few of them had ever set eyes on him.

Tobe lived in a five-story apartment building. The landlord lived on the top floor and rented out all the others. There was residents' parking and a single rental office unit on the first floor; the upper floors contained four apartments each, with Tobe in room 302 on the third floor. The other residents were average families with normal nine-to-five jobs. They never laid eyes on Tobe, because he lived his life on a timetable wholly different from theirs.

When Sergeant Toyama and his partner went to Tobe's apartment, they discovered that he shared the place with a thirty-two-year-old bar hostess. She hadn't changed her lifestyle after moving in with Tobe: she left for the club where she worked at half past four and returned home either by taxi late at night or by the first train in the morning. Tobe had now been gone for two weeks. While such a long absence was unusual, it wasn't unprecedented, so his girlfriend wasn't unduly worried.

"Hey, for all I know, he could be popping back here while I'm out at work," she told the two detectives with a laugh, as they stood in the doorway.

The two of them had been living together for two years. Sergeant Toyama got the distinct impression that the temperature of the relationship had cooled considerably with time.

•

While Kusaka was conducting his investigation around Tokyo, he and his partner were also on call for relief surveillance duties.

The investigators working the Tobe angle had to keep tabs on quite a number people. First, there were the women Tobe knew, ranging from insurance saleswomen to girls in local bars and massage parlors. There were his friends, and then there was the Ogawa Mansion. The Ogawa Mansion was the residence of Miyuki Ogawa, Tobe's biological mother (despite what his family register said).

Kusaka was heading toward the Ogawa Mansion to take over stakeout when his cell phone rang. He looked at the display: an unregistered number.

"Kusaka here."

"It's me, Makihara."

Lieutenant Takeo Makihara was the head of TMPD Organized Crime Unit.

"What's up?"

"I need to speak with you, Kusaka. You're in the Ogawa Mansion neighborhood?"

Was Makihara following him?

Kusaka was in a quiet residential area near Jiyugaoka Station. He looked up and down the street he was in, but couldn't see anyone.

"Where? Out here?"

"No. Keep walking and you'll hit a one-way street. Turn

in and you'll find a coffee shop. The place is called Lichere."

"Got you."

Kusaka told Sergeant Satomura to go ahead without him, and then he set off for the coffee shop.

The cowbell attached to the inside of the coffee shop door emitted a mournful clunk when Kusaka pushed it open. There was only one other customer, who was sitting right at the back. It was Lieutenant Kubota of the Criminal Investigation Division. His unit specialized in election law violation, bribery, corruption, and corporate crime. The crimes his unit and Makihara's unit investigated overlapped often.

"Long time no see," said Kusaka, sliding into the seat opposite. Kubota didn't bother to reply. A few seconds later, Makihara came in and marched over to their table.

"What exactly is the point of this little gathering?" asked Kusaka, once Makihara had sat down.

Makihara raised his hand and ordered three coffees. Kubota chose that moment to finally open his mouth.

"The investigators you've got on Tajima and Nakabayashi—pull them out right now. All of them."

Kubota and Makihara were a few years older than Kusaka was. That didn't mean he was prepared to let them boss him around.

"Shelve the high-and-mighty tone, will you? I don't work for you. You want me to do something, you need to give me a reason. A good reason."

Makihara leaned over the table and glared at him.

"You guys treading on the toes of the Tajima-gumi is the last thing we need right now, so be a good boy and back the fuck off."

"You should go through the proper channels. Talk to my superiors. This isn't how I'm meant to get orders."

"Listen," Kubota hissed. "We're talking to you like this because we *can't* go through the normal channels."

Kubota and Makihara were both lieutenants. If they were worried about their immediate superiors, that meant captains, directors, and, one level up, department chiefs and station commanders.

"Why can't you take it to your bosses?"

"We can't share that information with you," said Kubota.

"You're just going to have to trust us," Makihara chimed in. "There are certain issues we can't take to them. That's just how it is."

That had to mean that someone high up in the force had some sort of corrupt relationship with the Tajima-gumi or the Nakabayashi Group, and that Makihara and Kubota were discreetly investigating the matter. *But isn't this sort of thing usually handled by Internal Affairs?* Kusaka thought to himself.

"We're not just poking into Tajima and Nakabayashi for our own goddamn amusement, you know," added Kubota.

"We heard you're on the case of that chopped-up body found in the Tama River," said Makihara. "And that Makio Tobe's your suspect."

That was information he could only have gotten from inside the force. Who'd fed him the intel?

"Tobe's not yet an official suspect. We just want him to help us with our inquiries."

"You won't flush Tobe out by putting the heat on Tajima and Nakabayashi," growled Kubota.

"Oh no?"

Kubota waited for the waitress to move away.

"The Tajima-gumi cut its ties with Tobe years ago. He's not allowed near their offices. He's under a life ban. Since the time Nakabayashi kicked him out and he joined Kinoshita Construction, Tobe's been completely on his own."

"He's still doing business with lenders connected to the Tajima-gumi," protested Kusaka.

"The head honchos don't know about that. Tobe's flying under the radar, freelancing. The big guys aren't interested in that sort of nickel-and-dime loan-sharking shit."

"I need to warn you," interrupted Makihara, raising a cautionary finger. "If you make a move on the Ogawa Mansion, you may well get Tobe killed."

Kusaka cocked his head in surprise.

"I thought Miyuki Ogawa was his mother? The gang wouldn't dare touch him, surely?"

"You heard of Aiko Ogawa?"

Kusaka shook his head.

"Aiko is the daughter of Miyuki and Michio Ogawa. She's seriously ugly. Anyway, the story goes that Miyuki went through a phase of trying to be a good mom to

SOUL CAGE

her bastard boy, and Tobe was popping into the Ogawa
Mansion on a regular basis. Good old Tobe decided to
repay mommy's hospitality by raping his younger half-
sister. Rumor is that Tobe's such a lecher, he'd fuck a dog if
you stuck a wig on it. In his case, I'm prepared to give the
rumors the benefit of the doubt.

"That's why Tobe was kicked out of the Tajima-gumi
and the Nakabayashi Group. He's not allowed to set foot
in the Ogawa Mansion either. The guy somehow managed
to wriggle his way into Kinoshita Construction. Michio
Ogawa and high-up Nakabayashi people all know that he's
there, but if we pile the pressure on them because of Tobe,
there's no telling what they might do to him. He likes to
flaunt his Tajima and Nakabayashi connections, but they've
hung him out to dry. He means nothing to them."

It sounded plausible, but Kusaka still wasn't ready to
abort his own operation based on their story alone.

"The thing is, I don't have the authority to cancel the
operation myself," he explained mildly. "At the very least,
I'm going to have to involve the captain."

Makihara scowled.

"You're Unit Ten, right? Who's your captain? Is it
Zoom-zoom?"

The veteran cops on the force all referred to Imaizumi
by his nickname.

"That's right."

"Who's your director?"

"Hashizume."

307

Kubota shook his head violently.

"That man's dangerous. Hashizume doesn't know how to keep his mouth shut. Keep this between you and Zoom-zoom."

"I understand what you want me to do. But I know there's no way the captain will play ball if I just go and tell him we've got to pull back just because you guys met me in a café somewhere and asked me to. I'll need a written order with your names on it. It'll be handled discreetly, I promise. No one outside the unit will see it."

"You bastard," growled Makihara.

Kubota waved for him to back off.

"It'll take a little time, but we can do that. The one thing we cannot do is go into any detail about why we need you to withdraw your surveillance."

"That shouldn't be a problem. Now, I have a little favor of my own I'd like to ask from you gentlemen in return."

Makihara just scowled, but Kubota's response was more encouraging.

"Fire away. What can we do for you?"

"I want to apply for a search warrant for Tobe's apartment. Can you give me probable cause?"

"What sort of thing?"

"Anything—firearms, drugs, whatever. I just need the warrant to be issued for something I can be a hundred percent sure will be on the premises."

"I don't get it. Why not get a warrant for documents connected to Tobe's insurance scams? That's a safe bet."

Kusaka shook his head.

Tobe didn't seem like the kind to keep well-organized records. Searching his apartment for documents and finding none could set the case back seriously. Kusaka was most interested in random bits of miscellaneous information—photographs, fingerprints—that might end up being useful but couldn't be listed on the warrant. He needed a rock-solid probable cause to minimize the risk to the case.

"You guys tell me something I can be sure of finding in there, and I'll play ball. That's my one condition."

"Understood," grunted Kubota.

Makihara gave a surly nod.

Kusaka got to his feet.

"Thanks for your help. Oh, and thanks for the coffee too."

Outside a light rain was falling.

Kusaka's cell phone buzzed as he was walking down the street. The caller ID said "home." Noriko, his wife, was under strict instructions not to disturb him at work, and she normally had the good sense not to. It had to be something important.

"Hello."

"Hi, can you talk?"

"Provided you keep it short."

There was a sigh at the other end of the phone.

"It's Yoshihide. He came back from school early today. He's asleep upstairs in his room."

Kusaka looked at his watch. Twenty past three. Yoshihide must've skipped sports.

"Is he feeling okay?"

"He says he's got a tummy ache. I don't think it's anything worth leaving early for."

"Whatever it is, why not let him sleep it off?"

Kusaka did a quick mental review of his schedule.

"Chances are I won't be able to make it home at all this week. I want to talk to you about this, but you're going to have to be patient. I'm sorry."

"Ah."

Yoshihide was highly-strung—timid, even. He'd been slipping out of school early more and more often lately. Kusaka knew that bullying must have something to do with it.

"Yoshihide didn't say anything else?"

"He said everything was fine except for his tummy ache."

"Did you ask him if the other kids were bullying him?"

"Yes, well . . . sort of."

"Bullying's an issue you've got to tackle head on. The worst thing a parent can do is to look the other way."

"I don't see *you* looking out for your son at all."

Kusaka had no comeback to that.

"Look, it may be late at night, but I promise, I'll do my best to come home tomorrow, or, failing that, on the weekend."

"Please do."

"Don't make Yoshihide go to school if he really doesn't want to. He can do his coursework without going to school. Studying's something you can do anywhere."

"That's what I've been telling him too."

"Great. Make sure he eats properly, once he feels a bit better. Oh, and don't let him hole up in his room. Get him to come downstairs and eat in the kitchen with you. You can watch TV together. Okay?"

"Okay."

"I'm depending on you."

"You promise you'll come back soon?"

"Promise. I'm going to hang up now."

"Okay, see you soon."

Kusaka ended the call and put his phone back in his pocket.

He always ended up hating himself after conversations like that with his wife. God, he was such a coldhearted bastard!

For the most part, he loved his job. That wasn't how he presented things to his family, though. With them, he always moaned about being forced to take on all sorts of burdensome tasks against his will.

The train trip from his home in suburban Saitama to the TMPD headquarters in central Tokyo was already long enough. Now that he was on a task force out in Kamata, commuting home on a daily basis was outright impossible.

But he could certainly make it home for a single night. His son was stressed and worried. He had to go back, talk to the boy, cheer him up.

So why didn't he? Why had he started out by coldly informing his wife he wasn't able to go back? There was no "able" about it; he simply didn't *want* to go back home.

The thought that something terrible might happen to his son before he made it back made him physically flinch. He also knew that as soon as he was back amongst his colleagues on the force, he'd forget about his family in five minutes.

I'm a coldhearted bastard.

The words went round and round in Kusaka's head as he headed back to the Ogawa Mansion stakeout.

4

Sergeant Kikuta was on the team assigned to search Makio Tobe's apartment. The brass had announced the search at the meeting the night before, just before announcing that the surveillance on the Tajima-gumi and Nakabayashi Group was going to be withdrawn. Kikuta, who'd been keeping an eye on the offices of Nakabayashi Real Estate, was sent to Yutenji instead.

Reiko guessed that pressure had been brought to bear.

"You take on the Tajima-gumi and you expect to get pushback," she explained to Kikuta the next morning. "Someone complained. Someone pulled a few strings. And the string-puller got something in return. That's how it works. I don't think money's involved. My guess is that they got a tip that they could use as probable cause for the search. The higher-ups claimed that 'someone on the task force' told them about Tobe's woman being an amphetamine junkie. I hadn't heard anything about that until just then."

The search warrant came with an accompanying document that permitted the police to dust for fingerprints and to confiscate firearms and knives, as well as any insurance-related paperwork they thought relevant to the case. Illegal drugs also featured on the list, with a note to the effect that the search team had the right to examine articles linked to the suspect's girlfriend as much as those connected to the suspect himself.

They're probably after something else entirely.

"What good will it do us going after Tobe's girlfriend? I guess they went for a scattershot approach to avoid legal complications. The drugs and firearms are a respectable pretext to search the apartment, and if they stumble onto anything else interesting while they're there, that's covered under the warrant. I think that that 'anything else interesting' is what they're really after. Good luck, Kikuta. Do a good job. While you're busy with that, I'm going to conduct a second interview with Michiko Nakagawa."

Tobe's apartment consisted of a large kitchen, living room, a couple of bedrooms, and a separate bathroom. Tobe's hostess girlfriend, Mikako Kobayashi, was sitting at the dining table with a female officer watching the officers at work when she noticed Kikuta kneeling in front of a dresser in a bedroom.

"Hey, there's only my things in there," the woman

objected. "It's nothing to do with Tobe."

Mikako started getting to her feet. One of the investigators pushed her gently back into her chair. She might as well have issued a press release that she kept her stash in there.

Sure enough, Kikuta came across a nylon pencil case in the middle drawer of the dresser. Unzipping it, he discovered five sachets of white powder inside.

"I've got some suspicious packages here."

Kusaka, who was examining the bathroom, walked over to the bedroom where Kikuta was, shooting a sidelong glance at Mikako as he passed by.

"Ijizu, could you come with me?"

"Yes, sir."

Lieutenant Ijizu of Forensics brought a camera over. After first photographing Kikuta holding the case, he got Kikuta to return the package back to the drawer where he had found it. He got him to point at it, pick it up, unzip it, and take out and display the sachets as well as a syringe that was in the bottom of the case, and he carefully photographed every stage of the process.

"Okay. I've got what I need."

"Thanks, Kikuta," said Kusaka. "I'll take that."

Kusaka stuck out his hand and Kikuta passed him the case and its contents. Kusaka went back into the living area.

"Ms. Kobayashi, can you tell me who this belongs to?"

The woman said nothing.

"That's how it is? Okay, we can conduct a test right

here. What we do is dissolve this white powder here in water and then stick a piece of litmus paper in it. If the paper turns blue, that tells us we've got a psychoactive drug. In that case, we'll be asking you to do a urine test for us. That won't be a problem, will it?"

She still said nothing.

"Lieutenant Ijizu, would you do the honors?"

"Yes, sir."

Kusaka was relieved when the paper turned blue.

"Lieutenant, I think we've got a firearm up here. Looks like a .32-caliber."

Officer Shinjo had climbed onto the upper level of the closet. One of the forensics staff came and took photographs.

Back in the bedroom, Kikuta doggedly went on with his own search, when he came across an unopened tube of Dior lipstick.

The memory of Reiko's lips came rushing back. The soft lips that had in an instant wiped out the childish jealousy he was feeling toward Ioka; the weight of her hands on his shoulders; the springiness of her breasts as they pressed against him; the smell of her hair; the smell of her skin; the long lashes of her closed eyes; the ears, so delicate when seen up close; the white nape of her neck.

What did that kiss of hers mean?

Had she just felt sorry for him when she saw how angry Ioka was making him and kissed him out of pity? Or was she giving him a signal about the direction she wanted their relationship to go? Which was it?

It had happened twelve days ago. Reiko hadn't mentioned it since. Nor had Kikuta.

They saw each other at the morning meeting. After that, everyone dispersed and headed to their different tasks. Since Reiko was keeping an eye on Michiko Nakagawa and Kikuta was trying to track down Tobe, they never crossed paths during the day. They were both back at the station for the evening meeting. They always got back to the station just before the meeting kicked off at eight o'clock, so they didn't have time to chat beforehand.

Besides, Ioka was always tagging along after her. How could Kikuta discuss anything personal with him there? He knew he'd probably back off as soon as Ioka butted in, with some muttered excuse about it not being anything urgent.

It was pathetic, but Kikuta knew how he was likely to behave.

Back in high school, he'd only managed to come out and declare his feelings to one of the girls he had a crush on. It was at the school festival at the end of his third year. He'd been in a group of five boys and five girls who were playing a sort of Valentine's game. He'd summoned up the courage to pin his rosette on the object of his secret love. She hadn't responded well.

Straight after finishing high school, he did his stint at the Police Academy. His first posting was the Senju Precinct. He seemed to spend a great deal of time going to hostess bars and soapy massage parlors, largely because his senior colleagues liked to go and he was expected to tag obediently along.

There'd been this young officer in Traffic who told him straight out that she fancied him, but he'd sent out mixed signals, and it had gone nowhere. When a high school pal had asked him along on a group date, he'd hit it off with one of the girls there and promised to call her the next day—but he never did.

It was after his transfer to the Omori Precinct that he finally had his first relationship at the age of twenty-four. The girl was the daughter of the landlady at a local bar he liked. Everything about her—her looks, her figure, her character—was average, normal.

It was the mother who got the ball rolling.

"Hey, Officer Kikuta, why don't you take my daughter on a date? Seems like she's got zero interest in men."

At first he thought the woman was joking, but he took the daughter for a date, and the two of them ended up going out. It lasted for about a year, until the bar shut down and the mother moved back to her hometown up north in Hokkaido, taking the daughter with her. He never saw the girl again. She wrote him for about a year. He only replied to her once, and the letters eventually stopped coming.

That was the full and complete story of Kazuo Kikuta's love life.

"Is there something particularly suspicious about that lipstick?"

Kikuta started at the sound of Kusaka's voice. He must have been daydreaming. Looking over his shoulder, he saw all the investigators standing in a semicircle around him.

"This? Uh, no."

In a panic, he tried to put the lipstick back in the drawer, but he was all thumbs. The tube shot out of his hand, hit the wall, rebounded, and hit Sergeant Toyama on the forehead.

"Ouch."

"Sorry.

"Get a grip, Kikuta."

It looked as though the search was well and truly over.

After the litmus test, Mikako Kobayashi was made to take a urine test in the apartment. When that also gave a positive result, she was arrested for possession and use of controlled substances.

Lieutenant Kusaka watched the unmarked patrol car that was taking her to the station drive away. The forensics van soon followed. He ordered all the investigators to head back to the precinct.

All except one, that is.

"Want to grab a coffee with me, Sergeant Kikuta?"

Kusaka clapped Kikuta on the shoulder and set off toward the main road.

Kikuta was surprised. Kusaka had never spoken to him before. What the heck was going on?

The two men walked side by side. Kusaka didn't say anything. From the corner of his eye, Kikuta tried to read the other man's face. Was Kusaka going to tear a well-deserved strip off him for daydreaming on the job? It didn't look like it.

"What is it, Lieutenant?"

"What, can't I invite a subordinate out for a cup of tea without having an agenda?"

A subordinate?

Kikuta was a sergeant in Homicide Unit 10. Kusaka was a lieutenant in the same unit. Technically, that made Kikuta his subordinate, even if he was part of a different squad. It was standard operating procedure—but Kikuta didn't like it.

In his mind, Lieutenant Reiko Himekawa was his only real boss. He had a good idea that his colleagues Yuda and Hayama felt the same way, though he wasn't sure about Ishikura, who was older than the rest of them.

Reiko and Kusaka were like oil and vinegar. Over the last few months, they'd conducted their investigations independently of one another. Since both squads produced good results, the higher-ups weren't interested in knocking their heads together and forcing them to collaborate. If anything, they seemed to like the flexibility of the current arrangement. Kikuta knew that Reiko certainly liked it that way.

Did Kusaka see things differently? If that was what Kusaka wanted to talk to him about, then Kikuta had some opinions of his own.

"No, sir. Of course you can, sir," mumbled Kikuta. He'd got off on the wrong foot and decided to try another tack. "By the way, Lieutenant, what exactly were you after in that search?"

"Oh, nothing too specific," said Kusaka, pressing his

lips together. "I suppose I wanted to find some of Tobe's fingerprints, although they're not that important either."

"They're not?"

The vagueness of the reply took Kikuta by surprise. It was very much out of character. Kusaka's was legendary for his hatred of woolly thinking.

"What's wrong, Sergeant? You can't cope with the idea of going after something nonspecific?"

"It's not that, sir. It just seems . . . not very *you*."

Kusaka gave wry grin. That was out of character too.

"You want to know exactly what I was after in there? I don't know. Twist my arm, and my answer would probably be that I was looking for a motive—for why Tobe killed Takaoka. Finding that handgun is a kind of result, I guess. We know that Tobe had a gun, but the fact that he didn't take it with him when he left his apartment suggests that the murder was unplanned, a spur-of-the-moment thing— which doesn't really help us get any closer to his motives."

Kikuta broke into a smile.

Kusaka gave him a jaundiced look.

"Did I say something funny?"

"Yes, sir . . . a bit."

"What?"

"It's just that I never thought of you as the kind of person who did anything 'on the off chance.'"

Kusaka grinned back at him.

"A cop needs to have a sixth sense or intuition or what- ever you want to call it. I accept that. I just think that it's dangerous to follow your gut slavishly and narrow the focus of an investigation too far and too fast. Frankly, that's what I worry about with Himekawa. I'm wondering when she'll make some terrible mistake."

Kikuta was full of surprises today.

"I'd no idea you felt that way about Lieutenant Himekawa."

"That's probably because I've never verbalized it before. Maybe I'd never even thought it through properly until today. Believe me, having Himekawa steal a march on me is the last thing I'm worried about. I'm worried that someone might get hurt if her instincts take her in the wrong direction. That someone could be the suspect or the family of the victim; it could be Himekawa herself, or Hashizume or Imaizumi. If her instincts mislead her, she could end up wrecking people's lives. Doesn't that bother you?"

Kikuta nodded wordlessly.

"The real problem is that Himekawa can't explain the judgment calls she makes," Kusaka continued. "If she took the time to sit down and think it all through, there might turn out to be perfectly sound logic underpinning her thought process. She won't accept that she has any responsibility to explain herself. Her view is that results are the only thing that counts. That's the thing about her I find hard to stomach. I dislike her approach—and I wish she'd change it."

They had already walked past several cafés. Apparently, Kusaka hadn't even noticed them.

"Have you got any ideas about what underpins

Lieutenant Himekawa's thought process?" Kikuta asked.

Kusaka shook his head.

"I don't think I do. You know how she always stares into the middle distance before coming out with one of her theories? One minute she's all glassy-eyed and gazing into space, the next she's sprung to her feet and is propounding some wild idea. You ask her to explain herself, and she comes back at you with, 'That's what I think, so that's what I think.' For her, that's good enough. I simply can't follow. It drives me crazy."

"Do you think it's something psychic? You know, 'Lieutenant Reiko and her reiki powers.'"

"Spare me the silly puns, please."

Kikuta apologized, but he really wanted to shoot back that that sort of brusqueness was exactly what Reiko loathed in Kusaka.

They walked past yet another coffee shop.

"Tell me, Lieutenant," asked Kikuta. "Why did you bring this matter up with me today?"

Kusaka frowned.

"Probably because you made such an ass of yourself in there."

Kikuta gasped. He felt as though he'd been sucker punched.

An ass of myself!

A cyclist was approaching Kikuta at speed on the sidewalk. It gave him an excuse to duck behind Kusaka and conceal the fact that his face had turned beetroot red.

"Are you two seeing each other? If you are, then I

recommend that you get married sooner rather than later. Otherwise, it could have a negative impact on your career—and hers."

"No. I mean, that's not—"

"What are you babbling about, Sergeant Kikuta? You trying to tell me that it's hard for a sergeant like you to propose to a lieutenant like her?"

Go right ahead, Lieutenant! Who needs tact or delicacy? It's not like this is a difficult subject for me.

"You need to pull yourself together, Kikuta. If you're seeing her, then being upfront about it is the least you can do."

"Yes, but—"

"What, man? Don't tell me you haven't got around to telling her how you feel about her? Is that it?"

"Uhm, uh . . . that's right, sir."

Kusaka sighed with disgust.

"Oh, for God's sake! A great hulking fellow on the outside and such a little wimp on the inside—Kikuta, I'm disappointed in you."

Disappointed in me! What am I supposed to do?

In the end, they didn't go to a café. They bought a couple of cans of coffee from a convenience store and drank it on the street.

As he gulped down the hot, sweet liquid, Kikuta felt himself relax a little. He decided to ask Kusaka a question.

"Being married, Lieutenant. What's it like?"

Kusaka looked at the sky and exhaled with a hiss.

"Let's see.... Imagine you've got two balls of different colored clay that you knead together to form another bigger ball."

Kikuta felt he sort of understood what Kusaka was getting at. Or maybe he didn't.

"The different colors represent the husband and the wife. What will happen when they're kneaded together? The colors could mix; they could divide neatly down the middle; one color could completely overwhelm the other—whatever happens, the two smaller balls are going to smash together and recreate themselves as a one, slightly bigger ball. That's my take on marriage."

"What about kids?"

"Well, a child is like a third, smaller ball that appears as part of the big one. You've no way of knowing what color it will be."

"How old is your son, Lieutenant?" Kikuta asked.

"He's fourteen. Second year in junior high."

Kusaka gulped down the last of his coffee.

"Kids become independent, so I guess the role of parents is to make their kids as well-rounded as possible, so they can roll off successfully on their own."

Kusaka was gazing off into the middle distance as he spoke, rather like Reiko when she was having one of her inspirations. Kikuta felt that he had gotten a glimpse of the true face of Mamoru Kusaka—a face that the man almost never revealed to anyone at work.

5

Reiko and Ioka had been assigned to the surveillance of Michiko Nakagawa.

Michiko was studying at Kawasaki Beauty College. The college was only a three-minute walk from her house, while the Royal Diner, where she worked in the evenings, was just five minutes' walk away. The Kawasaki Station area, where she did most of her shopping, was a little over a kilometer away. With everything so close, she almost never took public transport. As a subject, she was extraordinarily easy to keep tabs on.

She'd only met up with Kosuke Mishima once since the task force put her under twenty-four-hour surveillance.

On Thursday, December 18, Michiko followed her usual routine. When she left her apartment in the morning and headed for school, Reiko followed at a discreet distance. The girl wasn't a suspect, so there was no point in panicking her by making their presence felt. She was wearing a black down jacket with a fur collar. Luckily for them, the fur of her collar was white, and she was easy to pick out.

"Are you going to ask her about Tobe today?" Ioka asked Reiko.

"If we can. We do need to talk to her about that."

They'd have to talk to her after school ended at 4:40 and before she went to work in the evening.

Reiko and Ioka caught up with her as she was walking home.

"Miss Nakagawa?"

Michiko turned. She didn't seem surprised to see them. "Yes."

"Can you spare us a minute?"

"Sure."

Reiko was planning to do the interview at a coffee shop along the way, but when Michiko suggested they come back to her place, she was happy to go along.

"I just need a minute to tidy up."

She kept them waiting outside for a minute or two, then let them into her apartment.

The room was just as tidy—or, if you wanted to be uncharitable, just as dreary—as on their last visit.

They all sat down in the same places, and Michiko prepared some tea. She seemed more relaxed: perhaps having a couple of detectives drop by for a chat was no longer such a big deal the second time it happened.

"We're here today because we wanted to ask you a few questions about your late father," began Reiko, when everyone was comfortable.

Michiko, who was peering into her teacup, raised her

head and looked first at Reiko and then at Ioka.

"Uh–huh."

"Last time we spoke, you told us that your father died in an accident while working at one of Kinoshita Construction's construction sites. After the accident, did a Kinoshita employee by the name of Makio Tobe contact you to talk about insurance?"

She was calm. Quite abnormally so.

"Yes, he did. And he kindly helped to arrange my move to this new apartment. Is there a problem?"

She sounded like she was reading from a script.

"Am I right in thinking that Kinoshita Construction had an insurance policy on your father that listed themselves as beneficiary in the event of his death, and that a proportion of the payout they received made its way through them back to you?"

Michiko was looking at her blankly. No wonder. Reiko knew her question had been long–winded and hard to understand. She tried again.

"Did Kinoshita Construction give you money from your father's life insurance to help you move?"

"Yes. At least, I think that's where the money came from."

"And you met with Makio Tobe?"

"Yes," Michiko said, no longer looking confused. "I met him several times."

"Where?"

The girl's eyes froze.

Was she scrambling to come up with an answer?

"At a café in Kawasaki."

Really? Or did you come up with that just now?

"Which café?"

A pause.

"I think it was a chain, probably a Doutor."

"Doutor's got five or six stores in the Kawasaki station area. Which one was it?"

I think she's floundering.

"The one near Marui department store . . . I think."

"When did you meet him?"

"Very soon after my father died."

"What sort of man was he?"

The girl's eyes went momentarily blank.

Does that mean . . . ?

Reiko remembered what Saito, the manager at the Royal Diner, had told her. Michiko had been behaving strangely on the night of the third. She was nervous and distracted, and loud noises made her jump.

That was typical behavior of someone who'd just been the victim of violence. Reiko knew all about post-traumatic stress from her own sexual assault: she'd been acutely sensitive to loud noises or anything even slightly reminiscent of conflict or violence.

Was Tobe responsible for Michiko's behavior on the third?

According to Kusaka's reports, Tobe was an indiscriminate chaser after women. It was hard to imagine that he wouldn't have tried his luck with a frail and good-looking girl like Michiko.

Michiko said that Tobe had arranged for her to move to this apartment. So he knew her address. If Tobe had assaulted her, likely as not this place was ground zero.

"Scratch that. Let me ask you something quite different. Did or did not Tobe come here on the evening of December third?"

Michiko shook her head furiously from side to side.

Reiko knew exactly what that meant.

When Yuda and his partner took over surveillance duties at 6:30 p.m., Reiko and Ioka headed back to Kamata Police Station.

"I feel so sorry for that kid," Ioka kept muttering as they made for the main street. His words stirred something in Reiko's memory: how as a girl she had been knocked down and pressed against the hard, dank earth in the park.

That's over and done with. It's my past. It's finished.

"According to Kusaka, Tobe dropped into the offices of Kinoshita Construction briefly on the afternoon of the third, then played the slots until early evening. Do you think he went around to the girl's place after that?"

"Yes. The scumbag."

"And you think he went to Middle Rokugo after that?"

"Yes. But I don't want you to say anything about any of this at tonight's meeting, okay?"

Ioka's brows shot up, and he groaned with frustration.

"I'm reasonably confident that we can clear up this

case without needing to bring up the question of what, if anything, happened between Michiko and Tobe."

Ioka groaned again, but Reiko wasn't interested in his objections.

"If we arrest Tobe and he makes a confession, there's nothing we can do. From our side, though, I don't want to make the girl a key figure in the case. Tobe's our murderer, and Takaoka's our victim. Anything else, we should let sleeping dogs lie. I don't want to put the spotlight on the girl any more than we have already. Tell me you're on board with that, Ioka. *Please.*"

"Uh, okay, boss," Ioka stammered. "Sure."

They found a taxi as soon as they reached the main boulevard. Throughout the short journey to the station, Ioka kept his mouth uncharacteristically shut.

In her report, Reiko noted Michiko's movements and the fact that she and Ioka had interviewed her and established that she'd met Makio Tobe.

With many of the investigators out on surveillance duties, the turnout for the meeting was low. The most important topic was the search of Tobe's apartment. Tobe's girlfriend, Mikako Kobayashi, had been arrested for the possession and use of controlled substances. Tests confirmed that the .32-caliber handgun found in the futon closet—it was a Colt Pocket—had never been fired. The gun wasn't loaded, and nine rounds of ammunition were found in a separate place. Mikako Kobayashi had given a statement in which she denied knowing anything about the gun.

Forensics also reported that fingerprints found in Tobe's apartment matched the prints found on the pole-hook in the Middle Rokugo.

Kusaka took it from there.

"From the way that the prints on the pole-hook overlap, it is clear that Tobe handled it just prior to the dismembering of the body. While that by no means constitutes proof that Tobe murdered Takaoka, we can say that he very probably did visit the garage on the day of the crime. There is another point I would like to bring to your attention: Tobe was in possession of a handgun, but he didn't take it with him when he left the apartment. If Tobe is the perpetrator, he must have acted on impulse. That brings my report for today to an end."

Reiko felt that Kusaka was both on and off target.

"Any questions?" asked Captain Imaizumi.

No hands went up.

That evening's meeting ended relatively early.

A full two weeks had passed since the setting up of the task force in Kamata, and many of the investigators were starting to look worn out. Even Kusaka dashed out as soon as the executive meeting came to an end, explaining that he had to nip back home. He lived way out in suburban Saitama and Reiko wondered if he'd get to the station in time to make his train.

She looked at her watch. It was 10:37. It would take just under an hour to make it to her parents' place in Minami-Urawa.

"Think I'll go home today too."

Kikuta half got up.

"Right, well I'll ... uh. ..."

Reiko waited for him to finish his sentence. She wasn't expecting him to offer to see her all the way home. He'd not be able to make it back this late, and she could hardly offer him a bed at her parents' house.

"I'll go with you ... as far as the station."

That's about as good as it's going to get.

"Great," said Reiko with a smile. "Thanks."

It was lucky that Ioka wasn't nearby. Had he popped out to the convenience store? Or was he in the bathroom? Either way, they needed to make tracks before he spotted them.

It was 11:00 p.m. The area around the station, with all the bars and restaurants, was still bustling.

Kikuta was walking to Reiko's right. He hadn't said anything, but Reiko was getting the feeling that he wanted to talk about their recent kiss. Was it going to be the start of something new? Or was it a meaningless one-off?

Reiko genuinely liked Kikuta. She felt closer to him than anyone else, and she trusted him implicitly. It was too early to think about going out with him. That was nothing to do with him; it was a personal issue. She needed to feel a little more secure in her identity as a detective on the force before she could take the next step.

They walked into the station and came to a halt just outside the ticket barrier. When they realized they were getting in the way, they edged off to the side.

"Thanks for walking me here."

Kikuta's face turned scarlet. Reiko had a flashback to the guardian deities outside the temple in Asakusa. She wondered if the other people in the station were getting the wrong idea: they probably thought he was angry with her.

"Lieutenant, I . . ."

"Yes?"

She knew Kikuta was hopeless at expressing himself. Putting any pressure on him would only be counterproductive. She needed to be patient; give him space.

"Lieutenant, I think you know how . . ."

Hurry up or I'll fall into a goddamn coma. Spit it out while I'm sugar and spice.

"I mean, I . . ."

Things weren't looking good. Reiko could feel her expression changing. Now she was frowning.

Come on, girl. Be patient. Be nice.

She looked at Kikuta's stubble-covered jaw. At his puckered lips, the texture and color of a sweet potato.

"You see, I really li—I really li—"

You really like me, right? I know you do. But I still want to hear you say it. Come on, spit it out! I want to hear it from you. That's why I'm waiting here. Are you going to make it worth my while? Will you finally come out and tell me today? How much longer do I need to wait, for God's sake?

It was not to be.

"Ah, Lieutenant Reiko, found you at last!"

Oh shit!

"Good night," she said.

She didn't look around but pushed past Kikuta and headed for the ticket gate.

His broad shoulders seemed to be shaking. *Real men don't cry*, she thought to herself, *but maybe red-faced guardian deities shed man-tears now and again.*

"Hey, Lieutenant Reiko!"

The voice rang out again behind her. That man was the bane of her life!

"Kaz Kikuta, my man! What are you doing here . . . with her?"

There was a thump, then a yelp.

She got on the escalator and went up to the platform without looking back.

It was a little after midnight when she finally made it to her parents' home. The hallway was dark, but the light in the living room was still on.

"Hi, it's me."

She dumped her bag, bulging with a change of clothes, in the hall, and stuck her head into the living room. Her father was sitting on the sofa.

"Oh, hi there," he said, swiveling around to face her. "You should have called. I could have picked you up."

"No problem, Dad. Our meeting ended earlier than normal today, so I thought, why not pop home? It was very spur of the moment. Where's Mom? Asleep already?"

"Yeah, she went upstairs a while ago."

Reiko's mother had had heart trouble in the summer. She'd given up staying up late.

"Had dinner?"

"I had a snack earlier."

She noticed that her father was enjoying a nightcap with his late-night TV.

You're drinking, Dad. You could hardly have come and gotten me in the car.

"So you've not eaten properly?"

"I had fried chicken and a rice ball."

"That all? Let me rustle up something."

"I'm fine. Anyway, eating late makes you fat."

Oh yeah? Then how come you're happy to stay out late in bars all the time, Reiko?

"If you say so, darling. Got the day off tomorrow?"

"Nah, it's too soon for that. Maybe another week."

Her father looked concerned.

"Look here, Miss Lieutenant, we don't want you overdoing things."

Her father was a regular working stiff with a regular office job. He'd probably never even heard the word *lieutenant* till Reiko got promoted.

"Okay for me to do some laundry?"

"It's too late now. Dump it by the machine and Mom'll deal with it tomorrow."

"How's she doing?"

"Not so bad. Pretty good, actually."

"You're sure?"

Reiko peered briefly up the darkened staircase. When she looked back into the living room, her father had returned his attention to the television.

He was wearing a navy blue dressing gown. Reiko always found the sight of her dad's rounded shoulders in a dressing gown oddly comforting.

No, *always* wasn't the right word. She wasn't thinking about her childhood. She was thinking of something that had happened almost exactly twelve years ago. It was a winter's night back when Reiko was starting to put her life back together after having been assaulted.

It was late. Reiko, unable to sleep, had come downstairs only to find the kitchen light on. She'd assumed that someone had forgotten to switch the thing off, and then she noticed someone in the room. She realized it was her father just in time not to shriek.

He was wearing a dressing gown, and he was squatting in front of the sink.

Through her surprise, Reiko had realized that her father was staring at a carving knife that he was holding with both hands. He was gazing intently at the light glinting off the blade as though he could see through it

338

to something else on the other side.

Some time passed. Then he lifted the knife above his head and held it there. His rounded shoulders quivered. Was Dad crying?

"Reiko . . . I'm sorry . . . I . . . I just can't."

For a moment, she'd thought he was talking to her. Then she realized he was talking to himself.

And that was when she had realized what was going on.

Her father was fantasizing about killing her assailant. He was trying, if only in his imagination, to kill the man who'd raped his daughter.

It was something he'd never be able to do in real life.

And it was something he couldn't do in his imagination either.

Daddy!

She had felt an overwhelming urge to throw herself on those convulsing shoulders and hug him tight.

Her dad—who wanted to avenge her. Her dad—who couldn't hurt a fly, even in his imagination.

"Daddy?"

She had only spoken in a whisper, but her father leaped to his feet, his face turned to one side.

"Oh . . . uh . . . I'd no idea you were up."

His voice had trembled as he hid the knife by dumping it in the sink.

"What's wrong, darling? Can't you sleep?"

"No, I'm fine," she had said, anxious not to upset him further.

"You should hurry back to bed."

"I guess," she had murmured.

She hadn't been able to bring herself to leave him alone down there. She wasn't sure why, but she desperately wanted him to know how she felt about him at that moment.

He had let out a long, drawn-out sigh. He didn't want her to know he'd been crying. Reiko knew she'd seen a side of him she wasn't supposed to see. It only made her love him more.

"Daddy."

"Yes."

"Thanks for that."

Her father hadn't replied that night.

"Oh gosh!"

Reiko snapped back to the present at her father's exclamation.

"What is it, Dad?"

"I just remembered that we've got some cream puffs in the refrigerator. Mom told me on her way up to bed."

You've got to be kidding me, thought Reiko. Tempting though it was, no way was she going to have a cream puff this late at night.

"I told you, Dad, I'm fine. A quick bath and then I'm going straight to bed."

"Oh well, suit yourself," murmured her father, picking up his whiskey glass and turning back to the TV.

Reiko thought she'd try him.

"Hey, Dad?"

"Yeah?"

"Thanks for that."

"Thanks? Thanks for what?"

He hadn't picked up on her reference.

"Oh, nothing."

She went upstairs to get changed.

When she came back downstairs to take a bath, her father was no longer in the living room.

PART
FIVE

1

I knew that the father of the girl Kosuke was going out with had died in a fall at one of Kinoshita Construction's building sites. My work buddies told me all about it. Apparently, Kosuke had been asking them about the dead man—the guy's name was Noboru Nakagawa—and trying to get contact details for his surviving family.

Still, I made out like I had no idea what was going on.

Wanting to treat Kosuke like an adult was only half the story. I also felt kind of hobbled by my position: I was *like* a father to him, sure, but I wasn't his real dad.

I was also plain thrilled that my Kosuke had got himself a girlfriend. Maybe he'd get hitched any day now. I was over the moon just thinking about it.

I wondered what sort of girl Michiko Nakagawa was. I'd only seen her in the diner where she worked as a waitress. What the hell, I thought—if Kosuke likes her, she can't be bad.

Her background and experience were similar enough to his: she knew the value of money and the importance of family. Kosuke wouldn't have time for anyone who didn't have basic values of that kind.

I knew that Kosuke was taking the place of my own son, who'd effectively died at the age of five. That was my problem, not his. That was why I made up my mind not to say anything to him about the girl's father. Maybe I was just being selfish, clinging to the joy I felt in watching the boy grow up.

Kosuke looked happier with every passing day. It was like his life was finally getting going and he could feel it in every nerve of his body. I was a wee bit jealous, but mostly I was excited. I wanted to do whatever I could to help him.

That evening, when work was over and done with, Kosuke helped me put all the gear back in place on the garage shelves, said a hasty good night, and hurried back to his place. It was raining, but somehow the drizzle seemed to land everywhere but on my boy.

I grinned ruefully to myself. Heck, I'd be lying if I said that I wasn't upset by the boy's eagerness to get away. But that's the way it goes: parents have to accept that the kids will eventually fly the nest.

I pulled down the garage's metal gate and went back to my place. I'd been living alone so long now, I could hardly remember when coming back to an empty house made me feel lonely.

I stuck the key into the rickety doorknob, pulled open the door, and switched on the light. In the living room, I picked up the remote control on the table and switched on the heater unit—the only piece of modern technology in the whole apartment.

I followed the same routine every winter night. I'd do a bit of house cleaning, perhaps a load of laundry, and prepare my dinner—which meant defrosting something I'd made earlier—while I was waiting for the bath to fill up. Then it was time for a nice long soak in the tub to wash away the cold and the weariness. Touch wood, my body's still holding together. I don't know how much longer I can keep working, but when my body goes, it'll be game over for me.

When I got out of the bath, I usually opened a beer to have with my dinner. On the menu tonight was vegetable stew cooked how my old lady used to make it. A big-screen TV was my only dinner companion. I watched a report about a scandal in the police force and a variety show with a bunch of TV personalities horsing around. I was enjoying myself until some news came on about a big pile-up on an expressway somewhere. I couldn't bear to watch, and I changed the channel. That was when I remembered something.

I'd been cutting up some lumber with a circular saw earlier that afternoon. Work was winding down for the day, and I must've gotten sloppy. With a saw, it's important to stand close and put your whole body weight behind the thing. I had wanted to cut this piece from a little further away, and I just swiveled and stretched in close. It was the sort of mistake I'd never make normally, but, like I said, it was late and I was tired—or maybe I was just getting old.

Anyway, the electric cord snagged, and the saw blade went through it like butter.

The saw gave a sad sigh. The blade stopped rotating, and the cord plopped to the ground.

I swore.

"You're an amateur, boss," laughed Kosuke. "You don't know what you're doing."

"Shut it, kid. Get the handsaw and deal with the last three pieces of wood yourself."

I needed to repair the saw. Tomorrow morning would have been fine, but now that I'd remembered the thing, I couldn't get it out of my head.

It was nine o'clock when I slipped a sweater over my tracksuit and headed over to the garage. It was still raining a little, but the garage was close enough that I didn't need to bother with an umbrella.

The garage was bigger than necessary for a minivan, but after I put in the shelves around the walls, the space became quite tight. I had to drive the van out into the road just to open the hatch.

I parked the van outside to free up space for my repair work. If any of the other garage owners came back, it would be easy to move it and let them in.

I grabbed the circular saw and its broken length of cord from the back of the van. I also grabbed an extension cord and a tool belt with a cutter knife, a tape measure, a hammer, and other stuff in it.

I went back into the garage, switched on the lightbulb,

and squatted down in the middle of the empty garage floor.

The first thing I needed to do was to strip the broken cord. Five centimeters should be long enough, I reckoned. I carefully sliced around the black rubber insulation covering the wires and slid it off.

Now I had two smaller wires sticking out, one red and one green. I repeated the process for them, cutting through the colored rubber and sliding it off. The metal electric wire splayed out like little tufts of blond hair.

I did the same for the other end of the broken cord, then I reconnected the wires, the red to the red, and the green to the green. I had some green insulation tape in my tool pouch. I cut a couple of lengths of it and wound it around the bare wires to stop the different ones touching and causing a short circuit.

Then I grabbed the extension cord and plugged it into a wall socket along the back wall. After plugging it into the outlet, I then plugged in the repaired saw cord.

I was just about to turn on the saw to see if my repair had done the trick, when I heard a voice.

"Yo!"

He was a dark silhouette framed in the open garage doorway. The trademark long coat was soaked through and sticking to his body.

"What the hell happened to you? What are you doing here this time of night?"

It was Tobe. Out of the blue. The guy never came to my part of town. Wait, that's not quite true; he'd dropped in a couple of times when I first moved here, but not once in all the years since.

"Oh, nothing special, Mr. Ta-ka-ok-a."

I looked at Tobe more closely. His face was spattered with mud. He looked like he'd crawled around to see me as some sort of stupid practical joke.

I smiled at him in an effort at being friendly.

"Don't think the look does a lot for your sex god persona," I said.

"I'm not in the mood for your dumbass jokes," Tobe shouted, launching a kick at the shelves on the side of the garage.

A square of laminate slid down the space between the shelf and the back wall, making a warbling sound as it flexed and settled that would have been comical at any other time. A can of glue toppled off the top shelf and crashed down onto the cement floor. So did the metal pole-hook for opening and closing the shutter of the garage.

"Sorry, Takaoka. Didn't realize it was serious. . . ."

Tobe bent down and picked up the pole-hook, then turned to look at the shutter box above his head.

"That fellow you work with, the kid . . . he's the son of Tadaharu Mishima, the guy I . . . uh . . . *dealt* with."

Fear rushed into every cell of my body. I broke out into goose bumps. I felt like I was about to physically burst.

Tobe thrust the pole-hook into the loop on the roller shutter and yanked violently. The shutter unrolled, hitting the concrete of the floor with an almighty crashing sound. The interior of the garage was cut off from the outside world.

Tobe unhooked the pole-hook from the door but didn't put it down.

"I had no fucking idea. All this time, you've been lying to me."

Something sliced through the air right by my ear. Pain exploded in my shoulder.

I groaned.

I couldn't have avoided the blow even if I'd known it was coming. I crashed down, face forward. My shoulder blade was burning.

"What the hell were you thinking, Takaoka, doing something like that? Have you forgotten the shit you pulled yourself?"

Tobe was raining blows on my back. It was excruciating. Moaning, I rolled onto my side in an effort to protect myself.

"You stole the family register of a dead man. You faked your own death. You arranged for your sister to get a nice fat insurance payout. But who set the whole gig up for you? Who got your sister on board? Huh? Who?"

He whacked me. On the hip this time.

"What are you up to now? Training the son of one of our debt-ridden jumpers to become a carpenter? What the fuck is that about? Don't try and tell me that you're doing it out of the kindness of your heart. Kindness is not what you're about, my friend."

The pole-hook came down on my thigh. Agony all the way down to my knee.

"You want to do *anything*, you get my permission first, okay! You're a fucking ghost, my friend. You died, and I, Makio Tobe, I brought you back to life again. You're the walking dead, my pet fucking zombie. Looking after people, caring for people—normal shit like that is a complete no-no for you, pal."

He hit me again. And again. And again. My whole right side was numb from the pain. It was like it just wasn't there anymore.

"And you know about that Noboru Nakagawa guy. Another loser who did the high dive for us. His daughter—"

My mind suddenly snapped back into focus.

Noboru Nakagawa's daughter.

"I paid for her. That makes her *my* bitch, see. Straight outta high school, that is one fresh little piece of pussy."

Tobe made an obscene pumping motion with his crotch. There was a smirk on his mud-spattered face.

"I've been getting my money's worth out of the girl, believe me, I have. Then tonight, that dipshit Mishima boy, your precious protégé, shows up out of nowhere and he's like, 'The bitch is mine, brother. Move over.' Think I enjoyed that?"

Another blow on my shoulders. Pain drowning in a sea of numbness.

"Two little lovebirds and their match made in high-dive heaven! Don't fucking make me laugh. I made a woman of the Nakagawa girl. I fixed her up with a place to live. She's mine—one hundred goddamn percent. That pissant kid's got no business fucking her or lecturing me with his high-and-mighty bullshit. You're gonna tell that kid to get the fuck out of my face. Okay, Mr. Ta-ka-o-ka?"

Tobe was now stomping on my arms. I checked. I could still move my hands. So no broken bones . . . yet.

"You don't help, then I'll unleash some crazy shit your way. I've still got all of Mishima's and Nakagawa's IOUs. *I* say their debts are paid, then their debts are paid. *I* say their debts are outstanding, then, hey, presto, their debts come magically back again. You get that? If the girl doesn't fall into line, I'll send her to a soapy massage parlor and the cunt can screw herself to death there. And what about your dear sister's restaurant? You want me to send some of my yakuza buddies over to frighten off her regulars? Then there's your kid in the hospital. Want me to drop by and fuck with his life-support machine? Pull a few tubes out of the wall? Huh? Which way you want to play this? Yours or mine? It's up to you, fuckbrain."

I'd dreamed about life without Makio Tobe in it before that day. Back when I started my new life as Kenichi Takaoka. Back when I met Kosuke and started to love the boy. And the more I loved Kosuke, the more I hated Tobe. The more I wanted him out of my life.

Every time he showed up on a building site where I was working, I'd fantasize about his death.

I hope you get cancer. I hope you get hit by a car. I hope one of your slut girlfriends stabs you to death. I hope your yakuza pals beat the shit out of you, stick you in a drum full of concrete, and shove you into Tokyo Bay. Anything—just so long as I never have to see you again.

But today was the first time I realized that I could do the job myself.

"Hey, get the fuck off me."

I'm gonna get this bastard out of my life.

"You weigh a fucking ton. That hurts. Hey! *Hey!*"

I want him dead, so Kosuke can be free.

"Enough. This ain't funny no more. Let me go."

Kosuke and the girl.

Tobe screamed.

Now they *can escape from the cycle of misery and poverty and* I *can bring this fucked-up life of mine to an end.*

2

Reiko was still in her room at her parents' house when her cell phone rang early the next morning. It was her pal Kunioku, from the medical examiner's office.

"Hiya, sweetie. That thing you asked me to take a look at? I've got one or two ideas. How's about you take me out to lunch?"

"Sure. What are you in the mood for?"

"Eel and rice at Owada's would hit the spot."

Typical, choosing the most expensive seasonal delicacy. Still, needs must. . . .

"Great. I'll head your way straight after the morning meeting."

"Looking forward to it."

Reiko crammed a few articles of clothing into her bag, strapped on a new watch, and set out for Kamata.

The task force meeting got under way. She told Officer Yuda that she had something to take care of and would need him to handle surveillance on Michiko Nakagawa for her, then left the station with Ioka in her wake.

Ioka asked if what they were doing had anything to do with the case file Reiko had mailed out the day before.

"That's right," said Reiko. "We're going to the Tokyo Medical Examiner's Office in Otsuka. I hope Kunioku's got something good for us."

She had a hunch that things were about to get interesting.

At reception, Reiko was informed that Kunioku was waiting for them in the meeting room on the second floor.

"Morning?"

Reiko peered into the room and saw Kunioku: he was catching forty winks in a seat over by the window.

"Good morning, Doctor," she repeated, rapping her knuckles briskly on the door a couple of times. Looking rather bilious, Kunioku opened his eyes.

"Oh, it's you."

"Sleeping on the job?"

"Outrageous!" Kunioku growled, his voice congested with phlegm. "I've just come off the night shift and was sitting by the window awaiting a glimpse of my girlfriend."

Kunioku's glasses had slid down his nose. He pushed them back into place.

"Who's the anthropoid with the funky bone structure?"

Reiko had to stifle a laugh. Ioka replied as if Kunioku had said nothing out of the ordinary.

"I am Hiromitsu Ioka, Major Crime Squad, Kamata Precinct CID. Lieutenant Reiko and I—"

"Forget about him," interrupted Reiko. "He's a nobody."

Ioka winced.

"Why, my dear, do you insist on surrounding yourself with underevolved specimens of the male of the species?"

Kunioku referred to Kikuta as Reiko's "pet gorilla," a nickname that grated, given Reiko's feelings for the man.

What species are you then, doc?

With his unruly tufts of gray hair and his sunken face like a wizened sweet potato, Kunioku looked fairly prehistoric himself. He hadn't yet hit retirement age, so he had to be less than sixty-five—but he looked well past seventy.

Kunioku insisted on telling everyone he met that Reiko was his "girlfriend." No one seemed to take him seriously. It nonetheless made things awkward for Reiko: she couldn't very well humiliate him and make a scene by contradicting him in public. Still, being cast in that role was humiliating for *her* too. The only solution was to plaster a forced smile on her face.

"Since you're making me take you for eel at Owada's, you must have something important to tell me."

Kunioku was sitting at one corner of the table. Reiko sat opposite him, and Ioka pulled out a chair to sit beside her.

"Hey, chimp, don't crowd my girlfriend! I need two empty seats between you and her."

Ioka wasn't going to be a pushover.

"Can't you compromise on one, Mr. Director?"

"I'm not the director here. I'm just chief medical examiner."

"And a man of great modesty, obviously."

Kunioku snorted and lapsed into silence. Reiko, who knew the doctor well, had the impression he'd taken a shine to Ioka.

"That's enough monkey business, Doctor. Tell us what you learned from the file."

"Being ordered around by a beautiful woman is one of life's greatest pleasures," he chuckled, leafing through his papers with his wrinkled hands.

"Let's see what we've got here . . . ah, yes. Now, while I have, of course, nothing but the greatest respect for the talents of Dr. Umehara, the pathologist at Tomei University Hospital's forensic medicine department—"

"Can we skip all the niceties, Doctor?"

"Very well," Kunioku said. "I read the report and looked at the photographs. I found nothing to disagree with in my colleague's findings. There are no visible external wounds on the torso or any damage to the internal organs such as could have caused death. The report is accurate . . . so far as it goes."

This sort of pussyfooting around must be part of doctors' professional etiquette. . . .

"It is regrettable, however, that the report fails to offer any explanation of this gouged-out semicircle of epidermis on the left of the pharynx."

Exactly!

"I was wondering about that too," she said.

"You're very observant, my dear. So much so that I'm

prepared to use my influence to help you on the path to promotion. You'd make a wonderful Special Assistant to the Director of the Ministry of Justice."

"Thanks, but no thanks. Staring at dead bodies day in, day out, isn't really my bag. What I like is working cases out in the field. Anyway, now's not the time. What's your theory about that gouged-out patch?"

Kunioku ran his finger thoughtfully over the neck in the photograph.

"Take a good look. It's a semicircle, a perfect arc. Don't you think that's strange?"

"Absolutely. It's like it was drawn with a compass."

"Nicely put. I believe that this semicircle here was actually part of a complete circle, which was sliced in half when the head was cut off."

"You mean that if we could locate the head, we'd find a matching semicircle of missing flesh on the upper part of the neck too?"

"Precisely. I believe that a circular stimulus was applied to the neck. Like to hazard a guess what it was, sweetheart?"

A circular stimulus? A stimulus that gouges out a circular hole in the skin?

"The body's been in the river for over ten days. That's why the actual damaged skin has dissolved. Still, we're looking for an external stimulus that causes circular blistering of the skin. I believe this stimulus was also the direct cause of death. Got any ideas?"

Gouging of the epidermis was a fairly standard

physiological reaction. All sorts of external stimuli could cause it. Something as straightforward as a blow from a blunt object or a gash from a sharp one could tear the skin off in a similar way. It was the fact that the wound was a perfect circle that was so extraordinary.

"Ready to give up, sweetheart?"

"What do I forfeit if I admit defeat?"

"I get to upgrade from the second-most expensive eel dish to the most expensive one."

"Give me a couple more minutes then."

A gouged-out patch of skin . . . a stimulus that causes circular epidermal exfoliation . . .

Heating a small saucepan—a milk pan, say—and pressing it to the skin would probably cause a burn that would peel off in a neat circle. It was hardly enough to kill anyone, though.

"What about *my* lunch?" blurted out Ioka.

Reiko's mind was on other things, and the question didn't register immediately.

"Huh? You?" she retorted eventually. "You damn well pay for yourself."

Circular epidermal exfoliation . . .

"Need a clue?"

"Not if I have to fork out for the most expensive lunch to get it."

"Don't worry. I'm a nice guy, so just this once, I'll accept the second-best lunch."

"Don't know why you think the standard menu isn't good enough for you."

"Don't try to nickel-and-dime me! The standard menu comes with miso soup; I prefer clear suimono soup."

"Oh, all right. Give me my first clue."

Kunioku adjusted his glasses on his nose.

"The circular epidermal exfoliation is *not* the direct result of an external stimulus. What do I mean by that? I mean that the actual weapon used wasn't circular in shape. Something was done to the victim; the circular lesion was a secondary effect of that."

So I'm looking for an external stimulus that causes circular epidermal exfoliation as a secondary effect. . . .

The burn idea seemed like a good one. Kunioku, though, had been very specific about the weapon itself not being circular. Reiko needed to get that shape out of her mind.

An external stimulus—a weapon—whose effect on the body has no relation to its own shape. . . .

"I've got it," she exclaimed. "Electrocution."

"Is that your best guess?"

"Yes. With electrocution victims, there's no internal damage, just like this case. The circular epidermal exfoliation is what's left of an electric mark."

"Bravo, my dear," said Kunioku.

"Hang on a minute," interrupted Ioka. "Was there a high enough current at the crime scene to cause actual death?"

Kunioku gave Reiko a look: "Go on, justify your theory."

"All right, Ioka. The standard domestic voltage here in Japan is one hundred volts. That's quite enough to kill someone—*provided the conditions are right*. In this case, the point of entry for the electricity was the pharynx, close to the carotid artery. Skin resistance to electric current in this part of the body is extremely low. The circular burn on the neck is what is called an electric mark or a Joule burn. In most cases of electric shock, electric marks are often the only visible sign of injury.

"The next thing is the current," she went on. "Now, your typical household electric current is certainly not high. Paradoxically, though, that can be more dangerous. The heart is a tangled mass of muscle fibers called myocardial fibers. As with any other muscle, not all the fibers in the heart are aligned in the same direction. When you apply a standard household electrical current to the body, it flows down the myocardial fibers pointing in one direction, but not down those pointing in the other. What do you think the result is?"

Ioka meekly shook his head.

"Ventricular fibrillation. Unable to beat at a fixed rhythm, the heart muscles start to twitch erratically rather than pump blood. When the current is high, the heart gets a single, massive shock, but it can recover—provided the shock doesn't last long. That's why plenty of people who get electrocuted live to tell the tale. If ventricular fibrillation takes place—remember, that's what an ordinary household current causes—it's almost impossible for the heart to resume normal function. Some parts of the heart are moving and other parts are paralyzed, so the heart stops working as a pump. When the blood's no longer being pumped around the body, death happens in a matter of minutes."

"Superb. Ten out of ten."

"Thank you. You've been a wonderful audience."

But speechifying had made Reiko aware of something. It was that vague sense of unease that the sight of the torso had given her. She realized now that it had nothing to do with the riddle of how the man had been killed. She had successfully pinpointed the cause of death, but the gray fog shrouding her mind showed no sign of lifting.

What's bugging me?

"Help me with something, Doctor. I'm not sure how to put this . . . Killing someone by pressing into them an electrode that would cause such a large electric mark is hardly an easy way to commit murder. In physical and technical terms, I mean."

Kunioku's brow wrinkled in thought.

"I think there's only one commonsense explanation possible. The murderer straddled the victim; he was holding an exposed electrode that was plugged into a power source in his right hand; he pressed this electrode for thirty seconds, maybe more, to the victim's throat. Depending on whether the skin was wet or dry, the effect varies. When the skin's wet, death occurs faster."

No, that's not what's bugging me, dammit.

Beside her, Ioka groaned. Was he a psychic, feeling her pain?

"So you think the murder took place in the garage?" Ioka said.

That's another issue we need to sort out.

"I think the flow of events justify our making that assumption," Reiko replied.

"There was a power outlet in there."

"What about an exposed electrode?"

Hang on a moment!

"Now that you mention it. . . ."

Reiko pulled the investigation file out of her bag and started flipping through it.

"What are you looking for?"

"Be patient."

It was something they'd found in the garage.

"There was an exposed electrode. See this electric saw here? See how the cord's been repaired halfway along? What if it was still broken when the crime took place, with no insulation tape on it?"

Kunioku peered at the photograph.

"Then we'd have our exposed electrode."

No, that's not it. That's not what's bugging me either. It's something about the torso itself.

Turning her attention back to the photograph of the body, Reiko stared at it intently.

This is what's left of the body of Kenichi Takaoka—electrocuted, chopped up, and thrown into the river. The body of Kenichi Takaoka—cut into pieces and dumped in the river, with one hand left in the van. This is his torso. Kenichi Takaoka's torso.

The three words went round and round in her head like a mantra.

"Lieutenant Reiko, are you all right?"

Kenichi Takaoka's torso.

Kenichi Takaoka's torso.

Kenichi Takaoka's torso.

"Sweetheart!"

"Lieutenant, hello? Can you hear me?"

That's it! There, on the right of the abdomen, just below the chest, a scar. Looks like it could be from gallbladder surgery.

"Lieutenant? Hello?"

"Hey, sweetheart, we're talking to you."

He's got a surgical scar. A surgical scar.

"Are you listening to us?"

"Lieutenant, I love you," crowed Ioka.

A surgical scar on Takaoka's torso? That doesn't make sense.

"It's hopeless. She's not hearing a word we're saying."

"Lieutenant, do you mind if I touch your titties . . . like so?"

Ioka, you filthy worm!

There was a crunch as Reiko's hand plowed into Ioka's nose.

Bizarrely, that was also the moment she found what she'd been groping after all this time. She felt as though a gust of fresh air had blown through her mind.

That's it! I remember now. The autopsy report mentioned scarring from surgery. But it doesn't make sense.

"I can't believe you did that," Ioka was whimpering. "That really hurt."

"The old backhand chop," said Kunioku, chortling

merrily. "You got the good old backhand chop. Serves you right."

That's what's been bugging me all this time. It was weird how the report mentioned the cholecystitis—but absolutely nothing else.

The gray mist evaporated. Her mind was clear now.

"Hey, monkey man, your nose is bleeding."

"Funny thing is, doc, I'm kind of enjoying it."

She now knew exactly what mystery she needed to solve: the torso in the river wasn't Kenichi Takaoka's after all.

Reiko snatched her cell phone out of her pocket.

"Ah," Kunioku exclaimed. "She's back in the land of the living."

"Sure looks like it," said Ioka.

Reiko was calling Hayama.

"Hi, Nori. It's me."

"Hi, boss. What's up?"

Out of the corner of her eye, Reiko noticed that Ioka was clutching his nose and that his eyes were wet with tears. What was wrong with him now?

"Which precinct was it that handled Kazutoshi Naito's car crash?"

"Kawaguchi in Saitama."

"Who went there to collect Naito's fingerprints from the accident report? Was it you?"

"It was Sergeant Ishikura."

Of course it was. Of course. Of course.

"Oh, right. What are you up to right now, Nori?"

"Same old, same old. Keeping an eye on Kimie Naito."

"Ask your precinct partner to handle that by himself, or call the case coordinator and get them to send out a replacement team. I want you to find Ishikura and go with him to Kawaguchi Precinct. The fact is . . ."

Hayama seemed to grasp the meaning of what Reiko was asking him to do almost before the words were out of her mouth.

3

Kusaka paid another visit to the offices of Kinoshita Construction.

"Do you know anything about the sort of places Tobe hangs out in?"

Kinoshita, the CEO, tilted his head to one side, a puzzled expression on his face.

"I think Tobe has a live-in girlfriend. She might know."

"Yes he does. We arrested her yesterday for the possession and use of amphetamines."

Kinoshita looked shocked.

"Amphetamines? That's not good."

"What about women *apart* from Tobe's girlfriend? Can you think of any?"

"Other women?" repeated Kinoshita in a pensive voice. After a brief pause, he gave Kusaka the names of several insurance saleswomen, but none of them were new to Kusaka.

"What I'm after are women who work in bars and hostess clubs—those sorts of places."

"Tobe once took me to a club in Shinjuku called Rose, if that's any help."

Kusaka had already been there.

"How about other people—friends, business associates? Or how about a lawyer? Tobe may not have a criminal record, but he must have been on the verge of criminality from time to time."

"A lawyer? I'm afraid I don't know of one."

In the end, Kusaka got no new information from his visit to Kinoshita Construction that morning.

After lunch, Kusaka returned to Kamata Police Station and dropped in on the Organized Crime Squad. Lieutenant Makihara had just got back to his desk after interrogating Mikako Kobayashi.

"How did it go?"

Makihara made a sour face.

"She works in a bar in Shibuya and claims to have bought the drugs nearby. Before I take things any further, I'm going to have to contact Shibuya Precinct. If we move independently on this, they'll have our balls. The people at Meguro Precinct are already bellyaching about us arresting the Kobayashi woman on their patch. They're trying to make out that we muscled in on a case of theirs. . . . It's complete bullshit. If they were onto the woman, they wouldn't have to keep asking me what the broad's address is. They're just kicking up a great big stink over nothing."

Kusaka did his best to crank out a sympathetic smile.

"Would it be okay if I had a quick word with her?"

"Yeah, sure, be my guest. You'll need her to consent to it too."

"Of course. Thanks."

Kusaka went up to the task force room on the sixth floor and completed all the necessary paperwork. Then he went back down to the second floor where the holding cells were.

In Japanese police hierarchy, there was a clear separation between the divisions like Homicide, CID, and Organized Crime, which conducted investigations, and the Administrative Division, which managed the holding cells. Split responsibility was intended as a safeguard to prevent detectives from violating the rights of people in custody.

In the office, Kusaka showed his forms to the senior officer in charge of the cells.

"You will be interviewing Ms. Kobayashi on a voluntary basis, I presume?" he inquired, eying Kusaka sternly.

"That's right. On a purely voluntary basis."

"Follow me. She's this way."

The officer led Kusaka down to the end of the passage where there was a bathroom and, just opposite, the special holding area for women. The guard seated just inside the door examined Kusaka's paperwork, then passed it in to Mikako Kobayashi in her cell.

"This is a request for a voluntary questioning," the guard explained. "That means you're free to withhold your cooperation. What do you want to do?"

Through the steel bars and reinforced Perspex, Mikako eyed Kusaka and the guard dubiously.

"Will you be questioning me this afternoon, Lieutenant Kusaka?"

Kusaka had flashed his ID at Mikako before they began their search of Tobe's apartment. He'd never expected her to remember his name. Perhaps it was a side effect of her profession: keeping track of customers' names and jobs was part of a hostess's skill set.

"Yes. As the guard mentioned, it's not a formal interview. It's a voluntary questioning, so you have the right to say no."

"What do you want to talk to me about?"

"About Makio Tobe."

"I don't believe it," she snorted contemptuously. "You're going to try and drag him into this mess now too."

Kusaka smiled wanly and shrugged his shoulders.

"Can you get me a nice deep-fried pork cutlet on rice?" she said, making beseeching eyes at him.

"I'm sorry. That's against the rules. You can order in food only if you pay for it yourself."

Kusaka knew that playing along with her could be risky. He'd expose himself to accusations of having traded favors for false testimony.

"How about a pack of smokes, then?"

"I can probably give you a couple of cigarettes."

The woman's face brightened.

The guard shot a disapproving look Kusaka's way.

Kusaka ignored him. A cigarette or two was hardly the end of the world.

"All right, I'll talk to you," Mikako said. "It's not fair, anyway—me banged up in this shithole while he's free as a bird."

The guard jerked his chin at her.

"Good. Stand back, please. I'm going to unlock the door."

Mikako obediently stepped away from the door, yawning and stretching as she did so.

Kusaka led the woman upstairs to an interview room on the third floor. He poured her a cup of tea and pushed an aluminum ashtray and his own pack of cigarettes across the table.

"You got any menthol ones?"

Kusaka shot an inquiring look over his shoulder at Sergeant Satomura. Satomura shook his head.

"I'm sorry. That's all there is."

With a sigh, Mikako picked up the pack. She stuck a cigarette between her lips, and Kusaka lit it for her with Satomura's lighter.

Mikako inhaled deeply, held the smoke in her lungs for a while to get the full taste, then slowly breathed it out. She seemed to be enjoying it so much that Kusaka felt like lighting one up himself.

"Ironic, isn't it? A hostess like me gets banged up, and what's the first thing that happens? Suddenly men are lighting my cigarettes instead of the other way around."

"Very funny."

Mikako took another drag on her cigarette, then flicked the ash into the ashtray, which rattled on the tabletop. Kusaka noticed that the woman's nails were still nicely painted.

"Let's talk about Tobe," Kusaka began. "You don't know where he's got to?"

She jerked her chin emphatically to one side.

"I told the detective I spoke to earlier where I thought he could be. Did you check those places out?"

"We did. All of them."

Kusaka held up his hand, and Satomura, who was sitting a short distance behind him, pulled a sheet of paper from a file and passed it to him over his shoulder.

"Can you think of any places not on the list you gave us earlier? How about a movie theater he liked to go to when he had time to kill?"

"Oh sure, Tobe the movie buff," the woman sneered. "Give me a break! He'd never actually *go* anywhere to see a movie, not even a damn porno flick. Guy's only interested in cum shots anyway."

"What about bars where he's a regular? Love hotels maybe, that sort of thing?"

"Well, he sure as shit hasn't taken *me* to any love hotels lately! Back in the day, when we still had the hots for each other, we always did it at his place. I may not look it, but I'm a pretty mean cook. I think that's why he liked me in the first place. I cook him a meal or two, and then he's all like, 'Move in with me. Let's live together.' What a joke! I was all for it at the time, though. I was thinking, you know, 'Maybe he's the one.' That phase didn't last much over three months."

Kusaka remembered that she had been living with Tobe for two years.

"What about interests, hobbies, things like that? He could have made friends that way."

Mikako tilted her head to one side. Although she wasn't a beauty, Kusaka could see that she had sex appeal. She'd probably look quite glamorous when she was all made up.

"He used to be into tropical fish."

"How come we didn't see any in the apartment?"

"Because they died. I didn't look after them right. Tobe went through the roof. I stood my ground, though. I was like, 'Hey, if you love your stupid fishy-wishies so darn much, why don't *you* take care of them, asshole.' He stormed out of the house, and since then—no more tropical fish."

"Know any tropical fish stores he used to go?"

"There was one near Yutenji Station, but it closed down."

"Was he friends with the owner?"

"After all the fish he bought there died? Not likely."

The more Kusaka learned about Makio Tobe, the more he felt he was dealing with a man who specialized in screwing up all his relationships.

"Doesn't he have any friends?"

"Not really. The guys in the gang wanted nothing to

do with him. How about the girlfriend angle? Did you investigate that?"

Kusaka nodded.

Mikako had smoked her cigarette down to the filter. She stubbed it out in the ashtray.

"He went through this phase of going to bet on motorboat races. I don't think you make real friends in places like that."

"You never know."

"Well, I can't think of anyone. Hang on. I remember there was this guy called Yoshiro—at least, I *think* it was Yoshiro—he was friends with for a while. I've no idea who this Yoshiro is, where he lives, anything."

That wasn't much help.

"Can I have another cigarette?"

"Help yourself."

Mikako lit a second cigarette. It didn't seem to give her quite as much pleasure as its predecessor. She looked rather fed up as she puffed out the smoke.

"I'm trying to come up with something. I feel bad that I'm being no help."

"That's not true at all."

"All I've done is bummed a couple of cigarettes."

"If you're feeling guilty, the best thing you can do is talk to us some more. We're interested in everything you have to say."

Mikako crossed her arms and looked pensively up at the ceiling, the cigarette clamped between her lips.

"How about his glad rags?"

"His clothes?"

"Yeah. There's this shop in Shibuya he's crazy about. Kane, the place is called. It's a bit 'gangster,' but not too over the top. He's really into their stuff."

Kusaka gestured for Satomura to make a note. He didn't think it was a very promising lead.

"Anything else?"

"He's really careful about his health."

"That sounds intriguing. How do you mean?"

"Like, well, maybe it's just common sense, but he told me that when he screws other girls, he's always careful to use a skin. 'I've had my share of STDs,' he told me. 'Gonorrhea, chlamydia, you name it. It's no fucking fun. That's why I always rubber up before sticking it in.'"

"You know which hospital he goes to?"

"In Shibuya. Dogenzaka Central Clinic. I use it too now."

"Does Tobe have any medical conditions you know about?"

If he had some chronic ailment, there was always the chance he'd have had to drop into a hospital over the last couple of weeks.

"A preexisting medical condition? Don't think so."

"Does he take any drugs regularly?"

"Uh-uh. He's not into speed or dope, no."

"I'm talking about medicine, not illegal drugs."

"Whoops, sorry! He's a good sleeper, so he certainly

doesn't need sleeping pills. No problems down there either." She pointed toward her crotch. "'Won't be needing Viagra till I'm ninety,' he says. 'Your balls will have rotted and dropped off long before then,' I tell him."

Kusaka wasn't ready to buy into Mikako's image of her boyfriend as a paragon of healthy living.

"I heard that Tobe likes a drink. How's his liver?"

"Likes a drink? Tell me about it. His liver seems to be okay. Still, they call it the silent organ, don't they? Maybe it's gone to shit and he hasn't realized it yet. He has to take that annual health check through his company; so far he's always gotten a clean bill of health. That's what he told me, anyway."

"By 'company,' you mean Kinoshita Construction?"

"Yes. Everyone there takes a health check in the spring."

Kinoshita, the CEO, hadn't mentioned that.

Mikako's tea had gone cold, and she started drinking it. Her tongue was very sensitive, she explained, and she didn't like anything too hot.

"What's Tobe supposed to have done, Lieutenant?"

Kusaka didn't reply.

"Is it murder? It said Homicide on the ID you showed me yesterday. . . . Has Tobe killed someone?"

Kusaka was skeptical that telling Mikako the truth would elicit any useful information from her, but he wasn't getting anywhere, so why not give it a go?

"Tobe is suspected in the murder of a forty-three-year-old building contractor by the name of Kenichi Takaoka."

"A building contractor?"

The woman eyed him dubiously.

"Any ideas?"

"Me? Nope. None at all."

Just as he'd expected: a waste of time.

Mikako's eyes widened suddenly. She leaned over the table toward him.

"I just remembered something about Tobe's health. He told me that he'd had this big operation just before we met and the doctor had done a bang-up job on him."

"Any idea what the operation was for?"

"I don't know, but he had a scar around here."

Mikako jabbed a finger just below her right breast.

The lung? No, no. That's the gallbladder area.

Something that felt like a gust of icy air surged up from the soles of Kusaka's feet to the crown of his head.

A scar from a gallbladder operation?

Kusaka turned to Satomura.

"Have you got the photographs of the body?"

"Just a minute."

Satomura, visibly tense, flicked through the file until he came to the photographs. The one he slid out of its plastic pocket was the one where the scar was most visible.

Kusaka pushed the picture toward Mikako, using the cigarette packet to cover the arm stumps.

"Could you take a look at this for me?"

Mikako's face contorted with revulsion.

"What the hell is that?"

"This scar here. Have you seen it before?"

Located beneath the right breast, the scar was a little away from the belly, and as such its appearance had probably not changed that much in death. And although loss of blood could have changed the coloration of the scar, its shape would be more or less the same.

"What?" Mikako eventually stammered. "What is this?"

She was looking wildly around the room like a person stumbling through darkness. She was casting around for a rational explanation that could save her from her own dire imaginings.

"Do you recognize the scar?"

She gave a wordless, curt nod. Her face was a blank.

"You know who this is?"

She nodded again.

"Who is it? Who does the scar belong to?"

The tears welled up in her big almond eyes.

Kusaka wasn't expecting her to cry—least of all for a bum she'd fallen out of love with years ago.

"It's Tobe," she whispered. "Makio Tobe."

She pushed Kusaka's hand and the cigarette pack it was holding off the photograph and stared at it.

"Oh, my poor, poor darling," she wailed.

Kusaka got up.

"Satomura, take care of this."

"Yes, sir."

Kusaka left the room. He'd been brutal, but you can't make an omelet without breaking eggs.

The murder victim's Tobe, not Takaoka! I need to go back to square one. What did I do wrong? Where did the investigation go off track?

Too agitated to stand around waiting for the elevator, Kusaka charged headlong down the stairs.

4

A promise is a promise.

Reiko was at Owada's with Kunioku and Ioka. They'd all ordered broiled eel on rice. Before going in, Reiko had called Yuda to tell him that she wouldn't be taking over surveillance on Kimie Naito that afternoon either.

"You're sure we've got time for this?" Ioka asked, looking around the old-fashioned restaurant with its low tables and tatami-mat floor.

"Don't worry. We won't get the results of the second analysis for hours yet."

Reiko had called the crime lab at TMPD headquarters and ordered them to do a rerun of the DNA test. She knew that getting the okay from the top brass would be a hassle, so she'd made the decision without consulting them. There'd be plenty of time to explain things to them when she was back at the precinct.

Before calling the crime lab, Reiko had grilled Kunioku on the best way to conduct DNA tests. She'd relayed his advice to the lab technicians, instructing them to follow it to the letter.

"Guess you're right, boss," Ioka said.

Reiko consulted the Longines watch she'd bought on credit. It was still only 12:30.

"I called the lab about an hour ago. Whichever way you slice it, we won't hear from them till midevening."

Kunioku's face was wreathed in smiles as the lacquered box containing the rice and eel was placed in front of him.

"You don't mind me ordering the most expensive option after all?"

"Not at all. Your input was extremely valuable."

"What about me, Lieutenant?"

Why are men so damn needy? Always me, me, me.

"You? What've you done to deserve it?"

She and Ioka had the cheapest of the three lunch menus. It came with miso soup—quite good enough, in Reiko's opinion.

"The doctor's soup's got whitebait in it."

"Well, ours has mitsuba leaf. It looks fantastic."

Reiko wasn't really in the mood for leisurely gourmandizing. She wanted to scarf her lunch and get the hell out of there.

"*Bon appétit.*"

"Hey, chimp, pass me the pepper."

"Here, let me serve you, Doctor," Ioka replied.

"Whoa! Easy, boy. You want to blow my head off?"

Reiko reckoned she could polish off the whole lunch in about three minutes.

"Slow down, sweetheart. You've got to *enjoy* your food."

"Thanks but no thanks for the advice. Good cops eat fast.

Comes with the territory. Come on, Ioka. Pick up the pace."

"Lieutenant, you're spilling food all over the place."

"Come on, Ioka. It's time for us to go."

"I haven't touched my pickled vegetables yet."

"Doctor, you just take your time and enjoy yourself."

"You're not really going to up and leave me, are you?" Kunioku said in his most cajoling voice. "You're breaking my heart."

"Look, when we've solved the case, we'll go out to that dobin mushi place you've been talking about. Is that a deal? See you, Doc."

"Sweetheart," Kunioku moaned.

Reiko pulled her down jacket over her shoulders, slipped her shoes back on, and handed the bill to Ioka.

"Huh?" he gaped. "Why me?"

"Got no cash on me. You handle it."

"You're joking, right?"

"I'm serious. You pay."

"Promise you'll pay me back?"

"Cross my heart and hope to die. Come on, man up and stop making such a fuss about nothing."

"How can you!"

Time to get back to work.

They got back to the big room in Kamata Precinct at two on the dot.

Captain Imaizumi, who was at the table at the front of

the room, looked up from his paperwork.

"What's going on, Himekawa? You're back early."

Reiko pulled a file out of her bag, then deposited it at her usual place.

"I need to talk to you, captain. Urgently."

Reiko ran her eyes around the room. No sign of Director Hashizume anywhere. He must be gracing some other task force with his presence. The only other people in the room were a couple of the Kamata administration staff.

Imaizumi must have seen that she was serious from the look in her eyes. He frowned up at her.

"Okay, what's this all about?"

"It's about the torso they found in the river. The first thing is the damage to the neck here."

She opened the file and pointed at the photograph.

"I have it on expert opinion that this scar is an electricity burn and has nothing to do with water degradation."

Imaizumi shut his eyes. His head sagged forward slightly.

"Been talking to Dr. Kunioku again?"

"Yes, sir. In an individual capacity. I approached him for a second opinion."

"What about the documentation?"

"I copied the file, sir, and posted it to him."

"Goddammit to hell, Himekawa! Have you any idea how much trouble you cause by refusing to go through proper channels?"

"I'm very sorry, sir."

Reiko knew that a simple apology would be enough. That

was the sort of frank relationship she had with Imaizumi.

"You think electrocution was the cause of death?"

"May I explain, sir?"

Imaizumi sighed. He nodded.

"You need two things to electrocute a person: the first is a power source, and the second is an electrode that's portable. That suggests to me that the crime is more likely to have been committed indoors than out. As things stand, the most probable location is the garage—meaning that the perpetrator committed the murder and dismembered the body all in the same place."

Ioka was breathing loudly through his nose. What was he getting so excited about now? Reiko shot him a sour look. It failed to register.

"The power source is straightforward enough: there are two electrical sockets in the garage. That brings us to the next question: what was the exposed electrode that served as the murder weapon? I propose that it was this."

Reiko flipped a page in the file to reveal a photograph of the electric saw that had been found in the garage.

"Notice how the power cord has been repaired about halfway down its length. We need to figure out exactly when this repair was made. I'd like to start by getting your permission to have the insulation removed and the wires examined."

If she handled the saw without the proper clearance, she could get in trouble for evidence tampering.

"You want me to send the saw to the TMPD crime lab?"

"Yes, sir."

"Anything else?"

"Yes, sir. I've got more. Could you just give me a minute, please?"

She performed a quick mental calculation. Hayama should be getting in touch any minute now. She decided to call him, just to be on the safe side.

He picked up. "Hayama here."

"It's Himekawa. Any joy?"

"Yes. I learned that Kazuyoshi Naito was seriously injured in the crash. The car he was in didn't have airbags; he suffered multiple fractures when his chest hit the steering wheel. According to the accident report, some of the broken bones actually punctured his lungs. The name of the hospital he was taken to is in the report. I need a little more time to track down the surgeon who treated him and find out the kind of surgery he had."

"Good. Get all the information you can, but you must be back in time for the evening meeting. Photocopy the accident report; if they won't let you, just make a list of the key points. I'm already at the precinct. If anyone starts giving you grief, patch them through to me here and I'll get Captain Imaizumi to have a word with them."

"Understood. I'll do my best."

Reiko snapped her phone shut.

Imaizumi cleared his throat.

"Can we resume?"

"Yes, sir."

"Now look at the torso," she said, again pointing at the photograph. "The report mentioned no surgical scars other than this one here, where the gallbladder was removed. If, however, Kenichi Takaoka is in fact Kazutoshi Naito, we would expect to find some visible traces of the medical care Kazutoshi Naito received in the wake of his car crash thirteen years ago."

Imaizumi narrowed his eyes and gave her a sharp look. "Meaning what?"

"Meaning that this body may not be who we think it is."

"The victim isn't Kenichi Takaoka, aka Kazuyoshi Naito?"

"No."

"Then who in God's name is it?"

"I believe it is Makio Tobe."

"What are you talking about?" Imaizumi spluttered. "The DNA analysis definitively proved that the torso is Takaoka's."

"I don't think so. In fact, sir, I believe that is where the mistake originated."

Reiko flicked through her dossier until she came to the notes she had made in the course of a phone call with Dr. Umehara of Tomei University Hospital earlier.

"At Tomei, they collected the DNA from a blood sample. The blood sample came from *inside* the torso, for the simple reason that getting a sample from the exterior of the torso was next to impossible due to the length of time it had been in the water. Apparently, collecting DNA from blood samples is standard operating procedure in autopsies."

"I don't think it's only limited to autopsies," objected Imaizumi.

Whoops! Careful, girl!

"You're right, sir. It's standard for *all* DNA testing. Anyway, Dr. Umehara and his team compared the DNA sample they extracted from the torso with the data of the DNA extracted from the blood left at the two crime scenes and from blood from the severed left hand. Because it matched, they concluded that the torso and the severed left hand belonged to the same person."

"Why do you think otherwise?"

"I believe that *how* the DNA sample was extracted from the hand lies at the root of the problem. I spoke to the people at the crime lab earlier today. They confirmed that they extracted the DNA sample from blood adhering to the severed base of the wrist. Let me go into a bit more detail about the whole process: they applied a special cotton swab to the bone protruding from the hand to collect a blood sample; they then isolated a single blood cell from which they extracted a DNA sample: they then amplified this DNA sample using PCR amplification equipment and used the MCT118 method to analyze its profile. They then compared it with the DNA profile of the blood from the garage floor and the back of the van. They concluded that it was the same. However . . ."

Reiko paused to catch her breath.

"What if the perpetrator had soaked the severed hand in someone else's blood? What would the effect of pouring a large amount of *somebody else's* blood into the carrier bag containing the severed hand be? That's the question we should be asking ourselves. When the hand was found, you may recall, it was covered in blood; the whole thing was a lurid pinky-red color, rather like pickled ginger."

Imaizumi was too busy trying to read Reiko's notes upside down to respond.

"That means that the DNA that the crime lab actually collected from the severed wrist bone was actually the DNA of a completely different person."

"Why should anyone do that?"

"The 'anyone' in this case is Kenichi Takaoka—and he wanted to create the false impression that he was dead."

Imaizumi scowled. A sound that was half sigh, half groan came out of his mouth.

Reiko pushed on.

"We don't know what Kenichi Takaoka knew about the subject of DNA, but it probably wasn't much. What, then, if we dial things down a notch? The idea of soaking the hand in someone else's blood to falsify the *blood type* is simple enough. Not so simple, of course, that we didn't fall for it, hook, line, and sinker . . ."

She flipped back through the file to a photograph of the torso.

"Faking fingerprints is a much more difficult thing to do. And every man and his dog know that the police check fingerprints. How did Kenichi Takaoka choose to deal with that? He chopped off *his own hand* and dunked it in Tobe's blood. He then chopped up Tobe's body and disposed of all the pieces, but by making sure that we found *his* hand and *his* fingerprints, he tricked us into thinking that the blood in the garage and the van—not to mention the torso that turned up later—all belonged to him, Kenichi Takaoka. Admittedly, I don't think that our finding the torso was part of his original plan."

Imaizumi uncrossed his arms.

"There you go again. Same damn story every time. Your theory's riddled with holes. There are way too many unknowns in there. Out of everything we currently know about this case, you've chosen to construct an elaborate scenario based on a single fact: the fact that this torso, which we originally thought to be Kazutoshi Naito's, lacks the surgical scars from an operation or operations that he had thirteen years ago."

"That's correct, sir. That's why I ordered the TMPD crime lab to redo the DNA test on the hand."

Imaizumi swallowed audibly.

"You did *what*? Without consulting me?"

"I'm very sorry, sir. It was urgent. Also—this is a little difficult for me to have to say—I suspect that Director Hashizume may be partially responsible for what happened. He was pressuring the crime lab to complete the first DNA test faster than normal. If the lab technicians say it's going to take nine hours, he should just shut up and wait nine hours."

"If they extract the DNA sample in the same way they

did last time, we'll get the same result. How long you wait's got eff-all to do with it."

"I think I've addressed that issue, sir. Based on Dr. Kunioku's advice, I instructed the lab to slice open one of the fingertips, take a cell from inside the finger, and extract the DNA sample for amplification and analysis from that cell. There's no way that the other person's blood could have made its way all the way up to the fingertips of the severed hand."

Imaizumi's head lolled on his shoulders incredulously.

"The whole damn shebang, eh?"

"I apologize, sir. Sincerely."

Reiko gave a deep bow of contrition. Ioka, beside her, bowed too.

What have you got to apologize for? she thought to herself.

"Officer Hayama should be returning with a full report on the surgeries that Kazutoshi Naito underwent thirteen years ago and the scars that those surgeries left him with. The results of the DNA test rerun should be out at around eight thirty."

The door flew open with a bang. Reiko turned. Kusaka was barreling toward them, an uncharacteristically agitated expression on his face.

"Captain!"

There was a tremor in his voice.

"What's the problem, Lieutenant?"

Kusaka was panting heavily. Reiko wondered where he'd run from.

Kusaka placed his hands flat on the table and leaned down toward Imaizumi. There was a tinge of hysteria in his eyes.

"Captain, listen to me."

"I'll be happy to. After you've calmed down."

"I am calm," Kusaka countered.

Perhaps Imaizumi's comment had struck home. Kusaka took a deep, steadying breath before proceeding.

"Mikako Kobayashi has just made a highly significant statement concerning the torso found in the Tama River. She identified it as the torso of Makio Tobe, based on the surgical scar from a gallbladder operation beneath the right breast."

Reiko kicked herself for missing that angle.

Whatever. Let it go.

Kusaka looked between Reiko and Imaizumi. His face was the picture of incredulity.

"What's going on here? Why aren't you even surprised?"

Surprise wasn't at the top of the list of emotions Reiko felt at that moment. Mostly she was enjoying a nice sense of smugness: she had got to the truth ahead of Kusaka, even if not by much.

5

Kusaka lost no time in contacting Kosuke Mishima. He told Mishima that he needed to ask him some questions and would appreciate him coming to the Kamata Precinct as soon as possible. Mishima promised to finish work early and come around right away.

In the meantime, Hayama came back, ready to share the results of his research in the Kawaguchi area. After phoning to let Reiko know that Kazutoshi Naito had suffered injuries in the chest area, he had gone to Saitama Central Hospital to interview the surgeon who operated on Kazutoshi after the crash.

"I'm sorry to say that the hospital had disposed of Kazutoshi's medical records. However, the surgeon who operated on him, Tatsuo Ikejiri, is still working there. He clearly remembered the accident—the wife killed, the son in critical condition and unconscious—and he provided me with a statement about Kazutoshi Naito's surgical scars. Apparently, Kazutoshi had a substantial amount of scar tissue in the chest area."

Reiko was so pleased that she clapped Hayama heartily on the back.

"Good work, Nori, my boy."

The corners of Hayama's mouth twitched up one, maybe two millimeters.

Did Nori just smile? Is there such a thing in nature?

Ishikura, who accompanied Hayama on his fact-finding mission to Kawaguchi, beamed happily in the background.

The phone rang. It was the downstairs lobby: Kosuke Mishima had arrived.

"I'll be right down," said Kusaka.

Reiko grabbed his elbow as he was putting down the phone.

"Lieutenant, can I sit in while you interview Mishima?"

Sergeant Satomura, who was standing next to his partner, gawped at her.

"Please," she begged. "I promise not to interfere. I can take notes, if you like."

With a frown, Kusaka glanced across at Satomura. The sergeant nodded discreetly. Done deal.

"We're fine with that," said Kusaka. He swung around to Imaizumi. "Is it okay with you, Captain?"

Imaizumi crossed his arms over his chest.

"If it's okay with you, it's okay with me," he said gruffly.

"Thank you."

Reiko bowed three times: once to Imaizumi, once to Kusaka, and once to Satomura.

"What about me, Lieutenant Reiko?" said Ioka.

Reiko had something important that she needed her partner to do for her.

"Ioka. I need you to get the circular saw out of the evidence room here and take it over to the crime lab at TMPD headquarters. If the precinct's got the budget, take a cab; otherwise, take the train. Is that all right, Captain?"

Imaizumi gave the okay. As Reiko headed for the door, she could hear Ioka grumbling behind her. His emotional state was the least of her worries right now.

Reiko's initial impression of Kosuke Mishima dovetailed with everything she'd heard about him so far: he was an attractive young man with a frank, honest air.

His shoulders and chest were broad—the result of working with his hands from a young age, she assumed—and he exuded dependability. He wasn't tall by any means, but the interview room felt a great deal smaller with him inside it.

"We've learned that we made some serious mistakes in our handling of this case. I need to talk to you today to see if you can assist us with the new direction of the investigation."

Kusaka's voice was the same as ever, but Reiko knew that he had to be feeling panicky underneath. Making a bad situation worse, at a second press conference the day before, the task force executive had announced that DNA analysis had proven without a doubt that the hand and the torso both belonged to the same man. To have to walk that back, almost before the journalists had left the building, was acutely embarrassing. Kusaka probably felt it more than most.

It's no skin off my nose.

Mishima said he was happy to cooperate. Kusaka, who'd been anxious, emitted a discreet sigh of relief.

"As of today, we now believe that the severed left hand that we discovered in the minivan and the torso that was found in the river on the fifteenth could belong to two different people."

Puzzled, Mishima stared at him.

"We cross-checked the fingerprints. We know that the hand belongs to Kenichi Takaoka. That fact is beyond doubt. However, the blood in the van and in the garage, and, as I mentioned just now, the torso, could be somebody else's."

"Somebody else?" Mishima parroted in a dazed voice.

"We're still reviewing all the data; however, we suspect that the other person is Makio Tobe."

Mishima's jaw dropped. He sat quite motionless. He almost seemed to have stopped breathing.

"Our current take on what happened goes like this: on the evening of December third, Kenichi Takaoka and Makio Tobe got into some kind of argument at the garage. The argument escalated and culminated in Takaoka murdering Tobe. It appears that he electrocuted him and that the murder weapon was the broken power cord of an electric saw. Would you know anything about that?"

Mishima told them how Takaoka had accidently sliced through the cord that very evening and taken the saw home to repair it.

"Thank you. That's very helpful indeed. Anyway, getting back to our take on the sequence of events. We think that Takaoka repaired the power cable after murdering Tobe, used the saw to chop up Tobe's body, and loaded all the body parts into the van. It was at that point that he cut off his own hand."

"That's insane," burst out Kosuke. "Why would he do a thing like that?"

"To make us think that Tobe was the murderer and that he was the victim."

Mishima's confusion was visible on his face: *Takaoka was the killer, not the victim. And Makio Tobe was the one who'd been killed. Why? Why? Why?*

"In conclusion, we believe that Kenichi Takaoka is still alive somewhere, but missing his left hand. If he hasn't received any medical care, we should assume that his physical condition is critical."

Why had Takaoka killed Tobe? That was the big question—and the question Mishima was probably best equipped to answer.

Reiko had her own ideas on the subject. A powerful sense of paternal responsibility was what had driven Takaoka to "end" his life as Kazutoshi Naito after the terrible road accident thirteen years ago. Similar paternal feelings had then turned him into a surrogate father for young Kosuke Mishima. Surely that was where they'd find his motive for murder? Surely Mishima knew that.

Reiko was sure of it.

399

Look at his eyes!

Kosuke's eyes were clear, frank, and straightforward, despite his difficult childhood. From the way he looked at people, you could tell that he'd been raised in a caring, loving atmosphere; that he knew someone loved him; and that he reciprocated the feeling.

Kenichi Takaoka was there for Mishima throughout his life. Family doesn't have to be about blood.

People raised in loveless homes, thought Reiko, their eyes were quite different: sluggish, listless, cold. Their eyes hid their feelings and acted as a barrier between them and the world outside. People like that could sometimes be very cruel. Reiko suspected that Makio Tobe probably fit that particular bill.

It was just so tragically sad. Takaoka only did what he did because he'd been driven into a corner, because he had no choice. His fatherly feelings had compelled him to commit the crime.

The police couldn't turn a blind eye to what Takaoka had done. At the same time, as a person, Reiko couldn't just stay detached and disengaged.

Takaoka and I—we're of a kind.

Unlike him, Reiko hadn't broken any laws. But if harboring murderous impulses were a crime, then, God knew, she was doubly guilty. She wanted to kill the man who'd raped her. She wanted to kill the man who'd murdered Otsuka from her squad. Those feelings were still smoldering and festering inside her.

Even Reiko's father, with his desire for revenge, was guilty. She felt bad that he'd become like that because of her, and she felt good because those feelings were also an expression of his love for her.

"Have you any idea where Takaoka might have gone?" said Kusaka.

Reiko didn't relish the idea of being on the same wavelength as Kusaka, but that was precisely the question she wanted to ask.

However, there was something she was desperate for Mishima to understand: *they were asking the question because they wanted to help Takaoka, not to punish him.*

"I've got no idea."

Of course he didn't. The incident had taken place more than two weeks ago now. Mishima had been struggling to come to terms with the loss of the man with whom he spent most of his time and who meant more to him than anyone, when suddenly they announced that actually he'd been alive all along. He needed to get his head around that fact before he could answer their question. Perhaps he wanted to ask them the same thing.

"In the course of the investigation, we found out that Kenichi Takaoka has an older sister and a son. I believe you know about the sister; her name is Kimie Naito. The son's name is Yuto. He's a couple of years younger than you are and is permanently hospitalized here in Tokyo. We've dug pretty deeply into Takaoka's past, and those two people are the only family of his we could find. As far as we can tell,

Takaoka hasn't tried to make contact or see either of them. We're just beefing up our surveillance of Kimie's restaurant and Yuto's hospital room, but we have no reported sightings of Kenichi Takaoka yet."

Mishima's eyes were blinking uncontrollably. He looked bewildered. It was too much new information, too fast. He was having trouble taking it in.

"The only other person who has a special relationship with Kenichi Takaoka is you, son. We want to hear your ideas about where he could have gone. Any ideas you may have."

Reiko's mind drifted off as she watched Mishima. She began ruminating about the state of mind Takaoka had been in on the night of the murder.

What was he thinking when he sawed off his own hand? What was he thinking when he loaded Tobe's chopped-up corpse into the minivan and drove over to the embankment? What was he thinking as he trudged through the rain and the dark up and down the steep slope and through the weeds to the river's edge?

Takaoka had had to do it all with just one good hand while enduring excruciating pain. Reiko imagined him willing himself to stay conscious as he went between the embankment and the river. She imagined him gritting his teeth, wiping the sweat out of his eyes, fighting off the shivering fits. She imagined the thoughts of Yuto, his quadriplegic son, and of Kosuke that must have kept him going.

Oh. My. God.

A black spark ignited in her brain.

I've been a fool. A total, utter idiot.

402

She felt tears welling into her eyes.

Takaoka had disposed of an entire adult body in the river after *he had chopped off his own left hand. After so much exertion, he wouldn't have the energy left to go anywhere else. He hadn't left the minivan on the embankment and run away because someone had seen him. By that stage, Takaoka would have been too weak to do any more driving. The only place that he could run to was—*

Mishima was the first person there to notice the change that had come over Reiko. Kusaka turned to see what the young man was staring at.

"What's got into you, Himekawa?"

Reiko shook her head, though she didn't know what she was trying to say by doing so.

"Kosuke, I need you to come with me."

She got to her feet, reaching out and grabbing hold of his meaty hand on the table as she did so. Mishima looked at the others in bewilderment.

"Come on, get up. Let's go and find Takaoka right now."

Mishima leaped to his feet, sending his chair flying.

PART
SIX

1

I looked down at Tobe. He was quite motionless. For some reason, I thought of Yuto, my son.

I'd arranged for my sister to get a fifty-million-yen insurance payout when Kazutoshi Naito "died." Even after embarking on my new life as Kenichi Takaoka, I still sent her seventy thousand yen every month.

But after my "death," I'd had to cut off direct contact. We couldn't communicate with each other. Even so, occasionally watched her from a distance: she looked careworn, haggard.

She'd been a stylish woman back in the day; she had this clear white skin she was so proud of. Maybe she drank too much at the bar she ran—her face became all red, and she didn't mind going out in unfashionable, even shabby, clothes.

It was obvious that life wasn't easy for her. Still, she did a great job taking care of Yuto.

She always brought his pajamas back home from the hospital to wash them. I remember seeing them flapping on the drying rack on the second-floor balcony, a bigger size every year. I felt bad about the burden I was putting on my sister, but the knowledge that my boy was growing up made my chest go all warm.

And now—

I'd murdered another man. I'd insured my life again—for fifty million yen this time—but there was no way that money would make it to my sister now.

Dying held no terrors for me. I'd always thought that dying a second time was the only way I could give any meaning to this phony life of mine.

Now I'd blown that chance.

Or had I . . . ?

Perhaps I could sort this mess out.

Maybe it was simple after all.

I knew that Tobe and I shared the same blood type: type A. That was nothing wildly unusual, but to me, at that moment, it was a precious ray of hope.

What if I exploited that coincidence and stage-managed the crime scene? If I did a good job, I could make it look like *I* was the one who'd been killed and *he* was a murderer who'd made his getaway.

The first thing I needed to do was to complete my repair of the saw. When that was done, I pulled on a pair of cotton gloves and set to work chopping Tobe's body up to make it easy to carry.

I decided to start with the head. Using a box cutter with the blade at full extension, I sliced around the neck just below the jaw. The mechanics of the job were the same as stripping the power cord of the saw. That, at least, was what I told myself to encourage myself as I began to carve him up.

When I cut through the main artery, the blood spurted out and spread all over the cement floor. It reminded me of honey pouring out of a knocked-over jar—viscous, sticky, unstoppable.

The muscles and cartilage were hell to cut through. Just beneath the skin there was this layer of fat. The fat made its way into my gloves and stuck to my fingers; it made my tools slippery and hard to grip; it really slowed me down.

Thanks to the circular saw, cutting through the bones was simple. All I had to do was squeeze the trigger and push. It would grind its way through even the thickest bones in a matter of seconds.

Switching between the cutter knife for the soft parts and the circular saw—occasionally supplemented by a chisel—for the bones, I manage to chop Tobe into pieces. I was careful to save some of his blood as I knew I was going to need it later. I found a plastic shopping bag in the garage, so I collected as much blood as I could in that.

By the time I'd finished cutting Tobe up, the garage floor was awash in gore. I slipped and fell a couple of times. I was covered in blood and as red as a daruma doll.

I wrapped Tobe's body parts in the plastic we used for protective sheeting. I'd stripped the body before I started working on it and stuffed the clothes into a paper bag. I put Tobe's shoes on my own feet: the footprints I left would help create the illusion of Tobe still being alive.

Then I opened the shutter of the garage and reversed

the van so it was about halfway into the garage. I opened the back hatch and carefully slid the body parts onto the lower deck, leaving the head and the left hand on the floor for the time being. They were in line for special treatment.

Now for the crucial stage!

I drove the van outside and parked it in the street. Then I went back into the garage and pulled the shutter down behind me.

I removed the glove from my left hand. I stuffed it into my mouth. I then twisted a towel I'd got out of the van into a rope and put it over my mouth to make a makeshift gag. I tied a knot in the towel at the back of my head and pulled it as tight as I could. The glove in my mouth was sodden with gore. As Tobe's blood and fat forced their way oozily down my throat, I imagined that I was drinking a toast to all the crimes that the two of us had committed together.

I wound thick annealing wire around my left wrist, over and over again. I pulled it so tight that the hand felt ready to drop off right there and then—and then I used a pair of pliers to twist it even tighter.

I reached for the cutter knife.

My hand was numb and heavy. I held it over a bucket positioned to catch the blood.

Here goes.

I made an incision. I was planning to use the same technique on myself I'd used on Tobe, but I kept losing my nerve. My wrist was quickly crosshatched with abortive cuts. My heart was pounding audibly; the blood was careening madly around my veins.

It's no good. I can't do it.

I forced myself to take a series of deep breaths. I started counting. I told myself I would make the cut when I got to the twentieth breath.

I heard myself moaning. I had sliced halfway around my wrist.

Every pore on my body burst opened and gushed vile, greasy sweat. The nerve endings inside the wound were screaming. Screaming. Screaming.

I had to stay conscious.

Summoning my reserves of strength, I picked up the electric saw. I carefully slipped the blade into the gaping wound in my inert wrist as it spurted blood.

I'd already come so far. Why was I being such a pussy now? I wiped my face on my upper arm to get the sweat out of my eyes, then stared at my drooping wrist and the blood-soaked saw blade.

Do it! Just fucking do it! Squeeze the trigger and push.

My teeth closed on the glove inside my mouth.

I screamed.

My throat ruptured.

My head split.

My guts turned over inside me.

Tears exploded from my eyes.

But I kept squeezing, kept pressing down.

The frenzied vibration of the saw traveled up through my elbow to my shoulder and from there around my whole body.

Aargh!

I screamed.

Aargh!

I bit deeper into the glove.

Aargh!

I wanted to escape into madness.

Aargh!

At long last, the hand dropped.

Escape into madness? There was no need. I was mad enough already.

Reiko, Kusaka, and Mishima all climbed into a taxi outside the police station. Reiko asked the driver to take them to the Tama River embankment.

Throughout the journey, Mishima didn't say a word. Nor did Kusaka, who was in the passenger seat beside the driver.

Reiko got the driver to turn right off National Route 15 after Zoshiki Station. Did the road lead to a temple right by the river? He shot a quick glance at the GPS. "That's right," he replied. "Anmyoji Temple." That was the temple the investigators had used as a base the first night of the case.

The road ended at the base of the sloped embankment. It stretched off in both directions. "Let us out here," said Reiko. The taxi came to a stop.

While Kusaka paid the driver, Reiko and Kosuke got out. They walked a few meters until they found some stone stairs. They began to climb them while, behind them, Kusaka ran to catch up.

From the top of the embankment, they all looked down on the riverbank. It was pitch black.

While the surface of the river reflected a few lights from the buildings on the opposite side, the area below them was unlit; it was a dark, flat, silent expanse.

Kusaka pulled out a flashlight. It only lit the ground around their feet, but that was all they needed. Reiko felt conflicted: half of her wanted to solve the case fast, half of her wanted to delay the resolution as long as possible. Whatever happened, she needed to take things one step at a time.

She discovered that she was still holding Mishima's hand. Had she been doing so ever since she'd dragged him out of the interview room? No. She'd let go of it when they got into the taxi, then grabbed hold of it again when they got out.

The skin was rough, the palm thick, the fingers chunky. Reiko's overwhelming impression was one of warmth.

It's the hand of a man who truly works for his living.

They went down the stairs on the other side of the embankment and then walked left across the flat bank. Reiko was confident that they were heading more or less in the right direction. They could use the flashlight to figure out exactly where to go once they got to the overgrown patch of ground.

Reiko slipped and nearly lost her footing. Mishima

tensed his arm, held her upright. She thanked him. He didn't reply.

When they arrived at the overgrown area at the river's edge, Reiko soon found the gap where the grass was all trodden down. She stopped, turned, and nodded at Kusaka. She'd been intending to go first, but when Kusaka lifted the flashlight and plunged into the gap, she was happy enough to follow him.

Kusaka was a black silhouette against the white side of the tent. He raised a hand, gesturing for Reiko and Mishima to halt.

Reiko noticed that the three pairs of socks from her last visit were still hanging on the line. Kusaka stepped up onto the raised patch of ground on which the tent was pitched and peered cautiously inside.

The flaps at the front of the tent were open, just as on Reiko's previous visit. Kusaka pointed his flashlight inside. The dancing beam was swallowed up. The whole tent emitted a hazy glow.

It looked like a cube of white light on the riverbank. Reiko thought of those floating lighted lanterns people set adrift in memory of the dead.

Mishima squeezed her hand.

Kusaka went in. The beam of his flashlight worked its way methodically around the tent's interior. A foul stench suddenly assailed her nostrils. Had the wind changed direction? Today she wasn't going to breathe through her mouth. She was going to take whatever came her way.

Kusaka eventually stuck his head out of the flap. He nodded wordlessly at Reiko.

She let go of Mishima's hand. He turned toward her, a questioning look on his face.

"Go," she murmured. Mishima walked toward the tent. Fearfully. Slowly.

He climbed up onto the raised patch of ground and squeezed past Kusaka into the tent. Kusaka remained by the door, directing the flashlight inside. When Reiko climbed up and stood next to him, he turned to face her, then looked down and quietly shook his head. Reiko noticed that he had a white latex glove on one of his hands.

"Boss!"

The cry, which sounded like it had been torn from the physical fabric of Mishima's body, slowly sunk into the dark waters of river.

"Oh my God, boss!"

The wailing became gradually quieter, as if the damp ground were absorbing the sound and breaking it down.

Kusaka stepped to one side. He gestured for Reiko to come and hold the flashlight for him. She held it pointed into the tent, illuminating Mishima and the area just behind him.

Kusaka went a short distance away and pulled out his cell phone. Reiko could see his profile against the screen light. His jaw was clenched tight.

"Kusaka here. We've located the suspect, Kenichi Takaoka. He's dead. Looks like he died several days ago."

Reiko heard Imaizumi's tinny voice at the other end of

the line: "Hand the scene over to Forensics and come back here," it said.

Kusaka snapped his phone shut and walked back to where Reiko was standing. He sighed.

"Takaoka was clutching an old photo in his good hand: it was him and the kid there, at an amusement park together."

He peeled off his latex glove and crammed it into his pocket.

Reiko could still feel the vestigial warmth where Mishima's hand had been gripping hers.

When Forensics went to process the scene the next day, they dug up a head and a left hand—Makio Tobe's, they assumed—from the ground immediately below the tent.

Kenichi Takaoka's body was taken to Tomei University Hospital's forensic pathology unit for an autopsy.

Dr. Umehara estimated that Takaoka had been dead four, possibly five days. Amputating his own hand had driven him into a state of circulatory shock; shock had then led to minor thrombosis, low blood pressure, hypoxemia, vasoconstriction, and capillary blockage. Eventually, his internal organs ceased to function properly, culminating in heart failure.

Takaoka's face—exposed to the cold dry air outside his blanket—was in the early stages of mummification. In a normal, heated environment, the process of decay would have been advanced enough that he would have been unrecognizable by the time Mishima saw him.

Further tests confirmed that the severed left hand from the van and the body in the tent both belonged to Kenichi Takaoka. A second search of Tobe's apartment was conducted the day after the body was found in the tent. This yielded a hairbrush with follicles that the lab tested to prove that the torso belonged to Makio Tobe.

However, nothing could alter the fact that their murder suspect, Kenichi Takaoka, was dead. They could forward the case to the Public Prosecutor's Office, but obviously there would be no indictment and no legal resolution to the case. The police were nonetheless obliged to put together a watertight case to properly establish Kenichi Takaoka's guilt. This would be forwarded to the Public Prosecutor's Office, which would review all the documents, before officially abandoning the case on the grounds of the suspect being dead.

Getting all the paperwork ready was a job that fell to the investigators who'd worked the case: Captain Imaizumi, as the head of Unit 10; Lieutenant Kusaka, the lead field investigator; and finally Reiko. While they were busy on that, all the other investigators on the case were placed on Level C, the lowest level of readiness. As their colleagues enjoyed the equivalent of a vacation, the three of them were stuck in Homicide's office on the sixth floor of the Tokyo Metropolitan Police headquarters, frantically cobbling together the necessary documents.

There were mountains of documentation to produce. They had to compile and index all the reports turned in by all the individual investigators. They had to do the same for all the witness statements and interview transcripts, as well as summarize all the expert forensic opinions and test results, including the recent report on the tent where Takaoka's body had been found. There was also a forensics report on the cord of the electric saw, which Ioka, following Reiko's instructions, had dropped off at the crime lab for testing. Kusaka personally put together all the documentation related to the various searches.

The necessity of proving that the suspect Kenichi Takaoka was in fact Kazutoshi Naito added a layer of complexity to everything. They had to draw up a detailed timeline with a comprehensive list of references. Even a minor factual error could produce an inconsistency that might undermine the entire case. The case they sent to the prosecutors had to be watertight. Only then would the police be officially allowed to close the book on this one. The result was reams and reams of paper for what was, after all, only a single murder.

I'm sick to death of this. It's so darn boring.

Reiko found herself scowling at Kusaka, who was working opposite her, three desks down.

It annoyed her that Kusaka was so good at this kind of work. He sat there, tapping away at his computer keyboard as though data entry were his full-time job. How could a man his age be so proficient at touch-typing? Most detectives over forty struggled even with the basics of a PC.

Bet the guy took evening classes. Creep.

Reiko was compiling a document that listed all the new

information uncovered subsequent to finding Takaoka's corpse.

On the night of the third, Takaoka had gone to the white tent after dumping Tobe's remains in the river. He had presented the original occupant, a certain Daisuke Tanaka, with two bundles of banknotes of one million yen each, and asked him to get out and give him the tent.

Tanaka willingly complied. He subsequently showed up in the homeless community beside the baseball ground a little further along the river. He won their acceptance by turning up with large quantities of food and alcohol. He was living alone because the other homeless guys didn't want him around. Two million yen, however, can change minds. Suddenly, the returnee was everybody's best friend; he even began to emerge as a leader in the group.

When the investigators asked Tanaka what he'd felt about Takaoka missing a hand, his response had been quite matter of fact. Most people who are sleeping rough have some sort of hard-luck story, he explained, and you soon learn not to pry.

They hadn't managed to establish where the two million yen came from yet. They suspected Tobe might have had it on him. They'd asked the public prosecutor if they could quietly drop their inquiries into the matter.

The matter of Takaoka's driver's license was an issue that puzzled Reiko, so she went and made some inquiries herself.

Takaoka was on file at the Driver's License Renewal Center. He was on record as having a standard vehicle driver's license under the name of Kenichi Takaoka, though the photograph was of himself, Kazutoshi Naito. His actual license was real, not counterfeit. Reiko couldn't understand how he had tricked the authorities into issuing and then renewing a license with an ID photo that didn't match.

The answer turned out to be surprisingly simple. The real Kenichi Takaoka, who had indeed committed suicide, never had a driver's license. As a result, when Kazutoshi Naito moved to Middle Rokugo, he'd been able to apply for a license under his new identity because the authorities had no record of the real Takaoka's appearance.

That was a wild goose chase.

Reiko looked at her watch. It was already three.

Imaizumi was away from his desk at a meeting with Wada, the chief of Homicide. The investigators of Unit 2, who were at Level A readiness, were based at the far end of the room. Ironically, Kusaka was the only person anywhere near Reiko.

Just my luck.

Reiko went over to the coffee machine and poured a couple of cups. She gave one to Kusaka—he took his black—on the way back to her desk.

"Here you go."

"Oh . . . cheers," he murmured.

His eyes never strayed from the documents on his desk in front of him, and his fingers continued speeding over the keyboard. The stuck-up, self-righteous little prig.

Damn, there I go again!

Reiko had never liked Kusaka's face—the cold, emotionless eyes, the beaky nose, the tight, thin lips—but there was more to it than that. *Kusaka looked like the man who raped her.* He wasn't a dead ringer by any means, but still, the resemblance was close enough to trigger nasty memories.

She wondered if having to work with Kusaka was some sort of test.

At a personal level, Reiko condoned what Takaoka had done: she had wanted to bump off both her rapist and Otsuka's murderer, so she was a potential murderer herself. Forgiving Takaoka was, for her, a simple matter of "do as you would be done by."

As a cop, though, things were different. However deeply she empathized with Takaoka, the fact remained: the man had broken the law. The same would be true for her, if she went one step further and actually killed the man who raped or the one who'd killed Otsuka, her squad member. That was right and proper. That was the law.

So where did that leave her?

Reiko was looking for a more compelling reason than the cold, logical tenets of the law to reject the vengeful impulses inside her. She wanted to achieve self-restraint based on something that came from her, as a person, and had nothing to do with the cold prohibitions of the law.

She peered at the monitor of Kusaka's computer. It looked like he was drawing up a list of all the articles they'd impounded during the two searches of Tobe's apartment.

Reiko found some comfort in the thought that, at least in this case, Kusaka, aka Mr. Guilty Verdict, wasn't going to get his way this time.

"Hey, Kusaka."

Can he hear me?

In silence, Kusaka kept typing until he got to the end of his sentence, then pressed enter, clicked on the save icon, and pressed enter again, before he turned to look at her.

"Yes, what?"

He was blinking. Reiko wondered if his eyes were hurting.

"I wanted to ask you what you thought of Takaoka."

"Think of him? How do you mean?"

"Well, you're about the same age as him, and you've got a son too."

"Thanks for the coffee," he said perfunctorily, picking up the cup with a peevish sigh. That attitude of his was precisely what got on Reiko's nerves.

"I suppose I can sympathize and understand some of what he did. I can't endorse it, though."

"Which bits can you understand?"

Kusaka sighed for a second time. Reiko assumed it meant something like, "Why must you ask me such idiotic questions?"

"As a man and as a father myself, I completely understand Takaoka's desire to support his quadriplegic son and to take care of Kosuke Mishima, despite their not being related by blood. Equally, I can't help but sympathize with him when it was only his commitment to doing right by Mishima and his son that led him to murder Tobe."

"And what can't you endorse?"

He heaved yet another sigh. The guy was a piece of

work. He didn't even try to hide his sense of superiority. His head drooped a little, and he said nothing.

"Come on, Kusaka, tell me."

"Why do you care what I think?"

"Like I said, because you're the same age and have a kid."

Reiko started feeling guilty. Perhaps she was pressing Kusaka harder than she should.

"Because whenever we get talking, I always seem to end up saying something trite and corny."

"Oh, so it's my fault?"

"That's not what I said. Let's end this conversation. I'm pretty sure I don't have any valuable insights to share."

"Don't be bashful. Trite and corny is fine by me. You're not a TV commentator."

"Trite and corny is the stock-in-trade of most commentators on TV. Exactly what I want to avoid here with you."

Kusaka took off his glasses and began massaging his closed eyes with his thumb and index finger. Was it some kind of signal? "Leave me alone"? "Give me a minute to collect my thoughts"? Reiko found the man discombobulating: the way he paced his remarks and gestures was so damn unpredictable. How did Kusaka behave when he was alone with his wife? What was the atmosphere like in the Kusaka family home? There was something morbidly fascinating about such questions.

"You know that line about how children are formed through watching their parents?"

With his flawlessly bad timing, it looked as though Kusaka had finally decided to open up, kicking things off with a nice stale cliché.

"Yeah, I know the line."

"I don't think it's just saying that children copy what their parents do. It's also saying parents can serve as a good example of what *not* to do. Takaoka 'died' twice, once as Kazutoshi Naito and once as Kenichi Takaoka, and then became a homeless nobody with no name."

That's not strictly true, thought Reiko. *On the first day of the investigation, he introduced himself to me as Takeshi Iizuka.* But she decided now wasn't the time for silly comments.

"Children are always keeping an eagle eye on their parents, even when you think they're not paying attention. My take on the matter is that parents should never do anything they wouldn't want their children to see or that they couldn't justify to them, whether the child is physically present or not. Anyone who wants to bring their kids up right has to live right themselves."

Hardly a revolutionary point of view, thought Reiko. She wondered how many parents would pass the Kusaka test. Probably not many. Adults committed the vast majority of crimes—and plenty of them had children to whom they were setting a bad example. And then—admittedly, this had nothing to do with criminality—you had those awful parents who expected much from their children when they had achieved little themselves. That wasn't right either.

"I told you I'd say something boring."

"I don't think you did," she protested halfheartedly.

Why did she always end up treating Kusaka so dismissively? It was an unattractive trait. She needed to do as she would be done by—otherwise, they'd never escape the vicious circle they were in.

Should I make the first move?

In effort to be friendly, Reiko cast around for a new conversation topic.

"Say, Kusaka, you've been married a long time. What's it like?"

She'd meant to lob him a conversational softball. Why was Kusaka scowling at her like that?

"What's wrong now?"

"You're so goddamn hopeless, you two."

You two?

"What do you mean?"

"'What's it like being married?' How am I supposed to answer a question like that? Everyone's different, so everyone's relationships are different too."

"So?"

"Go and ask Kikuta, if you're so desperate to know. I've already had a word with the guy. I'm not so in love with the sound of my voice that I want to make the same speech twice. You want to know what I think, go talk to him."

What the hell did Kikuta have to do with anything? And why was Kusaka suddenly so worked up?

Kusaka abruptly returned his gaze to the documents on his desk.

"There's something I need to ask you. Your explanation of how you figured out that Takaoka was holed up in the tent by the river—I've gone through it I don't know how many times, and it still makes no sense."

What's with changing the subject?

"I can follow up to the bit about Takaoka being too physically weak to drive his van, but I don't see how you go from there to him being in the tent. He could equally well have chosen to leave the scene on foot or chuck himself headfirst into the river. I don't want you progressing your cases through guesswork; I want you to refer to the fact of your having seen the guy and questioned him and develop a proper case that I can incorporate into a proper written report. This episode is typical of you: You make a random guess that just happens to be right, and you think that's good enough. I know I've said this to you before, but successfully identifying the perpetrator doesn't mean you can just forget about everything that led you to that point. If you can't give an accurate, watertight account of your own thought process, your case is at risk of being overturned in court—"

Kusaka's cell phone began to ring inside his jacket. He pulled it out and looked at the exterior screen.

"Excuse me a second."

Flipping open his phone, he stood up and wandered off toward the windows. Reiko guessed that the caller was from someone in his family.

"Hi, it's me.... Uh-huh, I see.... How's the other kid? ...What about Yoshihide? Is he doing all right ...?

Good ... No, I'm back at TMPD headquarters now....
I'm not sure...."

Kusaka consulted his watch.

"All right, I'll do it. I'll leave right now. I should be
there by five....Yes, yes, I understand. I'm going to hang
up now.... I'm going to hang up.... Bye, then."

Kusaka walked back to his desk and sat down. He
carefully saved all the files that were open on his desktop,
then began to close them, one by one.

"I've got to head home, Himekawa. Something urgent has
come up. Sorry, but I've got to go immediately. Tell Imaizumi
not to worry. I'll get everything finished up on time."

"Uh, sure.... Is there a problem at home?"

An expression of pain flashed across Kusaka's face. Reiko
had never seen anything like it before.

"It's my son—one of the other kids was bullying him,
he couldn't take it anymore, and he snapped. There was a
fight, and both of them got hurt."

Kusaka switched off his computer and locked away the
case documents in his desk drawer.

"Oh, that's awful.... Don't you worry, I'll let Captain
Imaizumi know."

Kusaka was on his feet and had his coat halfway onto
his shoulders.

"I was indiscreet just now. There's no need to tell him
anything about the bullying or my boy getting hurt."

Reiko nodded.

Kusaka glared at her sternly.

"What I was saying just now about your report—we'll discuss that some more tomorrow."

Must we really?

"Thanks, and good night."

Kusaka snatched up his briefcase and headed for the door, pulling his coat collar into place.

You're not playing fair, Kusaka.

The alarm in his eyes when he heard about his boy being hurt was plain to see. Even when what he was saying to his wife sounded cold and unsympathetic, there had been warmth in his eyes. *Maybe he isn't all bad*, she thought to herself, as she watched his retreating back.

Have a heart, Reiko. The man's a husband and a father.

The thought that she was beginning to hate Kusaka less—if only by a microscopic degree—annoyed her.

Why, if she was annoyed, did she feel so happy? That only made it even worse.

ABOUT THE AUTHOR

Tetsuya Honda is one of Japan's best-selling authors with the on-going crime series featuring Reiko Himekawa, a Homicide Detective with the Tokyo Metropolitan Police. *The Silent Dead* (Japanese title: *Strawberry Night*), is the first of five novels, and has sold over 4 million copies in Japan alone, and is the basis for two TV mini-series and a major theatrical motion picture. Honda lives in Tokyo.